THE IDEA OF THE GENTLEMAN
IN THE VICTORIAN NOVEL

The Idea of the Gentleman in the Victorian Novel

ROBIN GILMOUR
Lecturer in English, University of Aberdeen

London
GEORGE ALLEN & UNWIN
Boston Sydney

© George Allen & Unwin (Publishers) Ltd, 1981.
This book is copyright under the Berne Convention. No reproduction
without permission. All rights reserved.

George Allen & Unwin (Publishers) Ltd.
40 Museum Street, London WC1A 1LU, UK

George Allen & Unwin (Publishers) Ltd.
Park Lane, Hemel Hempstead, Herts HP2 4TE, UK

Allen & Unwin Inc.,
9 Winchester Terrace, Winchester, Mass 01890, USA

George Allen & Unwin Australia Pty Ltd.
8 Napier Street, North Sydney, NSW 2060, Australia

First published in 1981

British Library Cataloguing in Publication Data

Gilmour, Robin
   The idea of the gentleman in the Victorian novel.
  1. English fiction – 19th century- History and criticism
  2. Upper classes – England
 I. Title
823.809;352   PR830.S6

ISBN 0–04–800005–1

Library of Congress Cataloging in Publication Data

Gilmour, Robin
   The idea of the gentleman in the Victorian novel.
   Bibliography: P.
   Includes index.
  1. English fiction – 19th century – History and criticism.
  2. Conduct of life in literature. 3. Manners and customs
in literature. 4. Men in literature. 5. Middle classes in
literature.
 I. Title
PR878.C64G5   823'.8'0803520631   81–10869   AACR2

Jacket Illustrations: George IV *by* George Cruikshank, courtesy of the
Victoria & Albert Museum.
Pip and Joe from Great Expectations *by* Marcus Stone.
Dr Arnold from Tom Brown's Schooldays *by* Arthur Hughes.

Set in 10 on 11 point Press Roman by Janice Buchanan, Gerrards Cross
and printed in Great Britain
by Richard Clay (The Chaucer Press) Ltd., Bungay, Suffolk.

Contents

Preface and Acknowledgements	ix
Note on Main Texts	xi
Introduction: The Idea of a Gentleman	1
1 The Legacy from the Eighteenth Century	16
2 Thackeray and the Regency	37
3 The Mid-Century Context	84
4 Dickens and *Great Expectations*	105
5 Trollope and the Squires	149
Epilogue	182
Additional Bibliography	185
Index	187

Preface and Acknowledgements

In the nineteenth century, Dr Kitson Clark observed in *The Making of Victorian England* (Methuen, 1962, p. 253), deciding who were and were not gentlefolk was an 'agonizing problem' which possibly 'caused more trouble and heartburning in well-nourished bosoms than any other secular problem'. I have been continually aware in the course of writing this book that most modern readers are unlikely (for perfectly understandable reasons) to have much sympathy to spare for Victorian heartburning on this matter, and aware therefore of the need to recover the historical perspective from which the idea of the gentleman can be seen for what I believe it was: one of the most important and far-reaching of Victorian preoccupations. Three books in particular have helped me in this task, and I am happy to acknowledge my indebtedness to them here. One is Dr Kitson Clark's book, which taught me the value of an evolutionary approach to Victorian society and its institutions. The second is Gordon Ray's splendid biography of Thackeray, *Thackeray: The Uses of Adversity, 1811–46* and *Thackeray: The Age of Wisdom, 1847–63* (OUP, 1955, 1958), which, in addition to its obvious relevance to my argument, has been a source of much pleasure and instruction. And the third is Ellen Moers's classic study *The Dandy: Brummell to Beerbohm* (Secker & Warburg, 1960), which helped me to see the significance of the dandy, and of the Regency in general, for an understanding of early Victorian attitudes.

Of more personal debts, I should like to thank Keith Ashfield of Allen & Unwin for his interest in this project and for his patience. I am especially grateful to the following friends and colleagues at Aberdeen: to Wendy Craik and Paul Schlicke for the stimulus of their conversation on Victorian matters generally, and to Paul for his careful and helpful reading of the Introduction and Chapter 4; to George Watson for his incisive comments on Chapters 1 and 2, which saved me from several errors and infelicities; and to Len Hunt, David Longley and George Watson for their advice and encouragement. They have all contributed substantially to this book but are in no way responsible for its shortcomings.

Some of the material in Chapters 3 and 4 appeared in a rather different form in my chapter 'Dickens and the self-help idea', in *The Victorians and Social Protest*, ed. J. Butt and I. F. Clarke (David & Charles, 1973). I am also grateful to the English departments of the Universities of St Andrews and Strathclyde for the opportunity to air some of the issues in this book, and for the stimulus of their response.

My greatest debts, apart from that to the dedicatees, are to my wife Liz, for her constant belief in this enterprise, her encouragement, and her help in typing the manuscript; and to Peter Wood, from whom I learnt a love of literature, and of Victorian literature in particular.

Aberdeen
October 1980

In Grateful Memory of my Parents
Agnes Bell Gilmour (1906–64)
William Gilmour (1905–74)

Note on Main Texts

Writers and works which figure frequently in the text are not mentioned in the references. The following editions have been used:

Lord Chesterfield: References are to the *Letters* in the Everyman edition (London: Dent, 1929).

Dickens: All references are to *The Oxford Illustrated Dickens* (London: Oxford University Press, 1947–58), with the exception of *Oliver Twist*, for which the Clarendon text, edited by Kathleen Tillotson (Oxford: Clarendon Press, 1966), has been used.

Ruskin: References are to *Works*, ed. E. T. Cook and A. Wedderburn, 39 vols (George Allen, 1903–12).

Spectator: References are to *The Spectator*, ed. D. F. Bond, 5 vols (Oxford: Clarendon Press, 1965).

Thackeray: With the exception of *Vanity Fair*, all references to Thackeray are to *Works*, ed. George Saintsbury, 17 vols (London: Oxford University Press, 1908). References to *Vanity Fair* are to the edition of the novel edited by Geoffrey and Kathleen Tillotson (London: Methuen, 1963).

Trollope: With the exception of the Palliser novels, for which the Oxford University Press edition (1973) has been used, all references to the novels, as well as to *An Autobiography*, are to the World's Classics edition (London: Oxford University Press, various dates).

Introduction:
The Idea of a Gentleman

> Nothing is more certain, than that our manners, our civilisation, and all the good things which are connected with manners, and with civilisation, have in this European world of ours, depended for ages upon two principles; and were indeed the result of both combined; I mean the spirit of a gentleman, and the spirit of religion.
> (Edmund Burke, *Reflections on the Revolution in France*, 1790)

I

'By the by if the English race had done nothing else,' the poet Hopkins wrote in 1883, 'yet if they left the world the notion of a gentleman, they would have done a great service to mankind.'[1] It is hard to imagine anyone writing like this today. Where Hopkins saw a unique value, we are more likely to be aware of what Harold Laski called, in a famous essay,[2] 'The Danger of Being a Gentleman' — the damaging social exclusiveness of the gentlemanly ethic, its anti-intellectual and anti-democratic bias, its elevation of respectability and good form over talent, energy and imagination, and its perpetuation (through such institutions as the Victorian public schools) of the values of a leisured elite long after these had ceased to be relevant to the needs of British society. Or rather, since by now the reaction against the gentleman is as much a matter of history as his Victorian popularity, we are perhaps conscious only of his quaintness, of an old-fashioned social image. If the gentleman survives he does so only in the ghostly form of inherited attitudes and assumptions; the notion of a gentleman as Hopkins and other Victorians understood it, as a cultural goal, a mirror of desirable moral and social values, has been in a steady decline since at least the end of the First World War. And the decline of the notion is reflected in our changing use of the word 'gentleman' itself which, according to Fowler's *Modern English Usage* (1965), 'like that of ESQUIRE, is being affected by our progress towards a classless society; but in the opposite way: we are all esquires now, and we are none of us gentlemen any more'.

There is no doubt much to be thankful for in this development. The English cult of gentility has been responsible in its time for many blighted lives and a great deal of snobbery, and we are in no danger of forgetting or underestimating that fact today. The danger is rather that in remembering only the harmful legacy, we forget the serious content in the gentlemanly idea and the civilising role it played in the genesis of Victorian Britain. For the idea of the gentleman is in fact one of the most important of Victorian notions, 'the necessary link', as Asa Briggs says, 'in any analysis of mid-Victorian ways of thinking and behaving'.[3] Hopkins's 'notion of a gentleman' lay at the heart of the social and political accommodation between the aristocracy and the middle classes in the period, and was a powerful implicit assumption behind many of the characteristic reforms and innovations which were the fruit of that accommodation: the growth of the professions and of a professional class, the reforms of the Home and Indian Civil Services, the overhaul of the old public schools and the creation of the new, geared to the production of an administrative elite capable of serving and administering an increasingly complex industrial society and, later, an expanding empire. If they agreed on little else, the makers of Victorian opinion shared their society's high valuation of the gentleman, however differently each may have interpreted it: Ruskin and Samuel Smiles, Cardinal Newman and Dr Arnold, Thackeray and the Prince Consort – strange bedfellows, but each was engaged in defining, or redefining, what Tennyson in *In Memoriam* (1850) called 'the grand old name of gentleman' (lyric 111). And the idea of the gentleman is manifestly important in the Victorian novel; one cannot read very far in Thackeray, Dickens, or Trollope, without realising that they were fascinated by the image of the gentleman and its relation to the actual and ideal possibilities for the moral life in society. Our failure to come to terms with this aspect of their work is, I believe, a conspicuous gap in our understanding of the mid-Victorian novel. This study is an attempt to fill that gap.

As I hope the following chapters will show, I am concerned with the ways in which the idea of the gentleman helps to focus – in the society and in its literature – the experience of the Victorian middle classes during the period of their emergence and consolidation, the years from roughly 1840 to around 1880. The story begins earlier than that and ends later, but it was in these years that the nature of gentlemanliness was more anxiously debated and more variously defined than at any time before or since. Such intensity of preoccupation had its ridiculous side, but it also reflected the needs and aspirations of new groups struggling to establish themselves in a society which was, and remained for most of the nineteenth century, dominated by the land-owning aristocracy. More detailed discussion of the various Victorian images and definitions of the gentleman must wait till later chapters; the purpose of this Introduction is to clear the ground (at the risk of some simplification) by setting the idea of the gentleman in its broad historical and literary context. In attempting to disentangle the overlapping threads in the Victorian preoccupation with the gentleman, two factors need to be kept in mind: that the Victorians themselves were, if not confused, then at least much more uncertain than their grandfathers had been about what constituted a gentleman, and that this uncertainty, which made definition difficult, was an important part of the appeal which gentlemanly status held for outsiders hoping to attain it. The uncertainty was only relative, it was true: the man of noble birth, or of good family, was a gentleman by right (this is what the word 'gentle' in its original sense means), as was the Church of England clergyman, the army officer, the member of Parliament. But between these and other time-honoured ranks, and those who aspired to the status, lay the universal assumption that gentlemanliness was important and that its importance transcended rank because it was a moral and not just a social category. 'I'll mak' your son a baronet, gin ye like, Luckie,' James I is reputed to have said to his old nurse, 'but the de'il himsel' could na mak' him a gentleman.'[4] The moral component in gentlemanliness, and its social ambiguity, made it open to debate and redefinition in a way that the concept of the aristocrat was not, and if the issue became problematic in the nineteenth century as never before, it was because in a rapidly changing society more and more people were becoming wealthy enough to sense the attainability of a rank that had always, in theory, been open to penetration from below. The relative accessibility of gentlemanly status is a fact of considerable historical importance, as foreign observers were quick to perceive. Thus Tocqueville, in *The Ancien Regime and the French Revolution* (1856), made the word 'gentleman' his point of distinction between an open and a caste-based ruling class:

> A study of the connexion between the history of language and history proper would certainly be revealing. Thus if we follow the mutations in time and place of the English word 'gentleman' (a derivative of our *gentilhomme*), we find its connotation being steadily widened in England as the classes draw nearer to each other and intermingle. In each successive century we find it being applied to men a little lower in the social scale. Next, with the English, it crosses to America. And now in America it is applicable to all male citizens, indiscriminately. Thus its history is the history of democracy itself.
> In France, however, there has been no question of enlarging the application of the word *gentilhomme*, which as a matter of fact has, since the Revolution, dropped out of common use. This is because it has always been employed to designate the members of a caste — a caste that has never ceased to exist in France and is still as exclusive as it was when the term was coined many centuries ago.[5]

He was right, and Bagehot made substantially the same point when he defined English society as 'the system of *removable inequalities*, where many people are inferior to and worse off than others, but in which each may *in theory* hope to be on a level with the highest below the throne'.[6] The openness of the English aristocracy has been one reason for its remarkable historical survival. But while the history of the word 'gentleman' may be, as Tocqueville suggests, the history of democracy itself, gentlemanliness was not a democratic notion, nor could it have exercised its power over the imagination of the Victorian middle classes if it had been. Its appeal for them lay in its dignified and partially independent relationship to the aristocratic order, and in its potential for moralisation and modernisation. They wanted to widen the basis of qualification to include themselves, without sacrificing the exclusiveness which gave the rank its social esteem.

The origins of the gentleman lie deep in feudal society and the qualification of birth: 'the *essence* of a gentleman', Ruskin wrote, 'is what the word says, that he comes from a pure *gens*, or is perfectly bred. After that, gentleness and sympathy, or kind disposition and fine imagination' (*Works*, Vol. XXXVII, p. 197). The common mistake that 'gentleman' means a man of gentle disposition reflects a long-standing ambivalence in the usage of the word: as early as Chaucer 'gentil' means 'charming', 'mild' and 'tender', as well as 'noble' and 'well-bred'.[7] Birth was significant in so far as the man of family and liberal education would have greater opportunity for acquiring gentle manners and practising gentle behaviour, but every courtesy writer agreed that birth alone could not make the complete gentleman. Nor was that other criterion often cited in dictionary definitions, the right to bear a coat of arms, ever absolute, for the science of heraldry fell into disrepute in the eighteenth century and never recovered its prestige in the nineteenth. Even Lord Chesterfield had mocked pedigrees by hanging portraits of 'Adam de Stanhope' and 'Eve de Stanhope' in the family gallery, and the ease with which bogus coats-of-arms were devised and purchased is a standing joke in the Victorian novel. The idea of the gentleman could never have fascinated the Victorians as it did if it had been limited by caste or by a strict science of heraldry, nor, on the other hand, if it had been a totally moralised concept, a mere synonym for the good man. It was the subtle and shifting balance between social and moral attributes that gave gentlemanliness its fascination, the sense — it is perhaps what we mean by that elusive quality 'charm' — that in the perfect gentleman a habitual moral considerateness has been translated into such grace of manner that, as Hopkins said in the letter already quoted, 'to be a gentleman is but on the brim of morals and rather a thing of manners than of morals properly'. By the mid-century, however, the moral element was generally acknowledged to be in the ascendant, as Fitzjames Stephen recognised in 1862: the word 'gentleman', he wrote in the *Cornhill Magazine*, implies the combination of a certain degree of social rank with a certain amount of the qualities which the possession of such rank ought to imply; but there is a constantly increasing disposition to insist more upon the moral and less upon the social element of the word, and it is not impossible that in the course of time its use may come to be altogether dissociated from any merely conventional distinction.[8]

But it was not its susceptibility to moralisation alone which made the notion of the gentleman appealing to the Victorian middle classes; the process of moralisation, as we shall see in the next chapter, had been going on since the start of the eighteenth century. A significant part of its appeal lay in the special position the gentleman occupied in the traditional social hierarchy, a position − or rank − which shared in the prestige of landed society while being, in important respects, distinct from the aristocracy itself. Bertrand Russell, himself an earl, thought that 'the concept of the gentleman was invented by the aristocrats to keep the middle classes in order'.[9] But this is at best only a half-truth. All aristocrats are gentlemen, but not all gentlemen are aristocrats, and strictly speaking the social and historical origins of the gentleman lie in the gentry, not the aristocracy. In the traditional social hierarchy, the gentleman ranked beneath the baronet, the knight and the squire, but above the yeoman; and between the gentry and the aristocracy, for all that they were bound together by a common interest in the land and a similar way of life, there was according to the former's most recent historian 'always a measurable social gulf'.[10] Moreover the rank of gentleman was the point of entry for those seeking to penetrate gentry society; it was through this elastic and expanding category that the gentry 'were constantly being replenished and revitalised by the arrival of new families from office, trade, finance, farming and the professions'.[11]

The historical significance of the gentleman's location in the hierarchy of the gentry, rather than the aristocracy, was that it provided a time-honoured and not too exacting route to social prestige for new social groups. In terms of the older society of 'rank' and 'degree' it was a station which aspiring members of the middle classes could hope to penetrate and, to some extent, make over in their own image. The moral dimension in the gentlemanly idea made it accessible to reinterpretation and modernisation, while its relative independence of the aristocratic code on the one hand, and the grosser associations of 'trade' on the other, meant that in the rapidly changing and increasingly class-conscious society of the nineteenth century it provided a social standing-ground which could be occupied with dignity. It was theoretically possible for the self-made man to get into the aristocracy, if he had a great deal of money, some luck and not too thin a skin, but it was more comfortable (and cheaper) to buy a place in the country and set himself up as a weekend squire; this might not gain him entry to the higher county society, but he could reasonably expect to find acceptance somewhere in the ramifications of the gentry network. And acceptance, after all, was the final test and certificate of gentility.

For this reason middle-class apologists tended to stress the gentleman's origins in the gentry rather than the aristocracy; by doing so they were attempting to prise the concept away from the aristocracy, often indeed making it a concept critical of aristocracy, while retaining the prestige of its landed associations. This is an attitude which underlies the whole treatment of landed society in works like *Pride and Prejudice* (1813), Trollope's Barsetshire novels, Mrs Gaskell's *Wives and Daughters* (1866) and many others in the nineteenth century. One form it takes is the widely canvassed notion that a duke can never be more than a gentleman (though few were prepared to suggest that he might be less). Thus Frank Gresham, the squire's son in Trollope's *Doctor Thorne* (1858), reacts to the condescending behaviour of the Duke of Omnium by saying, 'I don't care if he be ten times Duke of Omnium; he can't be more than a gentleman, as such I am his equal' (ch. 19). (It was part of the peculiar prestige of the gentlemanly notion, as Tocqueville perceived, that the Duke of Omnium would have agreed – in theory, at any rate, and in public.) Another is the mythology of an indigenous 'Saxon' squirearchy, rooted in the land and exercising responsibility for it (and by implication sympathetic to the equally 'responsible' middle classes), which is both older established and morally superior to an irresponsible, parvenu 'Norman' aristocracy – Jane Austen's Lady Catherine de Bourgh and Trollope's De Courcys, with their Norman names and insolent manners, are both cases in point.

But while the Victorian middle classes might identify with the gentry against the aristocracy, the gentry remained a club that was run by old-fashioned rules. The very social forces which were bringing new groups knocking on the door of gentility were rendering problematic the qualifications on which they could be admitted. These had changed little since the sixteenth century and reflected the social priorities of a pre-industrial society. William Harrison's definition of 1577 sets out the main credentials:

> Whosoever studieth the laws of the realm, whoso abideth in the university (giving his mind to his book), or professeth physic and the liberal sciences, or beside has service in the room of a captain in the wars, or good counsel given at home, whereby his commonwealth is benefited, can live without manual labour, and thereto is able and will bear the port, charge and countenance of a gentleman, he shall for money have a coat and arms bestowed upon him by the heralds, and thereunto, being made so good cheap, be called master, which is the title that men give to esquires and gentlemen, and reputed for a gentleman ever after.[12]

This might seem a sufficiently capacious and flexible category, but to the rising men and groups of the early industrial revolution it presented a system of subtle exclusions. It conferred gentility on the army officer; on the clergyman of the established church, but not the Dissenter; on the London physician, but not the surgeon or attorney; on the man of 'liberal education', but only if he had received that education at Oxford or Cambridge, from which Dissenters were excluded and which was, in effect, a training-ground for Church of England clergymen. The one respectable 'trade' was the service of a wealthy merchant, who in any case had usually escaped from the office and bought himself a landed estate.

This system of exclusions seems bizarre to us now but it had its own logic, ensuring the prestige of those occupations which reinforced the stability of a social hierarchy based on the ownership of land. But it had little to offer the new men who were creating the industrial revolution and the increasing number of those who were needed to serve and administer a society that was rapidly becoming industrialised and urbanised — the engineer, the first-generation mill-owner, the general practitioner in an expanding town, the able but patron-less young man seeking a career in the Home or Indian Civil Service. For these and other social groups the rank of gentleman, though theoretically open, was put effectively out of reach by the abiding separation of work and income on which the social exclusiveness of the traditional gentleman was based. It was considered essential that a gentleman should not only be able (in Harrison's words quoted above) to 'live without manual labour', but also without too visible an attention to business, for it was leisure which enabled a man to cultivate the style and pursuits of the gentlemanly life. Thus, while gentlemanly status offered respectability and independence within the traditional social hierarchy, at the same time it challenged the dignity of the work which made the new industrial society possible.

It is this conflict, more than anything else, which explains why the early and mid-Victorian period saw such an anxious debate about the idea of the gentleman, and why that debate was so ambiguous and inconclusive, producing so many conflicting images of true gentlemanliness. The conflict lies behind, on the one hand, the assertion of men like Ruskin and Samuel Smiles that, in Ruskin's words, 'Gentlemen have to learn that it is no part of their duty or privilege to live on other people's toil' (*Works*, Vol. VII, p. 344); and on the other, the uneasy Victorian fascination with the figure of the dandy, the perfectly useless man who makes of his uselessness and disdain for work an exquisite style. It is the central thread in the long struggle for professional status on the part of new social groups, and it helps to explain why some groups, like the doctors and civil servants, succeeded, and others, like the more utilitarian engineers, failed. It can even be discerned at the heart of the personal quarrel between Dickens and Thackeray — Dickens who believed passionately in the dignity of literature, Thackeray who tended to feel that to earn one's living by writing novels was not a fit occupation for a gentleman.

In the end the Victorians solved the problem by a characteristically effective compromise: a new professional and administrative elite was necessary to run a new society, it was desirable that such an elite should be able to think of themselves as gentlemen and so recognise a bond with the values of the old society, and this could be achieved by broadening the basis of gentility in the public schools. By the last quarter of the nineteenth century it was almost universally accepted that a traditional liberal education at a reputable public school should qualify a man as a gentleman, whatever his father's origins or occupation. This had the effect of removing some of the ambiguities, but at the cost of standardising the product, and we need to get back beyond the image of the late Victorian public schoolboy if we are to understand the significance of the gentlemanly idea in the earlier period.

There it was the very flexibility and elasticity of the concept that formed the basis of its appeal, making it adaptable to the needs of rising social groups. If the Victorians failed to arrive at a single and authoritative answer to the question 'What is a gentleman?' until the public schools provided it for them, then this in itself is perhaps the most important point about the historical significance of the gentlemanly idea. As Marx and others recognised, the Victorian bourgeoisie was a revolutionary class: that its emergence did not result in a revolution, or that the revolution took a gradual rather than violent form, was due in large part to the fact that it was able to find a *modus vivendi* with the aristocratic ruling class. What has come to be called the Victorian Compromise had for one of its central features the gradual supersession of one kind of social structure by another. The older structure was the hierarchy of 'rank' or 'degree', a social pyramid reaching down from the monarchy and aristocracy at the peak to the unenfranchised many at the base. The new structure was that of class, in which society is seen as divided into a number of mutually antagonistic groups, each united by a common series of economic interests. Conflict is present in both structures, but in theory the notion of 'ranks' implies an interdependent hierarchy based on the exercise of responsibility downwards and deference upwards. Historians are divided as to when the class society took over from that of rank, if indeed it ever did so entirely. What is certain is that the two categories overlapped for most of the nineteenth century, and it is questionable if the older hierarchy was ever supplanted in the minds of men and women who had some direct experience of the old society, as most had. In these terms the historical importance of the idea of the gentleman was that it was a 'rank' from the older hierarchy which was capable of making the transition into the new society of 'class'. As such it can be seen as a bridging element, perhaps indeed the salient feature in the notion of 'deference' which historians from Bagehot onwards have seen as ensuring the stability and continuity of English society throughout the turbulent changes of the nineteenth century.

Introduction: The Idea of a Gentleman

The idea of the gentleman was crucial because its ambiguities answered to the conflicting needs of the nascent middle classes in the eighteenth and nineteenth centuries, their desire to be accepted by the traditional hierarchy and at the same time to make their impact upon it. Based upon the social divisions of a stratified society, but capable of transcending these divisions; upon the principle of exclusion (for when Adam delved and Eve span, as the Peasants' Revolt slogan had it, who was then gentleman?), yet deriving its special character from the ideal of courtesy, which involved treating all men with equal respect; upon the possession of money, though offering an ideal of disinterestedness by which a materialistic society could be criticised; upon historic origins in military service and landed society, though adaptable to the domestic values of suburban man — it is not surprising that the essential flexibility of the gentleman (the idea, the image, the social fact) made it attractive to different social groups at a time of profound transition.

II

The English novelist's relationship to this process has been intimate and complex, and historically the idea of the gentleman is bound up with the whole evolution of the modern novel of manners out of the courtesy book and the polite essay. As David Daiches says, 'the great theme of the eighteenth and often of the nineteenth century novelist is the relation between gentility and virtue'.[13] This is partly a matter of the English novel's inheritance from earlier courtesy writing. The gentleman has traditionally been the chief focus for literary discussions of secular virtue, the concern alike of courtesy book writers and of poets like Spenser, whose *Faerie Queene* (1596) had set out 'to fashion a gentleman or noble person in vertuous and gentle discipline'. It is no accident that the rise of the novel should coincide with the decline of the courtesy book, for the novel, with its immensely more complex registration of manners, was capable of fashioning a gentleman in altogether more lifelike and engaging ways. Nor is it an accident that Samuel Richardson, whose *Sir Charles Grandison* (1753–4) had been written in conscious reaction to the 'natural man' hero of *Tom Jones* (1749), and who by the end of the eighteenth century was the acknowledged authority on true gentlemanliness, should have been a London printer and therefore a member of what we would now call the middle classes. Richardson's interest in the relation between gentility and virtue goes deeper than the dramatisation of ideal types like Sir Charles Grandison; his intense preoccupation with the niceties of polite behaviour in his novels is, essentially, the preoccupation of a middle-class man of conservative tastes with the moral possibilities inherent in the courtesies of a high civilisation, who also perceived an inevitable gap between those possibilities and the actuality of most social behaviour. His heroes and heroines struggle to close that gap by their scrupulous lives and their intense emotional and spiritual investment in the idealised forms of their civilisation. Their mission is the moralisation of gentry society, and in his greatest novel, *Clarissa* (1747–8), the heroine dies after being raped by her aristocratic seducer because her respect for her 'honour' is inseparable from her deepest sense of her integrity as a human being.

In Richardson the forms of social life, manners, are inescapably related to the drama of the moral life. His vocabulary insists on the relation, where words like 'decorum', 'punctilio', 'propriety', are inseparable from 'dignity', 'sincerity', 'integrity'. This moralised view of manners is defined in resistance to aristocratic exploitation, and finds its natural ally and embodiment in the true gentleman. Clarissa reflects:

> Gentleness of heart, surely, is not despicable in a man. Why, if it be, is the highest distinction a man can arrive at, that of a *gentleman*? A distinction which a prince may not deserve. For manners, more than birth, fortune, or title, are requisite in this character. Manners are indeed the essence of it.[14]

Manners are certainly the essence of *Sir Charles Grandison*. The significance of this novel is that it presents an image of a baronet who answers completely to the middle-class expectation of what a landed gentleman ought to be; Sir Charles is a fictional embodiment of the ideal gentleman as Addison and Steele had conceived him at the start of the eighteenth century:

> When I consider the frame of mind peculiar to a gentleman, I suppose it graced with all the dignity and elevation of spirit that human nature is capable of. To this I would have joined a clear understanding, a reason free from prejudice, a steady judgment, and an extensive knowledge. When I think of the heart of a gentleman, I imagine it firm and intrepid, void of all inordinate passions, and full of tenderness, compassion and benevolence. When I view the fine gentleman with regard to his manners, methinks I see him modest without bashfulness, frank and affable without impertinence, obliging and complaisant without servility, cheerful and in good humour without noise.[15]

To the taste of a modern reader there is something so insipid in this that it is difficult to understand how it could have offered a challenge to the prevailing manners of the time. Yet the challenge lies in its very moderation and restraint: it is a middle-class image in the sense that it constitutes a rebuke to the pride and ostentation of aristocratic manners, and as developed in the *Spectator* (1711–14) it becomes part of a brilliant campaign to replace the gentleman of tradition — the rake, the beau, the bucolic Tory squire, the duelling man of 'honour' — with a more sober and domesticated type, suited to a society that was emerging from the violence of civil war and foreign conquest and coming to terms with its destiny as a trading nation. The type is realised in the idealised figure of Sir Charles Grandison, and Richardson's novel thus provides an important link between the *Spectator's* influential critique of Restoration manners and the nineteenth-century novel of manners developed by Jane Austen, herself an admirer of Richardson and of *Grandison* in particular.

Addison has been called the 'first Victorian', and in Chapter 1 I shall examine some of the ways in which the Victorians' preoccupation with the gentleman is partly anticipated by, and partly defined in reaction against, the images of gentlemanliness which they inherited from the eighteenth century. This forms a necessary prelude to the discussion of Thackeray in the second chapter. Like many men of his generation Thackeray was steeped in the eighteenth century, and he found a powerful creative stimulus in its literature. Several of his novels are set in this period, *The History of Henry Esmond* (1852) in the years of Marlborough's French wars and the heyday of the *Spectator*. Addison and Steele appear in person, and Esmond's mock-*Spectator* paper is at once a witty pastiche and a pointer to the informing presence of the *Spectator's* values in the novel. Esmond is a 'modern' gentleman in traditional clothes, and his story develops a private, domestic sense of honour within the setting of the old public code of duels, warfare and court intrigue. But it was not only temperamental affinity and a sense of historical continuity that linked Thackeray to the eighteenth-century essayists. In one important respect, the early Victorian reaction against Regency dandyism, Thackeray and his contemporaries were engaged in a very similar kind of cultural struggle. The history of English manners is cyclical, periods of middle-class sobriety and restraint alternating with periods of upper-class licence. The Restoration is a reaction against Puritanism, and is in its turn challenged by the new sobriety of Augustanism; the dandyism of the Regency is routed by the seriousness of the Victorians, only to reappear in *fin-de-siècle* aestheticism, and so on. What the Restoration was to the early eighteenth century, the Regency was to the first generation of Victorians. Where Addison and Steele had mocked the fashionable inanity of the beau and the fop, *Fraser's Magazine* and Carlyle and Thackeray were to attack the dandy. In both periods the idea of the gentleman becomes an essentially reforming concept, a middle-class call to seriousness which challenged the frivolity of fashionable life and reminded the aristocracy of the responsibilities inherent in their privileges. In the novels of Thackeray, and the early novels of Dickens, gentlemanliness is on the side of decency, the values of family life, social responsibility, the true respectability of innate worth as opposed to the sham respectability of fashionable clothes.

The literary image of the gentleman, then, is intimately related to the historical evolution and ambitions of the English middle classes, and both come together in the literary form which most adequately reflects and interprets their experience in the Victorian age. But of course the Victorian novelists' attitude to gentlemanliness was a good deal more complex than that of Addison or Richardson, and for the same reasons that make *Great Expectations* (1860–1) a greater and more interesting book than *Sir Charles Grandison*. Just as in society at large the gentlemanly idea exercised its fascination because it was neither a socially exclusive nor an entirely moralised concept, so too the novelists move naturally and easily between the moral and social attributes of gentlemanliness: they are never pinned down, as Richardson is in *Grandison*, to a strictly moral formulation, and their novels are the better for it. Thus Thackeray could denounce dandyism with the best of the Fraserians, but his novels record the ways in which the moral gentlemanliness he admired was haunted by the dandy elegance it seemed to have replaced, and as the features of Victorian commercial respectability hardened he could respond to the freedom and capacity for enjoyment of the old unreformed Regency gentleman: 'There is an enjoyment of life in these young bucks of 1823', he wrote in 'De Juventute', 'which contrasts strangely with our feelings of 1860' (*Works*, Vol. XVII, p. 433). Dickens, too, as Ellen Moers demonstrates in *The Dandy*, was fascinated by the dandyism which as an energetic middle-class author and self-made man he also abhorred. These conflicts and ambiguities were shared by the novelist and his reading public; they complicate (without invalidating) the moral element in the Victorian preoccupation with the gentleman; and out of them come some of the deepest social insights of the Victorian novel. *Great Expectations* is a masterpiece not because it denounces gentlemanliness as a sham, or argues that only a good man can be a gentleman, but because it shows that Pip's struggle to become a gentleman is at once a justified aspiration to a better and finer kind of life and an ambition that inevitably gets snarled in the trammels of class; and Dickens could write the novel because he had lived through such a struggle and understood its representative pathos and complexity.

For this reason the novelists were reluctant to theorise; working closer to the social reality they were more aware of the ways in which reality conflicted with the moral ideal. Systematic minds like Newman and Ruskin might attempt comprehensive definitions, where a novelist like Trollope would fall back on intuition. Challenged to define what he meant by a gentleman, he wrote in his *Autobiography* (1883), a man 'would fail should he attempt to do so. But he would know what he meant, and so very probably would they who defied him' (ch. 3). Like his own Dr Stanhope in *Barchester Towers*, Trollope was content with the fact that he 'knew an English gentleman when he saw him' (ch. 10). Yet, curiously, it is Trollope who comes closest to capturing in a phrase the interdependence of morals and manners, the ethical and the social, in the Victorian concept of the gentleman. Praising Thackeray in the

Autobiography for his portrayal of a 'perfect gentleman' in Colonel Newcome, he speaks of 'this grace of character' (ch. 13). The perfect gentleman must have qualities of character, of course, but he must also carry them with a grace that is beyond the reach of art or affectation.

This study begins with Addison and ends with Trollope. Throughout it I have attempted to relate the literary image of the gentleman to the wider cultural context of social, educational and ethical debate – to Lord Chesterfield's letters and the *Spectator* essays in Chapter 1, for example, or to the ideology of self-help and contemporary Victorian discussions of the professions and the public schools in Chapter 3. The other chapters are devoted to the major novelists in whose work the idea of the gentleman is a central preoccupation – Thackeray, Dickens and Trollope. The pattern which I shall be tracing is, in broad outline, the development of the idea of the gentleman from an image of moralised social conduct, a weapon of middle-class invasion, through its institutionalising in the mid-Victorian period, to its later, elegiac, manifestation as a rallying-point for older values threatened by the establishment of modern industrial society. The story begins with Addison's tender farewell to the old Tory squire, Sir Roger de Coverley, which ushers in the era of the middle-class gentleman; it ends with the return of Sir Roger when the middle-class revolution seems to be complete. Once the basis of qualification has been broadened to the extent that almost anyone can claim to be a gentleman who is accepted by his neighbours as one, the old distinction – Trollope's 'grace of character' – evaporates and writers return to the earlier image to express their sense of a lost courtesy and integrity. Sir Roger rides again in Colonel Newcome and the childless squires of Trollope, doomed victims of the modern world who have their twentieth-century heirs in the novels of Ford Madox Ford and Evelyn Waugh.

For this reason, among others, I have chosen to end with Trollope. As Walter Allen says, 'his view of life is hierarchic: every one of his characters has his place in a graduated social order. Trollope may on occasion mildly satirize it, but he accepts it as fully as Jane Austen does; and he is probably the last English novelist to do so.'[16] Everywhere in Trollope the old hierarchical landed order is under pressure from a new commercial society which threatens its pre-eminence and dilutes its values, gentlemanliness among them. When the Duke of Omnium's daughter protests in *The Duke's Children* (1880) that the man she loves is a gentleman, her father replies:

'So is my private secretary. There is not a clerk in one of our public offices who does not consider himself to be a gentleman. The curate of the parish is a gentleman, and the medical man who comes here from Bradstock. The word is too vague to carry with it any meaning

that ought to be serviceable to you in thinking of such a matter.'
'I do not know any other way of dividing people,' said she. (ch. 8)

This is Trollope's dilemma too: not knowing 'any other way of dividing people' he also suspects that the idea of the gentleman is becoming diluted to the point where it is in danger of losing its distinction, and so accurately perceives the destiny of the idea in the later nineteenth and early twentieth century. The history of the word, Tocqueville had said, is 'the history of democracy itself'. The very openness of the category meant that it could be claimed by more and more people lower and lower down the social scale, and with the standardising of gentlemanliness through the public schools the concept gradually lost its shape and meaning. Trollope is the last English novelist for whom the idea of the gentleman still draws strength from its traditional roots in landed society, and he is also, I think, the last great novelist in whose work the idea is a major informing presence. Later novelists like Meredith, James, Gissing and Conrad are clearly interested in the gentleman, but with the exception of Gissing, it can hardly be called a central preoccupation in their work as it is in Thackeray and Trollope. So there is critical point, as well as chronological neatness, in ending a study of this kind with Trollope.

The English gentleman did not die, or simply fade away; he was overtaken by social inflation. By the twentieth century the words 'gentleman' and 'gentlemanly' have largely lost the force they had in Jane Austen or Thackeray, and have become part of the conditioned reflexes of class. In one of his letters Sir Edward Elgar recorded his disgust at the vulgarity of the 1924 Wembley Exhibition and his relief on discovering a bunch of daisies on the turf: 'Damn everything except the daisy — I was back in something sane, wholesome & *gentlemanly*.'[17] One understands what he meant, but when the qualities of gentlemanliness can be attributed to a daisy then something has gone seriously wrong, and the concept was obviously ripe for the ridicule that has since been visited upon it. There was much that was snobbish and absurd in the Victorian obsession with the gentleman, but there was something important at stake too. As this book will argue, the idea of the gentleman carried some of the best hopes as well as the deepest contradictions of Victorian experience; behind the snobbery, the anxious debates about who did and did not qualify as a gentleman, the uneasy relationship to the aristocracy, there lies the struggle of a middle-class civilisation to define itself and its values, a process in which the novelists were intimately and sympathetically involved. The Victorian preoccupation with the gentleman needs to be seen in that context if its importance is to be understood, and as with so much else in the Victorian age, this means starting in the eighteenth century.

Introduction: The Idea of a Gentleman 15

REFERENCES: INTRODUCTION

1 C. C. Abbott (ed.), *The Letters of Gerard Manley Hopkins to Robert Bridges* (London: Oxford University Press, 1935), p. 176.
2 H. Laski, *The Danger of Being a Gentleman and other Essays* (London: Allen & Unwin, 1939).
3 A. Briggs, *The Age of Improvement 1783–1867* (London: Longman, 1959), p. 411.
4 Quoted in E. W. Stratford, *The Making of a Gentleman* (London: Williams & Norgate, 1938), p. 29.
5 A. de Tocqueville, *The Ancien Regime and the French Revolution*, trans. S. Gilbert (London: Fontana, 1966), p. 109.
6 W. Bagehot, 'Sterne and Thackeray', in *Literary Studies*, 2 vols (London: Dent/Everyman, 1911), Vol. 2, pp. 125–6.
7 F. N. Robinson (ed.), *The Works of Geoffrey Chaucer* (London: Oxford University Press, 1957), p. 953.
8 F. Stephen, 'Gentlemen', *Cornhill Magazine*, vol. V (1862), p. 330.
9 Quoted in W. L. Arnstein, 'The survival of the Victorian aristocracy', in *The Rich, the Well Born, and the Powerful*, ed. F. C. Jaher (Urbana, Ill.: University of Illinois Press, 1973), p. 236.
10 G. E. Mingay, *The Gentry: The Rise and Fall of a Ruling Class* (London: Longman, 1976), p. 4.
11 ibid., p. 5.
12 ibid., p. 2.
13 D. Daiches, *Literary Essays* (Edinburgh and London: Oliver & Boyd, 1956), p. 35.
14 S. Richardson, *Clarissa*, 4 vols (London: Dent/Everyman, 1932), Vol. II, letter 21, p. 73.
15 R. Steele, *Guardian*, no. 34 (20 April 1713).
16 W. Allen, *The English Novel* (Harmondsworth: Penguin, 1958), p. 203.
17 M. Kennedy, *Portrait of Elgar* (London: Oxford University Press, 1968), p. 251.

CHAPTER 1
The Legacy from the Eighteenth Century

> For manners are not idle, but the fruit
> Of loyal nature, and of noble mind.
> (Tennyson, 'Guinevere', 1859)
>
> Wherever it is spoken, there is no man that does not feel, and understand, and use the noble English word 'gentleman'. And there is no man that teaches us to be gentlemen better than Joseph Addison.
> (Thackeray, 'Charity and Humour', 1852)

I

It is tempting to say that what the Victorians most disliked in the eighteenth-century attitude to manners is epitomised by Lord Chesterfield's *Letters to his Son* (1774). Certainly the *Letters* were fatal to Chesterfield's reputation, and probably fatal to the reputation of the aristocratic fine gentleman ideal which he exemplified and tried to impose upon his illegitimate son. Looking back on Chesterfield at the end of the nineteenth century, the Victorian critic John Churton Collins had no doubt that to most of his countrymen 'his name is little more than a synonym for a profligate fribble, shallow, flippant, heartless, without morality, without seriousness, a scoffer at religion... Even among those who do not judge as the crowd judges there exists a stronger prejudice against Chesterfield than exists with equal reason against any other Englishman.'[1] Collins did his best to dispel the prejudice, but it is easy to see how it came about. The following comments from the *Letters* indicate what it was that stuck in the throat of posterity:

> When you go into good company (by good company is meant the people of the first fashion of the place) observe carefully their turn, their manners, their address, and conform your own to them. But this is not all, neither; go deeper still; observe their characters, and pry, as far as you can, into both their hearts and their heads. Seek for their particular merit, their predominant passion, or their prevailing

weakness; and you will then know what to bait your hook with to catch them. (5 September 1748)

The height of abilities is, to have *volto sciolto* and *pensieri stretti*; that is, a frank, open, and ingenuous exterior, with a prudent and reserved interior; to be upon your own guard, and yet, by a seeming natural openness, to put people off theirs...A prudent reserve is therefore as necessary as a seeming openness is prudent. (19 October 1748)

I recommended to you in my last an innocent piece of art — that of flattering people behind their backs, in presence of those who, to make their own court, much more than for your sake, will not fail to repeat, and even amplify, the praise to the party concerned. This is, of all flattery, the most pleasing, and consequently the most effectual. (22 May 1749)

Every man is to be had one way or another, and every woman almost any way. (5 June 1750)

These examples, and many more could be chosen, show Chesterfield at his very worst: the low opinion of human nature, the cynical attitude to women, the cold, calculating approach to human relations — this is Chaucer's 'smylere with the knyf under the cloke'. Dr Johnson's famous epigram about the *Letters* teaching the morals of a whore and the manners of a dancing-master catches the violence of the divorce between manners and morals in Chesterfield, as well as the shallowness with which he conceived of both. Less well known but if anything more pungent is Keats's comment in a letter of 1820: 'I would not bathe in the same River with lord C. though I had the upper hand of the stream. I am grieved that in writing and speaking it is necessary to make use of the same particles as he did.'[2] For Keats, and for the middle-class writers who came after him, Chesterfield's 'fine gentleman' was not fine or gentleman enough. In the contrast between the high polish of the 'modes' of civility and the low estimate of human nature which these concealed, they saw the cynicism of aristocracy and the heartless materialism of the previous century — both repugnant to people who had been touched by the twin influences of Evangelicalism and Romanticism, with their stress on the serious, the natural and the sincere. Dickens created a version of Lord Chesterfield in the character of Sir John Chester in *Barnaby Rudge* (1841), who is described as 'of the world most worldly, who never compromised himself by an ungentlemanly action, and never was guilty of a manly one' (ch. 25).

Between what Dickens understood by 'manly' and what Lord Chesterfield would have accepted as 'gentlemanly' an important change in attitudes has taken place. 'Manliness' is a key Victorian concept, as we shall see, and it connotes a new openness and directness, a new sincerity, in social relations. By the standards of manliness, Lord Chesterfield appears secretive, hypocritical, cold — and also comic. If his insidious cynicism could not be altogether laughed away, then his finicking regard for 'the Graces' could. The man who could write that 'there is nothing so illiberal, and so ill-bred, as audible laughter' because of 'the disagreeable noise that it makes, and the shocking distortion of the face that it occasions' (9 March 1748) was especially ridiculous to Dickens and Carlyle, who had encountered the same thing in the Regency dandies and responded to it with the cult of the hearty laugh, an essential feature of manliness. The criterion of sincerity, however, was a more tricky one to apply to Chesterfield, for as Churton Collins pointed out, he was nothing if not sincere; indeed the really unsettling — and interesting — aspect of the *Letters* is the contrast between the superficiality of the 'modes' and the earnestness with which they are recommended. They are unsettling because, uniquely in courtesy-book literature, they were not written to be published and therefore take us behind the scenes (the theatrical metaphor is appropriate) of aristocratic politeness in a way that the conventional manual of parental advice does not. In doing so they reveal something of the uncertainty at the heart of Augustan polite manners, and perhaps of all highly developed codes of manners.

Chesterfield was not, of course, the hypocritical villain that nineteenth-century mythology made him out to be, nor does a careful reading of his letters quite confirm the popular image. He was an aristocrat, a courtier, an admirer of French *moeurs*, and his letters to his son have a specific purpose: to educate him for a career in European diplomacy. Moreover, there is a good deal of sensible advice mixed up with all the fussing about 'the Graces'. The son is advised to use his time well, form regular habits, avoid dissipation, learn French, German and Italian, study modern history, pay attention to business. The Victorians were wrong to see Chesterfield as a fop and a snob. He had no pride in his birth as such, and he worked hard, ludicrously so, at the 'art of pleasing'. And if there is something comic in the spectacle of the Augustan 'great man' labouring away obsessively at the minor graces, there is also a certain pathos arising from our knowledge in reading them of the disappointment that lay in store for Chesterfield, when despite all the polishing the cherished son failed to shine. This makes for a disquieting directness of relation with Chesterfield and puts his *Letters* into a different category from the usual manual of parental advice got up for the market, like Dr John Gregory's popular and pietistic *Legacy to his Daughters* (1774). The *Letters* may advise 'dissimulation', the baited hook behind the 'pleasing address', but they are appallingly frank about recommending it. The message is the importance of not being earnest, but it is preached with insistent earnestness.

Chesterfield's real offence was twofold. He gave a handle to those who believe that manners are necessarily a system of insincerities, who share Mark Twain's view that 'good breeding consists in concealing how much we think of ourselves and how little we think of other persons'. The violence of the reaction against the *Letters* can be seen as in part a subconscious attempt to deafen such suspicions. And secondly, he may be said to have given the game away about the Augustan 'art of pleasing'. The disproportion between the triviality of the recommended modes and the seriousness of their recommendation reveals the enormous importance of sociability in eighteenth-century society. Urbanity, politeness, a 'pleasing address', were not vague social ideals; in a society run on the system of patronage they were the means by which influential 'friends' were attached and their 'interest' secured. Chesterfield's *Letters* revealed how manipulative the atttitude to social behaviour might be, how weak the links between manners and morals or between manners and sincerity, in a society which made dissimulation in some form necessary to self-advancement. 'Chesterfield caught the ambivalence within Georgian polite education', Sheldon Rothblatt writes: 'His own greatest vice was to reveal unequivocably how easily civilised behaviour could be reduced to the lowest common denominator. The public that read his posthumous writings neither applauded his candour nor forgave him for disclosing a cultural secret.'[3]

Dissimulation was the serpent among the flowers of polite manners. In calling Chesterfield a hypocrite it is as well to remember the derivation of the term from the Greek word for actor and the extent to which, in eighteenth-century fashionable life, all the world really was a stage. 'My anxiety for your success increases in proportion as the time approaches of your taking your part upon the great stage of the world', he wrote to his son on 29 October 1748. 'The audience will form their opinion of you upon your first appearance ... and so far it will be final, that, though it may vary as to the degrees, it will never totally change.' He was in effect training an actor, and here too the *Letters* raised one of the unspoken dilemmas of polite society. To quote Professor Rothblatt again: 'The Georgians realized that in order for their educational theory to succeed they must all be actors. They also realized that acting was a corruption of the values they wanted to profess.'[4] The high premium put upon manners as social performance meant that a successful but dishonest performance was always in danger of being mistaken for the real thing. No one was more aware of this problem than Jane Austen. All her villains are in this sense actors, young men of 'pleasing address' and masters of what Chesterfield called 'those lesser talents, of an engaging, insinuating manner, an easy good breeding, a genteel behaviour and address' (6 March 1747). Willoughby, Wickham, Henry Crawford, Frank Churchill — her novels progress towards an increasingly subtle registration of the ways in which plausible manners can mask moral realities, until in *Emma* (1816) the whole novel turns upon a sustained act of dissimulation by the ironically named Frank. It is interesting, too, that amateur theatricals should play such an important part in *Mansfield Park* (1813), her most ambitious exploration of late eighteenth-century landed society and the modern challenge to its values. The theatricals are introduced by outsiders who have caught the fashion from a Whig aristocracy flirting with dangerous radical ideas, but the enemy is within as well, where the prospect of acting exerts a fatal fascination over a bored gentry. In the symbolic absence of the father, 'Lovers' Vows' offers exciting rather than routine role-playing, an anarchic extension of the social performance which is polite manners. By contrast, the quietude of Fanny Price, her obstinate insistence on the integrity of heart and manner, looks forward to the criterion of sincerity that dominates Victorian notions of conduct.

The most famous Victorian portrait of Lord Chesterfield is that by Dickens in *Barnaby Rudge*. Sir John Chester is usually seen in his rooms in the Temple, sitting in bed or lolling on his sofa, sipping chocolate and reading Chesterfield's *Letters* – 'upon my honour, the most masterly composition, the most delicate thoughts, the finest code of morality, and the most gentlemanly sentiments in the universe!' (ch. 23). When challenged by his son Edward to be sincere – 'Let me pursue the manly open part I wish to take, and do not repel me by this unkind indifference' – Chester replies: 'Go on, my dear Edward, I beg. But remember your promise. There is great earnestness, vast candour, a manifest sincerity in all you say, but I fear I observe the faintest indications of a tendency to prose' (ch. 15). Appealed to later in the name of father, Chester affects to be shocked:

> 'My good fellow,' interposed the parent hastily, as he set down his glass, and raised his eyebrows with a startled and horrified expression, 'for Heaven's sake don't call me by that obsolete and ancient name. Have some regard for delicacy. Am I grey, or wrinkled, do I go on crutches, have I lost my teeth, that you adopt such a mode of address? Good God, how very coarse!' (ch. 32)

Churton Collins protested at 'the unspeakable vulgarity and absurdity of Dickens's caricature and travesty',[5] and the ironies here do seem heavily obvious. But as is often the case with Dickens, there is a less obvious point about fatherhood being made as well. His deeper insight is that a concept of gentility which has divorced itself from morality and the life of feeling leads not simply to the obvious vices of dissimulation and hypocrisy, but is itself subversive of the civilisation to which it lays claim. *Barnaby Rudge* is set in the late eighteenth century at the time of the Gordon Riots, and it is a nice moral and historical irony that Sir John Chester, who like Chesterfield disdains natural affection (Chesterfield thought the idea 'nonsense'), should father a 'natural' son, Hugh, an unkempt gipsy who is the antithesis of his well-bred father and becomes a ringleader of the riots. The heartless decorum of the eighteenth-century gentleman is seen to father anarchy, the exquisite manners when divorced from the moral life become brutalising.

The terms of Dickens's critique of Chesterfield set out the contrary values of a reforming middle-class approach to manners. The key words are frank, open, manly, earnest, sincere — acknowledging the possibility of a bridge between manners and morals, feeling and social form. 'As a man may be wise without learning,' one popular Victorian courtesy book put it, 'so one may be polite without etiquette; true politeness arises from the heart, not the head'.[6] The manly gentleman was felt to be above the petty rules of 'etiquette', which was what the flexible formality of Augustan manners had declined to by the mid-nineteenth century: 'what is good-breeding at St. James's would pass for foppery or banter in a remote village; and the homespun civility of that village, would be considered as brutality at court', Chesterfield wrote in his essay on 'Civility and Good-breeding'.[7] The Victorians tended to repudiate this 'sliding scale of manners', as one reviewer of a contemporary book of etiquette put it in the *Saturday Review* in 1862: 'The true gentleman is absolutely and unalterably the same in the cottage and in the palace, simply out of respect for himself and a noble scorn of appearing for a moment other than he is.'[8] They reached for something more constant than the Chesterfieldian modes of civility, free from affectation at court or foppery in the village, and involving (in Dickens's case at least) a reciprocal recognition of the natural courtesy of the humble. Stephen Blackpool, the Coketown workman in *Hard Times* (1854), is 'neither courtly, nor handsome, nor picturesque, in any respect', and yet his manner of accepting a gift of money from Louisa Gradgrind 'had a grace in it that Lord Chesterfield could not have taught his son in a century' (bk II, ch. 6). But by 1800 the Chesterfieldian courtier was a figure of history. If the Victorians failed to do him justice, mistaking his stoicism for simple hardness of heart and his educated worldliness for foppery, it is largely because his kind of fine gentlemanliness had merged for them into that of another — the Regency dandy. And as one contemporary reviewer reminded them, again in the *Saturday Review*, Chesterfield was at least something more than that: 'Chesterfield was not a man of the world in the sense in which Major Pendennis was a man of the world. This is to say, he was really a man of the world, and not a man about town — a very important distinction which the latter usually overlooks.'[9]

II

If Chesterfield survived in the Victorian consciousness as the supreme example of the cynical and worldly aristocrat, it was very different with Addison and Steele: they were welcomed as honorary Victorians. Macaulay's famous panegyric on Addison, Thackeray's hearty condescension to 'honest Dick' Steele, are gestures of solidarity with kindred spirits in a different age. In practice, there were probably few matters on which Chesterfield and Addison would have disagreed, from a detestation of duelling to a preference for 'Chearfulness' over 'Mirth' (*Spectator*, no. 381), and both were engaged in the business of polishing manners. The important difference was that while Chesterfield wrote in the tone and with the assumptions of a nobleman, Addison had shown himself sympathetic to the middle ranks and respectful of their domestic values. He had mocked the fopperies of the Town and praised the usefulness of the City and the decency of the Citizen, and above all he had done it with a wit and elegance that even the Town had found irresistible. 'He taught the nation', Macaulay wrote in his famous *Edinburgh Review* article of 1843, 'that the faith and the morality of Hale and Tillotson might be found in company with wit more sparkling than the wit of Congreve, and with humour richer than the humour of Vanbrugh.'[10] To a serious generation emerging from the Regency and its aftermath, this was indeed a valuable historical ally to claim.

To Addison, in particular, belongs the credit of having brought about a great reform of manners, whereby the wits were moralised and the puritans polished. If it is difficult to breathe much life now into this most limp of cultural cliches, it is partly because the very success of the enterprise eclipsed the insolent manners which Addison set out to tame. 'I sometimes catch myself taking it for granted', C. S. Lewis remarked in his essay on Addison, 'that the marks of good breeding were in all ages the same as they are to-day — that swagger was always vulgar, that a low voice, an unpretentious manner, a show (however superficial) of self-effacement, were always demanded. But it is almost certainly false.'[11] The sobriety of the new manners, and their extension into the negative gentility of Victorian 'good form', make Addison's achievement seem slight, but it was anything but slight to those like Dr Johnson who could remember the insolence of aristocratic manners and the need for an '*Arbiter elegantiarum*, a judge of propriety' at the time when the *Tatler* and *Spectator* started to appear; nor was Johnson in any doubt as to the historical importance of Addison's achievement: 'He has dissipated the prejudice that had long connected gaiety with vice, and easiness of manners with laxity of principles. He has restored virtue to its dignity, and taught innocence not to be ashamed. This is an elevation of literary character, *above all Greek, above all Roman fame*.'[12] Or as one of Addison's Victorian editors put it:

> It is no small triumph to have dissociated learning from pedantry, courage from the quarrelsomeness of the bravo; to have got rid of the brutalities and brutal pleasures of that older life, of its 'grinning

matches' and bull-baitings, its drunkenness and oaths, its rakes and its mohawks; to have no more Parson Trullibers, to have superseded the Squire Westerns by the Squire Allworthys, and to have made Lovelace impossible.'[13]

None of this posthumous praise, however, quite explains why Addison and Steele should have been so successful. The secret lay, I think, in their ability not only to make the amenity of the new manners fashionable, but to do so by making the old Restoration manners look comic and *passé*. 'So effectually', Macaulay wrote, 'did [Addison] retort on vice the mockery which had recently been directed against virtue, that, since his time, the open violation of decency has always been considered among us as the mark of a fool.'[14] Addison and Steele could not have performed this task unaided, of course; the spirit of the times was on their side in the early eighteenth century. The 'open violation of decency', for example, had also been the concern of the Societies for the Reformation of Manners which started to form in the 1690s. These moral vigilantes tried to clear the streets of the more flagrant manifestations of indecency, such as prostitution, drunkenness and swearing, and came down particularly hard on sabbath-breaking. But they were after small game, and one frequent accusation against them was that they prosecuted only those who could not afford to hide their vices. As Defoe put it in his *Reformation of Manners, A Satyr* (1702):

> The mercenry Scouts in every Street,
> Bring all that have no Money to your Feet,
> And if you lash a Strumpet of the Town,
> She only smarts for want of Half a Crown:
> Your Annual lists of criminals appear,
> But no Sir Harry or Sir Charles is here.[15]

Addison and Steele, on the other hand, had Sir Harry and Sir Charles very firmly in their sights. Their target was the dandyism, insolence, and licentiousness of so-called polite society — the genteel brutality of the rake and the mohock, the affectations of the beau and the gallant — and their campaign can be described as 'middle-class' to this extent, that they set up a standard of good breeding which in its sobriety and domestication was congenial to, and attainable by, men and women of the middle rank.

The new image of gentlemanliness which emerges in the pages of the *Spectator* takes its bearings from two contemporary phenomena: the surviving remnants of Restoration manners, particularly as those were perpetuated in the continuing vogue for Restoration comedy, and the then highly topical debate about the social status of the merchant; the two are closely related, as we shall see. By 1711, when the *Spectator* started to appear, the Restoration was a memory, but a memory which lingered on (so Addison and Steele saw it) in the cult of the 'fine gentleman' and the fashionable assumption that style and sobriety were somehow incompatible. The cult was kept alive by what seemed to Steele the inexplicable popularity of Etherege's *The Man of Mode* (1676) and its leading character, Dorimant, a calculating rake and man about town. The serious side of the *Spectator*'s redefinition of gentlemanliness can be seen in Steele's attack on Etherege's play (no. 65) and his subsequent piece on the 'Fine Gentleman' (no. 75), where he argues that 'what is opposite to the eternal Rules of Reason and good Sense, must be excluded from any Place in the Carriage of a Well-bred Man'. But this sober message is probably more effectively carried by the paper's witty mockery of foppery and false gallantry. Here the tactic is to make Restoration manners look quaintly out of date and therefore comic rather than menacing. Will Honeycomb, the ageing beau, is mocked by Addison for taking pride in his youthful exploits, which are typical of the would-be Restoration rake: 'fancies he should never have been the Man he is, had not he broke Windows, knocked down Constables, disturbed honest people with his Midnight Serenades, and beat up a Lewd Woman's Quarters, when he was a young Fellow. The engaging in Adventures of this nature WILL. calls the studying of Mankind, and terms this Knowledge of the Town the Knowledge of the World.' And then in a turning of the tables characteristic of Addison's wit, Will, who despises the 'Learning of a Gentleman' as pedantry, is himself labelled a pedant: 'What is a greater Pedant than a meer Man of the Town? Barr him the Play-houses, a Catalogue of the reigning Beauties, and an Account of a few fashionable Distempers that have befallen him, and you strike him Dumb' (no. 105). Sir Roger de Coverley is also introduced as having been a Restoration gallant once, before his rejection by the widow: 'Before this Disappointment, Sir Roger was what you call a fine Gentleman, had often supped with my Lord *Rochester* and Sir *George Etherege*, fought a Duel upon his first coming to Town, and kick'd Bully *Dawson* in a public Coffee-house for calling him a Youngster' (no. 2). It is perhaps fortunate for Sir Roger's later reputation as the good old English gentleman that this hint of licentiousness introduced by Steele was not taken up in Addison's subsequent development of the character.

On the other side, the *Spectator* showed itself in a general way sympathetic to the mercantile and commercial interests, and opposed to those who wanted to deny gentility to the merchant. There is Addison's admiring account of his visit to the Royal Exchange (no. 69), and the presence of the merchant Sir Andrew Freeport in the Spectator club to speak up for the importance of trade against the Tory views of Sir Roger. The debate between the two of them in no. 174 ends in victory for Sir Andrew, who argues that the 'Merchant' makes his workers independent of charity, whereas the paternalism of the 'Gentleman' can only create dependence: 'I believe the Families of the Artificers will thank me, more than the Households of the Peasants shall Sir ROGER. Sir ROGER gives to his Men, but I place mine above the Necessity or Obligation of my Bounty.' This paper was written by Steele, who was more consciously committed to the merchant's cause than Addison, although neither was so frankly propagandist as Defoe in his *Complete English Tradesman* (1726-7) and *Compleat English Gentleman* (unpublished till 1890). The latter attempted to reconcile the old criterion of gentility by birth with the 'bred' gentility of the lowly but accomplished self-made man, arguing that both should be accepted as gentlemen and that the title 'compleat' should be denied to the gentleman born who lacked a liberal education — which for Defoe meant an education in useful modern studies like geography and history, rather than the classics. The *Spectator* is never so specifically modernising as this. Sir Andrew Freeport is both merchant and gentleman: as a shipowner he qualified through one of the loopholes in the traditional code, which conceded gentility to the overseas merchant because of the risks he ran (like a naval officer, and in contrast to the mere desk-bound businessman), and he has the further assurance of his baronetcy and the 'Substantial Acres and Tenements' (no. 549) of his country estate. Addison and Steele were not concerned, as Defoe and others were, with the problematic gentility of the businessman who could not afford, or did not choose, to turn himself into a country gentleman. But then the *Spectator* was probably influential less for what it said in favour of the merchant than for what it refused to say against him. By mocking the attitude of the wits towards the 'cits', by allowing Sir Andrew to win the argument with Sir Roger, above all perhaps by bringing the merchant and the gentleman together at the same table, Addison and Steele were making the fashionable snobbishness towards trade look unfashionable.

In attempting to reconcile the Whig merchant and the Tory squire, the *Spectator* was arguing, characteristically, for a synthesis of the old and the new. Theoretically, Sir Roger de Coverley represented the bedrock opposition which Addison's party faced, yet the portrait is quite free of political menace (he is not, for example, a violent Jacobite like Fielding's Squire Western). Sir Roger is a good man and a kind master, a little superstitious and behind the times, perhaps, and touched with the pathos of his age and unrequited passion, but always Mr Spectator's 'good old Friend'. 'The enemy,' C. S. Lewis remarked, 'far from being vilified, is being turned into a dear old man.'[16] Nor was he the real enemy: from the point of view of the attempt to reform manners this was not the courteous old knight but the Restoration fine gentleman, and here the *Spectator* took sides in the theatrical controversies of the early eighteenth century. Steele's attacks on Sir George Etherege and *The Man of Mode* look forward to his famous play *The Conscious Lovers* (originally called 'The Fine Gentleman'), produced in 1722, which established the vogue for sentimental comedy and in the long run ended the popularity of Etherege's play. John Loftis[17] has shown how the early eighteenth-century stage was still dominated by the stereotypes of Restoration comedy, in which the merchant was portrayed as a griping usurer and cuckold outwitted by a libertine hero, and how out of touch these stereotypes were with the reality of the merchant's contemporary importance and influence. Apart from the standing insult to the mercantile interest, the continuing popularity of Restoration comedy and its offspring challenged the efforts of the dramatic reform movement dating from Jeremy Collier's *A Short View of the Immorality and Profaneness of the English Stage* (1698). This movement, yet another symptom of the climate of moral reform in which the essayists were working, was supported by Dissenting merchants who had inherited the Puritan distrust of the stage. Steele's achievement was to harness the moral force of the reform movement while rejecting the philistine bias of the reformers themselves. To say that he did this by flattering the merchants is perhaps unfair, but there is certainly a ring of propaganda about the well-known speech in *The Conscious Lovers* where the wealthy merchant Sealand turns on his aristocratic opponent:

> Sir, as much a cit. as you take me for, I know the town and the world; and give me leave to say, that we merchants are a species of gentry that have grown into the world this last century, and are as honourable, and almost as useful, as you landed folks, that have always thought yourselves so much above us. (Act IV, Scene 2)

And as Professor Loftis shows, with this change in social attitudes comes a change in dramatic values: the hard, bright wit of the Restoration gives way to a more mixed, sentimental drama, which in turn is welcomed by the Victorians. 'A touch of Steele's tenderness is worth all his finery', Thackeray wrote of Congreve in *English Humourists of the Eighteenth Century* (1853), 'a beam of Addison's pure sunshine, and his tawdry play-house taper is invisible' (*Works*, Vol. XIII, p. 522).

What is interesting in all this, looking forward to the Victorian period, is the extent to which the modern concept of gentility emerging from the eighteenth century is formed in reaction against the Restoration, or more precisely, against the image of Restoration manners projected by its literature. Starting with the dramatic reform movement, developed and refined in the writings of Addison and Steele, the critique of Restoration manners culminates in the work of their great novelist inheritor, Richardson. *Clarissa* is not only dramatic in its techniques; the book's significant antecedents, Professor Loftis suggests, 'are to be found, not in earlier prose fiction, but in the drama — in Rowe's *The Fair Penitent* and in Charles Johnson's *Caelia*';[18] and its hero-villain is a full-blooded rake named after a famous cavalier poet. Richardson's use of the Restoration stereotype (although needless to say Lovelace is much more than just that) so long after the event is a tribute to the power of the aristocratic rake to haunt the bourgeois imagination. Lovelace is necessary to define and display Clarissa's exquisite purity; she is the fine flower of her class and in her downfall displays a nobility greater than that of the nobleman's nephew who destroys her. From this point of view, *Clarissa* brings into the open the sense of middle-class superiority to aristocratic conduct latent in the new manners. 'Can *education* have stronger force in a woman's heart than *nature*?' Lovelace asks, 'Sure it cannot.'[19] But it can: Clarissa affirms the integrity unto death of an acquired nobility. At the same time, the novel would not be so compelling were it not for Richardson's fascination with the power, style and sexual assurance of his Restoration rake, and his ability to explore the complex sexual and psychological challenge, he presents to the idealised decorum of the heroine. In this way *Clarissa* sets a pattern for the conflict between the aristocrat and the bourgeois in later literature: the aristocrat may lose the moral argument but his style and power are not so easily dismissed. And as the rake gives way to the dandy and later the cad, we shall see how the Victorian novelists use these anti-types to explore the strengths and the limitations of the gentlemanly ideal.

The reaction against Restoration comedy, then, is an important factor in the emergence of a new genteel code in the early eighteenth century. The modern gentleman is born in the pages of the *Spectator*, not explicitly formulated as such, but implied in its treatment of contemporary manners. He is, one might say, the paper's ideal reader, a man of modesty, restraint, good humour and good sense; rather smugly aware that the really fashionable thing is not to seem too fashionable, tolerantly amused by the surviving relics of Restoration excesses, above the folly of duelling and the old snobbery against the cits (he may even be a cit himself), alert to the contemporary importance of the merchant, and able to laugh at the likes of Sir Roger de Coverley and Will Honeycomb because no longer threatened by them. In combination these attitudes have a Whiggish flavour, but it is very mild: the appeal of the new manners lay partly in their very reasonableness, and partly in the trick of making the opposition look endearingly out of date. For the *Spectator*'s readers, which included a significant proportion from the new City and professional middle ranks, they must have held a deep attraction. Addison and Steele were advocating a code of gentility answerable to conscience and domestic decency rather than the old public court of 'honour'.

Yet the old code of 'honour' died hard, and nowhere is this seen more clearly than in the survival of the practice of duelling. In its traditional meaning, honour was the code of a bellicose aristocracy for whom courage on the battlefield and in defence of family reputation was the supreme virtue. As such, it was never completely Christianised, despite the influence of the medieval chivalric ideal and the gradual softening of manners involved in the transition to modern civil society. The 'Christless code', as Tennyson called it in *Maud* (1855), which required a gentleman to respond to insult by a challenge to arms, was the linchpin holding together the highly selective principles of aristocratic gentlemanliness: 'honour' in this unreformed sense meant paying one's gambling debts, but not the tradesman's bill; deceiving a husband, if need be, but not cheating him at cards; insulting a servant with impunity, but one's equals only at the risk of a duel. The testing-ground for one's courage, and therefore the justification for the whole bizarre code, was the gentleman's readiness to defend his honour with his life. Paradoxical as it may seem, only by showing that honour was dearer than life itself could the ultimate disinterestedness of the gentleman's way of life be proved. In vain did reformers like Steele point out the absurdity of this code which, carried to an extreme, could involve the duellist in killing his best friend: 'by the Force of a Tyrant Custom, which is misnamed a Point of Honour, the Duellist kills his Friend whom he loves' (*Spectator*, no. 84). The 'Tyrant Custom' proved impervious to such exposures of its illogicality.

The problem the reformers faced was how to make a more civilised code of gentility attractive when it seemed to devalue courage, which everyone agreed was indispensable to the concept of honour. 'The great Point of Honour in Men is Courage,' Addison wrote in the *Spectator*, 'and in Women Chastity' (no. 99). Christianity enjoined the turning of the other cheek, but it was difficult to make such restraint seem heroic. 'Why is it that the Heathen struts, and the Christian sneaks in our Imagination?' Steele asked in *The Christian Hero* (1701), a pamphlet carrying the subtitle 'An Argument Proving that No Principles but Those of Religion are Sufficient to Make a Great Man'.[20] One solution to the problem, taken by Steele in *The Conscious Lovers* and by Richardson in *Sir Charles Grandison*, was to show, or attempt to show, that it takes *more* courage to refuse a duel than to fight one. When Sir Charles is challenged by the rake Sir Hargrave Pollexfen, he responds by inviting himself to breakfast and then arriving unattended and determined not to be provoked. This gives him an immediate moral advantage over his challenger, which he follows up with a display of such heroic dignity and restraint in the face of extreme provocation that he soon wins the ecstatic admiration of Sir Hargrave's seconds. But even Richardson had to hedge the issue by presenting Sir Charles as an expert swordsman who is only just keeping his temper in control, the implication being that this Christian hero would cut his opponent to ribbons if he let himself go. But Sir Charles does not let himself go, and so the novel points forward to the only solution for the incompatibility of 'honour' and Christianity, which is the internalisation of courage as moral virtue:

> I will not meet any man, Mr. Reeves, as a duellist. I am not so much a coward, as to be afraid of being branded for one. I hope my spirit is in general too well known for any one to insult me on such an imputation. Forgive the seeming vanity, Mr. Reeves: But I live not to the world: I live to myself; to the monitor within me.[21]

The monitor within was not strong enough to restrain some famous men in the next hundred years from fighting duels, among them six prime ministers, Wellington as late as 1829 over Catholic emancipation. It was only in the early Victorian years that the practice died out, and appropriately some of the credit for this must go to that great moderniser, the Prince Consort himself. Shocked by a recent duel, he used his influence to get the Articles of War amended in 1844 so that it became 'suitable to the character of honourable men to apologize and offer redress for wrong or insult committed, and equally for the party aggrieved to accept, frankly and cordially, explanation and apologies for the same'.[22] In this, as in so much else, Albert showed himself to be in sympathy with the reforming middle-class view. By the 1850s Cobden could threaten to hand over a challenger to the police without losing face.

The novelists follow the reformers in condemning the practice of duelling. Generally speaking, the question of how a gentleman is to respond to a challenge is a painful problem in eighteenth-century fiction, an embarrassing one in Scott, and not a problem at all by the time of Trollope. The one exception is Phineas Finn in Trollope's novel of that name (1869), but he proves the rule by being a reluctant duellist, forced to fight by his fierce aristocratic rival, and knowing all along that 'few Englishmen fight duels in these days. They who do so are always reckoned to be fools' (ch. 37).

The most remarkable treatment of the old and new codes of honour, and a work in which duelling plays a crucial part, is Thackeray's *History of Henry Esmond* (1852). Thackeray set this, the most complex of his fictional meditations on the eighteenth century, in the period of the Marlborough wars and the *Spectator*, and gave it a historical reach going back to the Restoration and forward to a new life in the American colonies. It is a novel in which the new code is seen breaking out of the petrified forms of the old. The melancholy Esmond is a character standing at the crossroads of his society, simultaneously an insider and an outsider. As the child of a secret marriage between a Restoration gallant and a Belgian girl, he is both a gentleman born and, in the eyes of the world, a bastard; he is the heir to the Castlewood estate yet prevented by a private sense of honour and obligation to the family from claiming it; a baptised Catholic, educated by a Jesuit, who ends up on the Protestant side; tied by emotional and family loyalties to the Stuart cause (associated in the novel with the Restoration), yet increasingly aware of its moral bankruptcy; conventionally in love with the worldly Beatrix, yet bound by deeper ties he only partly understands to her unworldly mother. The private history of Henry Esmond is at odds with the claims of the larger history in which he has to play his part, and the novel progresses towards a final disenchantment with the public role required of him by family destiny.

Esmond's progress along this road is marked by three carefully placed duels. The first, in which his cousin and patron, Viscount Castlewood, is killed by Lord Mohun, ends book I, where we have seen the growing but unacknowledged love between Esmond and Castlewood's wife, Rachel. The second occurs in book III, when Mohun kills Beatrix's suitor, the Duke of Hamilton, thus (on a psychological reading) removing Esmond's second rival in love. But the most significant duel in the novel can hardly be called a duel at all: it is the token, bloodless crossing of swords between Esmond and the Pretender in the last chapter, when the Prince, having deserted his supporters at a crucial stage to pursue Beatrix, offers the outraged Esmond the satisfaction of a gentleman:

> The swords were no sooner met, than Castlewood knocked up Esmond's with the blade of his own, which he had broke off short at the shell; and the Colonel falling back a step dropped his point with another very low bow, and declared himself perfectly satisfied. (bk III, ch. 13)

With this token duel, following on Esmond's bitter denunciation of the Stuart cause and the symbolic breaking of his sword, the old code of honour is renounced. The history of Colonel Esmond ends in a farewell to arms. The hero marries Rachel, his mother-mistress, and they emigrate to America, leaving behind Beatrix and the dying Restoration world she has come to symbolise. Thackeray's pastiche eighteenth-century memoir turns out to have a Victorian gentleman in its womb.

The continuity I have been tracing between eighteenth- and nineteenth-century notions of the gentleman is embodied in *The History of Henry Esmond*, with its resurrected 'Joe' Addison and 'Dick' Steele, mock *Spectator* paper, and numerous references to *The Christian Hero*, Congreve, and Restoration drama. The working out of the novel, too, shows Thackeray's endorsement of Esmond's private, domesticated conception of honour. Yet the pattern should not be made to seem too neat. Thackeray is no more unequivocal in his affirmation of unworldliness here than in his other novels. Rachel is loving, and the guardian of the values of hearth and home, but she is also jealous and possessive. Esmond may be the man of the future, but he is also a melancholy 'Knight of the Rueful Countenance' (bk III, ch. 2), and the Oedipal nature of his relationship with Rachel works against an easy dismissal of Beatrix as worldly. The *Spectator*'s values are upheld, yet 'Dick' Steele is presented as a sentimental, improvident drunkard, and the brilliant parody of the *Spectator* (bk III, ch. 3) mocks the coyness and artificiality of Addison's style. These equivocal undercurrents enrich and qualify the historical thesis the novel is advancing.

III

There is nothing equivocal, however, about the celebration of the new manners in Richardson's *Sir Charles Grandison*. The eighteenth century's most famous fictional gentleman is a monument to all that was most progressive in contemporary ideas of conduct, as Phyllis Patricia Smith[23] has convincingly demonstrated. The 'Man of TRUE HONOUR' promised in the preface is essentially a man of new honour. Steele's campaign against duelling, the *Spectator*'s mockery of the rake, here meet the anti-classical bias of Defoe's ideas on a modern liberal education and the Puritan emphasis on family life, to produce a gentleman designed to represent the ideal of the Christian hero. Sir Charles, like Richardson himself at the time of writing the novel, is surrounded by a circle of admiring women who provide both a chorus to the spectacle of his virtue and a little fireside school of courtesy wherein delicate points of honour and conduct are earnestly debated. In this way the novel brings to life the domestication of gentlemanliness which the new manners implied. But the coyness of the *Spectator*'s references to the 'fair sex' has gone; women in *Sir Charles Grandison* form the supreme court in which manners are judged, and as such are equal partners in the moralised community which grows up around the hero. This is an important development and one not lost on Jane Austen, for whom *Grandison* was a favourite book. While not exactly of the 'middle ranks' himself, Sir Charles is a morally refurbished fine gentleman calculated to win the hearts of Richardson's middle-class readers by his elevated conception of family life and his respectful attitude towards the merchants, whom he considers the most useful members of the community. Almost everything that gives offence in Chesterfield's type of fine gentlemanliness is reversed in Sir Charles Grandison (although Richardson valued Chesterfield sufficiently to send him a copy of the novel). The new respect for women is central to this redefinition, replacing the cynicism or condescension of earlier attitudes with an idealised vision of the lady as civiliser which looks forward directly to Jane Austen and the Victorian heroine.

The line that runs from Richardson through Fanny Burney to Jane Austen is a familiar one. In the process Richardson's heightened vision of ideal heroines and satanic seducers is brought down to earth in the daily life of the rural gentry. If Sir Charles Grandison is the grandfather of Mr Knightley, then Clarissa is the grandmother of Elizabeth Bennet and Fanny Price. The rake is transformed from a man who abducts heiresses and immures them in brothels to a dissembler who gives himself away by leaving doors open, like Frank Churchill in *Emma*: 'Do not tell his father,' old Mr Woodhouse says, 'but that young man is not quite the thing. He has been opening the doors very often this evening, and keeping them open very inconsiderately. He does not think of the draught. I do not mean to set you against him, but indeed he is not quite the thing!' (ch. 29). The art which can mediate a character's untrustworthiness through an old hypochondriac's sensitivity to draughts is a very subtle art indeed, and to talk of it in terms of a 'middle-class challenge to aristocracy' may seem crude. But the challenge is there, if not in *Emma*, then in the treatment of Lady Catherine de Bourgh in *Pride and Prejudice*; it can be heard in Elizabeth Bennet's reply to Lady Catherine's taunt that she is 'a young woman without family, connections, or fortune' who ought not to aspire out of her sphere to marry Darcy: 'In marrying your nephew, I should not consider myself as quitting that sphere. He is a gentleman; I am a gentleman's daughter; so far we are equal' (ch. 56). Again, the Richardsonian alliance between respectable trade and responsible gentry can be seen in the important role played in *Pride and Prejudice* by Elizabeth's trading uncle, Mr Gardner, who is the one member of her family to win the immediate respect of Mr Darcy: 'It was consoling', Elizabeth reflects, 'that he should know she had some relations for whom there was no need to blush' (ch. 43). And *Mansfield Park* is obviously a version of the *Clarissa* myth of the middle-class heroine who proves nobler than the *de facto* nobility, or in this case higher gentry: the moral proprieties of the Great House way of life are betrayed by the Bertram sisters but preserved in the much-tried integrity of their poor cousin, Fanny Price.

On the other hand, Richardson can hardly be considered an influential writer for the Victorian novelists discussed in this study, important as he is in the history of the idea of the gentleman. George Eliot, Tennyson and Macaulay all recorded their admiration for *Grandison*, but Thackeray was a Fielding man and Dickens was hostile: 'Richardson is no great favourite of mine', he wrote in a letter of 1847, 'and never seems to me to take his top-boots off, whatever he does.'[24] His elaborate code of manners was considered too fussy and theoretical, falling as far short of manly naturalness on one side of the target as Lord Chesterfield did on the other. Dickens and Thackeray would have agreed with Scott's comment on *Grandison* that the

> very care which the author has taken to deck his manners and conversation with every becoming grace of action and words, has introduced a heavy formality, and a sort of flourishing politeness, into his whole person and deportment. His manner, in short, seems too much studied, and his talk too stiffly complimentary ... to permit us to associate the ideas of gentleman-like ease and affability, either with the one or the other.[25]

In the Victorian novel he becomes a byword for a quaint and slightly comical antique courtesy, of the kind found in Thackeray's Colonel Newcome and Trollope's Squire Thorne; not so very different, in this respect, from Sir Roger de Coverley.

Fielding was a much more direct influence on Thackeray and Dickens than Richardson. In the first place, he was felt to be generously above the niceties of decorum on which the bourgeois Richardson got snagged.

This is another way of saying that Fielding was an aristocrat (in the best sense) and not really interested in redefining gentility. As William Empson says, his response to Richardson's 'new' fine gentleman would have been: 'But I know what a gentleman is; I am one.'[26] Then, and related to his freedom from the anxieties of gentility definition, he was a 'manly' ally. Thackeray's 'Harry' Fielding (a thoroughly simplified and sentimentalised amalgam of the historical man and the authorial persona, it must be said) is 'one of the honestest, manliest, kindest companions in the world...you fancy that you see the tears in his manly eyes, nor does he care to disguise any of the affectionate impulses of his great simple heart' (*Works*, Vol. III, pp. 384, 392). In *English Humourists* he is again slapped on the back as 'the manly, the English Harry Fielding' (*Works*, Vol. XIII, p. 655). And thirdly, there is the profound influence of *Tom Jones*, especially in its treatment of the figure of the orphan. Fielding created a hero who was illegitimate, ostensibly of low birth, yet possessed of a 'natural gentility' derived partly from good nature and a kind heart, who turns out in the end to have a genteel pedigree. To meditate on Tom Jones, as Dickens did in creating the young heroes of his novels, was to ask testing questions about the constituent elements of the gentleman. How important were birth and breeding in making a gentleman? Was heredity more important than environment, and could it survive, as Oliver Twist's does, a crushing environment? Could a 'natural gentility' exist without the patent of birth, and if so, how much was this a matter of moral qualities and how much a matter of education and fine clothes? These and other questions were perplexing to the early Victorians, and particularly so to a man like Dickens who had nearly lost his genteel birthright in the blacking factory (if, indeed, he ever had it in the first place). We shall see him make successive attempts to explore these issues in tracing the fortunes of his 'naturally' genteel orphan heroes.

IV

Finally, in considering the impact of these influences on later writers, it is necessary to go back to the *Spectator* and Sir Roger de Coverley. I have left discussion of him to the end, for literature's best-known old English gentleman stands out against the modernising current this chapter has been tracing. Not that there is anything unregenerate in the portrait, or boorish and violent as in Fielding's Squire Western. Sir Roger may have been conceived initially as a figure of country backwardness and as a foil to Sir Andrew Freeport, but he is portrayed as the soul of old-world courtesy, and the final Coverley papers are bathed in affection and sentiment. Perhaps, as C. S. Lewis suggested, Addison and Steele could afford to be so indulgent because his type was no longer felt to pose a threat to their cause. If so, then it is a nice historical irony that the Whiggish

Spectator should be remembered best for its Tory squire. But this is not really surprising, for the Coverley papers have something of the interest of a novel; there the modest aims of the polite essay are transcended. In the character of Sir Roger, Addison and Steele stumbled on one of the great English archetypes.

What was the source of his appeal? Partly it was that the character represented something robust and decent and generous, as opposed to the rather prim commercial rectitude of Sir Andrew Freeport. Sir Andrew argues against the 'gentleman's' charity on the grounds that he, the merchant, creates employment and therefore relieves poverty (no. 174); Sir Roger is simply charitable, going against the economic grain if need be. Solicited by the Thames watermen, he goes out of his way to choose one with a wooden leg — 'I wou'd rather bate him a few Strokes of his Oar, than not Employ an honest Man that has been wounded in the Queen's Service' (no. 383). What seemed quixotic in 1710 looked rather different in the century of political economy and the iron law of wages. Then Sir Roger is a model landlord, kind to his servants and tenants, generous to the poor. At Christmas he keeps open house, and sends 'a string of Hog's-puddings with a pack of Cards to every poor Family in the Parish' (no. 269). He is surrounded by ageing servants who love him for his goodness. At the county sessions he is the 'poor Man's Friend': 'I am afraid he caught his Death the last Country Sessions,' his butler writes in a letter to Mr Spectator, 'where he would go to see Justice done to a poor Widow Woman, and her Fatherless Children, that had been wronged by a Neighbouring Gentleman; for you know, Sir, my good Master was always the poor Man's Friend' (no. 517). In London he is an innocent at large; his virtue is rural, and squirearchical rather than aristocratic. All these characteristics combine to make Sir Roger the typical old English gentleman, but what gave him his mythical stature, at least in the nineteenth century, was surely his vulnerability. His personal simplicity and eccentricity, what Thackeray called in *English Humourists* 'that sweet weakness' (*Works*, Vol. XIII, p. 539), is a sign of the larger impotence of the type to which he belongs. It is important that he should be crossed in love and childless, and that when he dies a certain kind of old-world courtesy and integrity should seem to pass with him. Sir Roger is not simply the old English gentleman, he is the *last* old English gentleman.

He has many fictional heirs. There are several generations of 'last English gentlemen' in the English novel. Prominent among them is Thackeray's Colonel Newcome, who reveals his literary pedigree by his favourite reading: the *Spectator*, *Don Quixote* and *Sir Charles Grandison*. 'I read these, sir,' he used to say, 'because I like to be in the company of gentlemen; and Sir Roger de Coverley, and Sir Charles Grandison, and Don Quixote are the finest gentlemen in the world' (*The Newcomes*, ch.4). A short list of Sir Roger's heirs would include Dickens's Sir Leicester Dedlock, Trollope's Roger Carbury in *The Way We Live Now* (1875) —

and as we shall see, many more of Trollope's squires, Ford Madox Ford's Christopher Tietjens and Evelyn Waugh's Guy Crouchback. Common to them all is either childlessness or sexual disappointment or both, a distaste for the modern world and an old-fashioned code of honour, usually associated with the responsibilities of land or military service.

In the history of the gentlemanly idea in English fiction, Sir Roger and his heirs would seem to have had the final word. The sober, domesticated, middle-class gentility of the *Spectator* could capture the imagination of writers when it seemed, as it did to Richardson or Macaulay, a heroic defence of decency against the insolence of aristocratic power. Given the context of the Restoration or, later, the Regency, the new manners can be seen to have been a civilising force. But once they had hardened into the Victorian cult of good form and respectability, a writer like Thackeray was drawn again to the unworldliness of the Coverley archetype as a means of articulating what had gone wrong with his civilisation. Both attitudes to the gentleman, the reforming and the elegiac, can be seen at work in Thackeray, and it is to his fiction I shall now turn.

REFERENCES: CHAPTER 1

1. J. C. Collins, *Essays and Studies* (London: Macmillan, 1895), p. 195.
2. H. E. Rollins (ed.), *The Letters of John Keats*, 2 vols (Cambridge, Mass.: Harvard University Press, 1958), Vol. II, p. 272.
3. S. Rothblatt, *Tradition and Change in English Liberal Education* (London: Faber, 1976), p. 31.
4. ibid., p. 103.
5. Collins, op. cit., p. 200.
6. J. H. Friswell, *The Gentle Life: Essays in Aid of the Formation of Character* (London: Sampson Low, 1864), p. 43.
7. *The World*, no. 148 (30 October 1755).
8. *Saturday Review*, vol. XIV (1862), p. 158.
9. ibid., vol. XXII (1866), p. 367.
10. *Edinburgh Review*, vol. LXXVIII (1843), p. 231.
11. C. S. Lewis, 'Addison', in *Essays on the Eighteenth Century Presented to David Nichol Smith* (Oxford: Clarendon Press, 1945), p. 7.
12. S. Johnson, 'Addison', in *Lives of the Poets*, 2 vols (London: Oxford University Press, 1952), Vol. 1, pp. 407, 427–8.
13. J. R. Green, *Essays of Joseph Addison* (London: Macmillan, 1880), pp. xxii–xxiii.
14. Macaulay, op. cit., pp. 231–2.
15. Quoted in T. C. Curtis and W. A. Speck, 'The societies for the reformation of manners', *Literature and History*, no. 3 (1976), pp. 55–6.
16. Lewis, op. cit., p. 2.
17. J. Loftis, *Comedy and Society from Congreve to Fielding* (Stanford, Calif.: Stanford University Press, 1959).
18. ibid., p. 137.
19. S. Richardson, *Clarissa*, 4 vols (London: Dent/Everyman, 1932), Vol. II, letter 117, p. 462.
20. R. Steele, *The Christian Hero* (London: 1741 edn), p. 3.

21 S. Richardson, *Sir Charles Grandison*, ed. J. Harris, 3 vols (London: Oxford University Press, 1972), Vol. I, letter 39, p. 206.
22 O. F. Christie, *The Transition from Aristocracy, 1832–67* (London: Seeley, 1927), p. 134.
23 P. P. Smith, 'The eighteenth-century gentleman: contributing theories and their realization in *Sir Charles Grandison*', unpublished dissertation, Harvard University, 1947.
24 W. Dexter (ed.), *The Letters of Charles Dickens*, 3 vols (London: Nonesuch Press, 1938), Vol. II, p. 10.
25 I. Williams (ed.), *Sir Walter Scott on Novelists and Fiction* (London: Routledge & Kegan Paul, 1968), p. 39.
26 W. Empson, 'Tom Jones', *The Kenyon Review*, vol. XX (1958), p. 246.

CHAPTER 2
Thackeray and the Regency

> He is emphatically the true gentleman of our generation, who has appealed to our best and most chivalric sympathies, and raising us from the slough and pollution of the Regency has made us once more 'a nation of gentlemen'.
> (J. C. Jeaffreson, *Novels and Novelists from Elizabeth To Victoria*, 1858)

I

No writer is more central to this study than Thackeray, and in none is the issue of gentlemanliness likely to seem more problematic. Thackeray is, or should be, a figure of major importance in the history of the Victorian novel. He was the first novelist of real stature to seize on the fictional possibilities of the conflict between the aristocracy and the middle classes in the early Victorian years. He gave the word 'snob' in its modern sense to the vocabulary of the English novel, and his work from *The Book of Snobs* (1846-7) to *The Newcomes* (1853-5) is an unequalled record of the disturbing impact made by new economic and social forces on the traditional hierarchy of English society in the first half of the nineteenth century. The 'adored author of *The Newcomes*', as Milly Theale calls him in *The Wings of the Dove* (ch. 9), created the taste by which Trollope and later James himself were to be enjoyed. But today his reputation seems less secure than those of the other major Victorian novelists, and there is no doubt that 'gentlemanliness' has more than a little to do with it.

Thackeray has suffered, I suspect, largely because his contemporary reputation was so identified with what was felt to be the gentlemanly tone of his narration. 'It is impossible to appreciate either his philosophy, his style, or his literary position,' his friend James Hannay wrote, 'without remembering that he was a well-born, well-bred, and well-educated gentleman.'[1] In becoming the 'novelist as gentleman' treasured by his gentlemanly contemporaries, Thackeray was bound to suffer when the passage of time revealed how time- and class-bound that particular image of gentlemanliness was. In 1911 G. K. Chesterton was already noting the passing of 'that old world of gentility' and its implications for Thackeray:

'in comparison with Dickens he felt himself a man of the world. Nevertheless, that world of which he was a man is coming to an end before our eyes; its aristocracy has grown corrupt, its middle class insecure, and things that he never thought of are walking about the drawing-rooms of both.'[2] The consequence has been that a whole way of talking about Thackeray has passed too; its last echo can be heard on the final page of Saintsbury's *A Consideration of Thackeray*:

> I remember having, some thirty years ago, delight of battle for at least an hour by, and not far from, Kensington clock, on the subject of Thackeray, with the late Mr. Henley. At last, apropos of exactly what I have forgotten, I happened to say, 'And this, you see, is because he was such a gentleman'. 'No', said Henley, 'it is because he was such a genius.' 'Well', I said, 'my dear Henley, suppose we put it, that it is because he was such a genius who was also such a gentleman.' So we laughed and shook hands and parted. And really I am inclined to think that these words were, and are, 'the conclusion of the whole matter' about Thackeray.[3]

It is perhaps just as well that no one writes like this today: with friends like these, Thackeray hardly needs enemies. But Henley had a point; it is much more important to stress that Thackeray was a genius than that he was a gentleman. Nor is the 'novelist as gentleman' tag particularly helpful beyond a certain point. Obviously there are features of Thackeray's authorial persona which can be described as 'gentlemanly': his knowingness about the ways of the great world, for example, and his invitation to the reader to share that knowingness, or his habitual chivalry towards the weak and tender, or even the classical urbanity of his prose style. And as he grew older he did tend to retreat into the seeming safety of gentlemanly prejudice, in novels like *The Virginians* (1857–9) and *Philip* (1861–2). But the formula does not get to grips with the heights or depths of Thackeray's art, with either his unsettling irony or his equally unsettling melancholy, his note of *vanitas vanitatum*. Worse, by encouraging the notion that Thackeray was a kind of elegant lounger it has confirmed the modern suspicion that his view of life was superficial, offering only 'clubman's wisdom'. The temptation for Thackeray's admirers today has been to ditch the gentlemanly issue altogether, as John Carey did in his iconoclastic *Thackeray: Prodigal Genius*, where he spoke of 'the disastrous collapse of Thackeray's art, after *Vanity Fair*, into gentlemanliness and cordiality'.[4]

Yet this will not quite do either. Saintsbury's gentleman-genius may crumble in the critic's hands, but the idea of the gentleman remains a major, perhaps the major, thematic concern of Thackeray's fiction. In his great biography of Thackeray, Gordon Ray argued that he attained his 'high position among his contemporaries chiefly by redefining the gentlemanly ideal to fit a middle-class rather than an aristocratic context'.[5] This is a much more promising approach, forcing attention back on to the substance of his fiction, but again there are problems. One is the difficulty modern readers have in conceiving of middle-class gentility sympathetically, or in recovering the context that would enable them to do so, with the result that the sheer originality of what Thackeray is doing with Dobbin in *Vanity Fair* is apt to be missed. Another and more serious difficulty is his notorious ambiguity of attitude and tone. Even as he was creating them, Thackeray's inveterate scepticism was nibbling away at the clear outline of his good characters, so that a reader's growing impression that Dobbin, for example, is a noble gentleman has to contend with disparaging reminders of his lisp, yellow complexion and clumsy feet. Amelia is both a true lady and a 'tender little parasite' (ch. 67). A writer who so habitually seems to give with one hand and take away with the other invites the suspicion of his readers, even when, as in the case of Dobbin, the character carries most of the positive values of the novel. He wanted to affirm unworldliness but could never quite forget the judgement of the world. Thackeray is 'an uncomfortable writer', as Bagehot said,[6] and the idea of the gentleman was not immune from the ambivalence that marks his creative temperament: that is part of the problem.

To say that Thackeray was often ambivalent about gentlemanliness, however, is not to concede that he was necessarily confused about it. In fact, he understood the historical evolution of the gentlemanly idea better than any of his contemporaries, as we saw in the previous chapter, and it is with his historical sense that consideration of this topic should begin. Taking a hint from Professor Ray, I want to suggest that Thackeray's great achievement was to bring his version of the Addisonian analysis to bear upon the social experience of his own generation, specifically its experience of having lived through the Regency period and its aftermath. At the heart of his vision, and therefore at the heart of his interpretation of the gentlemanly idea, is his command of a long historical perspective, as David Masson recognised when he compared Thackeray with Macaulay:

> One of the many distinctions among men is as to the portion of the past by which their imaginations are most fondly fascinated and with which they feel themselves most competent to deal in recollection. Macaulay's real and native historic range began where he began his History — in the interval between the Civil Wars and the Revolution of 1688. Thackeray's began a little later — at the date of Queen Anne's accession, and the opening of the eighteenth century. And, as within this range he would have been a good and shrewd historian, so within this range his imagination moves easily and gracefully in fiction. A man of the era of the later Georges by his birth and youth, and wholly of

the Victorian era by his maturity and literary activity, he can go as far back as to Queen Anne's reign by that kind of imaginative second-sight which depends on delight in transmitted reminiscence.[7]

This is excellently put. It is the ease with which Thackeray can command the long historical perspective and the grace with which he moves, almost with the intimacy of personal memory, between past and present, that gives his record of changing manners its unique weight and authority. Masson was also right to see the significance of Thackeray's ability to keep one foot in 'the era of the later Georges' and the other in the Victorian period: so balanced, he was uniquely well placed to interpret for his own generation the transition from Regency to Victorian which they had lived through. Thackeray is peculiarly the novelist of the period 1815 to 1845, and it is against that background — the background of dandyism, the fashionable novel, the beginnings of the middle-class assault on aristocratic privilege — that his redefinition of gentlemanliness needs to be seen. He understood better than any of his contemporaries that the flamboyant Regency and its long aftermath had been the nursery of the Victorian middle classes, and in novels like *Vanity Fair* (1847–8) and *Pendennis* (1848–50) he portrays the interaction between the self-confident worldliness of the old order and the angular, domesticated morality of the new, struggling to define and assert itself in the early decades of the nineteenth century. He could not have done this so successfully had he not been able to call upon a long historical perspective, or to respond imaginatively to the worldliness of the old order and the domestic values of the new, enjoying the comedy of their interaction. Here, indeed, his ambivalence was a positive creative asset.

II

Thackeray was helped in this task by the fact that he could speak with authority about the gentleman's world. When friends and contemporaries like James Hannay observed that he was 'a well-born, well-bred, and well-educated gentleman' they were drawing attention, rather snobbishly no doubt, to the fact that he was not a parvenu like Dickens but a gentleman by all the best and most traditional criteria. Coming from a long-established family with a record of distinguished public service at home and in India, educated at Charterhouse and Trinity College, Cambridge, Thackeray was initiated into the rituals of the time-honoured 'education of a gentleman', which had changed little if at all since the eighteenth century — flogging and the classics at school, gambling, drink and debt at university. It is interesting to learn that he lost heavily at cards as an undergraduate (£1,500 in a single night on one occasion), and that he voted 'yes' at the Trinity Debating Society to the motion 'Has the institution of Duelling been of benefit to mankind?'. When he left university he could look forward to the usual life of gentlemanly ease on the strength of a comfortable private income. Yet there were aspects of Thackeray's history and subsequent experience which took him outside the conventional social pattern his education tended to impose. One was his Anglo-Indian background. Although he sailed from India at the age of 5 (appropriately on the *Prince Regent*), and never returned, he always retained something of what Gordon Ray called 'the curious point of view' of Anglo-Indian society: 'The humiliations endured by returned "Indians," whom half a lifetime of arduous service had sometimes made into personalities of formidable strength and eccentricity, gave them a detached and critical perspective from which to view the structure and customs of English society.'[8] From Major Gahagan to Colonel Newcome there is a mixture of mockery, affection and respect in Thackeray's handling of his 'Indians', until in *The Newcomes* the 'strange pathos' which accompanied 'all our Indian story' (ch. 4) colours his vision of England itself. Part of that pathos is his sense of the lonely decency and integrity which the Indian officer ideally possessed, a product of unselfish service scorned by a greedy, snobbish home society.

A more drastic exposure to the limitations of the gentlemanly ambience came with the loss of his fortune in 1833, when he was 22. Not having prepared himself for any career or profession, Thackeray was forced to earn a living at the unrespectable trade of literary journalism. This experience was undoubtedly a shock to him, and caused him to examine many of the assumptions of the rank into which he had been born. It was not so profound or so formative a shock as Dickens's experience in the blacking factory, nor so deeply humiliating as the genteel poverty which Trollope had to endure throughout his adolescence, but it can be seen as one of the roots of Thackeray's ambivalent attitude to the traditional gentlemanly ethos. On the one hand he could not help knowing, and feeling, that 'a literary man (in spite of all we can say against it) ranks below the class of gentry composed of the apothecary, the attorney, the wine-merchant, whose positions, in country towns at least, are so equivocal' (*Works*, Vol. II, p. 44). This led him to the affectation of genteel amateurism and that lukewarm attitude to his profession which so infuriated Dickens; and it may also explain why, when *Vanity Fair* made him famous, he was so quick to respond to the attentions of the great, and so gratified when they discovered that he was a gentleman after all. 'He [Hayward] seems and the great people too perhaps rather surprized that I am [a] gentleman', he wrote to his mother in 1848, 'they dont know who I had for my father & mother and that there are 2 old people living in Paris on 200 a year, as grand folks as ever they were. I have never seen finer gentlefolks than you two – or prouder.'[9]

On the other hand, while Thackeray could and did fall back on this pride of ancestry, the lean years in Grub Street taught him to see through the mystifications of rank, and in particular to understand the dependence of gentility upon money. The resulting double perspective is the source of some of his sharpest, most uncomfortable social insights:

> You and I, dear Miss Smith, know the exact value of heraldic bearings, — we know that, though the greatest pleasure of all is to *act* like a gentleman, it is a pleasure, nay, a merit, to *be* one; to come of an old stock, to have an honourable pedigree, to be able to say centuries back our fathers had gentle blood, and to us transmitted the same. There *is* a good in gentility; the man who questions it is envious, or a coarse dullard not able to perceive the difference between high breeding and low...
>
> In the matter of gentlemen, democrats cry, 'Pshaw! Give us one of nature's gentlemen, and hang your aristocrats.' And so, indeed, nature does make *some* gentlemen — a few here and there. But art makes most. Good birth, that is, good, handsome, well-formed fathers and mothers, nice cleanly nursery maids, good meals, good physicians, good education, few cares, pleasant easy habits of life, and luxuries not too great or enervating, but only refining — a course of these going on for a few generations are the best gentleman-makers in the world, and beat nature hollow. (*Works*, Vol. III, pp. 438–9)

This, from *The Second Funeral of Napoleon* (1841), must have seemed disquietingly closer to Thackeray's readers' real feelings on the matter than the rhetorical moralising at the end of *The Four Georges* (1861): 'What is it to be a gentleman? Is it to have lofty aims, to lead a pure life, to keep your honour virgin...?' (*Works*, Vol. XIII, p. 811). It is characteristic of him at his best to keep in an ironic balance the recognition that there is a distinction in gentility, and that money makes it possible.

Inevitably the balance proved difficult to sustain. Thackeray tended to swing from the one extreme of attacking 'this diabolical invention of gentility which kills natural kindliness and honest friendship' ('Chapter Last', *Book of Snobs*), to the other of affirming a bluff 'man and brother' stance of gentlemanly solidarity. The two attitudes can be found at all stages of his career, but the hostile one predominates in the early writings up to *Vanity Fair*. Thackeray began by attacking the aristocratic gentlemanliness he had encountered in his own social milieu and in his reading of eighteenth-century fiction. Count Galgenstein in *Catherine* (1839–40), the Hon. Algernon Deuceace in *The Yellowplush Papers* (1837–8), Brandon in *A Shabby Genteel Story* (1840), Barry Lyndon — these are all variations on the type of the gentleman-rogue, whose general characteristics are summed up by Thackeray in his comment on the ungentlemanly rogue Corporal Brock in *Catherine*:

In truth, it was almost a pity that worthy Brock had not been a gentleman born; in which case, doubtless, he would have lived and died as became his station; for he spent his money like a gentleman, he loved women like a gentleman, would fight like a gentleman, he gambled and got drunk like a gentleman. What did he want else? Only a matter of six descents, a little money, and an estate, to render him the equal of Saint John or Harley. (ch. 5)

The philandering, duelling, gambling, drinking gentleman was a stereotype of eighteenth-century literature (as Thackeray implicitly recognises by setting both *Catherine* and *Barry Lyndon* in that period). In *A Shabby Genteel Story* the type is brought up to date in George Brandon, a 'scoundrelly Lovelace' (ch. 8) who pursues the unworldly Caroline Gann: his heartlessness is laid at the door of 'that accursed system, which is called in England "the education of a gentleman"'. Here it is accused of teaching the young to be ashamed of their parents and their origins, and to forget 'the ties and natural affections of home': 'My friend Brandon had gone through this process of education, and had been irretrievably ruined by it — his heart and his honesty had been ruined by it ... and he had received, in return for them, a small quantity of classics and mathematics — pretty compensation for all he had lost in gaining them!' (ch. 2). It is perhaps significant that all these stories were published in *Fraser's Magazine*, a periodical of Tory-radical leanings but with pronounced and at times aggressively expressed sympathies for the middle classes. Certainly Thackeray's early writing is markedly anti-aristocratic: his noblemen are either rascals or nincompoops, and his middle-class characters are mocked for allowing themselves to be taken in by the mystique of aristocracy. Brandon knows that his friend Lord Cinqbars is a 'ninny' yet admires him because he is a lord: 'We pardon stupidity in lords; nature or instinct, however sarcastic a man may be among ordinary persons, renders him towards men of quality benevolently blind: a divinity hedges not only the king, but the whole peerage' (ch. 8). And Thackeray saw the same snobbishness at work in popular taste. *Catherine* is an attack on the practitioners of the Newgate novel, who pandered to their readers' snobbish susceptibilities by offering 'dandy, poetical, rose-water thieves' in place of the sordid reality, the 'real downright scoundrels, leading scoundrelly lives, drunken, profligate, dissolute, low', who 'don't quote Plato, like Eugene Aram; or live like gentlemen, and sing the pleasantest ballads in the world, like jolly Dick Turpin' (ch. 3).

Thackeray's most sustained anatomy of the gentleman-rogue is in *The Memoirs of Barry Lyndon* (as the 1844 serial was called when reprinted in 1856), a book which in the very thoroughness of its demolition work reveals both the limitations of his early attitudes to gentlemanliness and their origins in an outmoded literary convention. It is no accident that the book is set in the eighteenth century, for his target is the old bellicose code of 'honour' which *Esmond*, as we have seen, was to treat with much greater complexity. The novel is founded on the simple but skilfully maintained irony of an autobiographer recounting, boastfully and with an utter lack of self-consciousness, a life history which the reader quickly realises is shameful. The result is a condemnation of the eighteenth-century gentlemanly code from the mouth of a character who slavishly upholds it. From the start, when the humbly born Barry asserts his noble lineage and descent from the kings of Ireland (a spoof on the preoccupation with ancestry in eighteenth-century memoirs), the familiar features of the old manners are mocked. Barry boasts of his family, his skill as a duellist – 'A man of honour, Mr. Fagan...dies, but never apologizes' (ch. 2) – his success with women, his skill at cards. When he and his uncle begin a successful career as cardsharpers, Barry sees this as proof of his innate gentlemanliness: 'I knew I was born a gentleman, from the kindly way in which I took to the business, as business it certainly is' (ch. 9). He deplores the fact that 'in later times' (he is writing in the year 1814) 'a vulgar national prejudice has chosen to cast a slur upon the character of men of honour engaged in the profession of play' and blames it on 'a conspiracy of the middle classes against gentlemen – it is only the shopkeeper cant which is to go down nowadays' (ch. 9). His story is peppered with contempt for the business and professional classes, and he looks back on the days when gentlemen were gentlemen with regret: 'Yes, the old times were the times for *gentlemen*, before Bonaparte brutalized Europe with his swaggering Grenadiers, and was conquered in his turn by our shopkeepers and cheesemongers of England here' (ch. 10).

Barry Lyndon was the last of Thackeray's contributions to *Fraser's Magazine* and, artistically, it is clearly his best; but it is also a curious dead-end. The trouble is that Barry himself is too obvious a rogue for his exposure to hold the interest of a longish novel; Thackeray soon got bored with him, and the reader does too. Considerable creative inventiveness is spent on debunking a concept of gentlemanliness which by then was anachronistic, and which in any case the eighteenth-century novelists had exposed in their own day. Thackeray was banging on an open door. What he wanted to say about the snobbery of contemporary social and literary fashion could not be said by rewriting *Jonathan Wild*: Fielding's example, however deeply he may have identified with it, misled him into fighting the battles of the previous century and adopting a simplified satirical moralism which went against the grain of his genius. Thackeray needed to come closer to his own times and in doing so to recognise the ambivalence in his own attitudes. At one point in his lament for 'the chivalry of the old world', Barry says: 'Think of the fashion of London being led by a Br-mm-ll! a nobody's son; a low creature, who can no more dance a minuet than I can talk Cherokee' (ch. 13). The misconceived 'chivalry of the old world' was too easy a target for Thackeray; it was in pondering Brummell's legacy that he discovered his true subject and manner, which was not that of the impersonal satirist but of the involved spectator, the observer tainted by the vices he observes.

From this point of view Thackeray's contributions to *Punch* in the 1840s, notably 'The Diary of C. Jeames de la Pluche' (1845–6) and 'The Snobs of England' (1846–7), show an important development in attitude, as well as a new and sustained engagement with topical reality. 'The Diary of Jeames' is the story of a footman who makes a fortune from speculating in railway shares, and sets out to become a gentleman. As he tells us in his footman's English of being taken up by the Bareacres family and presented at court in the uniform of a deputy lieutenant in the Diddlesex Yeomanry, a contemporary reader would have recognised a comic parallel with the social rise of another wealthy upstart, George Hudson, the Railway King, who was at the peak of his social fortunes when Jeames was appearing in *Punch*. Slight as it is, the story catches exactly the social volatility of the 1840s and treats it in a way that is deeply characteristic of Thackeray himself, his class and his age. Considered as a satire, the 'Diary' mocks Jeames for his snobbishness and gullibility, while all the time suggesting that he is basically a good fellow; and more seriously attacks the mean and mercenary way the aristocrats sponge off him in his prosperity, and drop him when his shares collapse. Yet by having Jeames tell his own story in his aspiring Cockney idiom, Thackeray also pokes fun (snobbishly) at the idea of a man aspiring beyond his station in life. Radical and conservative at once, he offers his readers the double satisfaction of looking down on the aristocrats who leech on to Jeames, and of looking down on Jeames himself. Thackeray the snobbish anatomist of snobbery had emerged, and in 'The Snobs of England' he recognises it publicly, as it were, by giving these sketches the subtitle 'by One of Themselves'.

It is easy to point out the weaknesses of *The Book of Snobs*, as the sketches were called when collected and published in 1848. The definition of snobbery in the second chapter – *'He who meanly admires mean things is a Snob'* – has never pleased anyone, and this vagueness or uncertainty at the heart of the book perhaps accounts for the indiscriminate, repetitive nature of the satire: compared to his later novels *The Book of Snobs* has all the subtlety of a blunderbuss. In the end, however, this does not matter. The book is in fact one of Thackeray's most original works, a landmark not only in his career but in the history of Victorian fiction. In its entirety, it gives a vivid picture of an aspect of early Victorian society which no other writer, not even Dickens, had grasped so comprehensively – the hectic struggle for social position in a society rendered volatile by the influx of new money and ambition. In this context even the book's weaknesses are illuminating; the rawness of Thackeray's satire is of a piece with the social behaviour he is recording:

In the race of fashion the resolute and active De Mogyns has passed the poor old Clapperclaw. Her progress in gentility may be traced by the sets of friends whom she has courted, and made, and cut, and left behind her. She has struggled so gallantly for polite reputation that she has won it; pitilessly kicking down the ladder as she advanced, degree by degree. (ch. 7)

Dr Johnson had defended the principle of 'subordination' on the ground that without it 'there would be a perpetual struggle for precedence, were there no fixed invariable rules for the distinction of rank, which creates no jealousy, as it is allowed to be accidental'.[10] *The Book of Snobs* shows that 'struggle for precedence' coming to pass in a society where the 'rules for the distinction of rank' no longer seem fixed or invariable, at least to those with enough money and determination. The increased willingness of society to open its doors to the Jeameses and the Hudsons, as Thackeray saw it, had a fermenting effect on the middle classes who might otherwise be content to live happily in their own sphere. The same restlessness which impels the ruthless Lady de Mogyns to climb up the social ladder has its repercussions even in remote Mangelwurzelshire, among the Ponto family. Where she could be living a contented life as a country gentleman's wife, Mrs Major Ponto is reading the *Peerage* and bankrupting her husband by trying to keep up with the habits of county society. All middle-class England is writhing with snobbery.

When Thackeray describes Lady de Mogyns 'pitilessly kicking down the ladder as she advanced, degree by degree', there is a kind of gleeful relish in the writing, a positive enjoyment of the indignity he is describing, which has alienated many readers in his own time and since. That note of relish is of the essence of *The Book of Snobs*; it expresses Thackeray's excitement at having discovered what he saw to be the motive force of contemporary society. There is little room for sympathy as he builds up his natural history of snobbery. The characters are typed by their comic names — Lady Susan Scraper, Lady Clapperclaw, de Mogyns (from Muggins), the Reverend Lionel Pettipois, Sir George Tufto — and observed with an unrelenting eye. Mr Snob notices that the snobbish Miss Wirt, the Pontos' governess, has a finger 'as knotted as a turkey's drumstick' (ch. 25), or that the Marchioness of Carabas, on embarking for the Continent, 'looks around with that happy air of mingled terror and impertinence which distinguishes her ladyship' (ch. 21). No punches are pulled in describing 'Lieutenant-General the Honourable Sir George Granby Tufto, K.C.B., K.T.S., K.H., K.S.W., etc., etc.', who dresses 'like an outrageously young man to the present moment, and laces and pads his bloated old carcass as if he were still handsome George Tufto of 1800. He is selfish, brutal, passionate, and a glutton.' At table 'his little bloodshot eyes' can be seen 'gloating over his meal', he swears profusely 'and tells filthy garrison stories after dinner'. Lecherous, idle and ignorant, he is to be seen about Waterloo Place, 'tottering in his varnished boots, and leering under the bonnets of the women who pass by' (ch. 9).

The fierce comic light in which these and other characters are displayed led some of the first readers of *The Book of Snobs* to see Thackeray as a radical, and certainly the series ends with a scornful rejection of 'rank and precedence' and a plea for equality: 'Rank and precedence, forsooth! The table of ranks and degrees is a lie, and should be flung into the fire.' But his true position is, as usual, more complex than this. Just as the satire of 'The Diary of Jeames' was double-edged, simultaneously mocking and reinforcing snobbish attitudes, so the enterprise of snob-anatomy depends to some extent on the fact that Mr Snob is as intimate with the *Peerage* as his victims. The 'Snobographer' is forced to be a considerable genealogist himself, if only because his ironies require an intimate understanding of the processes by which wealth becomes rank:

> It used to be the custom of some very old-fashioned clubs in the City, when a gentleman asked for change for a guinea, always to bring it to him in *washed silver*: that which had passed immediately out of the hands of the vulgar being considered 'as too coarse to soil a gentleman's fingers'. So, when the City Snob's money has been washed during a generation or so; has been washed into estates, and woods, and castles, and town mansions, it is allowed to pass current as real aristocratic coin. Old Pump sweeps a shop, runs of messages, becomes a confidential clerk and partner. Pump the Second becomes chief of the house, spins more and more money, marries his son to an Earl's daughter. Pump Tertius goes on with the bank; but his chief business in life is to become the father of Pump Quartus, who comes out a full-blown aristocrat, and his race rules hereditarily over this nation of Snobs. (ch. 8).

This arresting passage encapsulates that feeling for time as social history which underlies Thackeray's major novels, as Jean Sudrann has shown.[11] To be able to command the knowledge of a time when the ancestor of the imposing Baron Pumpington swept the shop, or the Earl made that mercenary marriage between his daughter and Pump Tertius, gives a special kind of authority to Thackeray's attacks on the rich and the powerful. The long perspective enables us to see snobbery and pretension for what they are. At the same time it reinforces our sense of the gentlemanliness of the narrator himself, who by implication has nothing to fear from genealogical exposure and can therefore be trusted as a true, disinterested gentleman. In this way Thackeray was able to reconcile the conservative and radical sides of his temperament, his dislike for the heartlessness of society with his intense allegiance to his own long-established gentlemanliness.

But the fruits of that reconciliation between the satirist and the gentleman lay ahead. *The Book of Snobs* shows Thackeray's awareness of the process by which money is 'washed into estates, and woods, and castles, and town mansions', but only in *Vanity Fair* is the awareness integrated with a narrator who can command and orchestrate the panorama of English social life that the Snob papers intimate but never quite achieve. The crucial development is his discovery of what Percy Lubbock called his 'long retrospective vision',[12] enabling him to bring into play and harmonise the aspects of his talent which had hitherto been separate or unexpressed — the satirist, the parodist, the historian of manners, the moralist. And it is no accident that this development should coincide with his use of a particular historical period, the Regency, for his great novel. He had written about the eighteenth century in *Catherine* and *Barry Lyndon*, and about contemporary life in his contributions to *Punch*. By taking the Regency and its aftermath for his period in *Vanity Fair* he was tapping personal as well as literary memories, anatomising his own and his generation's origins. To understand the significance of that enterprise and its bearing on Thackeray's definition of the gentleman, it is necessary to look briefly at the Regency, at Thackeray's attitude to it, and at the literary genre which flourished in that curious interregnum between the Regency and Victorian ages: the fashionable or 'silver-fork' novel.

III

In 1828 Edward Bulwer (as he then was) published *Pelham; or, the Adventures of a Gentleman*, by common consent the best of the fashionable novels popular in the second quarter of the nineteenth century, and the one most frequently attacked by the enemies of dandyism. Its title page carried the following epigraph from Etherege's *The Man of Mode*:

> A complete gentleman, who, according to Sir Fopling, ought to dress well, dance well, fence well, have a genius for love letters, and an agreeable voice for a chamber.

The quotation is in fact incomplete. Careful as ever to hedge his bets, Bulwer left out the possibly *risqué* conclusion to Sir Fopling's definition, which in the original continues: 'be very amorous, something discreet, but not overconstant'.[13] None the less the choice of a Restoration epigraph was revealing, and its significance was not lost on one reader at least who was to become very influential as the scourge of Bulwer and dandyism: William Maginn, the editor of *Fraser's Magazine*. We have seen how *The Man of Mode* had been the most infamous of the Restoration comedies for the eighteenth-century reformers, the one singled out by Steele in his attacks on fashionable fine gentlemanliness for trampling 'upon all Order and Decency' (*Spectator*, no. 65). In his long and virulent review of Bulwer's novels in the fifth issue of *Fraser's*, Maginn quoted the Etherege epigraph and turned on Pelham and his kind the accusation that had been implicit in Steele's condemnation of Dorimant and Sir Fopling Flutter: their studied offensiveness to the middle classes. 'It would appear', Maginn wrote, 'that it was esteemed a mark of superior breeding with these vain young foplings, to express contempt of the middle classes of society.'[14] And he went on to defend the middle classes against what he saw as a snobbish and sinister alliance between high life and low, the dandy and the criminal, in the fashionable novel:

> It is from the middle classes that men of genius have in general risen. But it is a favourite notion with our fashionable novelists, to sacrifice the middle classes equally to the lowest and the highest. A gipsy, in particular, appears an especial favourite with the author of *The Disowned* [Bulwer]. There is a sort of instinct in this. The one class esteem themselves above law, and the other are too frequently below it. They are attracted, then, by a sympathy with their mutual lawlessness.[15]

This was a telling point, and the anti-dandiacals were to hammer it home throughout the long *Fraser's* campaign against Bulwer. Thackeray makes it the substance of his quarrel with Bulwer in *Catherine*, and again in his brilliant *Punch* parody, 'George de Barnwell'.

Against the 'lawlessness' of the dandy-criminal, Maginn set the conscience and 'heroic' self-denial of the middle classes: 'in these despised ranks, how frequent are the instances of generous devotion, and of ardent enterprise, of which the enervate candidates for place and patronage are utterly incapable!', achievements made possible because the middle classes practised 'the very first of virtues...that of self-denial'.[16] Bridling at the Etherege epigraph, he offered as the ideal of a true gentleman Dekker's description of Christ as

> A soft, meek, patient, humble, tranquil spirit;
> The first true gentleman that ever breathed.

— a definition which was to be offered many times in the Victorian period by advocates of the Christian gentleman ideal. 'Mr. Bulwer's gentleman is not of this *caste*; his qualities are, in every respect, the opposite of Dekker's.' There are, Maginn concluded, *'gentlemen* of two sorts; the natural, and the tailor-made. Let the reader judge to which class *Pelham* belongs.'[17] And to prove his point he quoted extensively from Pelham's lengthy digression on clothes in chapter 7 of the second volume, of which the following is a brief but typical example:

> I cannot sufficiently impress upon your mind the most thoughtful consideration to the minutiae of dress, such as the glove, the button,

the boot, the shape of the hat, etc.; above all, the most scrupulous attention to cleanliness is an invariable sign of a polished and elegant taste, and is the life and soul of the greatest of all sciences — the science of dress.

Bulwer expunged this passage and others from the second edition, but unfortunately for him Maginn had read the first edition, and Carlyle read Maginn. In *Sartor Resartus* ('The Tailor Re-clothed'), serialised in *Fraser's* from 1833 to 1834, Carlyle took Pelham's reflections on dress, savaged them, and made dandyism a metaphor for all the dead moral and intellectual habits which a serious new generation must cast off. It was a profoundly influential statement, and was to combine with other forces, like Evangelicalism, to turn a whole generation towards the values which the fashionable novelists seemed to disdain; work, earnestness, sobriety of style, social responsibility, manliness.

Carlyle could denounce dandyism so unequivocally because living in Edinburgh he had scarcely encountered it; indeed it is doubtful if he had read more of *Pelham* than appeared in Maginn's review. With someone of Thackeray's age and background, brought up in London and educated at Charterhouse and Cambridge, it was very different. He could hardly have avoided the fascination of the Regency because its ambience pervaded his youth and early manhood, lingering on after the formal end of the Regency came with George IV's accession to the throne in 1820. It was almost inevitable that, in common with his generation, he should take his cultural and historical bearings from the second decade of the century, the period in which *Vanity Fair* opens, when 'the present century was in its teens' (ch. 1). This was the heyday of the Regency and the dandy, the years of the Prince's pleasure-seeking court at Carlton House and those citadels of exclusivism, White's and Almack's, of Byron and Beau Brummell and Waterloo. The year of Waterloo, 1815, was its apogee: that year, the Beau is reputed to have said, 'was fatal to three great men — Byron, Buonaparte, and Brummell',[18] Byron having married in 1815 and Brummell been rejected by the Prince Regent. And that period was to cast a long shadow over the next twenty-five years, in the literary dominance of Byron and Scott, the social dominance of the dandies, and the political dominance of Regency grandees like the Duke of Wellington and Lord Melbourne.

The immense prestige of Wellington, linked as it was to the great historical landmark of Waterloo, a battle in which fashionable regiments had acquitted themselves bravely, served to complicate the early Victorian reaction to the Regency. 'The Duke's dandy regiments fought as well as any', Thackeray conceded rather grudgingly in *The Book of Snobs* (ch. 9). Otherwise this exclusive, court-centred world, bent on pleasure and disdainful of the useful and the serious, seemed in retrospect as frivolous as the Restoration — a historical parallel which the silver-fork novelists and their publishers were not slow to exploit. Disraeli compared the dandies to 'the fine gentlemen of our old brilliant comedy – the Dorimants, the Bellairs, and the Mirabels'; Mrs Gore, herself a silver-fork novelist, wrote that the genre arose 'from the ashes of our long-extinguished high-life comedy'.[19] Henry Colburn, who published most of the fashionable novels, brought out Evelyn's diary in 1818, and Pepys's in 1825. There were many points of similarity between the two periods. Prinny was no Charles II, but his Carlton House court offered a libertine alternative to the stodginess of the official court and an invitation, among his set, to return to the old insolent ways of aristocracy. The Regency dandy was the Restoration fine gentleman standing to attention and offering a calculated affront to utility and earnestness, to the 'cit' in the modern shape of banker or manufacturer; his style was an assertion of the aristocratic principle in the teeth of social unrest at home and the armies of the revolution abroad. But he was also a more embattled figure than his Restoration ancestor: not only were the middle classes more powerful (as the Reform Act was to show), but the enemy was within the gates as well, in the shape of the Evangelical revival sweeping through the upper classes at this time. In part this accounts for the ambivalence of the fashionable novel, delighting in the dandyism it satirises while at the same time showing an inevitable movement to some form of (usually secular) seriousness.

In one important respect, however, the Regency dandy differed from earlier types of unregenerate gentlemanliness. The beau, the fop, the macaroni, the buck, had all been recognisable from the ostentatious flourish of their dress. Brummell's innovation was a certain cool and austere elegance, a stylish simplicity which was not, however, to be confused with mere sobriety; it was said of him that 'one of his general maxims was, that the severest mortification which a gentleman could incur, was to attract observation in the street by his outward appearance'.[20] Naturalness of line and a minimum of ornament were the keynotes of his dress:

> Brummell's costume consisted of a coat buttoning tight over the waist, tails cut off just above the knee, lapels (perhaps lightly boned) rising to the ears and revealing a line of waistcoat and the folds of a cravat. Below the waist, form-following (rather than form-fitting) pantaloons tucked into Hessian boots cut almost to the knee. He used only two colours: blue for the coat, buff for the waistcoat and buckskins, these set off by the whitest white of his linen and the blackest black of his boots. The only ornaments he permitted himself were brass buttons on his coat, a plain ring and a heavy gold watchchain of which only two links were allowed to show ... For daytime wear Brummell abjured silks and satins, laces and ruffles. Wool, leather and linen were his materials.[21]

The crowning touch was the cravat, on which infinite care was expended to achieve just the right degree of unostentatious neatness. The story is told of a visitor meeting Brummell's valet on the stairs, his arms full of spotless white linen, and being told in answer to his inquiry 'These are our failures ...'. The cool elegance Brummell established marked the dandy off from the roistering buck and his grosser physical pleasures: it was, at least potentially, an *intellectual* pose. Such devotion to style as an end in itself had a kind of integrity, and came to be seen by the French inheritors of English dandyism as a possible stance for the intellectual in rebellion against bourgeois society.

Brummell's dandyism confronted (and affronted) the Victorians with the mystery of a triumphant style which was hostile to their earnestness and to the progressive momentum of their society. The fop was a timeless type who could be brushed aside as a drone and a fribble, but the cool self-possession of the dandy, his refusal to be earnest or useful, and the fact that he had enjoyed a brief but brilliant social dominance, these were puzzling to explain. How could Brummell have been considered a 'great man' in a society which contained such genuinely great men as Lord Byron and the Duke of Wellington? Yet Wellington had been a dandy himself, had been called 'the Dandy' by his troops in the Peninsula, and valued his position as an English gentleman above his military successes and honours. Byron, too, had accepted the social leadership of the dandies and adopted something of their pose in *Beppo* and *Don Juan*. Nor could Brummell's success be explained away simply by the friendship of the Prince Regent, for he continued to flourish after it ended and, indeed, his best-remembered *bon mot* was his famous remark when he cut the Prince and then asked his companion 'Who's your fat friend?'. He was ruined not by social ostracism but by debt, and even that was on the grand scale: he fled to Calais owing £50,000, 'in its way as great a fall as Napoleon's', Byron's friend Hobhouse remarked.[22] Nothing is so evanescent as style, yet it was the Beau's devotion to style, as recalled in a handful of anecdotes, that irritated and troubled the Victorians. Style as an end in itself, requiring a devotion which transcended the drives of sex, greed and ambition (contemporaries noted the cool, asexual character of Brummell's pose, and of course the dandy was by definition above the claims of the useful), perhaps this was what after all distinguished the gentleman. The Victorians wanted to moralise and Christianise the gentleman, to make the world's work compatible with gentility. The Brummellian dandy confronted this middle-class ambition with a challenge similar to that offered by the old code of honour in the previous century. The duellist proved his devotion to the code of gentlemanliness by his willingness to die for it; however absurd and self-destructive, this required courage and evinced a disinterested devotion to honour. Did not the dandy's devotion to style, his studied *nil admirari*, similarly demonstrate the ultimate disinterestedness that set the gentleman apart from the grocer?

The social uncertainty which made that question so troubling in the 1830s and 1840s gave the fashionable novelists their opportunity. With one eye on Brummell and his more ostentatious heirs, and the other on the seriousness of the rising generation, novelists like Bulwer, Mrs Gore and Disraeli exploited a genre which contrived to have it both ways, indulging a snobbish fascination with high life while showing their dandy heroes coming in the end to seriousness, or at least to disillusionment. In this the novelists and their publishers revealed an acute understanding of the market, as Bulwer himself recognised in *England and the English*:

> The novels of fashionable life illustrate feelings very deeply rooted, and productive of no common revolution. In proportion as the aristocracy had become social, and fashion allowed the members of the more mediocre classes a hope to outstep the boundaries of fortune, and be quasi-aristocrats themselves, people eagerly sought for representations of the manners which they aspired to imitate, and the circles to which it was not impossible to belong. But as with emulation discontent also was mixed, as many hoped to be called and few found themselves chosen, so a satire on the follies and vices of the great gave additional piquancy to the description of their lives. There was a sort of social fagging established; the fag loathed his master, but not the system by which one day or other he himself might be permitted to fag.[23]

One aspect of the market which the novelists exploited was the continuing appetite for Regency legend and gossip. Dandyism had moved on from Brummell's day, of course, departing from the exacting standard of crisp elegance he had set to become florid and exaggerated in the bearded, be-trousered Count D'Orsay and the ringleted young Disraeli. But the fashionable novel tended to look back to the Beau as the great originator of dandyism, re-creating or recollecting the circle which had acknowledged his social leadership: the Prince Regent, Wellington, Byron, the Marquis of Hertford (a model for Disraeli's Lord Monmouth in *Coningsby* as well as Thackeray's Lord Steyne), Theodore Hook. Hook, himself a silver-fork novelist, was the original of Mr Wagg in *Vanity Fair* and *Pendennis*, and Lucius Gay in *Coningsby*. Both Hook and Lord Hertford had been intimates of the Prince's Carlton House set. Brummell appears thinly disguised as Russelton in *Pelham*, and receives the extravagant homage of the young dandy who hopes to replace him as the leader of *ton*:

> the contemporary and rival of Napoleon — the autocrat of the great world of fashion and cravats — the mighty genius before whom aristocracy had been humbled and *ton* abashed ... the illustrious, the immortal Russelton stood before me. I recognised in him a congenial, though a superior spirit, and I bowed with a profundity of veneration, with which no other human being has ever inspired me.[24]

It is difficult to see how *Pelham* could ever have given offence, even in the unexpurgated first edition, for it is a witty, readable novel, and only the humourless and literal-minded, one would have thought, could fail to see the mockery (too light to be called satire) which plays over Pelham's dandyism. Perhaps the offensiveness lay in the very success Bulwer achieved in handling his hero's confessions. Beau Brummell remained a mysterious figure because no one knew what went on in that well-dressed bosom; his only life seemed to be a public life. But *Pelham* is a confessional novel in which the young dandy tells of his growth to maturity, and lays bare the motivating force of his life — ambition. Much the same is true of Disraeli's dandy heroes. The fictional dandy cultivates the arts of pleasing, but only to impress or insinuate himself with others so that he may advance his career in fashion or politics. The ghost of Lord Chesterfield stalks the pages of the silver-fork novel, with his uncomfortable message that manners are a means to an end:

> What a rare gift, by the by, is that of manners! how difficult to define — how much more difficult to impart! Better for a man to possess them, than wealth, beauty, or talent; they will more than supply all. No attention is too minute, no labour too exaggerated, which tends to perfect them. He who enjoys their advantages in the highest degree, viz., he who can please, penetrate, persuade, as the object may require, possesses the subtlest secret of the diplomatist and the statesman, and wants nothing but opportunity to become 'great'.[25]

This reflection of Pelham's is pure Chesterfield, both in elevating the 'ornamental' above the 'solid' and in the nakedness of the social ambition. It is the point the *Letters* hammer home *ad nauseam*:

> I repeat it, and repeat it again, and shall never cease repeating it to you, air, manners, graces, style, elegancy, and all those ornaments, must now be the only objects of your attention...The solid and the ornamental united are undoubtedly best; but were I reduced to make an option, I should, without hesitation, choose the latter. (11 February 1751)

Pelham readily admits to being reared 'in the art of *volto sciolto pensieri stretti*' and to practising 'dissimulation',[26] thereby recalling one of Chesterfield's favourite maxims and the infamous letter (22 May 1749) in which he recommends dissimulation to his son. And Chesterfield is obviously the model for the witty, worldly letters Pelham's mother writes to him, which are among the very best things in the novel.

So *Pelham*, light as it is, may have given offence not only by invoking Restoration comedy on the title page and in many of the chapter epigraphs, but also by touching the same raw nerve of middle-class sensitivity as Chesterfield's *Letters* had done. Thackeray mocked *Pelham* (Jeames has read it six times 'in horder to give myself a hideer of what a gentleman reely is') but it was not at the heart of his quarrel with Bulwer in the way that the latter's Newgate novels were, with their sinister blend of high fashion, low vice and metaphysical posturing. The fashionable novels which can tell us most about *Vanity Fair* are the second wave published in the 1840s, notably Mrs Gore's *Cecil, or the Adventures of a Coxcomb* (1841) and *Cecil, a Peer* (1841), and Disraeli's *Coningsby* (1844). These were the novelists he parodied so brilliantly in 'Punch's Prize Novelists', published concurrently with *Vanity Fair* in 1847 — Mrs Gore in 'Lords and Liveries' and Disraeli in 'Codlingsby' — so it is reasonable to assume they were in his mind at this time.

Thackeray perceived that there was a great novel to be carved out of the materials of the fashionable novel, which the novelists themselves lacked the historical sense and narrative skill to exploit. It is latent in the *Cecil* novels and to some extent explicit in the subtitle of *Coningsby*: 'The New Generation'. The first *Cecil* opens at the start of the Napoleonic Wars, and the epigraph to the first chapter is 'Vanitas, — vanitatis'. Like *Pelham* it is a fictional autobiography, with the important difference that Cecil Danby is older; the novel was published a decade after *Pelham*, but looks back to a period a decade or two before that in which Bulwer's novel is set, thus opening up a much longer temporal perspective. Cecil is introduced to Prinny at Carlton House ('the Carlton House of the Prince, not of the Regent'), knows Brummell in his prime, fights at Waterloo, and goes on the grand tour with Byron. Mrs Gore skilfully re-creates the persona of an ageing dandy, looking back from the early Victorian years to his prime 'when the present century was in its teens' and lamenting the lost splendours of his youth. He defends Prinny — 'It brings tears into my eyes to reflect how that last remnant of the Chesterfield school has since been vilified'[27] — and deplores the passing of the great Regency monuments:

> The Opera House is pretty nearly the only place of public amusement of the Prince's time, left standing. Carlton House, Buckingham House, Ranelagh, Lords, Commons, Whitfield's Chapel, Vauxhall, Fozard's Riding School, the Argyll Rooms, and the King's Mews, — all evaporated, — all flown off *in fumo*! This is the age of demolition, — the era of rubbish![28]

A tiresome *laudator temporis acti*, Cecil constantly evokes a past that dwarfs the present: '"There were giants on the earth in those days." Napoleon and Wellington were making war, — Metternich and Nesselrode making peace'.[29] Brummell is a 'great man' and compared to Napoleon:

> Napoleon is beginning to receive ample justice at the hands of a new generation; and our grand-nephews will behold in George Brummell a

great reformer, — a man who dared to be cleanly in the dirtiest of times, — a man who compelled gentlemen to quit the coach-box and assume a place in their own carriage... who will survive for posterity as Charlemagne of the great empire of Clubs.[30]

Mrs Gore had a much better historical sense than most of the fashionable novelists: *Cecil* is written for a 'new generation' and she skilfully builds this new generation into the novel in the shape of Cecil's elder brother, John Danby, an embryo Victorian in his bookishness, political seriousness and devotion to the domestic hearth. Cecil begins by despising his brother and ends by admiring him for his 'moderation' and 'modest good sense'; his brother's example helps him to see that the future belongs to the serious and the solid, and that he, Cecil, belongs to the past. 'As coming events cast their shadows before them, one felt already even in the early part of the reign of George IV a weary child of mind and body, foreshadowing the age of utilitarianism. The ornamental was about to pass away, — the graceful to evaporate';[31] he is left acknowledging the fragility of his *passé* dandy life-style:

> The longer we float along the stream of life, the better we begin to understand the fable of the vessel of iron and the vessel of clay; and if incompetent to convert our fragile materials into sterner stuff, the further we recede from contact with the hard and powerful the better.[32]

This, incidentally, is the fable used by Lord Steyne in *Vanity Fair* when he warns Becky about pursuing fashion without money: 'You poor little earthenware pipkin, you want to swim down the stream along with the great copper kettles' (ch. 48). *Cecil* was the first novel to exploit a perceived gap between the Regency and later generations, and in the sequel, *Cecil, a Peer*, the ageing dandy is brought into the Victorian age. Cecil is present at the death of George IV — 'The vail of the temple of worldliness was rent in twain!'[33] — witnesses the coronation of William IV, and then, as Lord Ormington, comes up from his country seat to attend the coronation of Victoria. The novel ends in the present (1841), with the hero a bachelor *roué* in his fifties like Major Pendennis.

It became something of a convention in fashionable novels of the 1840s to emphasise the gap between generations. Theodore Hook, for example, uses a pair of contrasted brothers in *Fathers and Sons* (1842) to make a point about changing manners: the unregenerate Sir George Grindle has two sons, George the elder, who is a dandy (George, after Brummell and the Prince Regent, was also used by Thackeray for his Cockney dandy, George Osborne), and Frank, who is serious and scientific. Needless to say, it is the serious Frank who overcomes the obstacles created by his father's preference for George to outwit the older generation and win the hand of the like-minded heroine. In *Coningsby* the cynical worldliness of Lord Monmouth represents pre-Reform Bill politics against the ardent Young Englandism of his grandson's 'new' generation. There is also the case of Lady Blessington's *Meredith* (1843), where 'a middle-aged reformed coxcomb passes on to the rising generation the lessons gleaned from his misadventures'.[34]

Vanity Fair clearly owes something to these silver-fork novels of the 1840s. The contrasted brothers motif reappears in Rawdon and Pitt Crawley, the one a buck who belongs to the old world, the other a 'serious' politician with designs on the new. The backward-looking Cecil may well have suggested to Thackeray the possibility of a reminiscential narrator ranging over the same stretch of time, but less indulgently. *Coningsby*, which he reviewed twice, perhaps alerted him to the fictional subject that lay in the interaction of 'old' and 'new' generations, as well as suggesting the mileage to be got from such notorious Regency survivors as the Marquis of Hertford. But in the end this likely indebtedness is less interesting than what Thackeray did with the themes and conventions of the fashionable novel, which was to dig through them to the rich soil of history, and excavate the world that had given rise, not just to the dandy novel, but to the dandy himself. By doing so he was able to teach his generation to see through their obsession with the Regency and recover respect for a more modest and attainable notion of gentlemanliness.

IV

Some light is thrown on Thackeray's thinking about the fashionable novel and dandyism past and present by an interesting series of reviews he contributed to the *Morning Chronicle* in the summer of 1844, shortly before he started writing *Vanity Fair*. On 6 May his review of Captain Jesse's *Life of Brummell* appeared, with an ironic invitation to the middle-class reader to take comfort from the Beau's lowly origins: 'It may be consoling to the middle classes to think that the great Brummell, the conqueror of all the aristocratic dandies of his day, nay, the model of dandyhood for all time, was one of them, of the lower order... Let men who aspire to the genteel, then, never be discouraged'.[35] The following week he reviewed *Coningsby*, passing from the great original of dandyism to its most ambitious contemporary literary representative, and gleefully exposing the dandyism behind Disraeli's political reformism:

> It is the fashionable novel, pushed, we do really believe, to its extremest verge, beyond which all is naught. It is a glorification of dandyism, far beyond all other glories which dandyism has attained. Dandies are here made to regenerate the world — to heal the wounds of the wretched body politic — to infuse new blood into torpid old institutions — to

reconcile the ancient world to the modern — to solve the doubts and perplexities which at present confound us — and to introduce the supreme truth to the people, as theatre managers do the sovereign to the play, smiling, and in silk stockings, and with a pair of wax candles.[36]

In this respect, Thackeray perceived, the 'New Generation' was not new at all, simply the old exclusivism disporting itself in the political colours of the day. His celebratory review of Stanley's *Life of Arnold* three weeks later is in marked contrast. Arnold is praised for his 'heroic' qualities, 'his lofty simplicity, his burning love of truth, his great heart so full of love and power'[37] — genuinely a man of a new generation, 'manly', serious and sincere. In his final review of 1844 for the *Morning Chronicle* Thackeray returned to Young England in a mocking notice (2 August) of *Historic Fancies* by the Hon. George Smythe, the Coningsby of Disraeli's novel.

Taken together these four reviews suggest how Thackeray's thinking about his version of the fashionable novel may have been influenced by contemporary publications. The old dandyism of Brummell, the new dandyism of the silver-fork novel and Young England, the Christian gentleman ideal of Dr Arnold — these form a spectrum of contemporary notions of gentlemanliness. Moreover, Thackeray realised that *Coningsby* had taken the silver-fork novel as far as it could go: 'It is the fashionable novel, pushed, we do really believe, to its extremest verge, beyond which all is naught.' Pushed any further, the fashionable novel would need to start examining its own conventions and presuppositions, in particular its ambiguous relationship to the dandyism it fed off; and if the writer of these novels were to deal with the new generation he could not do so as Disraeli had done, simply by giving the old dandies new clothes and a dash of political idealism, he would need to take account of the new middle-class seriousness of which Stanley's *Life of Arnold* was a portent. Thackeray clearly thought he could do better, and in late 1844 or early 1845 he wrote the first chapters of *Vanity Fair*.

Questions of literary stature apart, what strikes one most on coming to *Vanity Fair* after the fashionable novels is the immensely more complex historical understanding Thackeray brought to his treatment of roughly similar materials. Cecil fights at Waterloo but this gets only a passing mention; Thackeray places the battle, or rather the effects of the battle, at the centre of his canvas. It is not, however, Waterloo as the military novelists had treated it, all pageant and heroics, but Waterloo as a great symbolic event in English history. Thackeray saw it much as Matthew Arnold was to do, as the English aristocracy's finest hour, requiring and displaying the 'endurance and resistance' which are 'the great qualities of an aristocracy'.[38] Waterloo dominates the structure of the novel and the destinies of the main characters, and its long shadow falls across the domestic events with which the second half of *Vanity Fair* is largely concerned. As Avrom Fleishman says, it is

> the turning point in the lives of most of the characters, and becomes a memory which grandly and darkly hovers in the minds of all. Its presence serves to fix events in historical time more firmly than in any other novel of the age. Events are dated from Waterloo as though it were the turn of an era: Before Waterloo, After Waterloo. It is an epochal event that not only stands at the center of a nation's historical development, but shapes the destiny and character of all its members.[39]

Thackeray's treatment of Waterloo, ostensibly downbeat and offstage, also reveals the ways in which *Vanity Fair* can be called a historical novel. He is not concerned with the great set-pieces of history, or with introducing historical personages (no Napoleon, Wellington, or even Brummell); as in *Esmond*, he 'would have History familiar rather than heroic'. But he is very much concerned with what might be called history as cultural memory, with re-creating the changing features of his society as many of his readers would recall it. For instance, the characters on their way to Brussels are described as making 'that well-known journey, which almost every Englishman of middle rank has travelled since' (ch. 28), and the contemporary reader is reminded of a pilgrimage to Waterloo which he, like Mr Osborne later in the novel, or indeed Thackeray himself, may have made. In this way a link is established between the past with which the novel deals, the reader's own memory and the memory of the narrator.

There are many such links in *Vanity Fair*. Reading the novel in the Tillotsons' splendid annotated edition one is continually struck by Thackeray's knowledge of the Regency period and the care he took to bring it before his readers. This extends from the use of source-books like G. R. Gleig's *Story of the Battle of Waterloo* (1847), to detailed period accuracy in the clothes the characters wear, the books they read, the songs they sing, the plays they go to see, even the town landscape they inhabit. To take one example: when George Osborne drives down Piccadilly to his wedding, Thackeray peels away the recent architectural accretions and takes us back to a time and place 'where Apsley House and St. George's Hospital wore red jackets still; where there were oil-lamps; where Achilles was not yet born; nor the Pimlico arch raised; nor the hideous equestrian monster which pervades it and the neighbourhood...' (ch. 22). The 'hideous equestrian monster' was Wyatt's giant statue of the Duke of Wellington, a source of much controversy at the time *Vanity Fair* was appearing. As Joan Stevens points out, George is driving past Hyde Park Corner as it was in 1815, 'unconscious of the changes that will come, changes that will celebrate the battle in which he will be killed, six weeks beyond the present narrative moment',[40] and the irony is underlined for contemporary readers by mention of the Wyatt controversy. In such ways the reader's present is linked to a historical past still in living memory. Likewise, taking a hint from Disraeli, Thackeray drew on the Marquis of Hertford, whose death in 1842 was fresh in public memory because of the scandalous disclosures in the litigation over his will, for Lord Steyne, and of course the name Steyne had associations with Regency Brighton. Vauxhall Gardens were in sad decline at the time he was writing, but by re-creating them in their prime he was able to establish a poignant contrast with the pleasure-seeking Regency. Such suggestive interweaving of past and present is made possible by his use of a narrator for whom the period between the Regency and the 1840s is a stretch of lived experience. Thackeray was in his mid-thirties when he wrote *Vanity Fair*, but he usually comes forward (there are some inconsistencies) in the guise of a man twenty years older, the contemporary of the characters: 'Fifty years ago, and when the present writer, being an interesting little boy...' (ch. 39). The narrator's personal memory encompasses the historical memory of his novel, and this may explain why the original readers (to judge from the reviews) did not see *Vanity Fair* as a work of historical fiction: they were conscious of temporal continuity, not the discontinuity normally associated with the genre.

But if *Vanity Fair* does not fit neatly into the historical novel genre, it none the less has a grand historical subject. Thackeray's ability to command the transition from the Regency to the early Victorian period — a transition which he rightly saw in relation to the great landmark of Waterloo and characterised by the decline of an older heroic military code — shows his understanding of the essential historical movement of his society. Looking back across the same stretch of time as Harriet Martineau's popular *History of the Thirty Years Peace 1816–1846* (1849), he recognised the phenomenon to which her title draws attention, that the real history of England since Waterloo had been social and domestic rather than military and diplomatic. *Vanity Fair* is a central document in any consideration of what the Victorian critic E. S. Dallas recognised as the chief characteristic of his age, 'the withering of the hero and the flourishing of the private individual':

> The development of literature in our day...has led and is leading to many changes, but to none more important than the withering of the individual as a hero, the elevation and reinforcement of the individual as a private man. This elevation of the private life and the private man to the place of honour in art and literature, over the public life and the historical man that have hitherto held the chief rank in our regards, amounts to a revolution.[41]

And Dallas cites Thackeray's 'Novel without a Hero' as an example of this tendency. It is in such a context, the supersession of a military-heroic by a private and domestic notion of gentility, that Thackeray's redefinition of the idea of the gentleman needs to be seen.

V

Vanity Fair opens in Miss Pinkerton's Academy, a 'stately old brick house' with 'narrow windows', where Miss Pinkerton trades on her connection with 'The Great Lexicographer', Dr Johnson. The dying world of eighteenth-century gentility, resting on the Johnsonian doctrine of 'subordination', is deftly suggested. It is appropriate that Miss Pinkerton's parting gift to Amelia should be a copy of Johnson's *Dictionary*, and appropriate too that Becky should throw her copy (provided out of kindness by Miss Jemima) back over the wall, an act that establishes an unforgettable opening image of her spirit and cruelty. When she then exclaims 'Vive la France! Vive l'Empereur! Vive Bonaparte!', shocking Amelia with this 'blasphemy' (ch. 2), Thackeray means us to register the symbolism of her defiance: the little governess-to-be with her French mother and bohemian father is to challenge the fixed hierarchy of English society much as, on a larger scale, the little Corporal is challenging the old order in Europe. The Becky/Napoleon parallel works on both a serious and a comic-satirical level. Becky is a social upstart who, like the 'Corsican upstart' (as most of the characters in *Vanity Fair* call Napoleon), mounts a 'campaign' to penetrate the citadels of fashion, thus enabling Thackeray to revive and puncture one of the favourite cliches of the Regency memoir and silver-fork novel: the notion that the dandy was as 'great' a man in the sphere of fashion as Napoleon in war (one recalls Hobhouse's comment that Brummell's bankruptcy was 'in its way as great a fall as Napoleon's'). It was a master-stroke to make his adventurer not a posturing dandy but a 'sharp' woman and a social climber, thus opening up a whole new range of satirical possibilities: a more complex Lady de Mogyns is let loose in the world of *Cecil*. Yet the Napoleon analogy is not entirely mocking either, for there is something genuinely Napoleonic in Becky: she too is a portent of radical change within the old social order, and she has the daring to mount above her humble origins and the skill to exploit limited advantages. Moreover, by keeping Napoleon continually before us, the analogy becomes a steady drumbeat reminding us of the serious business to come, when the terrible reality of war will show up the pursuits of fashionable life for the vanities they are.

In leaving Miss Pinkerton's Academy, Becky moves from the world of Dr Johnson to that of Byron, or rather to a sub-Byronic world of stockbrokers' sons and Cheltenham dandies. Here again Thackeray is standing the fashionable novel on its head. In his *Morning Chronicle* review of *Coningsby* he had objected to 'these cheap Barmecide entertainments' where the novelists 'like to disport themselves in inventing fine people, as we to sit in this imaginary society'.[42] *Vanity Fair* mocks this compact of snobbishness and credulity by taking the reader back to the golden age of the silver-fork novel and introducing him to characters very like himself. Instead of Brummell we meet Jos Sedley, the fat, vain, bashful Collector of Bogley Wollah, who only pretends that he knows Brummell. Byron did appear in the first edition of *Vanity Fair*, but only in a footnote authenticating the description of Rawdon Crawley's brutish pleasures in chapter 11. In place of the elegant leaders of *ton*, we are given an insecure City dandy in George Osborne, and the clumsy, lisping Dobbin. Disraeli's cult of aristocracy is undermined in the portrait of the boorish Sir Pitt Crawley, who is described by Becky in terms which mock fictional stereotype:

> Sir Pitt is not what we silly girls, when we used to read *Cecilia* at Chiswick, imagined a baronet must have been. Anything, indeed, less like Lord Orville cannot be imagined. Fancy an old, stumpy, short, vulgar, and very dirty man, in old clothes and shabby old gaiters, who smokes a horrid pipe, and cooks his own horrid supper in a saucepan. He speaks with a country accent, and swore a great deal at the old charwoman, at the hackney coachman who drove us to the inn where the coach went from, and on which I made the journey *outside for the greater part of the way*. (ch. 8)

Substitute *Cecil* or *The Young Duke* for *Cecilia* and the assault on the reader's habitual expectations is as pointed as it is at the beginning of chapter 6, where Thackeray toys with the idea of telling his 'homely story' in 'the genteel, or in the romantic, or in the facetious manner'. His target is the mystique of aristocracy which the fashionable novels served.

> I know the tune I am piping is a very mild one, (although there are some terrific chapters coming presently,) and must beg the good-natured reader to remember, that we are only discoursing at present about a stock-broker's family in Russell Square, who are taking walks, or luncheon, or dinner, or talking and making love as people do in common life, and without a single passionate and wonderful incident to mark the progress of their lives. (ch. 6)

The great achievement of the novel will be to link that mild tune and those ordinary lives to the larger movements of history, so that from these 'modest...fountains', as James Hannay observed, 'spring[s] the stream of story that by-and-by expands into a mirror-like lake, reflecting the character of a whole generation'.[43]

The structure of *Vanity Fair*, as many critics have pointed out, is provided by the linked and contrasting destinies of the two heroines: Amelia, who is to live through and for the affections of home and motherhood, and Becky, who takes on the 'world'. Becky dominates the first half of the novel. She wins the reader's sympathy initially because, unlike Amelia, she has none of the conventional advantages (the loving mamma, the cushioning wealth) to launch her in life, and so must strike out for herself if she is to avoid the fate of being a governess. And the spectacle of her rapid social rise is exhilarating, revealing qualities of wit and resourcefulness which compel admiration all the more for being set against Amelia's passivity and the state of selfish brooding into which she sinks under misfortune. Becky takes her chances: by the time of the Waterloo Ball, after only 'three dinners in general society, this young woman had got up the genteel jargon so well, that a native could not speak it better; and it was only from her French being so good, that you could know she was not a born woman of fashion' (ch. 29). She is truly the brilliant strategist, the Napoleon of social life Rawdon takes her to be, who 'believed in his wife as much as the French soldiers in Napoleon' (ch. 34) — and as doomed to disappoint. Like Napoleon, she is cleverer than the denizens of the world she hopes to enter and from which she is excluded by low birth and lack of money. 'Birth be hanged,' Sir Pitt says, 'Your as good a lady as ever I see. You've got more brains in your little vinger than any baronet's wife in the country' (ch. 14). What she pursues may be worthless, but the skill she brings to the pursuit makes her progress through the novel into a satire on the great world. A brilliant actress herself, she exposes the hypocrisy behind the social performance; and in this she is like her creator, a subversive conformist mimicking the behaviour of others in order to amuse and satirise. Our experience of her as a character is inevitably complex, for although treacherous and unscrupulous she is also the source of too many of the keenest pleasures of *Vanity Fair* to be judged easily. The Becky who imitates Lady Southdown preaching the virtues of her quack medicine, so that 'for the first time in her life the Dowager Countess of Southdown was made amusing' (ch. 41), or who taunts Lady Bareacres, trembling with impotent rage in her horseless carriage at Brussels, with the family diamonds she has sewn into the cushions — 'What a prize it will be for the French when they come! — the carriage and the diamonds I mean; not the lady' (ch. 32) — thus taking an exquisite revenge for the Bareacres family's insolent treatment of Amelia; this Becky transcends her role as scheming adventuress. There is a saving grace in her ability to shrug off setback, to laugh at defeat or at herself. Her talent for the unexpected and unpredictable, even at times for a good-humoured indifference to self-interest, wins our sympathy and makes her, for all her faults, Thackeray's ally in exposing the heartlessness and hypocrisy of the great world.

At the same time, it is important not to laugh away her faults, for there is a point at which the Napoleon parallel breaks down. Despite her initial 'Vive Bonaparte!' she is no revolutionary: the spectacle of her social rise is a source of subversive comedy, but her own ambitions remain conventional: to be accepted by the fashionable world. She is the means by which Thackeray exposes Vanity Fair, but she herself remains deceived by it. This is what makes her betrayal of Rawdon so terrible. His 'You might have spared me a hundred pounds, Becky, out of all this — I have always shared with you' (ch. 53) points to the robust companionship in roguery whose central tenet, loyalty, she breaks for the spurious and conventional social rewards Lord Steyne has to offer.

The interplay of fashion and war, comic and satirical in Becky's Napoleonic social campaign, takes on a more serious colour as the novel gathers momentum and moves with sombre inevitability towards Waterloo. In the chapters (26–32) which formed numbers 8 and 9 of the monthly serialisation, Thackeray's genius is in full flood, enabling him to give a sustained, many-sided treatment to his central subject. Coming at the midway point of the novel they provide a great climax to the fashionable life of the first half, while at the same time putting that life into a larger perspective and so pointing forward to the deeper but quieter realities which are increasingly to dominate in the second. Brussels seems the apotheosis of Vanity Fair, where the characters find themselves

> in one of the gayest and most brilliant little capitals in Europe... where all the Vanity Fair booths were laid out with the most tempting liveliness and splendour. Gambling was here in profusion, and dancing in plenty: feasting was there to fill with delight that great gourmand of a Jos: there was a theatre where a miraculous Catalini was delighting all hearers; beautiful rides, all enlivened with martial splendour... (ch. 28)

Here George Osborne achieves the social coup of entertaining the Bareacres family and is snubbed for his pains ('we needn't know them in England, you know'); and Becky, flirting with General Tufto, is a brilliant social success at the Opera and the Ball, making Amelia feel 'overpowered by the flash and the dazzle and the fashionable talk of her worldly rival' (ch. 29). And in making the Waterloo Ball the concluding event in this crescendo of fashionable activity, Thackeray was going one better than the fashionable novelists, for no ball could be more 'historical' (ch. 29) than this (it had after all been celebrated by Byron himself in a famous poem): 'All Brussels had been in a state of excitement about it, and I have heard from ladies who were in that town at the period, that the talk and interest of persons of their own sex regarding the ball was much greater even than in respect of the enemy in their front' (ch. 29). At this moment of triumph for Becky, Thackeray slyly reminds us how far she has come: 'In the midst of the great persons assembled, and the eye-glasses directed to her, Rebecca seemed to be as cool and collected as when she used to marshal Miss Pinkerton's little girls to church' (ch. 29).

Thackeray's command of his subject shows in the variety of perspectives he is able to present on the impact war makes on this pleasure-seeking society. There is the touching scene of reconciliation between George and Amelia when, stopped 'in the full career of the pleasures of Vanity Fair' by news of the French advance, he goes into her bedroom, sees her asleep, as he thinks, and is overcome by remorse and tenderness at the way he has neglected her for Becky at the ball. He stoops to kiss her, and her arms close round his neck, then 'a bugle from the Place of Arms began sounding clearly, and was taken up through the town; and amidst the drums of the infantry, and the shrill pipes of the Scotch, the whole city awoke' (ch. 29). One admires the economy of that detail: the 'shrill pipes of the Scotch' signal the end of the music and the dancing, and the end too of this brief moment of recovered tenderness; it is too late for George.

We are given glimpses of two other marriages facing war which offer implicit parallels and contrasts to Amelia and George. Thackeray had parodied Charles Lever's military novels in 'Punch's Prize Novelists' (1847), and here he outflanks them by deserting the military for the domestic realities of the battle: 'We do not claim to rank among the military novelists. Our place is with the non-combatants. When the decks are cleared for action we go below and wait meekly' (ch. 30). We see the courage and practicality of Peggy O'Dowd, staying up to pack the Major's gear, and the solicitude of Rawdon for Becky, as genuine in its way as George's last-minute regrets and perhaps more sharply moving because it reveals hitherto hidden depths of affection and stoicism in him. Marriage has domesticated this 'clumsy military Adonis', and he makes an inventory of his worldly goods for Becky which amounts in effect to a willing renunciation of the apparatus of the fashionable man: his dressing-case, duelling-pistols '(same which I shot Captain Marker)', horses, 'chain and ticker', fur-lined cloak, are carefully catalogued and priced so that 'they might be turned into money for his wife's benefit, in case any accident should befall him'. He goes off to war

> in his oldest and shabbiest uniform and epaulets, leaving the newest behind ... And this famous dandy of Windsor and Hyde Park went off on his campaign with a kit as modest as that of a serjeant, and with something like a prayer on his lips for the woman he was leaving. He took her up from the ground, and held her in his arms for a minute, tight pressed against his strong beating heart. (ch. 30)

The imminence of war and death has awakened the dandy soldier to seriousness: this short scene enacts in miniature the essential movement of the Waterloo chapters and indeed of the novel as a whole. A similar point is made at greater length in the high comedy of Jos Sedley's mounting panic and eventual ignominious retreat from Brussels. Here the dandy is literally re-clothed, as the 'stout civilian', who has affected a military-style coat and cap and grown soldierly moustaches, begins to fear that the victorious (as he thinks) French may take his clothes at face value:

> Then he looked amazed at the pale face in the glass before him, and especially at his mustachios, which had attained a rich growth in the course of near seven weeks, since they had come into the world. They *will* mistake me for a military man, thought he, remembering Isidor's warning, as to the massacre with which all the defeated British army was threatened; and staggering back to his bed-chamber, he began wildly pulling the bell which summoned his valet.
> Isidor answered that summons. Jos had sunk in a chair — he had torn off his neckcloths, and turned down his collars, and was sitting with both his hands lifted to his throat.
> '*Coupez-moi*, Isidor,' shouted he; '*vite! Coupez-moi!*'
> Isidor thought for a moment he had gone mad, and that he wished his valet to cut his throat.
> '*Les moustaches*,' gasped Jos; '*les moustaches — coupy, rasy, vite!*' — his French was of this sort — voluble, as we have said, but not remarkable for grammar.
> Isidor swept off the mustachios in no time with the razor, and heard with inexpressible delight his master's orders that he should fetch a hat and a plain coat. '*Ne porty ploo — habit militair — bonny — donny a voo, prenny dehors*' — were Jos's words — the coat and cap were at last his property.
> This gift being made, Jos selected a plain black coat and waistcoat from his stock, and put on a large white neckcloth, and a plain beaver. If he could have got a shovel-hat he would have worn it. As it was, you would have fancied he was a flourishing, large parson of the Church of England. (ch. 32)

This is a great moment in the novel, and an important one, for it is Thackeray's comic version of *Sartor Resartus*. What happens to the fat dandy here is prophetic of the sobriety that awaits Regency style and attitudes in the second half of the novel. And it is beautifully in keeping with Thackeray's debunking of the silver-fork and the military novel that the one blade we should see in the whole Waterloo section is the razor which shaves off Jos's moustaches.

VI

There is a marked change in tempo between the two parts of *Vanity Fair*: six weeks separate Amelia's marriage and George's death, fifteen or sixteen years Waterloo and her marriage to Dobbin. In these more leisurely expanses of time we witness the characters growing older, becoming parents, revealing latent but hitherto unsuspected capacities for selfishness or generosity. An increased emphasis on their private lives was inevitable in the story Thackeray had to tell, but he suggests that it is also characteristic of the way society is changing around them. This can be seen in his treatment of the Pitt Crawleys, father and son. Old Sir Pitt goes spectacularly to the dogs: 'His dislike for respectable society increased with age' (ch. 39); and Queen's Crawley falls into dilapidation as he takes up with the butler's daughter, 'Ribbons'. But this is shown to be the last flourish of an older unregenerate way of life, belonging more to the eighteenth than to the nineteenth century (and to Fielding's Squire Western, who is an obvious literary source for Sir Pitt). When his son takes over, this reforming politician repairs the estate and rebuilds the family's links with respectable society. The reign of 'Ribbons' gives way to that of the gentle-natured Lady Jane, and to a renewed emphasis on family life. The younger Sir Pitt is a man of a new age, with his 'serious' religion and his bluebooks, and in nothing more typical of the early Victorians than in his readiness to drop Evangelicalism when it suits his political ambitions. The unreformed Regency survives in Lord Steyne and Gaunt House, where Becky reaches the pinnacle of fashion, but even here Thackeray implies that it is a survival, its seigneurial arrogance now the exception rather than the rule. When Gaunt House is described in chapter 47 the impression is one of dreariness and emptiness: 'Brass plates have penetrated into the Square — Doctors, the Diddlesex Bank Western Branch' (further signs of a new age), but the chimneys are smokeless and Lord Steyne lives at Naples, in contrast to the days when the 'Prince and Perdita' (the Regent and his mistresses) used to pass through a 'little modest back door' in the Mews into 'the famous *petits appartements* of Lord Steyne'.

Perhaps the most interesting movement from Regency habits to the values and concerns of domestic life occurs in the case of Rawdon Crawley. Rawdon is changed first by his love for Becky, and then by his deepening love for the son who becomes the centre of his life as Becky leaves him behind in her pursuit of fashion. Thackeray does not sentimentalise this change as another Victorian novelist might have done, it remains in the grain of a character who is in other respects a 'rascal' (ch. 37), and indeed we first learn of his 'great secret tenderness' for his son in the chapter which shows Rawdon abetting Becky in ruining their landlord Raggles (ch. 37). But his inarticulate paternal fondness brings out a certain decency and simplicity of heart in Rawdon which exiles him from the heartless Steyne circle, and aligns him more and more with those who live by the affections. He becomes aware of his loneliness when Lord Steyne arranges for little Rawdon to be sent off to school:

The poor fellow felt that his dearest pleasure and closest friend was taken from him. He looked often and wistfully at the little vacant bed in his dressing-room, where the child used to sleep. He missed him sadly of mornings, and tried in vain to walk in the Park without him.

He did not know how solitary he was until little Rawdon was gone. He liked the people who were fond of him; and would go and sit for long hours with his good-natured sister Lady Jane, and talk to her about the virtues, and good looks, and hundred good qualities of the child. (ch. 52)

In this he is like Amelia, who has also had to send a treasured only son away (the novel is full of such satisfyingly unobtrusive links and parallels). In the postwar world Rawdon's occupation is gone, and Thackeray keeps reminding us of his Waterloo service. He becomes the 'Colonel'; he takes his son to the barracks, where 'the old troopers were glad to recognise their ancient officer, and dandle the little Colonel' (ch. 37); and when young Rawdon and little Georgy Osborne meet in the Park, it is stressed that they are both sons of Waterloo men (an emphasis brought out by Thackeray's illustration, 'Georgy makes acquaintance with a Waterloo Man'). Rawdon's status as a 'Waterloo man' is both an accurate historical detail, indicating a cultural legend which is already starting to grow only a few years after the event, and a kind of moral medal related to our awakened sense of his capacity for decent and honourable feeling.

Waterloo is a great landmark in the second half of *Vanity Fair*. The focus of sentimental memory for Amelia, a place of national pilgrimage for old Mr Osborne and others like him, a fund of boastful anecdotes for Jos Sedley in India (where he is known as 'Waterloo' Sedley), it finally comes to seem a badge of honour for those who fought in the battle. There is a telling moment in the novel after the great exposure scene with Lord Steyne in chapter 53 (where, incidentally, it is Rawdon's display of his soldier's strength and courage which wins Becky's involuntary approval: 'She admired her husband, strong, brave, and victorious'), when Rawdon goes to see his brother Pitt and asks him to look after his son. He sits down at the baronet's table, 'set out with the orderly blue books and the letters, the neatly docketted bills and symmetrical pamphlets; the locked account-books, desks, and dispatch boxes, the Bible, the *Quarterly Review*, and the *Court Guide*' (ch. 54) — all the apparatus, in fact, of the careful, aspiring Victorian politician. Sir Pitt thinks he has come to borrow money but Rawdon cuts him short:

> 'It's the boy,' said Rawdon, in a husky voice. 'I want you to promise me that you will take charge of him when I'm gone...Damn it. Look here, Pitt — you know that I was to have had Miss Crawley's money. I wasn't brought up like a younger brother: but was always encouraged to be extravagant and kep idle. But for this I might have been quite a different man. I didn't do my duty with the regiment so bad.' (ch. 54)

Here Thackeray goes against the grain of the contrasted brothers convention he took from the fashionable novel. Rawdon's 'I didn't do my duty with the regiment so bad' is a touchingly modest but effective retort to the ostentatious dutifulness of his brother, and it puts us even more on his side than we are already. Something honourable, robust, manly, associated with doing one's duty through physical courage, is being squeezed out between the typical bluebooks and *Court Guide* of a rising new generation. This may seem to contradict the general drift of the novel but in fact the contradiction is more apparent than real, because it is chiefly in his capacity as a father that we are being invited to see the positive side of the 'Waterloo man'. As Rawdon passes from the public, Gaunt House world to the private world of the affections, he brings with him the increasingly dignified associations of honourable regimental service.

The chief beneficiary of this development in our attitude to Waterloo is Dobbin, 'our friend the Major' (ch. 58), who has been absent in India during the Gaunt House section of the novel (chapters 47–56). He too has done his duty with the regiment, and it is not without significance that the narrator refers to him as 'Major Dobbin' in the second half of the novel. Like 'the gallant ––th', who return to England at the end after fourteen years soldiering abroad, the clumsy 'Figs' of the early chapters has come to acquire an unassertive dignity, his years of military service an index of his simplicity of heart and capacity for unselfishness and loyalty. And Thackeray reminds us that Dobbin has been a 'Waterloo man' at a critical stage of his affair with Amelia, when he reproaches her for her ingratitude and then leaves, for good as he thinks. Amelia watches his servant load the coach:

> Francis brought out the stained old blue cloak lined with red camlet, which had wrapped the owner up any time these fifteen years, and had *manchem Sturm erlebt*, as a favourite song of those days said. It had been new for the campaign of Waterloo, and had covered George and William after the night of Quatre Bras. (ch. 66)

Dobbin's love for Amelia was 'new' also at the time of Waterloo and has weathered many a storm since. It is in the same 'old cloak lined with red stuff' (ch. 67) that he wraps Amelia at the end. Details as resonant as these tow the great bulk of the novel behind them, and make Thackeray's affirmation of Dobbin's gentlemanliness seem earned and convincing in a way that such affirmations in Victorian fiction are generally not:

> Which of us can point out many such in his circle – men whose aims are generous, whose truth is constant, and not only constant in its kind, but elevated in its degree; whose want of meanness makes them simple: who can look the world honestly in the face with an equal manly sympathy for the great and the small? We all know a hundred whose coats are very well made, and a score who have excellent manners, and one or two happy beings who are what they call, in the inner

circles, and have shot into the very centre and bull's eye of the fashion; but of gentlemen how many? Let us take a little scrap of paper and each make out his list.

My friend the Major I write, without any doubt, in mine. He had very long legs, a yellow face, and a slight lisp, which at first was rather ridiculous. But his thoughts were just, his brains were fairly good, his life was honest and pure, and his heart warm and humble. He certainly had very large hands and feet, which the two George Osbornes used to caricature and laugh at; and their jeers and laughter perhaps led poor little Emmy astray as to his worth. But have we not all been misled about our heroes, and changed our opinions a hundred times? Emmy, in this happy time, found that hers underwent a very great change in respect of the merits of the Major. (ch. 62)

The whole course of the novel has separated out the special quality of Dobbin's gentlemanliness from the glitter of fashionable style, the posturings of bucks and dandies, the assertive mercantile gentility of the Osborne family, and embodied it in the clumsy Major. Why, then, does Thackeray need to rub home his clumsiness, lisp and yellow face in the second paragraph? For many readers this will be a prime example of Thackeray's notorious ambiguity. But there is, perhaps, a defence of his practice here if we remember the genre to which *Vanity Fair* belongs. It is very much to Thackeray's purpose that we should not only see through the fashionable novelists' idea of what a gentleman is, but come to respect an image of gentlemanliness which has nothing to do with fashion. Dobbin's clumsiness is to the point because it puts him at the opposite pole from the dandy-gentlemen of contemporary fiction, the Pelhams, Cecils and Coningsbys. One thinks of Auden's lines in 'In Praise of Limestone':

> The blessed will not care what angle they are regarded from,
> Having nothing to hide.

Dobbin's goodness, having its roots in humility and unselfishness, is not reduced by the sneers of the worldly, or even by that part of Thackeray's narrative persona which sees as the world sees.

So, while agreeing with Gordon Ray that Thackeray's achievement was to redefine the idea of the gentleman to fit a middle-class rather than aristocratic context, and while recognising this process at work in *Vanity Fair*, it is necessary also to enter a small but important qualification. Dobbin is certainly 'middle class' in the sense that he is a grocer's son who lacks the traditional three generations pedigree, and there is nothing aristocratic about him. But he is also a soldier, and there are hints in the novel, like Rawdon's 'I didn't do my duty with the regiment so bad', of a possible conflict between that older sense of honour and honour as it is understood by a rising Victorian man like Sir Pitt Crawley. In Dobbin the soldier and the middle-class man are reconciled. In Colonel Newcome a few years later the qualities symbolised by Dobbin's Waterloo cloak, or clumsily expressed in Rawdon's feeling for his son, have split off from 'bourgeois' values to constitute a kind of archaic gentlemanliness which can find no home in Victorian society. The seeds of that development are already present in *Vanity Fair*.

VII

Dobbin is Thackeray's least equivocal portrait of a gentleman, and his relative firmness of outline owes something to the fact that he is held in a long historical perspective, his virtue defined against the background of the early decades of the century where, I believe, Thackeray's imagination was most at home. This is the period, the pre-railway 'old world', celebrated with ironic nostalgia in his famous Roundabout paper, 'De Juventute'. It is when he approaches the mid-century and his own adult experience that one becomes aware of disabling uncertainties in his handling of the idea of the gentleman. Perhaps this may explain why his next novel, *Pendennis*, is not quite the masterpiece it might have been, given its intimate relationship to his own life and deepest concerns. *Pendennis* is an attempt to portray one of 'the gentlemen of our age ... no better nor worse than most educated men' (preface); it is partly autobiographical, drawing on Thackeray's memories of his undergraduate days and early career in the magazines, and it takes the story of Regency dandyism through the 1830s into the early Victorian period. Pen belongs to the second generation of nineteenth-century dandyism: with his 'partiality for rings, jewellery, and fine raiment' and 'perfumed baths' (ch. 18), he has something of that slightly epicene quality to be detected in Count D'Orsay and the young Disraeli. He is caught between the two worlds of the Regency, represented by his uncle, and Victorian domesticity, of which his mother is the harbinger and his 'sister' Laura the embodiment. Thus the conflict between worldly and unworldly values, which in *Vanity Fair* had been polarised in contrasting characters, here takes place in the heart and mind of a representative gentleman of the age.

There are other continuities with *Vanity Fair*, notably the use of clothes symbolism and the splendid Major Pendennis, who is not only one of the great comic creations of Victorian fiction but also a character marvellously appropriate to the historical thesis underlying both novels. If there is nothing in *Pendennis* quite to rival the scene of Jos Sedley's disrobing at Brussels, a comparable renunciation of fashion can be seen in the shaving of Pen's head during his illness and his comically rueful resort to the Major's wig-maker afterwards. Warrington's 'manly' gentlemanliness shows in his disregard for the cut of his clothes: 'He was dressed in a ragged old shooting-jacket, and had a bristly blue beard. He was drinking beer like a coal-heaver, and yet you couldn't but perceive that he was a gentleman' (ch. 28). In contrast to Warrington is the elaborately dressed Major:

> At a quarter-past ten the Major invariably made his appearance in the best blacked boots in all London, with a checked morning cravat that never was rumpled until dinner-time, a buff waistcoat which bore the crown of his sovereign on the buttons, and linen so spotless that Mr. Brummell himself asked the name of his laundress, and would probably have employed her had not misfortunes compelled that great man to fly the country. Pendennis's coat, his white gloves, his whiskers, his very cane, were perfect of their kind as specimens of the costume of a military man *en retraite*. At a distance, or seeing his back merely, you would have taken him to be not more than thirty years old: it was only by a nearer inspection that you saw the factitious nature of his rich brown hair, and that there were a few crows'-feet round about the somewhat faded eyes of his handsome mottled face. His nose was of the Wellington pattern. His hands and wristbands were beautifully long and white. On the latter he wore handsome gold buttons given to him by his Royal Highness the Duke of York, and on the others more than one elegant ring, the chief and largest of them being emblazoned with the famous arms of Pendennis. (ch. 1)

It is not just the Major but the Regency itself which is *en retraite* here. The references to Brummell, Wellington and the Duke of York fix him and his world in the past, but unlike that other old campaigner, Captain Costigan, he at least presents a proud silhouette: it is only on 'a nearer inspection' that you see the wig and the lined face. The Major is not a Waterloo man but his military appearance is not all surface either, like Jos Sedley's; inside there is a real toughness, a courage and authority which come out when put to the test by the Fotheringay and her father (the title of chapter 10 is 'Facing the Enemy') or later by his rebellious manservant Morgan. Besides, the Major is the real thing — if there can be reality in dandyism — for although one of his functions in the novel is to suggest the comic ephemerality of fashion and the sadness of a lifetime's devotion to it, he at least remains true to his chosen style to the end. By doing so he reveals the derivative, half-hearted nature of Pen's dandyism and the essentially *transitional* character of the gentlemanliness being portrayed in him.

Pen's problem is that he can be neither a full-blooded dandy like his uncle nor the kind of domesticated country gentleman his mother would wish, and the Major helps us to see why. His vanity is robust and worldly in the old Regency manner, Pen's is narcissistic, coming like his selfishness from the over-mothering of a proto-Victorian domestic 'angel'. The frequency with which he blushes in the novel is a sign of his incomplete dandyism, of a cosseted vanity easily surprised into bashfulness, and Thackeray is often at his best in *Pendennis* when he makes us share Pen's blushes, showing the irreconcilability of the models (the Major, his mother) available to him. His dilemma is brilliantly presented and developed in the opening sequence of the novel, from the moment when the Major at breakfast in his club turns from his fashionable mail (including an invitation from Lord Steyne) to Mrs Pendennis's letter lying 'solitary and apart from all the fashionable London letters, with a country post-mark and a homely seal' (ch. 1). The account which follows of the Major's successful 'campaign' against the Fotheringay serves to enrich and complicate this opening antithesis of worldly and unworldly values. The Major's man-of-the-world perspective frames our introduction to the Fairoaks world, not as an absolute judgement upon it, but as a reminder that unworldliness is not enough and that Helen's combination of unworldliness with maternal possessiveness is positively harmful to her son. At the same time the intensity of Pen's feeling for his actress, so out of keeping with the usual attitude of young men — as the Major says, 'a virtuous attachment is the deuce' (ch. 9) — reveals a capacity for deep and generous commitment beyond the ken of his uncle's worldly knowingness. He needs to escape the emotional claustrophobia of Fairoaks, but the tenderness of heart and mind he has learnt there subtly incapacitates him from following the Major's worldly path: caught between two moral and emotional possibilities, two styles of gentlemanliness, Pen at the outset taps some of the representative uncertainties of 'the gentlemen of our age'.

And yet this potentially interesting dilemma is not satisfactorily developed. It is difficult to put one's finger exactly on what goes wrong with *Pendennis* after, say, the Oxbridge chapters, but the failure is probably due more to what does not take place than to what does. Thackeray's subject is the subject of the fashionable novels on which *Pendennis* is partly based, the sentimental education of a young man living in the 'world'. In Pen's case this education hardly takes place: there is the long and sympathetic treatment of his infatuation with the Fotheringay, and after that almost nothing — an intermittent, cynical flirtation with Blanche Amory, a toying with the idea of an affair with Fanny Bolton (it can hardly be called an affair), then marriage to Laura. The conflict within Pen between the ways of the world and the holiness of the heart's affections never really takes place because the conditioning experience which would have given life to that conflict is not there. The Fotheringay affair has to do double service both as Pen's adolescent introduction to passion and as the explanation of his later world-weariness, which is not only psychologically improbable but makes nonsense of Thackeray's concluding pleas for Pen as an averagely stained man of the world ('let us give a hand of charity to Arthur Pendennis, with all his faults and shortcomings, who does not claim to be a hero, but only a man and a brother'), since none of the staining is seen to have taken place. It is, simply, hard to believe in the blushing Pen as a 'battered London rake' (ch. 63).

Obviously the censorship of Mrs Grundy played a part in this failure, but not perhaps as much as Thackeray's defensive preface would have us believe. ('Since the author of *Tom Jones* was buried, no writer of fiction among us has been permitted to depict to his utmost power a MAN.') Dickens, after all, had taken his novelist hero into an unhappy marriage in the contemporaneous *David Copperfield*, and was later to explore a Pen/Fanny Bolton affair much more successfully with Eugene Wrayburn and Lizzie Hexam in *Our Mutual Friend* (1864—5). A deeper reason for failure may lie, as John Sutherland has suggested,[44] in Thackeray's own reticence, his inability to explore in fiction the representative elements of his own personal, intimate experience as Dickens was able to do in both *David Copperfield* and *Great Expectations*. But whatever the cause, the half-hearted world-weariness into which Thackeray makes Pen slip betrays the rich tension of the early chapters, draining reality from both worldly and unworldly characters alike, and making his marriage to Laura seem a perfunctory full-stop rather than the natural destination of a sentimental education.

Another area of failure, or at least unresolved ambiguity, lies in Thackeray's treatment of the relationship between Pen's literary career and his status as a gentleman. The compatibility of work and gentlemanliness was a burning issue in the Victorian period, and played a central part in the 'dignity of literature' controversy which separated Thackeray from Forster and Dickens. Dickens followed Carlyle by making David Copperfield affirm the gospel of work as the basis of his success:

> I have never believed it possible that any natural or improved ability can claim immunity from the companionship of the steady, plain, hard-working qualities, and hope to gain its end ... Some happy talent, and some fortunate opportunity, may form the two sides of the ladder on which some men mount, but the rounds of that ladder must be made of stuff to stand wear and tear; and there is no substitute for thorough-going, ardent, and sincere earnestness. (ch. 42)

Thackeray was not sure that a gentleman should be quite so enthusiastic about the 'plain, hard-working qualities' or so earnest about his career, and the uncertainty shows in his handling of literary Bohemia in *Pendennis*. At one level the picture of Pen's dealings with the fashionable publishers Bacon and Bungay, the founding of the *Pall Mall Gazette*, and the publication of his worthless novel, *Walter Lorraine*, is the best insider's account we have of the fashionable novel industry in the 1830s. Thackeray reveals the mixture of snobbery and opportunism in Bacon, who 'liked to be treated with rudeness by a gentleman' (ch. 31), and the shameless name-dropping with which Warrington promotes Pen's work, or Shandon his new magazine: 'I have used the Duke of Wellington and the Battle of

Waterloo a hundred times, and I never knew the duke to fail' (ch. 32). The prospectus for the *Pall Mall Gazette* is written in the debtor's prison but beamed at 'the gentlemen of England – yes, *the gentlemen of England* (we'll have that in large caps., Bungay, my boy)...' (ch. 32). The cynical appeal to the snobbery of a new public is effectively satirised, but as so often with Thackeray, behind the anti-snobbery lurks a snobbish position. The publishing world's cynicism is seen as a sanction for Warrington's cynicism, which he passes on to Pen, and in turn as a justification for their implicit assumption that authorship is a pursuit which the true gentleman only tastes with half his mind. 'All poets are humbugs, all literary men are humbugs,' Warrington protests, 'directly a man begins to sell his feelings for money he's a humbug' (ch. 41). Warrington, who is Thackeray's mouthpiece elsewhere in the novel, confesses to embarrassment at having it known that he writes for a living (ch. 31), and the Major is only reconciled to Pen's doing so when his writings are praised by his fashionable friends. The Major's snobbery may be 'placed' but his creator is not free from it himself: the term of praise most frequently used to describe Pen's writing is that it is 'gentlemanlike' (ch. 35).

These areas of omission and uncertainty in *Pendennis* are none the less revealing, and what they reveal is the great difficulty Thackeray had in exploring a representative gentleman of the age. He could present the dilemma of his class and generation but not work it out to a satisfactory conclusion, because to do so meant confronting the ambivalence in his attitudes to rank, work, the 'world', sexuality, gentlemanliness – an ambivalence which worked to such rich creative effect when dealing with the Regency and its aftermath, but became self-conscious when faced with the prospect of an entirely moralised concept of the gentleman. Thackeray could criticise Major Pendennis but he could not forget him, or treat him with amused contempt as Dickens does Mr Turveydrop, the Regency hangover in *Bleak House*. In a letter written at the time of *Pendennis*, he said 'my vanity would be to go through life as a gentleman – as a Major Pendennis you have hit it'.[45] The result is that the modern young gentlemen of his novels, the Pens, Clives and Philips, represent a simplified side of himself, and engage his imagination at a relatively shallow level. In place of the critical exploration of the Pendennis type of young man which Dickens comes to in Eugene Wrayburn, Thackeray offers a hearty slap on the back for these blushing, manly, cigar-smoking young protagonists, and a plea for our indulgence on the score that they are, like Conrad's Lord Jim (though less problematically), 'one of us'. And when Pendennis as narrator of subsequent novels starts referring coyly to 'Mrs Pendennis', the mixture of self-satisfied geniality and cosy fireside gentility is almost unbearable. No aspect of Thackeray's work has dated more.

The truth seems to be that the social analysis of Thackeray's novels points to an ideal of mid-Victorian domesticated gentility and hearty manliness which he was incapable of realising convincingly, perhaps because he was not convinced by it himself. Amelia and Dobbin are the exceptions which prove the rule, because their kind of modest gentility draws force from the contrast it offers to the spectacle of human greed, snobbery and heartlessness which stimulated his imagination in *Vanity Fair*. Thackeray could celebrate it in recoil, as it were, from its opposite, or when he could contemplate it in the historical past. Often the two go together, as in his next novel, *The History of Henry Esmond, Esq.*, where the embryonic Victorian gentleman hero, the simple 'Esq.', interests Thackeray precisely because he is an embryo and stands out against the worldliness of the early eighteenth century. But Thackeray was happier with a less insipid type than Pendennis or Esmond, and his most famous portrait of a gentleman is not Esmond, the modern man in a historical setting, but Colonel Newcome, the old-fashioned man in a modern setting. With *The Newcomes* his preoccupation with the gentlemanly idea takes a final, fruitful turn back into archetype.

VIII

If *Pendennis* may be described as an attempt to redeem George Osborne, then *The Newcomes* is the story of a quixotic Dobbin adrift in the world of *The Book of Snobs*. Like Dobbin, Colonel Newcome is a first-generation gentleman and an officer, and the hints of unfashionable loyalty and simplicity of heart associated with Dobbin's years in India with 'the gallant ——th' become, in the Colonel, a major dimension of characterisation. The returned Indian officer, with thirty-five years of honourable service behind him, lean and tanned in his mustachios and loose-fitting clothes, is a standing rebuke to the sleek materialism and 'cold ways' (ch. 26) of the home society. As always in Thackeray, dress is important, and the Colonel's indifference to it is, like Dobbin's, a mark of integrity. 'His kit is as simple as a subaltern's' (ch. 26) when he returns to India, and he wears his old 'uniform of gold and silver' to be presented at court yet manages to look 'much grander than Sir Brian in his deputy-lieutenant's dress' (ch. 20). Of course the Colonel is much simpler than Dobbin, and his literary, if not his family, pedigree is much older: in India he is known as Don Quixote and his favourite reading, as we saw in the previous chapter, is the *Spectator*, *Don Quixote* and *Sir Charles Grandison*. Thackeray had been re-reading *Don Quixote* while writing *The Newcomes*, and his stress on the quixotic element in the Coverley type saves the character from sentimentality and makes the Colonel — part noble warrior, part foolish fond old man — a satisfying embodiment of doomed chivalry in the modern world. It is also significant that he considers Fielding 'low' (ch. 4), revealing his naivety and inflexible unworldliness; ironic, too, for there is a strong similarity between Tom Jones's struggles with Thwackum and Square, and the young Tom Newcome's resistance to his stepmother's Evangelicalism. Both are young men of natural decency in a society of hypocrites.

It is important to Thackeray's purpose that we should see the central character both as the old Colonel and as the young Tom growing up in the atmosphere of Clapham Sect Evangelicalism at the start of the nineteenth century. *The Newcomes* has the longest historical reach of any single Thackeray novel, ranging from the end of the eighteenth century to the 1840s, and encompassing the period of *Vanity Fair* and *Pendennis*. But the interest in dandyism has abated; instead the novel fleshes out the process of social climbing satirised in *The Book of Snobs*, whereby 'the City Snob's money' is 'washed during a generation or so...into estates, and woods, and castles, and town mansions' until 'it is allowed to pass current as real aristocratic coin' (ch. 8). The founder of the dynasty is a workhouse boy who comes to London in the reign of George III, does well, and marries his sweetheart from the factory back home. Thomas Newcome is the child of this love match, but after his mother's death his father marries the wealthy Sophia Hobson, and Tom is brought up in her 'serious paradise' at Clapham. A whole chapter of English social history is brilliantly caught in a few pages:

> As you entered at the gate, gravity fell on you; and decorum wrapped you in a garment of starch. The butcher-boy who galloped his horse and cart madly about the adjoining lanes and common, whistled wild melodies (caught up in abominable play-house galleries), and joked with a hundred cookmaids, on passing that lodge fell into an undertaker's pace, and delivered his joints and sweetbreads silently at the servant's entrance. The rooks in the elms cawed sermons at morning and evening; the peacocks walked demurely on the terraces; the guineafowls looked more quaker-like than those savoury birds usually do. (ch. 2)

Thackeray is particularly good at suggesting the ways in which Evangelicalism will condition the later Victorian cult of respectability (the subtitle is 'Memoirs of a Most Respectable Family'). The decorum which 'wrapped you in a garment of starch' contains the seeds of inhibition and hypocrisy; the rich living — 'in Egypt itself there were not more savoury fleshpots than at Clapham' (ch. 2) — indicates how compatible money-making and vital religion are, and how easy it will be for subsequent generations to compromise with the world. From the start Tom Newcome rebels against Clapham, he is an ordinary natural boy out of place in this 'serious' society. He loves the hearty life of Grey Friars School, and shows his dislike of home 'by insubordination and boisterousness; by playing tricks and breaking windows...by upsetting his two little brothers in a go-cart (of which wanton and careless injury the present Baronet's nose bears marks to his dying day); — by going to sleep during the sermons, and treating reverend gentlemen with levity' (ch. 2). Even as a youth, then, Tom Newcome is out of step with the future, and his decision to join the Indian Army confirms our sense of qualities in him which a new age will disregard: natural spirits, generous feeling, loyalty, an exalted sense of honour.

He is also disappointed in love, like his literary ancestor Sir Roger de Coverley. His love affair with Léonore de Blois is destroyed by their parents, and this baulked passion is kept before us as the source of the Colonel's melancholy and the mark of his loneliness. Some of Thackeray's finest touches are those shafts back into the past which remind us that the Colonel has always been lonely and starved of affection, as when he tries to understand Clive's artistic tastes by going to the National Gallery and puzzling before the ancient statues as he used to puzzle (Thackeray reminds us) over the Greek rudiments which made him cry as a child (ch. 21). The unhappy, rebellious childhood, and the bitterness of disappointed love, serve to universalise the Colonel at the same time as reinforcing his old-fashioned qualities, and make him something more complex than just a dear old boy.

The Newcomes is the rich culmination of Thackeray's satirical interest in the genealogy of his characters. The long perspective and the characteristic movement backwards and forwards in time mean that the reader never loses sight of the Newcome family's humble origins, and it is part of the Colonel's true gentlemanliness that he does not forget them either. Ancestry is important in this novel because true and false gentility are defined in terms of the ability to be honest about one's antecedents. Since gentility is but ancient riches, as the old saying has it, or in Lady Kew's words, 'except the Gaunts, the Howards, and one or two more, there is scarcely any good blood in England' (ch. 52), it is absurd as well as snobbish to furnish oneself with a bogus pedigree, like Sir Brian pretending to claim descent from Edward the Confessor's barber-surgeon. Much more sensible, and in Thackeray's view more truly gentlemanly, is the Colonel's belief that 'if we can't inherit a good name, at least we can do our best to leave one, my boy' (ch. 7). He is not ashamed to acknowledge his weaver father and through thick and thin is loyal to his humble old nurse, Sarah Mason, unlike his brothers. It is the bogus gentlemen who stand upon their state: Sir Brian who 'looked like the Portrait of a Gentleman at the Exhibition', a studied pose, or his brother Hobson with his affectation of being 'a jólly country squire' (ch. 6). True gentlemanliness in *The Newcomes* goes with a certain indifference to rank and money. The penniless, bohemian Fred Bayham belongs to a family which has 'seen almost all the nobility of England come in and go out, and were gentlefolks, when many a fine lord's father of the present day was sweeping a counting-house (ch. 11). (It is typical of Thackeray to keep the odd real pedigree up his sleeve to trump his snobs.) Or there is the Vicomte de Florac, habitually impoverished but a genuine aristocrat, who chooses not to take up the princely title he falls heir to, and who shows a true sense of honour in his reaction to the Colonel's poverty at the end:

> To be a Pensioner of an Ancient Institution? Why not? Might not any officer retire without shame to the Invalides at the close of his campaigns, and had not fortune conquered our old friend, and age and disaster overcome him? It never once entered Thomas Newcome's head, nor Clive's, nor Florac's, nor his mother's, that the Colonel demeaned himself at all by accepting that bounty. (ch. 76)

Thackeray's point is that poverty with honour is no disgrace to a gentleman; indeed, Florac, Bayham and the Colonel exemplify his further point, that the true gentleman was likely to be poor, given the way Victorian society was going.

The Victorians sentimentalised Colonel Newcome, but on the whole Thackeray does not. He is convincing because he draws strength from the central place he occupies in the novel's satirical vision and in Thackeray's rich awareness of middle-class evolution, and because he is a flawed character, capable of snobbery, as in his attitude to artists, of foolish obstinacy, of unreasoning prejudice. When he returns from India determined to make Clive's fortune so that he can marry Ethel, his very unworldliness makes him vulnerable to the corruption of the world, and he is chiefly responsible for Clive's loveless marriage to Rosey Mackenzie. The final impression is deeply mixed – generosity, an absence of meanness and hypocrisy, an un-Victorian simplicity of heart and manner, chivalry to women, loyalty, a scrupulous sense of honour; but also prudishness (as in his attitude to Fielding), obstinacy, a surprising streak of vindictiveness which surfaces in his pursuit of Barnes Newcome, and an innocence of the world that is dangerous to himself and to those close to him. Thackeray does not simply portray him, elegiacally, as doomed, he reveals the inner weaknesses and vulnerability which make him doomed. But what universalises Colonel Newcome, making him not just the most memorable last English gentleman in the literature but a true heir of Don Quixote, is the note of lonely austerity in Thackeray's conception of him. Even at the height of his 'corruption' by the world, when he is heaping the profits of the Bundelcund Bank in tasteless luxury on Clive's head, there is a sense of something untouched in the Colonel himself, a simplicity of style which is poignantly uncovered when the brokers move in to the new house after his bankruptcy:

> Bills are up in the fine new house. Swarms of Hebrew gentlemen with their hats on are walking about the drawing-rooms, peering into the bedrooms, weighing and poising the poor old silver coconut-tree, eyeing the plate and crystal, thumbing the damask of the curtains,

and inspecting ottomans, mirrors, and a hundred articles of splendid trumpery. There is Rosey's boudoir which her father-in-law loved to ornament — there is Clive's studio with a hundred sketches — there is the colonel's bare room at the top of the house, with his little iron bedstead and ship's drawers, and a camel trunk or two which have accompanied him on many an Indian march, and his old regulation sword, and that one which the native officers of his regiment gave him when he bade them farewell. I can fancy the brokers' faces as they look over this camp wardrobe, and that the uniforms will not fetch much in Holywell Street. (ch. 70).

One thinks of Dobbin's Waterloo cloak. This passage could almost stand as an emblem of the Colonel's place in the world of the novel — downstairs conspicuous luxury, upstairs the bare room and the camp wardrobe which speaks mutely of lonely integrity and a lifetime's service.

The death of Colonel Newcome as a Poor Brother at Grey Friars School is such a famous example of Victorian pathos that it is still difficult to see it clearly and judge its effectiveness. But if we set aside the usual easy jokes about the Colonel saying 'Adsum!', such as Carey's 'Heaven was a public school',[46] then it is possible to make out a good case for its artistic rightness and inevitability. *The Newcomes* offers us the shape of a life, beginning with the rebellious little boy at Clapham, passing by the thirty-five years in India, returning to England first with honour and hope and then with increasing disillusionment, and ending in penury in the early Victorian age. It is a representative life and death because it shows a certain temperament and a certain kind of honour failing to adapt to new conditions. The return to Grey Friars at the end illuminates that failure by reminding us of the young Tom Newcome who had loved Grey Friars and hated to return home, and who has retained through life the boy's simplicity of heart. As for the famous death itself, there too we are reminded of the young man and the roots of loneliness in him when he calls in his delirium for Léonore:

> She went into the room, where Clive was at the bed's foot; the old man within it talked on rapidly for awhile: then again he would sigh and be still: once more I heard him say hurriedly, 'Take care of him when I'm in India;' and then with a heart-rending voice he called out 'Léonore, Léonore!' She was kneeling by his side now. (ch. 80)

Thackeray added this passage as an afterthought in the manuscript, but as John Sutherland points out in *Thackeray at Work*, it makes all the difference. 'The effect is complex: blank, childish innocence and adult passion combat in the Colonel to the very end.'[47] This reminder of a lifetime's unappeased hunger in the Colonel's heart sharpens our sense of his loneliness and throws a light back over his past life — we see that he has never been at home anywhere. Like his portable 'camp wardrobe', the Colonel's death in a charitable institution is appropriate for a man who has always been a homeless warrior.

In these and other ways Thackeray strengthens and deepens his portrait of a gentleman by drawing on an archetypal pattern of human experience. Behind Colonel Newcome stand Sir Roger de Coverley and Don Quixote and ultimately all those victims of the modern world whose archaic sense of honour cannot adapt, made poignant in the Colonel's case by his loneliness and baffled need. The Victorians were right to see him as a triumph of characterisation, and Trollope, himself much influenced by *The Newcomes*, put it best when he recognised the rarity of the art which could so convince of his gentlemanly virtue:

> I know no character in fiction, unless it be Don Quixote, with whom the reader becomes so intimately acquainted as with Colonel Newcombe [sic]. How great a thing it is to be a gentleman at all parts! ...It is not because Colonel Newcombe is a perfect gentleman that we think Thackeray's work to have been so excellent, but because he has had the power to describe him as such, and to force us to love him, a weak and silly old man, on account of this grace of character. (*Autobiography*, ch. 13)

The 'grace of character' makes the Colonel an enduring image of what was best, and weakest, in the older idea of the gentleman. It is not, and could not be, a completely moralised image, nor was it likely to help the Victorians in their task of redefining gentility, except by reminding them of what they were in danger of losing. 'If the art of being a gentleman were forgotten,' Stevenson wrote in 1888, 'like the art of staining glass, it might be learned anew from that one character.'[48] But the image of stained glass reveals that what Stevenson and others chiefly relished in the character was his archaic simplicity. If the Colonel is at home anywhere it is not in the nineteenth century but in the eighteenth, at Coverley Manor.

This in turn suggests that Thackeray's success in *The Newcomes* may be related to his failure in *Pendennis*. The uncertainty which afflicted his attempt to explore a typical gentleman of the age vanished when he could return to an earlier type; and although I consider *The Newcomes* to be a very great novel, and its modern neglect scandalous, there is a sense in which the creation of Colonel Newcome was easier for Thackeray than that of Pendennis. As I have argued, he was at his best when he could hold the figure of the gentleman at a slight historical distance — too far back and one has the simplifications of *Barry Lyndon* or the somewhat wooden solemnity of *Esmond* and *The Virginians* (1857—9), too close to his own time and one has the reticence which mars *Pendennis* and the painful self-consciousness of *Philip* (1861—2). It is because they engage most fully his imagination of the origins of his own society and his own experience, and are not simply period pieces, that *Vanity Fair* and *The Newcomes* seem to me his great achievements. In these novels he made two decisive contributions to his generation's debate about the nature of gentlemanliness: he taught his contemporaries to see through their unhealthy preoccupation with the Regency, and he offered them in Colonel Newcome an image of antique courtesy that was to resonate through all their later attempts to modernise gentility. What he did not do, and perhaps could not do, was to resolve their dilemma about work and the occupations a gentleman could honourably pursue; the nature of his involvement with Regency dandyism was such that he could never make Dickens's unequivocal affirmation of 'the steady, plain, hard-working qualities'. In this respect at least, Thackeray is the novelist as gentleman. But, to return to Saintsbury, it is doubtful if his genius and his gentlemanliness can be equated. 'Only a minor talent can be a perfect gentleman', W. H. Auden wrote; 'a major talent is always more than a bit of a cad.'[49] Thackeray was not a cad, but he was not a minor talent either. Whether we value his gentlemanly tone or not, his greatness goes deeper than that and lies in his densely imagined pictures of early nineteenth-century society, in which gentlemanliness played such an important, and ambiguous, role.

REFERENCES: CHAPTER 2

1 J. Hannay, *A Brief Memoir of the late Mr. Thackeray* (Edinburgh: Oliver & Boyd, 1864), p. 7.
2 G. K. Chesterton, *Criticisms and Appreciations of the Works of Charles Dickens* (London: Dent, 1911), p. viii.
3 G. Saintsbury, *A Consideration of Thackeray* (London: Oxford University Press, 1931), p. 273.
4 J. Carey, *Thackeray: Prodigal Genius* (London: Faber, 1977), p. 11.
5 G. Ray, *Thackeray, the Uses of Adversity* (London: Oxford University Press, 1955), p. 13.
6 W. Bagehot, 'Sterne and Thackeray', in *Literary Studies*, 2 vols (London: Dent/Everyman, 1911), Vol. 2, p. 128.
7 G. Tillotson and D. Hawes (eds), *Thackeray: The Critical Heritage* (London: Routledge & Kegan Paul, 1968), pp. 345–6.
8 Ray, op. cit., p. 67.
9 G. Ray (ed.), *The Letters and Private Papers of William Makepeace Thackeray*, 4 vols (London: Oxford University Press, 1945–6), Vol. II, p. 334.
10 J. Boswell, *Life of Johnson*, ed. R. W. Chapman (London: Oxford University Press, 1970), pp. 316–17.
11 J. Sudrann, ' "The philosopher's property": Thackeray and the use of time', *Victorian Studies*, vol. X (1967), pp. 355–88.
12 P. Lubbock, *The Craft of Fiction* (London: Cape, 1965 edn), p. 96.
13 G. Etherege, *The Man of Mode*, ed. W. B. Carnochan (London: Edward Arnold, 1967), Act I, 11. 362–7.
14 W. Maginn, 'Mr. Edward Lytton Bulwer's novels; and remarks on novel-writing', *Fraser's Magazine*, vol. I (1830), p. 514.

15 ibid., pp. 514–15.
16 ibid., p. 515.
17 ibid., p. 516.
18 W. Hazlitt, 'Brummelliana', in *Collected Works*, ed. P. P. Howe, 20 vols (London: Dent, 1934), Vol. 20, p. 152.
19 E. Moers, *The Dandy: Brummell to Beerbohm* (London: Secker & Warburg, 1960), p. 74.
20 ibid., p. 34.
21 ibid., pp. 33–4.
22 ibid., p. 29.
23 E. Bulwer (later Bulwer Lytton), *England and the English*, 2 vols (London: Bentley, 1834), Vol. II, pp. 103–4.
24 E. Bulwer (later Bulwer Lytton), *Pelham; or the Adventures of a Gentleman*, 1st edn, 3 vols (London: Colburn, 1828), Vol. II, p. 284.
25 ibid., Vol. I, p. 92.
26 ibid., Vol. II, p. 291.
27 Mrs C. Gore, *Cecil, or the Adventures of a Coxcomb*, 3 vols (London: Bentley, 1841), Vol. I, p. 228.
28 ibid., Vol. I, pp. 264–5.
29 ibid., Vol. I, p. 162.
30 ibid., Vol. I, p. 225.
31 ibid., Vol. III, p. 168.
32 ibid., Vol. III, p. 285.
33 Mrs C. Gore, *Cecil, a Peer*, 3 vols (London: Bentley, 1841), Vol. I, p. 279.
34 R. Colby, *Fiction with a Purpose* (Bloomington, Ind., and London: Indiana University Press, 1967), p. 167.
35 G. N. Ray (ed.), *Thackeray's Contributions to the 'Morning Chronicle'* (Urbana, Ill.: University of Illinois Press, 1955), p. 32.
36 ibid., p. 39.
37 ibid., p. 51.
38 M. Arnold, 'England and the Italian question', in *Complete Prose Works*, ed. R. H. Super, 11 vols (Ann Arbor, Mich.: University of Michigan Press, 1960–76), Vol. I, p. 85.
39 A. Fleishman, *The English Historical Novel* (Baltimore, Md: Johns Hopkins University Press, 1971), p. 146.
40 J. Stevens, '*Vanity Fair* and the London skyline', *Costerus*, n.s., vol. II (1974), p. 39.
41 E. S. Dallas, *The Gay Science*, 2 vols (London: Chapman & Hall, 1866), Vol. II, pp. 323–6.
42 Ray (ed.), *'Morning Chronicle'*, p. 40.
43 J. Hannay, *Studies on Thackeray* (London: George Routledge, 1869), pp. 19–20.
44 J. Sutherland, *Thackeray at Work* (London: Athlone Press, 1974), pp. 45–55.
45 Ray (ed.), *The Letters*, Vol. II, p. 511.
46 Carey, op. cit., p. 28.
47 Sutherland, op. cit., p. 84.
48 R. L. Stevenson, 'Some gentlemen in fiction', in *Lay Morals*, in *Works*, Skerryvore edn (London: Heinemann, 1925), Vol. 22, p. 279.
49 W. H. Auden, *The Dyer's Hand* (London: Faber, 1962), p. 21.

CHAPTER 3

The Mid-Century Context

> In this age of rivalry, money worship, and spurious equality ... we all seek to be gentlemen and gentlewomen. The pursuit is laudable, the aim is noble; and what is more, in running this race, we may be all winners: for we each can reach the goal from our own point, and bear off our crown. To be a gentleman admits of such various interpretations, that whilst, on the one hand, nothing is so difficult, on the other nothing is so easy.
> (James Hain Friswell, *The Gentle Life*, 1864)

I

'I can't tell you what it is,' Clive Newcome says to his father, 'only one can't help seeing the difference. It isn't rank and that; only somehow there are some men gentlemen and some not, and some women ladies and some not' (Thackeray, *The Newcomes*, ch. 7). One great strength of the novelist as a historian of manners is that he can do justice to that element of the *je ne sais quoi* which has always been so important and so elusive in the appeal of gentlemanliness. Thackeray is at his best not when providing a moralistic answer to the question 'What is it to be a gentleman?', as he attempts to do in *The Book of Snobs* (ch. 2), at the end of *The Four Georges* and elsewhere, but when he succeeds in embodying this 'grace of character' in Dobbin or Colonel Newcome. The sociologist must try to resolve the contradictions of the English class system, but the novelist will have been there before him, pouncing on these contradictions and making them a source of ironic comedy:

> 'I don't know why it should be a crack thing to be a brewer; but it is indisputable that while you cannot possibly be genteel and bake, you may be as genteel as never was and brew. You see it every day.'
> 'Yet a gentleman may not keep a public-house; may he?' said I.
> 'Not on any account,' returned Herbert; 'but a public-house may keep a gentleman ...' (Dickens, *Great Expectations*, ch. 22)

Such witty registration of social reality leaves the theorist of manners limping far behind, which of course is the reason why the rise of the novel meant the end of the courtesy book. None the less, the very frequency with which the question 'What is it to be a gentleman?' was being asked in the 1850s and 1860s is a fact of some importance for the student of the novel, because it testifies to a growing uncertainty about the old landmarks of gentlehood which the fiction itself reflects. The problem of the self-made or would-be gentleman is the subject of several novels: *Great Expectations*, Mrs Craik's *John Halifax, Gentleman* (1856), Meredith's *Evan Harrington; or, He Would Be a Gentleman* (1861). Trollope's *Doctor Thorne* (1858) contains a vulgar self-made man as well as an illegitimate heroine who puzzles over her humble birth: 'If she were born a gentlewoman! And then came to her mind those curious questions; what makes a gentleman? what makes a gentlewoman?' (ch. 6). In this chapter I want to examine some of the answers which were found to these vexing questions in the mid-Victorian years.

Among Meredith's rejected titles for *Evan Harrington* can be found *Gentle and Genteel*.[1] A clear indication of changing attitudes is the declining status of the word 'genteel' in the early Victorian period, and to some extent that of 'gentility' also, and the increased prestige of 'gentle' and 'manly'. In Jane Austen 'genteel' is still used in its old un-ironic sense, and as late as 1838 one finds Dickens in *Nicholas Nickleby* describing Kate Nickleby (un-ironically if defensively) as possessing 'true gentility of manner' (ch. 28). Ten years later in *Dombey and Son* (1846–8), when he describes Mrs Blockitt as a 'simpering piece of faded gentility' (ch. 1), or Mr Dombey's 'tall, dark, dreadfully genteel street' (ch. 3), the words have acquired their negative modern connotations of primness and exaggerated propriety. 'Manly', as we have seen, was a key epithet of the period, deriving much of its force from the attack on the supposed effeminacy of dandyism and being used generally to connote a wholesome masculine disregard for the niceties of etiquette and the cramping decorum of the 'fine gentleman' ideal. It is in this sense that Mr Thornton, the northern mill-owner in Elizabeth Gaskell's *North and South*, uses the word in the chapter 'Men and Gentlemen':

A man is to me a higher and a completer being than a gentleman ... I am rather weary of this word 'gentlemanly,' which seems to me to be often inappropriately used ... while the full simplicity of the noun 'man,' and the adjective 'manly' are unacknowledged – that I am induced to class it with the cant of the day.[2]

But Thornton was being less daring than he thought: 'manly' had already established itself in the terms he meant. Nor was it initially the synonym for tough masculinity that Muscular Christianity and the public school games cult were later to make it seem. In *The Manliness of Christ* (1879) Thomas Hughes tried to distinguish 'true manliness' from simple animal courage and athletic prowess, arguing (contrary to the surviving image of him as a public school hearty) that it was 'as likely to be found in a weak as in a strong body'³ and involved 'tenderness and thoughtfulness for others'⁴ and self-restraint as well as courage. Before the growth of the stiff upper lip in the late Victorian public school, manliness was also associated with the capacity to show feeling. 'A man is seldom more manly than when he is what you call unmanned', Thackeray wrote in his essay on Steele; 'the source of his emotion is championship, pity and courage; the instinctive desire to cherish those who are innocent and unhappy, and defend those who are tender and weak' (*Works*, Vol. XIII, p. 572). In *North and South*, again, Mr Hale gives way to 'deep, manly sobs' at the news of his wife's fatal illness.⁵

Gentleness, then, and manliness went together, and both received equal stress in the new Victorian concept of the gentleman. More problematic was knowing what weight to give to 'gentle' in its meaning of 'gentle birth' and what to its more modern sense of 'tender'. The great popularity of James Hain Friswell's *The Gentle Life*, which went through thirty-eight editions between 1864 and 1892, indicates that there was a receptive audience for the message that good birth was not essential for the gentleman or gentlewoman. Friswell was an ardent Thackerayan (he published a sentimental 'conclusion' to *The Newcomes*), a self-styled latter-day Addison whose essays preached the consoling doctrine that all that mattered was moral conduct: 'In the following pages but one idea of a gentleman is endeavoured to be instilled, and that is of one who is indeed gentle, who does his best; who strives to elevate his mind, who carefully guards the very beatings of his heart; who is honest, simple, and straightforward.'⁶ Such a bland definition simply avoids the problem, however, by ignoring the existing ambiguity in the word 'gentle'.

The boldest attempt to resolve this ambiguity is the famous chapter 'Of Vulgarity' in volume V (1860) of Ruskin's *Modern Painters*, one of the two great non-fictional definitions of the gentleman in the period. Ruskin starts from the contemporary confusion about the word 'gentleman', and offers, as he always does, this primary definition: 'Its primal, literal, and perpetual meaning is "a man of pure race"; well-bred, in the sense that a horse or dog is well bred.' But a false meaning of the term has grown up, 'that of "a man living in idleness on other people's labour"; – with which idea the term has nothing whatever to do' (*Works*, Vol. VII, p. 343). The lower classes resent this interpretation, quite rightly in Ruskin's view, but they are wrong to think 'that race was of no consequence. It being precisely of as much consequence in man as it is in any other animal' (p. 344). Both errors must be got rid of. Gentlemen 'have to learn that there is no degradation in the hardest manual, or the humblest servile, labour, when it is honest'; and the 'lower orders' need to learn that good breeding matters and that 'by purity of birth the entire system of the human body and soul may be gradually elevated, or, by recklessness of birth, degraded' (p. 344). Ruskin means 'good breeding' literally, as coming of a good stock and 'purified' by moral habit, and it follows that this will not necessarily be the prerogative of the nobility or gentry, although the nature of their lives gives them greater opportunity to acquire it. We must not confuse 'race with name': it is 'an error to suppose that, because a man's name is common, his blood must be base; since his family may have been ennobling it by pureness of moral habit for many generations, and yet may not have got any title, or other sign of nobleness, attached to their names' (p. 345).

So far one admires Ruskin's clarity of mind in separating the notion of 'breeding' from class, and the notion of the gentleman as a 'born' man from the assumption that he was born to live in idleness. The difficulties for a modern reader arise when he goes on to link fineness of inherited constitution to the capacity for fine feeling and sensitivity:

> A gentleman's first characteristic is that fineness of structure in the body, which renders it capable of the most delicate sensation; and of structure in the mind which renders it capable of the most delicate sympathies – one may say, simply, 'fineness of nature'. (p. 345)

The purely bred gentleman in Ruskin's view will be more sensitive than others:

> And, though rightness of moral conduct is ultimately the great purifier of race, the sign of nobleness is not in this rightness of moral conduct, but in sensitiveness. When the make of the creature is fine, its temptations are strong as well as its perceptions; it is liable to all kinds of impressions in their most violent form; liable therefore to be abused and hurt by all kinds of rough things which would do a coarser creature little harm, and thus to fall into frightful wrong if its fate will have it so. (p. 346)

At this point one hears the voice of Dickens's Steerforth in *David Copperfield*: 'Why, there's a pretty wide separation between them and us', he says of the Yarmouth boat-people, 'They are not to be expected to be as sensitive as we are. Their delicacy is not to be shocked, or hurt easily' (ch. 20). Ruskin, of course, does not mean this, but his correlation of fine 'make' with the capacity for fine feeling leads in the end to a caste theory of morals: gentlemen are set over us and they deserve to be, because they are finer – spiritually, morally, emotionally – than we are. In fact, this is not too much of a caricature of Ruskin's final position. The true gentleman was for him a superior creature, but one who must justify his lofty position by extending the 'sympathy' which was the result of his sensitiveness to caring for those beneath him, and practising the 'largesse' of a revived chivalry. It is worth noting in passing that both Thackeray in *Vanity Fair* and Dickens in *Great Expectations* make a pointed separation between fineness of 'make' and the capacity for fine feeling, Dobbin being given a lisp and clumsy feet, and Pip his coarse hands and blacksmith's arm.

The other famous Victorian definition of the gentleman is, of course, Cardinal Newman's in *The Idea of a University* (1852, published under that title 1873), and this is worth considering both for its great intrinsic interest and for the light it sheds on one of the most popular and least examined of Victorian assumptions — the concept of the Christian gentleman. Dekker's description of Christ as 'the first true gentleman that ever breathed' has already been mentioned, and it was frequently quoted. The notion of the Christian gentleman was vague enough to be claimed by all sections of church opinion, and each had its own courtesy book. For the Evangelicals William Roberts's popular *Portraiture of a Christian Gentleman* (1829), fulsomely dedicated to Hannah More, argued the essential compatibility of gentlemanliness and vital religion. At the other extreme was Kenelm Digby's *The Broadstone of Honour: or, Rules for the Gentlemen of England* (1823), a key work in the Anglo-Catholic revival which has been described as 'the breviary of Young England'.[7] Digby was a Catholic convert who addressed his work to the 'order' of the 'Gentlemen of England' in the hope that they would learn from his compendium of medieval chivalric lore to see the responsibilities inherent in their privileges, and his book played an important part in the development of the idea of chivalry in the period. The Broad Church too had its saint's life in the shape of Stanley's *Life of Dr Arnold* (1844), another enormously influential book which advanced an ideal of gentlemanliness best summed up, perhaps, by a comment in one of Arnold's letters: 'A thorough English gentleman, — Christian, manly, and enlightened, — is more, I believe, than Guizot or Sismondi could comprehend; it is a finer specimen of human nature than any other country, I believe, could furnish.'[8] 'Christian, manly, and enlightened' were just the qualities to appeal to a new generation impatient with social and theological conservatism, and dismayed by party divisions within the churches.

What none of these and other apologists for the Christian gentleman ideal asked themselves was the question Newman put to his audience so intelligently in *The Idea of a University*: how compatible *are* gentlemanliness and Christianity? 'An infidel gentleman is an impossible character', Digby wrote, 'or rather the expression is an error of language, since the very act of rejecting Christianity must exclude us from the order.'[9] So accustomed were the Victorians to an unthinking association of gentility with Christianity that one High Church headmaster, William Sewell of Radley, could actually preach a sermon in the school chapel on the subject of 'Rank' and deliver himself of the following sentiments:

> A gentleman, then, and a Christian, whether boy or man, both knows, and is thankful that God, instead of making all men equal, has made

them all most unequal ... Hereditary rank, nobility of blood, is the very first condition and essence of all our Christian privileges; and woe to the nation, or the man by whom such a principle is disdained, who will honour no one except for his own merits and his own deeds![10]

If that seems bizarre, then Sewell's sermon on 'Gentlemanly Manners' is even more so. Here the snobbery of Thackeray's fashionable clergyman Charles Honeyman is communicated in the tones of Dickens's Mr Podsnap:

We have, I think, in England, owing to the freedom of our constitution, and the happy providential blessings which God has heaped upon us, followed the division of mankind which God himself has made, and struck the line between those who are gentlemen, that is, of a higher and superior class, and those who are not, where He himself has struck it. Some men He has made to rule and govern; some to be ruled and governed. And in England, the term gentleman is generally given to all those who are in those positions of society, in which they are trusted with power and authority, and are required to exercise the higher faculties of nature, in influencing, guiding, and benefiting others. And now you can see that in this sense, the term gentleman is applicable to every one of you. You are all the sons of gentlemen, of persons who, at least, are in liberal, respected professions and occupations. This place is not intended for any others.[11]

It is hardly surprising that when Sewell sent a volume of his Radley sermons to Dickens, 'his reply though courteous indicated that we were far too widely apart on fundamental principles'.[12]

Newman's famous definition needs to be seen against this background of easy assumption. He valued the gentleman for his cultivation and courtesy, and he saw the promotion of these qualities — the old Augustan notion of 'civility' — as the chief goal of a liberal education. But he was led by his own deep and thoughtful Catholicism, and partly by the occasion on which the original discourses were delivered, to insist upon the ultimate distinctness of gentlemanliness and Christian virtue. The occasion was the proposal to found a Catholic university in Dublin, and in lecturing there on the subject of education Newman was walking an intellectual tightrope, as he knew. On the one hand his task was to persuade a Catholic audience, in a Catholic country not historically well disposed to the English gentleman, that a university education ought to be an end in itself and that the cultivation and disinterestedness of the educated gentleman were worthwhile goals. On the other he had to assure his hearers, and in particular the Irish bishops, that such an enterprise would not conflict with the truths of the Catholic religion. This delicate task may well have led him to exaggerate the contrast between Catholicism and what he calls the 'Religion of Reason' or 'Religion of civilized times, of the cultivated intellect, of the philosopher, scholar, and gentleman'.[13] The distinction between these two 'Religions', the religion of the Catholic and the religion of the gentleman, forms the subject of Discourse VIII, 'Knowledge Viewed in Relation to Religion'.

Newman begins by conceding that intellectual culture may help the cause of religion by encouraging detachment from the senses, because it 'generates within the mind a fastidiousness' which will 'generally be lively enough to create an absolute loathing of certain offences, or a detestation and scorn of them as ungentlemanlike, to which ruder natures, nay, such as have far more of real religion in them, are tempted, or even betrayed'.[14] But such fastidiousness is shallow-rooted because it is founded on a subtle sense of self-esteem rather than the love of virtue. Gentlemanliness on its own offers a simulacrum of Christian virtue which is all the more insidious because it makes a hidden appeal to man's pride, substituting the sense of shame for fear, and a secretly prideful 'modesty' for true humility: 'conscience tends to become what is called a moral sense; the command of duty is a sort of taste; sin is not an offence against God, but against human nature'.[15] He illustrates the pagan nature of 'this intellectual religion' from Gibbon's account of the death of the Emperor Julian, and quotes from Shaftesbury's *Characteristics* (1711) to show the replacement of true religion in the eighteenth century by 'a doctrine which makes virtue a mere point of good taste, and vice vulgar and ungentlemanlike'.[16] This doctrine is essentially superficial, Newman argues, because by putting the emphasis on appearances it enables pride to return in the guise of self-respect, and vice (in Burke's famous words) to lose half its evil by losing all its grossness. He makes the telling point that it is self-respect, not religion, which is bringing to an end 'the unchristian practice of duelling, which it brands as simply out of taste, and as the remnant of a barbarous age'.[17] Then follows the famous 'definition of a gentleman' as 'one who never inflicts pain':

> His benefits may be considered as parallel to what are called comforts or conveniences in arrangements of a personal nature: like an easy chair or a good fire, which do their part in dispelling cold and fatigue, though nature provides both means of rest and animal heat without them. The true gentleman in like manner carefully avoids whatever may cause a jar or a jolt in the minds of those with whom he is cast; — all clashing of opinion, or collision of feeling, all restraint, or suspicion, or gloom, or resentment; his great concern being to make every one at their ease and at home. He has his eyes on all his company; he is tender towards the bashful, gentle towards the distant, and merciful towards the absurd; he can recollect to whom he is speaking; he guards against unseasonable allusions, or topics which may irritate; he is seldom prominent in conversation, and never wearisome. He makes light of favours while he does them, and seems to be receiving when he is

conferring...He is never mean or little in his disputes...He is patient, forbearing, and resigned, on philosophical principles; he submits to pain, because it is inevitable, to bereavement, because it is irreparable, and to death, because it is his destiny...Nowhere shall we find greater candour, consideration, indulgence: he throws himself into the minds of his opponents, he accounts for their mistakes. He knows the weakness of human reason as well as its strength, its province and its limits. If he be an unbeliever, he will be too profound and large-minded to ridicule religion or to act against it; he is too wise to be a dogmatist or fanatic in his infidelity. He respects piety and devotion; he even supports institutions as venerable, beautiful, or useful, to which he does not assent; he honours the ministers of religion, and it contents him to decline its mysteries without assailing or denouncing them. He is a friend of religious toleration, and that, not only because his philosophy has taught him to look on all forms of faith with an impartial eye, but also from the gentleness and effeminacy of feeling, which is the attendant on civilization.[18]

It is a superb, searching definition, feeling its way, as no other definition of the period does, into the nuances of the gentlemanly character. Justice is done to the courtesy and stoicism of that character, but Newman also mercilessly lays bare the pride at the heart of the gentleman's self-effacement. Behind the seeming selflessness lies a real selfishness; the gentleman will surrender the outworks of his personal convenience in order to preserve the citadel of his self-esteem intact. Newman acutely perceives that there is an exquisite vanity at work in the gentleman's courtesy which works against deep commitment or self-surrender. Hence the strikingly *negative* character of the definition. 'Perhaps one-third of the sentences which describe the gentleman are couched in the negative form,' Dwight Culler observes, 'and another third imply a negative by the nature of their verb.'[19] Newman's gentleman is not a man who does but a man who refrains from doing, and it is revealing that his sources were from the eighteenth century: Shaftesbury's *Characteristics* and James Forrester's *The Polite Philosopher* (1734). Newman's commentators assume that Forrester's pamphlet (which Newman found bound in an edition of Chesterfield's *Letters*) belongs to the Chesterfield school, where in fact it was strongly influenced by Addison; but the spectre he raised, intentionally or not, was that of Chesterfield. Forrester, like Addison, set out 'to make Men ashamed of their Vices, by shewing them how ridiculous they were made by them, and how impossible it was for a bad Man to be polite'.[20] Newman, like Chesterfield, reminded the Victorians that it was not impossible. One by one he cut the many threads by which proponents of the new manners had attempted to bind gentility and virtue together: politeness was not piety, self-respect not conscience, good taste and civility were not virtue, shame was not a sense of sin, putting others at their ease not charity. He did not deny that the gentleman could be a Christian, only that he was *necessarily* one.

If there is a flaw in Newman's definition it is that he relied too exclusively on eighteenth-century models, overlooking (perhaps deliberately) the earnestness and purposeful Christian manliness propounded by his erstwhile opponent Thomas Arnold, who had attempted to teach the gentlemen of England that a graceful self-effacement was not enough. That apart, Newman is almost as relevant as Chesterfield to the student of manners. Among much else, his sense of the gentleman's secret vanity illuminates the bashfulness of the Pendennises of Victorian fiction, and helps to explain why, in literature and in real life, the type found commitment so difficult. 'Yet may we think, and forget, and possess our souls in resistance', Clough's narrator reflects in canto III of *Amours de Voyage* (1858), words which apply not only to the hesitant hero of the poem, but to elegant gainsaying Victorian gentlemen like Clough himself and Matthew Arnold. Newman helps us to see how much their gentlemanly stance was a refuge from commitment, from the prospect of surrendering oneself to the transforming power of sex or politics or religion, and so losing the self-conscious inner poise that made life possible:

> I do not like being moved: for the will is excited; and action
> Is a most dangerous thing; I tremble for something factitious,
> Some malpractice of heart and illegitimate process;
> We are so prone to these things, with our terrible notions of duty.
> (Canto II)

On the other hand Newman's net fails to hold a character like Dobbin, making one aware, again, of Thackeray's remarkable achievement in *Vanity Fair*. But whether one agrees with all of it or not, the great virtues of Newman's definition are that it is consistent and comprehensive, and that in questioning the notion of the Christian gentleman it sets down an important limit to the moralising of gentility.

II

Newman looked to the past for his image of the gentleman, but outside the walls of the Birmingham Oratory his contemporaries were becoming concerned about the gentleman's future, particularly in relation to the kind of work that was increasingly required to be done in a changing society. It is no accident that most of the famous Victorian definitions of the gentleman occur in the 1850s and early 1860s, for this is the period when the spirit of middle-class reform was making its challenge felt within the aristocratic framework of English institutions. The drive for professional status and recognition, the challenge to patronage, the campaign for

Civil Service reform, the re-examination of the old public schools: these were all linked developments in which the traditional understanding of the gentleman's role and possible occupations, although not his social prestige, was being questioned. Pressure from below from those seeking wider opportunities and surer status in an expanding society accelerated the growth of a professional elite, and led to a sustained attack on the system of patronage and the demand that government employment should be thrown open to competition. This movement for reform was implicitly (and sometimes explicitly) an attack on aristocratic dominance: competition would overthrow the old pattern of 'interest' whereby the government and diplomatic services, the church, the army and the navy provided a refuge for younger sons and dependants of noble families.

There are several important milestones. The Government of India Act 1853 established the principle of competition for the Indian Civil Service, and a year later the Northcote-Trevelyan *Report on the Organisation of the Permanent Civil Service* advocated competitive examinations and promotion by merit. Their proposals were given topical urgency by revelations of official incompetence in the handling of the Crimean War, which led to the formation of the Administrative Reform Association in 1855. Dickens and Thackeray were both involved in this campaign for reform, and *Little Dorrit* (1855—7) contains an attack on the Civil Service in the shape of the Circumlocution Office and the Tite Barnacles, the aristocratic parasites who run it. In 1854 Macaulay's *Report on the Indian Civil Service* proposed a system of written examinations which would test general education and a mastery of English rather than the classics which formed the staple of the traditional liberal education. Examination was coming to be important in the establishment of the professions too. The Medical Act 1858 created the registered medical practitioner as the heir of the old apothecary, and by so doing, as W. J. Reader argues, 'went a long way towards establishing the approved pattern of a Victorian profession, whether in medicine or in any other occupation that aspired to equal dignity';[21] namely, licence by examination, and registration by a professional body with powers of expulsion backed up by legislation. 'This is what every professional man and would-be professional man longs for', Mr Reader observes: 'the closed shop with an Act of Parliament to lock the door.'[22]

The remarkable feature of these reforms and proposed reforms is that while they should have challenged the social dominance of the gentleman ideal, their end-result was to consolidate and perpetuate it. Trollope need not have feared that open competition in the Civil Service would lead to the exclusion of gentlemen; as Gladstone accurately predicted in 1854, the change would confer 'an immense superiority [upon] all those who may be called gentlemen by birth and training'.[23] For this the reformed, post-Arnoldian public schools must take most of the credit — or blame. Reform of the public schools went hand in hand with Civil Service and administrative reform, since its original purpose was to brace the children of the old elite to face the challenges of a new society. In the long run open examinations were to favour those who had had a public school education, because the reformed public schools encouraged the spirit of academic competition, and the examinations themselves tested prowess in just those subjects the schools catered for. Reform weeded out from government service the lazy and stupid sons of noble families, the Tite Barnacles, whom the old system had catered for. The institutional framework was improved without damage to the social structure, for the primacy of gentlemanliness, and of the gentleman's traditional education in the classics, went largely unchallenged.

It is important to understand the nature of the 'reforms' which Arnold, and even more the Arnold legend, helped to bring about. These did not mean any widening of the curriculum; indeed Arnold was responsible for ending even the minimal science teaching (a triennial visiting lecturer) available at Rugby when he arrived. Nor did they mean a change in recruiting policy to bring in boys from outside the gentry and clergy class which provided the overwhelming majority of Rugby pupils: that was a task for the new schools which sprang up in the 1850s and 1860s. Arnold went so far as to discourage applications from sons of the nobility, on the grounds that they were not amenable to the discipline he was trying to inculcate; he saw his clientele neither in the aristocracy nor in the commercial middle classes, but among 'the sons of gentlemen of moderate fortune,' as his wife put it in a letter, 'who formed the mass of our boys'.[24] These he could hope to impregnate with his vision of their high destinies in a changing world. His ambition was to moralise and Christianise the English schoolboy, but his really influential achievement was probably to turn the sixth form into an elite within the elite, a missionary task force sent out to vitalise English society. Arnold was fanatically devoted to the sixth, and he gave them an exhilarating sense of new moral worlds to be conquered. 'I think this was our most marked characteristic,' Thomas Hughes said of his Rugby generation in 1891, 'the feeling that in school and close we were training for a big fight − were in fact already engaged in it − a fight which would last all our lives, and try all our powers, physical, intellectual, and moral, to the utmost.'[25] This attitude led Hughes to Christian Socialism; in others it encouraged the spirit of competition, which Arnold saw as a desirable and increasingly important feature of modern life. As early as 1831 he was telling the school (from the pulpit) that 'never was competition so active − never were such great exertions needed to gain success. Those who are in the world know this already; and if there are any of you who do not know it, it is fit that you should be made aware of it.'[26] Arnold's stated priorities were more traditional: 'what we must look for here is, 1st, religious and moral principle; 2ndly, gentlemanly conduct; 3rdly, intellectual ability'.[27] But his important legacy to the sixth was preparedness for a world of competition, and the moral earnestness and sense of communal responsibility encouraged by his other important reform, the development of the prefect system. The thirty or so boys in the sixth were chosen largely on intellectual criteria, and these took the full force of his powerful personality; to the majority of boys who failed to make this elite, he probably communicated no more than a vague sense that life was a more serious business than their fathers had thought. In either case, the traditional English gentleman who passed through his or his disciples' hands would never be quite the same again.

Arnold became a more influential figure after his death than he was in his years at Rugby, partly through the great popularity of Stanley's *Life* and *Tom Brown's Schooldays* (1857). Hughes's novel, indeed, deserves a passing mention in this study because it is a unique witness to the impact of Arnold's personality on an ordinary boy from the rank for which, above all others, Rugby catered: the gentry. It must always puzzle us to know quite why Arnold was, in Bagehot's words, 'an admirable master for a common English boy, – the small apple-eating animal whom we know',[28] and even more how the reforms initiated by this austere and intellectual man could have ended up in the cult of athleticism in the later Victorian public school. The answer is to be found in the pages of *Tom Brown's Schooldays*, which show how very amenable team games, especially football and cricket, were to the moral qualities Arnold wished to inculcate. Tom's development from apple-eating animal to Christian gentleman is portrayed in terms of a movement upwards from the 'lower' field sports, like fishing and bird's nesting, and the anarchic poacher-gamekeeper attitude to authority they encourage, and from the 'selfish' individualism of hare and hounds, to the 'higher' sense of communal responsibility involved in being captain of the cricket eleven. Arnold's message is seen to have sunk home at Tom's last cricket match, when he and the young master discuss the moral superiority of cricket:

> 'The discipline and reliance on one another which it teaches is so valuable, I think,' went on the master, 'it ought to be such an unselfish game. It merges the individual in the eleven; he doesn't play that he may win, but that his side may.'
>
> 'That's very true,' said Tom, 'and that's why football and cricket, now one comes to think of it, are such better games than fives' or hare-and-hounds, or any others where the object is to come in first or to win for oneself, and not that one's side may win.'
>
> 'And then the Captain of the eleven!' said the master, 'what a post is his in our School-world! almost as hard as the Doctor's; requiring skill and gentleness and firmness, and I know not what other rare qualities.'[29]

Here one sees the other side of Arnold's influence, the spirit of fellowship and responsibility which was to lead the Christian Socialist Hughes to the

Working Men's College and the Co-operative movement. 'The Doctor was not particularly interested in sport', the Trinidadian writer C. L. R. James observes, 'But Arnold's ideas of principled behaviour were so strong that they went into the games that the boys were playing. Dr Arnold's ideas were not easy for scholarship to incorporate, but on the cricket field and football field — and Hughes was very much aware of this — they were of great value and very important.'[30]

In 1895 one Rugby master asked another about the social origins of the new headmaster, H. A. James: 'Tell me, is James a gentleman? Understand me, I don't mean, Does he speak the Queen's English? but — had he a grandfather?'[31] The purpose of the new public schools was to take the sting out of that question by making membership of the public school community, and not 'ancestry', the agreed criterion of gentlemanliness. Arnold's mission had been to the existing elite; the newer schools responded to the expanding middle-class market in the second half of the century. The growth of the system around the idea of the public school gentleman meant that a working compromise had at last been achieved between the old aristocracy and gentry and the newer middle classes. Yet in the long run British society has paid a heavy price to have the sons of its entrepreneurs educated alongside the traditional elite, for it meant the alienation of the new men from the business, and particularly the technology, necessary for the continued advance of an industrial civilisation. By 1881 Hughes himself had begun to realise that the sort of gentleman the public schools were turning out was not the sort needed by society: he wrote that the 'spirit of our highest culture and the spirit of our trade do not agree together. The ideas and habits which those who have most profited by them bring away from our schools do not fit them to become successful traders.'[32] The sons of the trading classes were taught by the system to despise the origins of their parents' wealth, and they learnt little to equip them for the modern world owing to the predominance of the traditional notion of the liberal education with its almost exclusive concentration on Latin and Greek. It is astonishing to learn in Professor Honey's authoritative study of the Victorian public school system that 'the position of the classics, in public schools and in English education in general was if anything more powerful at the end of the nineteenth century than it had been at the beginning'.[33] This educational bias did not go completely unchallenged. In 1864 the Clarendon Commission objected mildly to the virtual exclusion of science from the public school curriculum, and a decade later the Devonshire Commission on Scientific Instruction expressed itself more strongly:

> The ommission from a Liberal Education of a great branch of the Intellectual Culture is of itself a matter for serious regret; and, considering the increasing importance of Science to the Material Interests of the Country, we cannot but regard its almost total exclusion from

the training of the upper and middle classes as little less than a national misfortune.[34]

The classic response to this criticism was that offered by Frederick Temple, then headmaster of Rugby, to the Clarendon Commissioners: 'The real defect of mathematics and physical science as instruments of education is that they have not any tendency to humanise. Such studies do not make a man more human, but simply more intelligent.'[35] In fairness to Temple it should be said that he was one of the few Victorian headmasters to make a place for science in the public school curriculum. None the less, his distinction between moral education and intellectual training is typical of his period and reveals the powerful link between the idea of liberal education and the gentlemanly ideal.

Defenders of the system could offer specific pedagogic justifications for concentrating on Latin and Greek — that these subjects disciplined the mind, developed the memory, laid a foundation of linguistic knowledge, and so on — but the educational *raison d'être* of classical studies was grander and vaguer. It might be explained along the following lines: a study of the classics familiarised a man with the cultural achievements, social, political, legal, literary, philosophical, of the most highly developed civilisations of antiquity; it not only offered access to a still-relevant body of inherited wisdom, but also freed the mind (hence 'liberal') to range beyond the narrowly technical and utilitarian to contemplate the complex interrelationships of civilisation itself. It was thus an education for citizenship generally, and for leadership in particular. Training was for the professionals who would do the ordinary business of society, liberal education was for the gentleman amateurs who would govern it. Such at least was the ideal, although in describing it one has to suppress a sense of its almost comical disparity with what must have been the reality for generations of uncomprehending ordinary schoolboys — an unenlightened grind through the grammar of Virgil with the aid of a crib. Even so, the mystique of the liberal education was powerful, and not just for the minority of clever boys who profited from it, because it turned upon a concept which is absolutely fundamental to an understanding of both the gentlemanly ideal and the Victorian elite: *disinterestedness*.

The idea of disinterestedness is the thread that links, if anything can, the various mutations of the idea of the gentleman from the gentleman-duellist to the Victorian public servant. The belief that a man's ultimate loyalty ought to be to something larger than his own pocket underlay the traditional gentleman's commitment to the honour of his name and of his country, and it was a characteristically Victorian achievement to broaden the basis of honour to include professional ethics as well. And more than professional ethics: disinterestedness at its highest meant an ideal intellectual and moral independence climbing above the pull of 'interest' and dogma. As G. M. Young put it, 'the function of the nineteenth century was to disengage the disinterested intelligence, to release it from the entanglements of party and sect — one might almost add, of sex — and to set it operating over the whole range of human life and circumstance'.[36] Intellectually, this meant that 'free play of the mind on all subjects which it touches', as Matthew Arnold defined disinterestedness when recommending it to the modern critic in his essay 'The Function of Criticism at the Present Time' (1864). Socially and morally, it meant the modern gentleman's ability to stand above self-interest and look to the good of his community. This is the justification, if there can be a justification, for the distrust of 'trade'. As Taine put it in his account of Victorian attitudes, 'the monied man and the man of business is inclined to selfishness; he has not the disinterestedness, the large and generous views which suit a chief of the country; he does not know how to sink self, and think of the public'.[37] The gentleman's moral (and financial) independence from the narrowing entanglements of trade was felt to be a guarantee of honour and patriotism. In *Shirley* (1849), Charlotte Bronte accused 'the mercantile classes' of wanting to make an ignominious peace with Napoleon so that trade with the Continent could resume: 'These classes certainly think too exclusively of making money: they are too oblivious of every national consideration but that of extending England's (*i.e.* their own) commerce. Chivalrous feeling, disinterestedness, pride in honour, is too dead in their hearts' (ch. 10).

The new generation of public school educated gentlemen was faced with the paradox of gentlemanliness: money was needed to sustain the rank, but the gentleman's highest quality, disinterestedness, presupposed an indifference to mere monetary considerations. Not for them the cultural pressure which forces Chad Newsome in Henry James's *The Ambassadors* (1903) to return from Paris to the family business in Woollett, Massachusetts. The pressure was in the opposite direction, to choose occupations which would be compatible with the habit of gentlemanly disinterestedness their education had encouraged: the professions, the Indian Civil Service, the home and colonial services. In the short run this development served Victorian society very well, for it broke the traditional connection between gentility and idleness, and provided a steady stream of able and principled young men to run the Empire. In the longer run, the balance is more difficult to strike. On the debit side there is the historical alienation of the educated elite from trade and technical knowledge, with consequences that were perceived by Matthew Arnold as early as 1868, when he reported for the Schools Enquiry Commission on upper- and middle-class education on the Continent: 'we have amongst us the spectacle of a middle class cut in two in a way unexampled anywhere else', he wrote of English education, with 'a professional class' which identified with the aristocracy 'but without the idea of science', and an 'immense business class...cut off from the aristocracy, and the professions, and without governing qualities'.[38] Against this must be set the high degree of probity which came to characterise British public and professional life after the abolition of the old patronage system, which is one of the most substantial, if today unsung, achievements of Victorian civilisation. Then there is the concept of 'fair play' inseparable from the gentlemanly ethic, old and new, which enabled the English gentleman to wield his powers with more justice, and surrender his privileges more peacefully, than any other national elite in modern history. And even the anti-utilitarian bias of his education had its positive side: 'In that materialistic England there was some value in an education which was not completely utilitarian and which produced at the lowest, particularly after Arnold had done his work, a greater sense of responsibility and a greater sense of freedom than existed in other systems.'[39]

III

So far we have been concerned with the idea of the gentleman in relation to the upper and middle classes of Victorian society, and to complete the picture of mid-Victorian attitudes it is necessary to look at the appeal of the idea to those lower down the social ladder. The greatly increased mobility of nineteenth-century society posed problems of adjustment for the established gentleman — what occupations could he pursue without injuring his gentility? — but for the enterprising self-made man it offered tantalising rewards, among them, if he was to believe Samuel Smiles, the goal of becoming a gentleman. The last chapter of *Self-Help* (1859) is entitled, significantly, 'Character: The True Gentleman'. Nothing illustrates better the hold which the gentlemanly idea had over the Victorian imagination than its ambivalent presence in the literature of self-improvement.

The popular image of Smiles is that he preached the gospel of worldly success, but this is far from being the case. Although he believed that 'every man's first duty is, to improve, to educate, and elevate himself',[40] it was the acquired character, not the material success of the self-made man, that he valued. The process of self-improvement, or 'self-culture' as he called it, was to be undergone not because it might bring worldly wealth — Smiles stressed that it might well not — but because it strengthened character and individuality and gave the working man a sense of dignity and independence. He was also in his way a critic of snobbery. In the chapter on 'Money: Its Use and Abuse' in *Self-Help* he deplored the cult of respectability and the social restlessness which wealth encouraged: 'There is a dreadful ambition abroad for being "genteel". We keep up appearances, too often at the expense of honesty; and, though we may not be rich, yet we must seem to be so. We must be "respectable", though only in the meanest sense — in mere vulgar outward show.'[41] The 'True Gentleman' was essentially classless:

The inbred politeness which springs from right-heartedness and kindly feelings is of no exclusive rank or station. The mechanic who works at the bench may possess it, as well as the clergyman or the peer... Riches and rank have no necessary connection with genuine gentlemanly qualities. The poor man may be a true gentleman – in spirit and in daily life. He may be honest, truthful, upright, polite, temperate, courageous, self-respecting, and self-helping – that is, be a true gentleman. The poor man with a rich spirit is in all ways superior to the rich man with a poor spirit.[42]

Smiles always protested that his message was not the vulgar, materialistic one of 'getting on', yet without questioning his sincerity or integrity, it can be seen that his argument implied more than he thought it meant. He could not really avoid the familiar problem that the idea of the gentleman was not and could not be entirely classless in Victorian society: there was an unavoidable sense of *social* mobility involved in the idea of 'raising' or 'elevating' oneself. If this is not entirely Smiles's fault, then his choice of language sometimes is. Consider the following passage from the final chapter of *Self-Help*:

The cheapest of all things is kindness, its exercise requiring the least possible trouble and self-sacrifice. 'Win hearts,' said Burleigh to Queen Elizabeth, 'and you have all men's hearts and purses.' If we would only let nature act kindly, free from affectation and artifice, the results on social good humour and happiness would be incalculable. Those little courtesies which form the small change of life, may separately appear of little intrinsic value, but they acquire their importance from repetition and accumulation. They are like the spare minutes, or the groat a day, which proverbially produce such momentous results in the course of a twelvemonth, or in a lifetime.[43]

Smiles's language here is soaked with the vocabulary of investment: courtesy is 'cheap', wins 'hearts and purses', produces 'results', forms 'the small change of life', of 'little intrinsic value' but growing by 'accumulation'. Courtesy is being recommended as the best share to have in one's portfolio, offering a high yield for a small outlay. At such moments the inevitable comparison, strange as it may seem, is with Lord Chesterfield. Courtesy is not an end in itself, it is a means to an end. Smiles preaches gentlemanliness as a disinterested and self-sufficient achievement of character, but his medium often betrays his message.

Nor could self-improvement be linked to the idea of the gentleman without involving questions of class, despite Smiles's disclaimers. In the real world the impulse to improve oneself was likely to be inspired by social and, even more, sexual ambitions, and success was almost bound to be judged, however unfairly, by traditional criteria. These are issues which hover in the background of several Victorian novels dealing with the theme of self-improvement, such as George Eliot's *Felix Holt the Radical* (1866) and Hardy's *The Mayor of Casterbridge* (1886) and *Jude the Obscure* (1896), and they emerge as the central subject of *Great Expectations*. But the classic novel of self-help, in the sense that it presents the ideology in its purest, least critical form, is *John Halifax, Gentleman* (1856), by Dinah Mulock, later Mrs Craik. This is the story of a poor boy who rises from being a tanner's lad to a prosperous mill-owner by practising the qualities Smiles was to codify three years later in *Self-Help*: hard work, perseverance, self-discipline and self-culture. At the start John Halifax is a penniless orphan of 14, almost illiterate, the only suggestions of his future destiny being his 'firm, indomitable will'[44] and his conviction that his father had been 'a scholar and a gentleman'. He carries with him a Greek Testament inscribed '*Guy Halifax, gentleman*' which inspires him to recover this lost status, but 'his lineage remained uninvestigated, and his pedigree began and ended with his own honest name — John Halifax'.[45] Even at the outset, then, the issue is clouded with a hint of 'ancestry', and the aggressive ring of the title, with its stress on *Gentleman*, suggests a recovered as well as an achieved rank. John Halifax works hard at the tanner's trade, and like Smiles's great hero George Stephenson uses his spare time to make models of the machinery he will later introduce into his factory. But he comes to feel ashamed of his 'ugly hands' when he meets and falls in love with a 'gentlewoman', Ursula March, and thereafter his efforts at self-culture are coloured by sexual desire and the social ambitions which in this case go with it. He earns her respect as a true gentleman when he responds with dignity and restraint to the publicly offered insults of her cousin, the local squire (no duelling for John Halifax): 'You have but showed me what I shall remember all my life', she tells him, 'that a Christian only can be a true gentleman'.[46] They marry and with her capital he leases the factory that is to make his fortune. Thereafter it is a steady upward graph of prosperity, celebrated with total lack of irony or criticism by the author. John Halifax is the Sir Charles Grandison of the cotton-mills:

> But my eyes naturally sought the father as he stood among his boys, taller than any of them, and possessing far more than they that quality for which John Halifax had always been remarkable — dignity. True, Nature had favoured him beyond most men, giving him the stately, handsome presence, befitting middle age, throwing a kind of apostolic grace over the high, half-bald crown, and touching with a softened gray the still curly locks behind. But these were mere accidents; the true dignity lay in himself and his own personal character, independent of any exterior.[47]

As one would expect with a novel so closely identified with the aspirations of the commercial middle class, the aristocracy comes in for some hard knocks. John Halifax's upward rise coincides with the downfall of Lord Luxmore and his family, ruined (as the French name would suggest) by luxury, extravagance and adultery. A not very subtle process of social displacement is being portrayed: as the stout 'Saxon' self-made man rises into county esteem, driving to his mills 'in as tasteful an equipage as any of the country gentry',[48] the 'Norman' nobleman dies in disgrace, his impoverished heir eventually marrying the daughter of the hero.

Yet it is just this uncritical involvement with her hero's ambitions that makes Mrs Craik's novel so revealing of the underlying ambiguities in the self-help ideology. Near the end of the novel John Halifax starts to tell the story of his rise from lowly origins, when his son interrupts him with the remark 'We are gentlefolks now'.[49] His father's reply, 'We always were, my son', says everything. For on the one hand the confidence that makes John Halifax feel that he can be a gentleman comes from the inner conviction that he is one already, so that the rank is not so much earned as retrieved; and on the other he can only be accepted as a gentleman when he has achieved the tangible certificates of rank to validate the inner character he has acquired by Smilesian self-culture − the carriage, the estate, the acceptance by county society, even the aristocratic son-in-law. Besides, these are presented in the novel as the *rewards* for practising self-help: success is measured in terms of breaking into the traditional hierarchy. *John Halifax, Gentleman* bears out the truth of Asa Briggs's observation that 'in the battle between the self-made man and the gentleman, the self-made man won in England only if he became a gentleman himself, or tried to turn his son into one'.[50]

'An Artisan, Yet a Gentleman' is the title of one of the *Talks with Young Men* (1884) by John Thain Davidson (1833−1904), a Presbyterian minister who wrote in the self-help tradition, adding a religious top-dressing to Smiles's largely secular message. In it he commends the example of the Apostle Paul, who although a gentleman by birth, education and manners, did not scruple to earn his daily bread as a working man. Davidson's message is that of Carlyle, Ruskin and Smiles, that gentlemen must learn to overcome their squeamishness about manual labour. But his title is slightly misleading; it should read, 'A Gentleman, Yet an Artisan'. There were many who agreed that gentlemen did not demean themselves by working with their hands. But artisans becoming gentlemen? That was more difficult to accept, for at the end of the day the rank depended upon exclusion, and was made possible by what Ruskin called, in a passage of fiercely honest irony in *Sesame and Lilies* (1865), the 'sacrifice of much contributed life':

> ...we live, we gentlemen, on delicatest prey, after the manner of weasels; that is to say, we keep a certain number of clowns digging and ditching, and generally stupefied, in order that we, being fed gratis,

may have all the thinking and feeling to ourselves. Yet there is a great deal to be said for this. A highly-bred and trained English, French, or Italian gentleman (much more a lady), is a great production, — a better production than most statues; being beautifully coloured as well as shaped, and plus all the brains; a glorious thing to look at, a wonderful thing to talk to; and you cannot have it, any more than a pyramid or a church, but by sacrifice of much contributed life. (*Works*, Vol. XVIII, pp. 107–8)

The novelist who understood this best was Dickens. In *Great Expectations* the ambiguities surrounding the idea of the gentleman in self-help literature are brought into the open, and traced in the history of an orphan boy who has no genteel birthright like John Halifax, no confidence that he 'always was' a gentleman, and who is forced to confront the sacrifice of contributed life which has made his acquired gentility possible. In Pip the problems of an artisan trying to become a gentleman are for once honestly faced.

REFERENCES: CHAPTER 3

1. L. Stevenson, *The Ordeal of George Meredith* (New York: Russell & Russell, 1953), p. 76.
2. E. Gaskell, *North and South*, ed. A. Easson (London: Oxford University Press, 1973), ch. 20, p. 164.
3. T. Hughes, *The Manliness of Christ* (London: Macmillan, 1879), p. 25.
4. ibid., p. 21.
5. Gaskell, op. cit., ch. 21, p. 169.
6. J. H. Friswell, *The Gentle Life: Essays in Aid of the Formation of Character* (London: Sampson Low, 1864), p. vi.
7. A. Chandler, *A Dream of Order: The Medieval Ideal in Nineteenth-Century English Literature* (London: Routledge & Kegan Paul, 1971), p. 160.
8. A. P. Stanley, *The Life and Correspondence of Thomas Arnold, D.D.*, 12th edn, 2 vols (London: John Murray, 1881), Vol. II, p. 339.
9. K. Digby, *The Broad Stone of Honour: or, Rules for the Gentlemen of England* (London: C. & J. Rivington, 1823), p. 41.
10. W. Sewell, *Sermons to Boys at Radley School*, 2 vols (Oxford: Clarendon Press, 1859), Vol. II, pp. 244–5.
11. ibid., pp. 453–4.
12. L. James, *A Forgotten Genius: Sewell of St. Columba's and Radley* (London: Faber, 1945), pp. 233–4.
13. J. H. Newman, *The Idea of a University*, ed. I. T. Ker (Oxford: Clarendon Press, 1976), p. 158.
14. ibid., p. 162.
15. ibid., p. 165.
16. ibid., p. 173.
17. ibid., p. 178.
18. ibid., pp. 179–80.
19. A. D. Culler, *The Imperial Intellect: A Study of Newman's Educational Ideal* (New Haven, Conn.: Yale University Press, 1955), p. 239.

20. J. Forrester, *The Polite Philosopher* (Edinburgh: 1746), p. iii.
21. W. J. Reader, *Professional Men: The Rise of the Professional Classes in Nineteenth-Century England* (London: Weidenfeld & Nicolson, 1966), p. 66.
22. ibid., p. 68.
23. R. Wilkinson, *The Prefects* (London: Oxford University Press, 1964), p. 23.
24. Quoted in J. R. de S. Honey, *Tom Brown's Universe: The Development of the Victorian Public School* (London, Millington, 1977), p. 16.
25. T. Hughes, *The Manliness of Christ*, 2nd edn (London: Macmillan, 1894), p. 194.
26. Quoted in Honey, op. cit., p. 14.
27. Stanley, op. cit., Vol. I, p. 107.
28. W. Bagehot, 'Mr. Clough's Poems', in *Literary Studies*, 2 vols (London: Dent/Everyman, 1911), Vol. II, p. 275.
29. T. Hughes, *Tom Brown's Schooldays* (London: Macmillan, 1889 edn), pt II, ch. 8, pp. 289–90.
30. 'Out of the air', *Listener*, vol. 96 (1976), p. 13.
31. Quoted in Honey, op. cit., p. 326.
32. Quoted in W. H. G. Armytage and E. C. Mack, *Thomas Hughes: The Life of the Author of 'Tom Brown's Schooldays'* (London: Ernest Benn, 1952), p. 227.
33. Honey, op. cit., p. 128.
34. Quoted in A. J. Meadows and W. H. Brock, 'Topics fit for gentlemen: the problem of science in the public school curriculum', in *The Victorian Public School*, ed. I. Bradley and B. Simon (London: Gill/Macmillan, 1975), p. 111.
35. ibid., p. 113.
36. G. M. Young, *Victorian England: Portrait of an Age*, 2nd edn (London: Oxford University Press, 1953), p. 186.
37. H. Taine, *Notes on England*, 2nd edn (London: Strahan, 1872), p. 172.
38. Quoted in Reader, op. cit., p. 113.
39. G. K. Clark, *The Making of Victorian England* (London: Methuen, 1962), p. 272.
40. S. Smiles, *Thrift* (London: John Murray, 1875), p. 94.
41. S. Smiles, *Self-Help* (London: John Murray, 1859), p. 226.
42. ibid., pp. 325, 328.
43. ibid., p. 323.
44. D. M. Mulock (Mrs Craik), *John Halifax, Gentleman* (London: Dent/Everyman, 1961), ch. 8, p. 81.
45. ibid., ch. 2, p. 11.
46. ibid., ch. 17, p. 163.
47. ibid., ch. 30, p. 310.
48. ibid., ch. 29, p. 293.
49. ibid., ch. 29, p. 301.
50. A. Briggs, *Victorian People* (Harmondsworth: Penguin, 1965), p. 142.

CHAPTER 4

Dickens and Great Expectations

> 'Biddy,' said I, after binding her to secrecy, 'I want to be a gentleman.'
> 'Oh, I wouldn't, if I was you!' she returned. 'I don't think it would answer.'
> (*Great Expectations*, ch. 17)

> 'My father was not a gentleman – he was too mixed to be a gentleman.'
> (Kate [Dickens] Perugini, *The Dickensian*, 1980)

I

It used to be said of Dickens that he could not describe a gentleman. Behind this charge often lurked the snobbish assumption that he could not describe gentlemen because he was not a gentleman himself. Thus when Forster's *Life* appeared in 1871 with its revelations of his father's imprisonment for debt and his own childhood employment in the blacking factory, the worst suspicions of the *Times* reviewer were confirmed: Dickens the man, he observed, was 'often vulgar in manners and dress... ill at ease in his intercourse with gentlemen... something of a Bohemian in his best moments'.[1] It was G. K. Chesterton who put the matter in its proper perspective:

> When people say that Dickens could not describe a gentleman, what they mean is... that Dickens could not describe a gentleman as gentlemen feel a gentleman. They mean that he could not take that atmosphere easily, accept it as the normal atmosphere, or describe that world from the inside... Dickens did not describe gentlemen in the way that gentlemen describe gentlemen... He described them... from the outside, as he described any other oddity or special trade.[2]

In this, as in so much else, Dickens contrasts with his great rival Thackeray. Thackeray took to the gentlemanly atmosphere naturally; it forms a shared basis of assumption between author and reader and is one source of the distinctive authorial tone in his novels. His ease in the traditional world of the gentleman gave Thackeray what seemed, to many of his contemporaries, a greater frankness when dealing with the peccadilloes of his young heroes, in contrast to the resolute respectability of Dickens's. 'In the very heart and soul of him this young man is *respectable*', Mrs Oliphant wrote of David Copperfield in *Blackwood's Magazine* in 1855, comparing him with the man-of-the-world heroes of Thackeray and Bulwer Lytton: 'Into those dens of vice, and unknown mysteries, whither the lordly Pelham may penetrate without harm, and which Messrs Pendennis and Warrington frequent, that they may see "life," David Copperfield could not enter without pollution.' And David Copperfield's purity, she recognised, stemmed from his creator's social orientation in the middle class:

> society down below here, in the third or fourth circle of elevation, is more exacting than that grander and gayer society which calls itself 'the world;' and while the multitude of novel-writers set themselves to illustrate, with or without a due knowledge of it, the life of lords and ladies, and the gay realms of fashion, Mr Dickens contents his genius with the sphere in which we suppose his lot to have been cast by nature, in the largest 'order' of our community — the middle class of England.[3]

Both Thackeray and Dickens, we can now see, were novelists of the middle-class emergence, but at opposite ends of the scale. Thackeray's province is that 'debateable land between the aristocracy and the middle classes', as W. C. Roscoe called it,[4] and his gentlemen for the most part have a public school education which qualifies them, whatever their origins, for entry to the traditional gentleman's world of the club and the fashionable regiment. Dickens is concerned with the lower reaches of the middle class in its most anxious phase of self-definition, struggling out of trade and domestic service and clerical work into the sunshine of respectability. His own background is almost a paradigm of that process: his grandfather had been steward to Lord Crewe, his grandmother became housekeeper at Crewe Hall, his father (probably through Crewe influence) got a clerkship in the Navy Pay Office, he himself became a successful author and a self-made gentleman who in later life assumed the right to use the crest of the old Dickens family of Staffordshire. He knew intimately the snobberies and social insecurities which the early Victorian hunger for respectability generated — all the more intimately, indeed, for having temporarily lost his own right to respectability when, after the family moved to London in 1822 (Dickens was 10), his father was imprisoned for debt and he himself sent to work in the blacking factory. This area of Dickens's biography is too well known to need any rehearsing here, but it is interesting to note that the autobiographical fragment he wrote in his thirties, and later partially incorporated in *David Copperfield*, identifies passionately with his younger self's shame at being set to work 'from morning to night, with common men and boys, a shabby child', and reveals the tenacity with which he held on to his status as 'the young gentleman': 'Though perfectly familiar with them, my conduct and manners were different enough to place a space between us. They, and the men, always spoke of me as "the young gentleman".'[5]

The man who wrote these words and suffered that experience of social disinheritance, however briefly, knew areas of nineteenth-century experience which were closed to Thackeray and all the other major Victorian novelists. Thackeray once wrote that 'an English gentleman knows as much about the people of Lapland or California as he does of the aborigines of the Seven Dials or the natives of Wapping' (*Works*, Vol. I, p. 132). Dickens's unique qualification was that he could not share the gentleman's conventional ignorance. The experience that had been personally humiliating and shameful was, from another point of view, an artistic opportunity. His ability to see the gentleman 'from the outside', as Chesterton recognised, gave him an insight into the Victorian pursuit of gentility, and the role of the gentleman in the structure of nineteenth-century society, which a born insider like Thackeray could never have. Dickens knew what the natives of Wapping were like, and how they saw the gentleman; he discovered for himself how thin and precarious was the partition that separated a lower-middle-class family from the abyss of urban poverty in the early nineteenth century; and he knew from his own experience how intensely that partition might be valued by those threatened with the drop into the abyss, how desperately an aspiring young gentleman would struggle to escape working 'from morning to night, with common men and boys, a shabby child'. For most of his life Dickens did not 'know' these things objectively, as a man more detached from middle-class aspirations might have done; he experienced them subjectively, in all their complexity and ambivalence. But in one marvellous novel, *Great Expectations* (1860–1), he found a fictional form capable of expressing the social ironies underlying both his own and his generation's preoccupation with the idea of the gentleman, and in doing so delivered what is in many ways his most profound commentary on Victorian civilisation and its values.

Dickens could write *Great Expectations* because he was so deeply involved in the process of social evolution which, I shall argue, lies at the heart of the novel. 'He typifies and represents, in our literary history', one contemporary critic said of him, 'the middle class ascendancy prepared for by the Reform Bill.'[6] Dickens came of age in the year after the 1832 Reform Bill, and he has all that parvenu generation's fascination with the idea of the gentleman. Not surprisingly we find him pulled this way and that by the conflicting images of gentlemanliness abroad in the early Victorian period. Ellen Moers has suggested that the young clerks and medical students in the early novels belong (as perhaps the young Dickens did himself) to the species known in the 1830s as 'The Gent'. The 'Gent' was 'a second-hand shop-worn imitation of the dandy'[7] — young men at the very bottom of the respectable class who wore flashy clothes and cheap jewellery and worshipped fashionable life at a distance (one thinks of Tony Jobling and the 'Galaxy Gallery of British Beauty' in *Bleak House*). And although she distorts some of the later novels to make her case, she shows how Dickens's growing revulsion from the stuffy, Podsnap side of Victorian middle-class life in the 1850s and 1860s inclined him to a more sympathetic portrayal of the dandy-type, in characters like Sydney Carton in *A Tale of Two Cities* (1859) and Eugene Wrayburn in *Our Mutual Friend* (1864—5).

More conventionally, Dickens shared to the full in the Victorian ambivalence about the relative claims of inherited and acquired status: like the fictional John Halifax who, as we saw in the previous chapter, was both a hero of self-help and (as he thinks) the son of 'a scholar and a gentleman', Dickens was capable of asserting his qualities as a self-made man as well as his claims as a gentleman's son. The latter tend to dominate in his treatment of the heroes in early novels like *Oliver Twist* (1837—9) and *Nicholas Nickleby* (1838—9), who struggle to recover and reassert a lost birthright of gentility, and can still be discerned in a letter written a year before he died, where he spoke of his father's coat-of-arms: 'I beg to inform you that I have never used any other armorial bearings than my father's crest; a lion couchant, bearing in his dexter paw a Maltese cross. I have never adopted any motto, being quite indifferent to such ceremonies.'[8] (The movement of thought here, from the modest assertion of inherited gentility — 'my father's crest' — to the protested indifference to 'such ceremonies', is of course characteristically ambivalent, simultaneously claiming the status and dissociating himself from those who take it too seriously.) On the other side Dickens could, and frequently did, align himself with the self-help virtues, particularly in his middle period — the years from *Dombey and Son* (1846—8) to *Bleak House* (1852—3) — when he was most in sympathy with the progressive momentum of what he called in *Bleak House* 'the moving age', against the 'perpetual stoppage' (ch. 12) of the moribund, tradition-ridden elements in mid-Victorian life. He knew by heart and liked to quote the lines from Bulwer Lytton's play *The Lady of Lyons*:

> Then did I seek to rise
> Out of the prison of my mean estate;
> And, with such jewels as the exploring mind
> Brings from the caves of knowledge, buy my ransom
> From those twin jailers of the daring heart —
> Low birth and iron fortune.[9]

This was the Dickens who was as successful an example of self-help as any in Smiles's book, and who throughout his career used his fame to champion the rights and dignity of his profession, an important campaign which helped to destroy the old patronage system and the snobbish assumption (to which Thackeray was prone) that a professional writer could not be a gentleman. It was the progressive, self-made Dickens who spoke of the rewards of self-help to those institutions of Victorian self-help, the Mechanics' Institutes and Athenaeums, and who identified with the 'manly' character of the reformed English gentleman which Dr Arnold and others had struggled to bring into being. Of Arnold himself, Dickens wrote to Forster in 1844: 'I respect and reverence his memory beyond all expression';[10] and in a speech twenty years later he praised 'the frank, free, manly, independent spirit preserved in our public schools'.[11]

The total picture is complex, as one would expect: the gent, the dandy, the traditional gentleman by birth, the self-made man, the manly Victorian gentleman – Dickens's imaginative response to these competing images of social style fluctuates with changes in his attitude to his own experience and to the life of a changing society. All of them were possible for him and none was final; he could try them on, as it were – and Dickens, a fine and obsessive actor, very nearly joined that least respectable of professions in his stage-struck youth – without feeling that any of them matched his identity. The bohemian streak which many contemporaries discerned in his showy dress was the outward sign of a defiant non-respectability deep inside Dickens; the famous coloured waistcoats were in deliberate rebellion against the cautious sobriety of mid-Victorian gentlemanly fashion. Seeing gentlemen from the outside he came to appreciate both the centrality of the gentlemanly idea in Victorian culture and its underlying irony, that however earnestly it might be moralised the concept depended for its existence upon exclusion, on separating gentlemen from non-gentlemen. *Great Expectations* is the fruit of that recognition. Dickens was in a unique position to write it because, looking back and coming to understand the ironies of the great expectations which had inspired his own social rise, he could see how central these expectations had been for the class and generation to which he belonged. 'A man's life of any worth is a continual allegory', Keats said in one of the more enigmatic passages in his letters, 'Shakespeare led a life of Allegory: his works are the comments on it.'[12] *Great Expectations* might be described as Dickens's fictional comment on the allegory, the representative fable, in his own experience.

II

Great Expectations comes at a crucial stage in Dickens's career. When he started to write it in the autumn of 1860, his life no longer conformed to the conventional pattern of men of his age and class, nor to the public image his readers had come to have of him. The novelist of domestic harmony, who more than any other Victorian writer had been identified with celebrating the values of hearth and home, had two years earlier broken up his own fireside circle, separating from his wife after twenty-two years of marriage and taking up with a young actress, Ellen Ternan. Partly to pay for the three establishments he now had to run, partly to assuage a desperate restlessness that plagued him for the last fifteen years of his life, he had started a series of public readings from his works which his old friend and biographer John Forster considered 'a substitution of lower for higher aims' that 'had so much of the character of a public exhibition for money as to raise, in the question of respect for his calling as a writer, a question also of respect for himself as a gentleman'.[13] But Dickens, who had fought so hard for his own respectability and so honourably for the respectability of his profession, was not to be restrained now by appeals to the concept of the 'gentleman': the old theatrical urge had surfaced again, made doubly attractive (despite Forster's warnings about the low associations of the stage) by the fact that he was in love with an actress and forced to live a life of secrecy and disguise. Besides, the influence of old friends like Forster was waning: Dickens's intimate companions were now younger men like Wilkie Collins, with whom he could lead a racier, more bohemian life and who would be more sympathetic to his affair with Ellen Ternan. The wheel had come full circle: Dickens the social outsider, who had identified in his early middle age with the moralised gentlemanliness of the emergent Victorian middle classes, was now an outsider again, but secretly so.

The wheel had come full circle in another sense too. In 1860 Dickens sold his house in London and came to settle in his country home, Gad's Hill Place, in Kent. In one way this move signalled a determined break with the life he had lived for the past twenty years (a determination symbolised by the bonfire of his private papers he made shortly after moving in); in another it was a return to the source. For Gad's Hill Place was, as Dickens described it when he bought it in 1855, 'literally "a dream of my childhood"'.[14] This old house, which was situated on the highest point on the road between Gravesend and Rochester, offered a virtual panorama of the landscape of his earliest memories, associated as these were with the happiest period of his childhood spent in Chatham and the adjoining town of Rochester. In 'Travelling Abroad', one of the autobiographical *Uncommercial Traveller* pieces written shortly before *Great Expectations*, Dickens tells the story of how as a small boy he used to go walking in this Kent countryside with his father, who would point out Gad's Hill Place to him and say, 'If you were to be very persevering and were to work hard, you might some day come to live in it' (p. 62). Now he was the owner of Gad's Hill, a successful self-made man who had realised this 'dream' of his childhood, and yet despite the success also a lonely and disappointed man. In another *Uncommercial Traveller* article written at this time Dickens described the 'distant river' he could see from his window, 'stealing steadily away to the ocean, like a man's life' (p. 114). And it is that sense of the whole direction of a life, of a man looking back in middle age on his childhood and youth, and speculating on how he came to be what he now is, which provides the dominant tone and perspective in *Great Expectations*:

> That was a memorable day to me, for it made great changes in me. But, it is the same with any life. Imagine one selected day struck out of it, and think how different its course would have been. Pause you who read this, and think for a moment of the long chain of iron or gold, of thorns or flowers, that would never have bound you, but for the formation of the first link on one memorable day. (ch. 9)

At this stage of his career Dickens was very much concerned with the links in the chain that bound him to his past, with the relationship between the successful middle-aged author and the small boy who had had great expectations of coming to live in Gad's Hill Place — concerned, too, with the irony that these realised expectations, in the shape of wealth and fame, seemed to have brought him no nearer happiness. Significantly, *Great Expectations* opens in the Kent countryside which Gad's Hill overlooked, and is set chronologically not in the contemporary world of 1860 but in the early years of the nineteenth century when Pip and his creator were children.

By 1860 Dickens was able to stand back from his own experience and see it in its totality. He could appreciate the irony of his own disappointed great expectations, but also the irony of the larger cultural pattern into which these expectations fell. As a man who had passed through and beyond his society's obsession with the gentleman, he knew from the inside how closely the great expectations of the class to which he belonged were bound up with the pursuit of gentility, but he also knew from the inside the contexts in which the gentlemanly code broke down. The small boy who had worked in the blacking factory, the middle-aged man who was prepared to risk his respectability in the search for personal fulfilment, were both outsiders, and the novel he wrote at this time combines the perspectives of both — the child-hero trapped in the lot of 'common men and boys', the older narrator looking back in troubled middle life on the struggles of his younger self.

Something of the narrator's tone can be heard, in a minor key, in 'Dullborough Town', another of the *Uncommercial Traveller* articles Dickens wrote at this time and to which he originally gave the Wordsworthian title 'Associations of Childhood'. Dullborough is Rochester and also 'our town' in *Great Expectations*, and in the article Dickens records with whimsical sadness the changes which have overtaken Rochester and himself since he left it with such high hopes as a boy: 'All my early readings and early imaginations date from this place, and I took them away so full of innocent construction and guileless belief, and I brought them back so worn and torn, so much the wiser and so much the worse' (p. 116). Disappointed expectations hang heavily over Dullborough: the golden Rochester of *Pickwick Papers* has shrunk to a backward provincial town, where the playing-fields remembered affectionately by Dickens have been swallowed up by the railway, and the old picturesque coaching-office has given way to a utilitarian warehouse. As Dickens passes through the town he turns an amused eye on such encroachments of the Victorian age as the Mechanics' Institute, a draughty monument to the self-improvement idea where, he is gratified to find, the more improving works moulder on the shelves; and he visits the old theatre only to discover that 'it was mysteriously gone, like my own youth'. Lightly enough touched as it is, this note of social change and personal loss anticipates the tone and point of view of the early chapters of *Great Expectations*, just as the opening of the article takes us back to the period in which the novel is set:

> I call my boyhood's home...Dullborough. Most of us come from Dullborough who come from a country town.
> As I left Dullborough in the days when there were no railroads in the land, I left it in a stage-coach. Through all the years that have since passed, have I ever lost the smell of the damp straw in which I was packed — like game — and forwarded, carriage paid, to the Cross Keys, Wood Street, Cheapside, London? There was no other inside passenger, and I consumed my sandwiches in solitude and dreariness, and it rained hard all the way, and I thought life sloppier than I had expected to find it. (pp. 116–26)

It is the same journey, by the same stage-coach, to the same destination, that Pip makes in chapter 20 of *Great Expectations* — and, one might add, written in the same tone of unsentimental reminiscence of a time long past. It comes as no surprise to learn that *Great Expectations* grew out of one of these autobiographical *Uncommercial Traveller* articles.

Yet *Great Expectations* is not in any obvious sense an autobiographical novel: the very irony which distinguishes Dickens's handling of Pip's story indicates a distancing objectivity, a complete imaginative mastery of personal elements and their transformation into representative fable. It is significant that whereas in previous treatments of the young man's rise in the world Dickens had made the central character's name the title of the novel — *Oliver Twist*, *Nicholas Nickleby*, *David Copperfield* — thereby emphasising the destiny of an individual, the title *Great Expectations* reaches out beyond Pip to suggest the expectations of a whole society. There are no simple autobiographical parallels or straightforward transferences of life into art of the kind that take place in *David Copperfield*, where Dickens had been able to incorporate almost verbatim sections of his unfinished autobiography. This is in keeping with all we know of Dickens's expressed attitudes to the two works. *David Copperfield*, his 'favourite child', could always inspire in Dickens an intense self-identification with the hero: 'To be quite sure I had fallen into no unconscious repetitions', he wrote to Forster when starting work on *Great Expectations*, 'I read *David Copperfield* again the other day, and was affected by it to a degree you would hardly believe.' His references to *Great Expectations* stress only the drollness of what he called his 'grotesque tragi-comic conception':

> I have made the opening, I hope, in its general effect exceedingly droll. I have put a child and a good-natured foolish man, in relations that seem to me very funny. Of course I have got in the pivot on which the story will turn too — and which indeed, as you remember, was the grotesque tragi-comic conception that first encouraged me.[15]

Dickens's comments on *Great Expectations* are hardly revealing, here or elsewhere, yet it is interesting that he should have expressed delight in the irony inherent in his 'grotesque tragi-comic conception', for this suggests the difference between the two works. *David Copperfield* is the story of a middle-class child who carves a successful career for himself despite early injustices, and its overall mood is correspondingly optimistic; the hero of *Great Expectations* is a blacksmith's boy whose efforts to become a gentleman bring him only frustration and disillusionment, and although Pip does achieve in the end a state of self-recognition and a measure of muted happiness, the controlling mood of the novel is one of resignation. At a more fundamental level these differences of mood can be traced to Dickens's radical revision of two subjects which had preoccupied him since the start of his career and have an intimate bearing on his treatment of the gentlemanly idea — the theme of inheritance and the relationship between respectable society and the social underworld.

As we have seen, Dickens the man was divided between the claims of inherited and acquired status, between the part of himself which wanted to believe that he was a gentleman's son and the part which took pride in having overcome Bulwer Lytton's 'twin jailers of the daring heart — Low birth and iron fortune'. Both attitudes are a perfectly natural response to the insecurities of his early years in London and the never-forgotten brief exposure, in the blacking factory and the debtors' prison, to the prospect of total social disinheritance. In *Oliver Twist*, his first fictional treatment of the orphan's story, this experience and his reaction to it can be discerned in two conflicting impulses at the heart of the novel: a horror of the criminal underworld when seen through the terrified eyes of the child Oliver, and a sympathetic understanding of the same underworld from a different, more realistic and socially compassionate perspective.

Dickens understands why underworld characters like Nancy, Bill Sikes and the Artful Dodger are the way they are. He shows impressively the environment out of which criminals grow, and he suggests — it is the most telling social criticism in the book — that when Oliver arrives in Fagin's den, degraded and degrading as it is, he finds there what had been denied to him in the workhouse which respectable society provides for its unfortunates — food, warmth, shelter, companionship, laughter. The conflict between horror and understanding in fact makes the novel more compelling than a consistently realistic treatment would have been. The shrinking Oliver becomes the respectable reader's point of entry into the social underworld: he is made to feel the menace of that world, its power to suck in the innocent and the vulnerable, and in this way Dickens is able to bring across his message more effectively than by overt denunciation — the message that it is the accident of birth which condemns a child to the workhouse, and the fault of society that the road from the workhouse should lead so naturally to the life of crime:

> What an excellent example of the power of dress, young Oliver Twist was! Wrapped in the blanket which had hitherto formed his only covering, he might have been the child of a nobleman or a beggar; it would have been hard for the haughtiest stranger to have assigned him his proper station in society. But now that he was enveloped in the old calico robes which had grown yellow in the same service, he was badged and ticketed, and fell into his place at once — a parish child — the orphan of a workhouse — the humble half-starved drudge — to be cuffed and buffeted through the world — despised by all, and pitied by none. (ch. 1)

The satirical intention of this passage is not carried through in the novel as a whole, however. Oliver is brought to rest in the genteel clothes provided by his fairy godparents, the Maylies and Mr Brownlow, and his improbable immunity from the environment which corrupts all the other underworld characters is justified by the discovery that he is after all the son of a gentleman. From Oliver's point of view the novel insists on the utter incompatibility between the underworld and the life of respectable society, as opposed as heaven and hell, and yet from another point of view suggests that if Fagin's den seems more human than the workhouse, the life of crime preferable to the official charity institutions of society, then the responsibility for this lies at the door of that same respectable society. *Oliver Twist* both makes this recognition and recoils from it, acknowledging the common humanity of Oliver and the Dodger and simultaneously vindicating the innate gentility of the hero: Oliver at the end is re-clothed and sent to school; the Dodger is transported.

This ambiguity surfaces again in Dickens's next sustained treatment of the orphan myth, *David Copperfield* (1849–50), although without the radical social implications of the earlier novel. Here the orphan's genteel inheritance is given a more credible narrative status, and the threatened loss of that inheritance forms only one episode in a much longer novel. David Copperfield is a gentleman's son who nearly loses his birthright when he is set to work in his stepfather's wine warehouse after his mother's death, but recovers it when he runs away to his Aunt Betsey's home in Dover, where he is recognised, accepted and (like Oliver) symbolically re-clothed and sent back to school. The nightmare of disinheritance appears only briefly, in chapters 11 and 12, which deal with David's work in the warehouse and his stay with the impecunious Micawbers (those chapters, in fact, which incorporate passages from the autobiography). As in *Oliver Twist*, the nightmare derives its compelling force from two related emotions: the inner conviction of gentility and thwarted potential which makes the hero miserable in the social underworld, and the terror that this innate superiority will not be recognised by those, like Aunt Betsey, who are capable of releasing him from bondage. Again, the novel both acknowledges the humanity of the lives lived in the underworld and insists that gentlemanliness involves climbing out of the abyss and putting it resolutely behind one.

David, being more humane and complex, does not have Oliver's horrified sense of the incompatibility of the two worlds, but he is troubled after his escape by the fear that he has been more deeply implicated in the underworld than is altogether compatible with his recovered middle-class status, a suspicion that his fellowship in social degradation has involved him in a secret complicity with the outsider which permanently taints him for respectable company. 'How would it affect them,' David thinks of his contemporaries at the respectable school to which his aunt has sent him, 'who were so innocent of London life and London streets, to discover how knowing I was (and was ashamed to be) in some of the meanest phases of both?' (ch. 16). This reaction is of course both psychologically accurate and historically all too understandable, but it is also symptomatic of David's inclination to keep the unrespectable Micawbers at arm's length in the novel, as when he advises Traddles not to lend them money – 'You've got a name, you know' (ch. 28). It is also interesting to note that while the novel shows abundant sympathy for David in his struggle back to respectability, little sympathy is given to the plight of Wilkins Micawber, the Micawbers' eldest son, who in age and situation is closest to David (and to Dickens himself in his own Micawber family).

David Copperfield is of course different from *Oliver Twist*: the underworld with which it deals is merely disreputable and not criminal, and David's rise in the world is accompanied by a convincing affirmation of the self-help values of hard work and earnestness congenial to Dickens at this stage of his career. But David is really not much more of a self-made man than Oliver: both are gentlemen by birth whose tenacious hold on an inner conviction of gentility throughout their sufferings is rewarded by fairy godparents. In *Great Expectations* this genteel underpinning to the orphan's story is knocked away and the fantasy exposed. Pip is always and only the blacksmith's boy, his struggle is to acquire rather than to recover gentility, and he is not allowed to forget or ever truly escape from his rude beginnings. The fairy godparents of the earlier novels reappear, but in an ironic reversal of the inheritance theme. Miss Havisham is a grotesque version of Aunt Betsey, an eccentric single lady who in taking Pip up seems to have recognised his innate fitness to become a gentleman, but as her name suggests she is a sham, a witch, while the money that makes Pip's pursuit of gentility possible comes from another 'witch', Magwitch, and thus from the underworld — literally the underworld of Australia where he has made his money, and symbolically from the social underworld of violent crime with which he is associated in Pip's mind for most of the novel.

And Dickens gives a further twist to the orphan myth in *Great Expectations*. The story of David Copperfield's threatened disinheritance still has power to move us partly because of the tension in the hero's mind between the world of the social outsider to which he feels condemned, and the comforts and decency of the middle-class family life for which he longs. This tension is interesting because it is not a simple question of black and white: the outsider's world undoubtedly has its seamy side, but qualities of sympathy and fellow-feeling also flourish there. Moreover it exhibits, at times, certain kinds of human attractiveness lacking in the more respectable society of the novel — one thinks of Micawber's gaiety and his liberating extravagance, and there is the strange paradox that in a novel so preoccupied with marital relations the disreputable Micawbers should provide almost the only example of a marriage that triumphantly works. Dickens's artistic fidelity to his material is such that he is compelled to record these things, and yet at the same time there is a powerful feeling in the book that the world of the outsider is most dangerous just when it reveals an endearing aspect: David would be lost to respectable living (like young Wilkins) if he allowed himself to be adopted by the Micawbers. It is perhaps significant, as John Bayley suggests,[16] that the villain in *Oliver Twist* was named after the real-life Bob Fagin, the boy whose very kindness to Dickens in the blacking factory must have threatened to reconcile him to his humiliation.

In *Great Expectations*, however, there is no such resistance on Dickens's part to the human claims of the underworld. Far from endorsing the sense of class division in Pip's mind, Dickens constantly undermines it; he is not concerned to justify Pip's rise in station but rather to suggest and analyse the guilt, the inhibition, the personal betrayals which this involves. While David succeeds through a combination of hard work and good fortune, Pip is given the economic basis of the genteel life only to discover in the end that he owes it to a man whose whole history and way of life seem a denial of the refinement to which Pip aspires. In this way the social contrasts which threatened the equilibrium of David's progress are made the very agents of meaning in the later work, and what had been implicit in David's sense of shame — that his middle-class status had somehow been compromised by his association with the likes of Micawber and the boys in the warehouse — these fears are brought into the open and given objective expression in the plot, in the secret bond of complicity between Pip and the convict Magwitch.

Gissing thought that 'no story in the first person was ever better told',[17] and the ironic, remorseful tone in which Pip recounts his life reflects (as the more nostalgic narrative tone of *David Copperfield* does not) Dickens's complete control of his material. The novel is shot through with a sense of the interrelatedness of human life which finds a focus in the narrator's troubled conscience: every incident arises from, and relates to, the ambiguities surrounding his rise in station. When Pip first returns to his home town, for example, he travels on the coach with two convicts, one of whom he recognises as the man who had given him the one-pound notes at The Three Jolly Bargemen in chapter 10. Herbert Pocket has come to see him off, and his response to these men is one of unqualified revulsion and disgust — 'What a degraded and vile sight it is!' And looking at them, Pip can share his friend's perspective:

> The great numbers on their backs, as if they were street doors; their coarse mangy ungainly outer surface, as if they were lower animals; their ironed legs, apologetically garlanded with pocket-handkerchiefs; and the way in which all present looked at them and kept from them; made them (as Herbert had said) a most disagreeable and degraded spectacle. (ch. 28)

To the born gentleman like Herbert the convicts in their manacled state are a species apart, something less than human. Yet Pip has reason to know that they are human, and in that secret part of his consciousness where so much of the essential action of *Great Expectations* takes place he can feel compassion for them, envisaging the ghastly prison-ship which awaits them at the end of their journey: 'In my fancy, I saw the boat with its convict crew waiting for them at the slime-washed stairs, — again heard the gruff "Give way, you!" like an order to dogs — and again saw the wicked Noah's Ark lying out on the black water' (ch. 28). On the journey down to Rochester the convicts start to discuss the forgotten incident, and although there is no likelihood that the man will recognise him, Pip is filled with a nameless and undefined terror. Torn between his sympathy for the men and his fear that the convict will somehow know him and discredit his new-found gentility, Pip leaves the coach on the outskirts of the town:

I could not have said what I was afraid of, for my fear was altogether undefined and vague, but there was great fear upon me. As I walked on to the hotel, I felt that a dread, much exceeding the mere apprehension of a painful or disagreeable recognition, made me tremble. I am confident that it took no distinctness of shape, and that it was the revival for a few minutes of the terror of childhood. (ch. 28)

The irony which informs such scenes is masterly in its control and manipulation of class attitudes. Dickens manages simultaneously to suggest and yet withhold the truth about the source of Pip's expectations, so that when Magwitch does declare himself the knowledge comes not only as a startling revelation but — like the catastrophe of *Oedipus Rex* — as something that has been immanent in the history and behaviour of the central figure. This unity is a feature of the inclusiveness of Dickens's vision. From being peripheral to the hero's progress in *David Copperfield*, the world of the social outcast becomes central in *Great Expectations*; it is conceived not as something apart but as the inseparable corollary, the moral counterpart, of middle-class life. And in this way the unreconciled ambiguities of the earlier works are recognised and redeemed. 'The reappearance of Mr. Dickens in the character of a blacksmith's boy', Shaw observed, thinking of the fictional name Dickens had given in *Copperfield* to one of the boys in the blacking factory, 'may be regarded as an apology to Mealy Potatoes.'[18]

And yet, in an important sense, Mr Dickens is *not* the blacksmith's boy. The personal dimension that shaped his treatment of the orphan myth in *Oliver Twist* and *David Copperfield* is here subsumed in a representative life-history which encompasses some of the deepest hopes, fears and fantasies of Dickens's class and generation. *Great Expectations* has been called 'the classic legend of the nineteenth century',[19] and to appreciate its legendary features more clearly it is useful to see the concerns of the novel in their contemporary context, in particular the context of mid-Victorian attitudes to self-betterment, civilisation and criminality.

III

The greatness of *Great Expectations*, as Lionel Trilling observed, begins in its title: 'modern society bases itself on great expectations which, if they are ever realized, are found to exist by reason of a sordid, hidden reality. The real thing is not the gentility of Pip's life but the hulks and the murder and the rats and the decay in the cellarage of the novel.'[20] Much modern criticism of the novel has been rightly preoccupied with the relationship between cellarage and drawing-room, between the gentility of Pip's life and the criminal outcast who makes it possible; and discussion has tended to focus on the hero's seemingly excessive sense of guilt and the encompassing 'taint of prison and crime' (ch. 32) which pervades his upward rise. 'Snobbery is not a crime', Julian Moynahan points out in an influential article and asks 'Why should Pip feel like a criminal?'[21]

It is an important question, because Pip's guilty conscience is the link between cellarage and drawing-room in the novel, but the terms in which Moynahan and others have phrased and answered it are questionable on both instrinsic interpretive and extrinsic historical grounds. How true is it, for instance, to say that Pip is a snob? The words 'snob' and 'snobbery' are used by Dickens's critics but not by Dickens himself in the text of the novel, although Thackeray and *Punch* had made them widely current by the time *Great Expectations* was written. One has only to compare Pip with the compulsive toadies in Thackeray's *Book of Snobs* to see how very different he is. The real snobs in *Great Expectations*, the characters blinded to human considerations by the worship of wealth and social position, are Pumblechook and Mrs Pocket, and Pip sees through them both from the start. What the view of the novel as a 'snob's progress' ignores, as Q. D. Leavis has convincingly demonstrated, is the sympathy and complexity with which Dickens treats Pip's predicament: to call him a snob is to suggest that he was wrong to feel discontented with life on the marshes and could have chosen to act otherwise than he did, whereas much of the energy of Dickens's imagination in the early part of the novel goes in showing how mean and limiting that life is, and how helpless Pip himself is in face of the contradictory forces at work on him – a point that will be discussed in greater detail a little later. Similarly with Pip's great expectations, the burden of most modern criticism has been to stress that these are *only* illusory, that the 'real thing' (as Trilling says) is not Pip's gentility but what goes on in the cellarage of the novel, that his expectations are indeed even dangerous and anti-social, as Moynahan argues. But such arguments are in varying degrees unhistorical, ignoring the fact that Pip's desire to become a gentleman is 'real' too and has a representatively positive element, in the sense that it is bound up with that widespread impulse to improvement, both personal and social, which is a crucial factor in the genesis of Victorian Britain. Here, indeed, *Great Expectations* partakes of a contemporary meaning which we have largely lost with the passage of time, some such meaning as Frederic Harrison shared when he looked back on the nineteenth century in 1882, and found it to be 'the age of great expectation':

> Mr. Carlyle, Mr. Ruskin, the Aesthetes, are all wrong about the nineteenth century. It is *not* the age of money-bags and cant, soot, hubbub, and ugliness. It is the age of great expectation and unwearied striving after better things.[22]

It may be that we still have a tendency to see the Victorian age through the eyes of Carlyle and Ruskin, and that in our readiness to discern a criminal potential in Pip's expectations we overlook that sense of hopefulness and promise, even idealism, to which Harrison testifies. For the optimism inherent in his description of the nineteenth century as 'the age of great expectation and unwearied striving after better things' plays an important part in *Great Expectations*, as it did in the real world out of which the book was written.

At this stage it may be relevant to recall what was said in the previous chapter about the creed of self-help and *John Halifax, Gentleman*. Ellen Moers has called Pip a dandy, but his dandyism is surely minimal: the immediately relevant context is self-help, which was very much in the air at the time with the publication of Smiles's famous book in 1859, the year before Dickens started work on *Great Expectations*. Dickens even makes an ironic reference to self-improvement literature in the 1868 edition of the novel, where 'The pursuit of Knowledge under difficulties' is the running title to the scene in chapter 2 in which Pip gets into trouble for asking persistent questions about the convict-hulks. The reference is of course to *Pursuit of Knowledge under Difficulties* (1831) by George Lillie Craik, who subsequently married the author of *John Halifax, Gentleman*. Dickens is making a familiar joke, but it might also alert a reader to the ways in which his story of the poor boy who wants to become a gentleman falls into a classic nineteenth-century pattern. Like Newcomen and Faraday, two of Smiles's heroes, Pip is a blacksmith's boy with a 'hunger for information' (ch. 15) which the dame-school in his narrow provincial world fails to satisfy. The fictional John Halifax had been ashamed of his ugly hands and employment as a tanner's lad, and wanted to marry a lady; Pip also learns to feel shame at his 'coarse hands and ... common boots' (ch. 8), and his social ambitions are similarly confused with a sexual motive.

But it is the Smilesian notion of 'self-culture', in relation to the idea of the gentleman in self-improvement literature, that is most relevant to *Great Expectations*. Instead of talking of snobbery, we should see the young Pip as engaged in an attempt at self-culture, and note that his efforts to improve himself precede his visits to Satis House and are sympathetically handled by Dickens:

> There was no indispensable necessity for my communicating with Joe by letter, inasmuch as he sat beside me and we were alone. But, I delivered this written communication (slate and all) with my own hand, and Joe received it as a miracle of erudition.
>
> 'I say, Pip, old chap!' cried Joe, opening his blue eyes wide, 'what a scholar you are! An't you?'
>
> 'I should like to be,' said I, glancing at the slate as he held it ...(ch.7)

There is a representative pathos and comedy here, and it establishes a sympathetic attitude towards Pip's struggle for self-culture which is never entirely absent from Dickens's conception of his character. He means us to see Mr Wopsle's great-aunt's dame-school as the hopelessly inadequate and frustrating educational institution Pip finds it to be, and to respect Pip for his determination to make something of it; even in the midst of debt and dissipation in London, Pip reminds us, 'through good and evil I stuck to my books' (ch. 25).

Humour plays an essential part too in defining Pip's predicament and awakening our sympathies for him. *Great Expectations* is an unequalled record of the small daily pains, embarrassments, gaucheneses, involved in self-culture for the poor boy trying to become a gentleman. From the moment when Estella's scorn awakens shame in Pip — '"He calls the knaves, Jacks, this boy!" said Estella with disdain... "And what coarse hands he has! And what thick boots!"' (ch. 8) — Dickens brings a wonderful comic tact to the portrayal of his education in etiquette and manners. There is Herbert's unobtrusive gentlemanly introduction to table manners:

> We had made some progress in the dinner, when I reminded Herbert of his promise to tell me about Miss Havisham.
>
> 'True,' he replied. 'I'll redeem it at once. Let me introduce the topic, Handel, by mentioning that in London it is not the custom to put the knife in the mouth — for fear of accidents — and that while the fork is reserved for that use, it is not put further in than necessary. It is scarcely worth mentioning, only it's as well to do as other people do. Also, the spoon is not generally used over-hand, but under. This has two advantages. You get at your mouth better (which after all is the object), and you save a good deal of the attitude of opening oysters, on the part of the right elbow.'
>
> He offered these friendly suggestions in such a lively way, that we both laughed and I scarcely blushed. (ch. 22)

And there is the comedy of Joe's awkward struggles with his hat when he comes to visit Pip in London, a scene which makes us share Pip's embarrassment at Joe's embarrassment, his uneasiness at this awkward reminder of his own recent awkwardness:

> [His hat] demanded from him a constant attention, and a quickness of eye and hand, very like that exacted by wicket-keeping. He made extraordinary play with it, and showed the greatest skill; now, rushing at it and catching it neatly as it dropped; now, merely stopping it midway, beating it up, and humouring it in various parts of the room and against a good deal of the pattern of the paper on the wall, before he felt it safe to close with it; finally splashing it into the slop-basin, where I took the liberty of laying hands upon it. (ch. 27)

I am sure, incidentally, that Dickens is poking fun here at his old enemy Lord Chesterfield and his exaggerated horror at displays of clumsiness. There is a passage in one of Chesterfield's letters which this scene seems to comment on:

> When an awkward fellow first comes into a room, it is highly probable that his sword gets between his legs and throws him down, or makes him stumble at least; when he has recovered this accident, he goes and places himself in the very place of the whole room where he should not; there he soon lets his hat fall down; and, taking it up again, throws down his cane; in recovering his cane, his hat falls a second time; so that he is a quarter of an hour before he is in order again... At dinner, his awkwardness distinguishes itself particularly, as he has more to do: there he holds his knife, fork, and spoon differently from other people; eats with his knife to the great danger of his mouth, picks his teeth with his fork, and puts his spoon, which has been in his throat twenty times, into the dishes again... His hands are troublesome to him, when he has not something in them, and he does not know where to put them; but they are in perpetual motion between his bosom and his breeches... All this, I own, is not in any degree criminal; but it is highly disagreeable and ridiculous in company, and ought most carefully to be avoided by whoever desires to please. (25 July 1741)

Physical clumsiness, and the difference between a working-class hand and a gentlemanly hand, are much emphasised in *Great Expectations*. Dickens uses Joe's clumsiness both as a means of indicating how far Pip has come (for good and bad) from the forge, and to make the anti-Chesterfield point that these rough blacksmith's hands, of which Pip has started to feel ashamed in himself, are truly gentle: the comedy of clumsiness modulates into Joe's dignified exit at the end of the chapter, when he gives Pip his hand and 'touched me gently on the forehead, and went out' (ch. 27).

But if Dickens was capable of doing justice to the positive moral dimension in self-culture, he was also aware of the ways in which it tended to overlap with class and sexual aspirations. I argued in the previous chapter that there is a basic ambivalence in self-help literature towards the notion of 'getting on'. The moral emphasis in Smiles is admirable: self-culture is to be pursued as the road to self-respect, dignity, the independence that comes from self-discipline, and so on; its end is character, not wealth or success. But he never faces squarely the possibility that these moral ends might be inseparable from more narrowly social and marital ambitions, nor does he seem to recognise the extent to which his own examples encourage the equation of self-help with worldly success. It was all very well for Smiles to say that 'even though self-culture may not bring wealth, it will at all events give one the companionship of elevated thoughts',[23] when often the motive behind self-culture, and its consequence, was to fit the self-helper for elevated companionship of a different kind — the company of gentlemen, in whose ranks, as Smiles argued in his final chapter, 'Character: The True Gentleman', the successful self-helper naturally belonged. In *Great Expectations* the ambivalence in the concept of self-culture is brought into the open. Dickens shows how, after Pip's visit to Satis House, his admirable ambition to improve himself gets caught up in social and sexual fantasies, which are then brought near to realisation by the news of his financial expectations. The real-life self-helpers elevated themselves by dint of perseverance and self-discipline, whereas Magwitch's anonymous gift instantly provides Pip with the economic basis for the genteel life. It is a significant twist, for by giving his hero the fruits of self-culture without the labour, Dickens is able to concentrate upon the social and sexual implications, and the inherent paradoxes, of the self-improvement idea.

Dickens's exploitation of these attitudes in *Great Expectations* is intimately related to his perception of another important feature of the contemporary scene. The struggle for individual refinement reflects a larger movement in society as a whole; men like Smiles were influential chiefly because they spoke to a generation which was itself acutely conscious of having made enormous advances in the civilisation of everyday life. Dickens's novel, it may help to recall, was published in the same year as the second volume of H. T. Buckle's *History of Civilization in England*, with its proclaimed faith in the 'laws of Progress' and the 'mighty career' of English civilisation. The belief in progress which inspired Buckle and his contemporaries was something more than vulgar optimism or self-congratulation, impressive as the record of social reform must have seemed to mid-century observers; behind it lay an awareness that the state of civilisation they had achieved was a unique and recent development, something that had taken place substantially within the lifetime of a large section of the Victorian public.

This historical fact suggests further ways in which Pip's story can be seen as representative of early nineteenth-century experience. His exaggerated allegiance to the concept of refinement is entirely characteristic of a culture which had barely emerged from the crude and violent society of the eighteenth century. The Victorians were proud, and rightly, of the improvements they had worked in the texture of daily living. As early as 1836 John Stuart Mill was contrasting the civilisation of his day to the 'rudeness of former times', and he noted that 'the spectacle, and even the very idea of pain, is kept more and more out of sight of those classes who enjoy in their fulness the benefits of civilization', whereas in former times everyone had been habituated to 'the spectacle of harshness, rudeness, and violence, to the struggle of one indomitable will against another, and to the alternate suffering and infliction of pain'.[24] By mid-century this process of civilisation had become so consolidated that G. R. Porter could write, in the 1851 edition of his *Progress of the Nation*, that 'it is in itself a proof, of no slight significance, as to the general refinement of manners, that in a work of this nature there would be found an impropriety in describing scenes that were of every-day occurrence formerly, and without which description it is yet impossible adequately to measure the advance that has been made'.[25]

The proximity to the Victorian age of a violent past, and the contrast which this made with the age's most treasured social achievements, is of the utmost relevance to *Great Expectations*. On the one hand there is the England of 1860, relatively stable, relatively prosperous, conscious and rightly proud of the considerable advances in civilisation which the previous forty years had seen; and on the other there is the recent memory of a very different world, the harsh and brutal society of the eighteenth century which the Victorian reformers set out to transform and which still survived as a background to their efforts — a source of congratulation but also of uncertainty and anxiety. Here one can begin to see the contemporary significance of the social ironies in the novel. By making Pip's benefactor a transported convict, and thereby setting his effort at self-culture within a framework of criminality, Dickens was touching the very nerve of a characteristic mid-Victorian dilemma. For if anything seemed to contradict the new civilisation it was the continued existence within it of violent crime: this raised the vexing question of the relationship between those classes who were 'civilised' and those who were manifestly not. (Magwitch is, of course, only a criminal in a technical sense, and Dickens sympathises with him because he has been neglected and oppressed by society. But the important point about him, in terms of the novel's treatment of 'civilisation', is the fact that he is violent and animal, and that for much of the book he is invested with the horrors of Pip's childhood vision of him as 'a desperately violent man', whom he had seen 'down in the ditch, tearing and fighting like a wild beast' [ch. 39] .) What responsibility did the civilised middle classes bear for the barbarity which still persisted at the fringes of their society? Was it a blot on their upward progress, or merely the work of a criminal underworld which the march of civilisation would eradicate?

These issues are raised in an article by W. R. Greg in the *Edinburgh Review* of 1851. Greg was reviewing William Johnston's *England as It Is* (1851) and, anxious to counter what he considered to be the pessimistic tenor of the book, set out to explain the increased crime figures Johnston had cited in support of his theory of national decadence. An increase in crime, Greg argued, did not necessarily betoken an increase in criminality, for '*crime is, for the most part, committed, not by the community at large, but by a peculiar and distinct section of it*' (his italics); these '*professional criminals*' constituted in Greg's view 'a *class apart*', and although they might have increased in number this 'in no degree militates against the idea of the progress of morality and civilisation among all other classes'.

The 'swollen return of crime is undoubtedly a blot upon our escutcheon and a drawback on our progress; not as impeaching the general honesty and virtue of the nation, but as showing the existence of a class among us which the advance of civilisation ought to have eradicated or suppressed'.[26] This view of the criminal as belonging to a *'class apart'* is a typical contemporary attitude and one which Dickens is holding up to scrutiny throughout *Great Expectations*; we have already encountered it in Herbert's response to the convicts on the coach, and Pip's uneasiness on this and subsequent occasions may be seen as a dramatisation of the ambiguity inherent in such a response. Greg might reassure his middle-class readers with the comforting view of an altogether separate and self-contained criminal population, but Dickens's vision reveals a world in which the hero owes his respectability to his involvement with a criminal outcast.

No amount of background material can take the place of a careful critical reading, but it can provide the context for such a reading; in the case of *Great Expectations* it puts us back into a world more sympathetic to the idea of self-culture than ours, where the dream of 'great expectation' — that 'unwearied striving after better things' which Harrison noted — had its positive side too. Moreover, these contemporary attitudes mirror the subconscious hopes, fantasies and uncertainties of a society which is still very close to a more primitive past: Pip's hankering after gentility takes on a dimension of pathos when we realise that Victorian snobbery and prudishness were often (to quote from Dr Kitson Clark) 'the result of a struggle for order and decency on the part of people just emerging from the animalism and brutality of primitive society'.[27] His extreme sense of class division should be related to the intensity of his need to civilise himself, and in this Pip is a true child of the early nineteenth century, his awareness of the civilised life sharpened by a knowledge of its very precariousness.

What has been said so far points to an interpretation of *Great Expectations* which sets it rather apart from Dickens's other novels, certainly from the great social satires of his middle and late period. *Bleak House*, *Little Dorrit* and *Our Mutual Friend* are frontal assaults on the ills of Victorian society, and while *Great Expectations* is still concerned with the nature of that society, it is concerned in a different way. The novel is unique among his fiction in that its real subject is not a specific social abuse, or a series of related abuses, but nothing less than civilisation itself; more accurately, it is a study in social evolution, a drama of the development of conscience and sensibility in a child who grows up in the early years of the nineteenth century. And in this, as I have argued, Pip's story is truly a representative one. Behind *John Halifax, Gentleman*, *Self-Help* and *Great Expectations* — works otherwise so different in attitude and imaginative quality — lies the social experience of the first generation of the Victorian age. *Great Expectations* is a novel of memory in a double sense: it deals with one man's recollection of his past, and in doing so goes to considerable lengths to re-create a period of the immediate past which must have survived in the memory of many of Dickens's original readers. This historical dimension reveals further ways in which the story of Pip is the 'classic legend' of the nineteenth century.

IV

Unlike George Eliot and Thackeray, Dickens is not usually credited with period consistency, and most of his novels combine topical material with biographical and topographical details drawn from Dickens's childhood and youth. But *Great Expectations* is the one exception: it is as carefully dated as *Vanity Fair*, and in the same period, except that Dickens's Regency is at the opposite end of the social scale. As Mary Edminson has shown in a fascinating article, the novel is consistently and, it would seem, deliberately set back in time from its date of composition to the first quarter of the nineteenth century. By examining many period details which a modern reader might overlook but a contemporary would have noticed, she has demonstrated that the internal dating is 'intended to represent a period for the main action of about 1807 to 1823 or at most two or three years later'.[28] It is of course history without dates and footnotes, but it can be shown to have been consciously evoked and consistently maintained. In the first place there are numerous asides throughout the novel which remind the reader that the world in which the action takes place is now past. Thus we are told in chapter 2 that Pip lived in a wooden house, 'as many of the dwellings in our country were — most of them, at that time'; and that 'there was no getting a light by easy friction then'. We learn that after the assault on Mrs Joe the Bow Street runners came down from London 'for, this happened in the days of the extinct red-waistcoated police' (ch. 16). When Pip moves to London, Dickens is careful to keep his reader aware of the difference between 'those days' and the present: 'It was Old London Bridge in those days' (ch. 46); Mr Wopsle's theatre 'was in that waterside neighbourhood (it is nowhere now)' (ch. 47); 'At that time, the steam-traffic on the Thames was far below its present extent, and watermen's boats were far more numerous' (ch. 54); and so on. There are many such parenthetical references in the novel; some are general reminders of time past, others conceal more specific dates. The reference to the Bow Street runners, for instance, suggests a date for the first section of the novel before 1829, when Peel established the Metropolitan Police; the mention of the impossibility of 'getting a light by easy friction' in chapter 2 dates Pip's childhood before 1827, when the 'lucifer' match was invented, and the fact that Orlick is still struggling with flint and steel in chapter 53, when Pip is 23, is one of the clues suggesting that the final section of the novel also takes place before 1827. The mention of Old London Bridge in chapter 46 confirms this dating, distancing the end of the novel to a period before 1831–2, when the old bridge was pulled down and the new opened, and possibly before 1824, the year in which work started on New London Bridge.

These details are slight, but telling, pointing up the historical dimension implicit in the carefully delineated landscape of the novel. In other places Dickens is more emphatic. When the soldiers burst into Mrs Joe's Christmas party in chapter 5, the sergeant announces five times that they are in the service of 'his Majesty the King', making quite clear that this takes place at a time before Queen Victoria's accession in 1837, and possibly before the death of George III in 1820. There is a similar underscoring of period in chapter 36 when Wemmick, advising Pip against lending money to Herbert, suggests that he would be as well to throw it in the river: 'I should like just to run over with you on my fingers, if you please, the names of the various bridges up as high as Chelsea Reach. Let's see; there's London, one; Southwark, two; Blackfriars, three; Waterloo, four; Westminster, five; Vauxhall, six.' As Miss Edminson has shown, Dickens carefully omits the two most recently constructed bridges, Chelsea (1858) and Hungerford (1845), and since he elsewhere makes clear that the London Bridge he has in mind is Old London Bridge, this draws attention to a date for this section (Pip is 21) not later than 1831–2, when the old bridge was pulled down, and probably before 1824, when there was still no question of an 'Old' or 'New' London Bridge.

It would be pedantic to insist on too precise a time-scheme, but if from these and other details we accept a chronology of the action extending from 1807 at the start of the novel (when Pip is 7) to 1823 or so at the end (when Pip is 23), we can see that these dates are congruent with much else in the novel which they help to bring into focus. Pip is born at the start of the nineteenth century into a world that is recognisably more violent and precarious than the world of 1860. Dickens's omissions are revealing: there are no railways in *Great Expectations*, where all travelling is by coach, and there is no mention of factories either. Joe Gargery is a blacksmith, the archetypal pre-industrial revolution craftsman, and we are told that his 'education, like Steam, was yet in its infancy' (ch. 7). The early chapters convey a powerful sense of the precariousness of human life, and here too the novel's mood is faithful to a period when the rate of human mortality was high: Pip and his sister are the only survivors of a family of nine. The 'Bloody Code', the brutal penal code which the early nineteenth-century reformers set out to overhaul, is still harshly operative. Although the infamous Hulks, condemned by a parliamentary committee of 1837, had ceased to exist by the time *Great Expectations* was published, the air of terror and mystery with which Dickens invests them – 'like a wicked Noah's ark' (ch. 5) – suggests the earlier years of their operation, when they came to symbolise for many contemporary observers all the ruthlessness of a barbaric criminal code. This is recognisably the Kent landscape through which Cobbett passed in August 1823, when he classed the hulks along with government spies, treadmills, and houses of correction, as evidence of the secret vindictiveness of the country's rulers.[29]

Indeed, Dickens's whole treatment of crime and punishment in the novel is clearly intended to suggest an earlier, more primitive and punitive state of society. 'At that time', he observes of Newgate, 'jails were much neglected, and the period of exaggerated reaction consequent on all public wrong-doing...was still far off' (ch. 32). When Pip arrives in London for the first time he is shocked by the filth and squalor of Smithfield and by nearby Newgate, where 'an exceedingly dirty and partially drunk minister of justice' offers him for half-a-crown the chance to witness a trial before the Lord Chief Justice:

> As I declined the proposal on the plea of an appointment, he was so good as to take me into a yard and show me where the gallows was kept, and also where people were publicly whipped, and then he showed me the Debtor's Door, out of which culprits came to be hanged: heightening the interest of that dreadful portal by giving me to understand that 'four on 'em' would come out at that door the day after to-morrow at eight in the morning to be killed in a row. This was horrible, and gave me a sickening idea of London...(ch. 20)

Dickens means his readers to be sickened too, both by the brutality of the criminal code and by the humiliatingly public and dehumanising way in which it is carried out — a point he makes continually throughout the novel, from the recapture of Magwitch in chapter 5 ('I thought what terrible good sauce for a dinner my fugitive friend on the marshes was') to his sentencing to death with thirty-one others at the end:

> At that time it was the custom...to devote a concluding day to the passing of Sentences, and to make a finishing effect with the sentence of Death. But for the indelible picture that my remembrance now holds before me, I could scarcely believe, even as I write these words, that I saw two-and-thirty men and women put before the Judge to receive that sentence together. (ch. 56)

The reader is invited to blink also, and if he is Dickens's contemporary, to look back from the relatively humane treatment of criminals in the mid-Victorian years to the bad old Regency days when such things were common practice. And to jog such a reader's memory he inserts several details which would convey the flavour of Regency manners — the 'Assembly Ball at Richmond (there used to be Assembly Balls at most places then)' where Pip takes Estella to task for encouraging Drummle's attentions (ch. 38); Wemmick's gothic cottage, reflecting the heyday of gothic fashion during the Regency; the pale young gentleman's obsession with the formalities of boxing when he challenges Pip to fight in chapter 11, his insistence on the laws of the game and on 'seconding himself according to form' suggesting a schoolboy's imitation of the prize ring, then enjoying its golden age.

It seems clear, then, that Dickens deliberately set the action of his novel within the first twenty-five or thirty years of the nineteenth century, and did so in such a way as to emphasise a gradual process of social change leading up to the date of publication. As Miss Edminson has said,

> the emphasis is on change, and this in itself serves to date the action... When the novel concludes, one is aware that there has been a definite movement in time during the unfolding of the plot, but also that the final years are not those of its composition and publishing. The reader is constantly brought up against transitions which at the time of publication, he might have been expected to remember.[30]

This conclusion is fascinating in itself, and it has an important bearing on our understanding of the gentility theme in *Great Expectations*. By tracing Pip's story back to the start of the nineteenth century Dickens is in effect offering his readers in the gentleman-conscious 1860s an exemplary life-history, the genesis of a Victorian gentleman out of a poor self-helping blacksmith's boy; and by evoking the earlier period so deliberately, and in particular by reminding his readers of the brutal way in which a primitive society treated its criminals, Dickens is able to show the complex origins of the Victorian preoccupation with refinement and gentility — how the desire to become a gentleman was not just a snobbish aspiration out of one's class, but was also a desire to be a gentle man, to have a more civilised and decent life than a violent society allowed for most of its members. It is this perception which is developed in the early chapters of the novel, to which we now turn.

V

Pip is at once the most completely individualised and the most typical of Dickens's heroes; he is also the most solitary. 'I was always treated', he records in chapter 4, 'as if I had insisted on being born in opposition to the dictates of reason, religion, and morality, and against the dissuading arguments of my best friends.' Cut off from the past by the death of his parents, and with no point of reference in the present beyond the harsh guardianship of a sister twenty years older, he is literally the author of his own identity: 'I called myself Pip, and came to be called Pip' (ch. 1). He experiences none of the childhood happiness and security that David Copperfield knows; his 'first most vivid and broad impression of the identity of things' is the perception of his own utter isolation in a hostile environment, epitomised by the lonely churchyard where his family lies buried and by the convict whose abrupt and insistent demands he is forced to fulfil:

> 'Hold your noise!' cried a terrible voice, as a man started up from among the graves at the side of the church porch. 'Keep still, you little devil, or I'll cut your throat!'
> A fearful man, all in coarse grey, with a great iron on his leg. A man with no hat, and with broken shoes, and with an old rag tied round his head. A man who had been soaked in water, and smothered in mud, and lamed by stones, and cut by flints, and stung by nettles, and torn by briars; who limped and shivered, and glared and growled; and whose teeth chattered in his head as he seized me by the chin. (ch. 1)

The convict represents human life at its closest to the animal creation, and thereafter he is inseparable from the savage marsh landscape out of which he erupts. 'I wish I was a frog', he says as Pip leaves, 'Or a eel' (ch. 1), and when food is brought for him he gulps it furtively like a dog, expressing his gratitude by a mechanical clicking in his throat, 'as if he had works in him like a clock, and was going to strike' (ch. 3).

This note of animality is struck at the outset of *Great Expectations* and its resonance pervades the whole novel. No other work of Dickens, not even *Oliver Twist* or *Our Mutual Friend*, is so impregnated with violence, latent and actual, or so imaginatively aware of the gradations between the primitive and the refined. Magwitch turns Pip upside down, calls him a 'young dog' (ch. 1), and threatens him with grotesque tortures, yet this intimidation is only an extreme version of the treatment he already receives at the hands of other adults. Pip returns home in chapter 2 to a household where he has to endure the rigours of his sister's 'hard and heavy hand', arbitrary thrashings from Tickler, violent dosings of Tar-water ('Some medical beast had revived Tar-water in those days as a fine medicine') which make him conscious of 'going about, smelling like a new fence'. Mrs Joe's system of bringing up by hand is sanctioned by a primitive rural society, and it is harsh, unjust, brutalising and morally diminishing. Pip is the product of a household in which physical contact predominates to the exclusion of any idea of mental or spiritual cultivation, and the effect of this upbringing is to make him timid and guiltily self-conscious of his own natural gifts of curiosity and intelligence. He is, variously, punched and scrubbed by his sister, bullied by Pumblechook, distrusted by Jaggers and openly despised by Estella; Wopsle pokes his hair into his eyes and uses him as a 'dramatic lay-figure' to be 'mauled' in his 'poetic fury' (ch. 15). At the Christmas dinner (surely the bleakest festivity in all Dickens) Pip is made to feel like 'an unfortunate little bull in a Spanish arena' (ch. 4), and the efforts of his elders to improve the occasion by comparing his lot with that of the pig they have just eaten only serve to emphasise the passive degradation of his life. Everyone, with the exception of Joe, conspires to thrust upon Pip the consciousness that he is little better than a young animal: unwanted, troublesome and — in Mr Hubble's phrase — 'naterally wicious' (ch. 4). When Estella slaps his face and calls him a 'little coarse monster' (ch. 11) she is only giving a social category to a sense of physical and moral humiliation which is already strong within Pip.

The strange meeting which opens the novel is thus of primary significance, not only for the action it initiates, but because it helps to establish a dominant mood and atmosphere for what follows. Pip's encounter with Magwitch brings to dramatic focus all the violence, the injustice, the physical and moral coercion inherent in his environment, while at the same time providing an emblem of Pip's relationship to his world. He is, we see, a child alone in a society of adults, a society which robs him of human dignity by impressing on him that he is merely a little animal, but which simultaneously makes complicated demands of him, as Magwitch does when he bullies him into stealing from the forge. Pip enlists our sympathies because of his helplessness, and also for his intelligence and pluck; despite the indignities of his upbringing there still burns within him a certain moral delicacy, a basic decency, and a dim perception that life could be otherwise than it is, that it might be possible to have an existence free from the oppression and intimidation which prevail in his sister's house. One might almost say that Pip in these early scenes experiences the basic predicament of the self-help hero, his awareness of his own potential kept alive by the affectionate companionship of Joe and, negatively, by a deep sense of outrage within him, an instinctive knowledge of radical injustice:

> Within myself, I had sustained, from my babyhood, a perpetual conflict with injustice. I had known, from the time when I could speak, that my sister, in her capricious and violent coercion, was unjust to me. I had cherished a profound conviction that her bringing me up by hand, gave her no right to bring me up by jerks. Through all my punishments, disgraces, fasts and vigils, and other penitential performances, I had nursed this assurance; and to my communing with it, in a solitary and unprotected way, I in great part refer the fact that I was morally timid and very sensitive. (ch. 8)

The tone of the opening chapters is perfectly adapted to expressing this tension between Pip and his environment. The first-person narrative is brilliantly sustained, registering both the remorseful probings of the adult mind and the immediacy of a child's conflict with strange and incomprehensible forces. The mood is tougher, less nostalgic, than the mood of *David Copperfield*, and the penitential character of Pip's recollections does not obscure a quality of real aggression in his response to the injustices of his childhood. He longs to pull Wopsle's Roman nose, or to fight back at the bullying Pumblechook, the mere sight of whom makes him 'vicious' in his reticence when asked to explain about his visit to Satis House (ch. 9).

Nor is there any tolerance for fools in *Great Expectations*. The comedy which characters like Wopsle and Pumblechook provide is invariably related to their capacity to frustrate or obstruct Pip's life, and even such an obvious comic set-piece as the description of the dame-school is firmly set within the context of his pursuit of knowledge: the very stupidity and ignorance of Mr Wopsle's great-aunt throws a sympathetic light on Pip's 'hunger for information' (ch. 15). We may laugh at her, but Pip's own reaction is sharply dismissive — indeed much of the comedy in the novel derives from the almost disproportionate savagery of the irony which the narrator turns upon these comic figures. She is a 'preposterous female' (ch. 15), a 'miserable old bundle of incompetence' (ch. 17); in her death she 'successfully overcame that bad habit of living, so highly desirable to be got rid of by some people' (ch. 17). Pumblechook is described with similar scorn as, variously, a 'windy donkey' (ch. 58), a 'fearful imposter', an 'abject hypocrite', 'that basest of swindlers', 'that diabolical corn-chandler' (ch. 13), and so on throughout the book.

Comic irony here expresses the verbal resistance of the physically powerless but sensitive and intelligent child; it is the medium through which his sense of outrage finds a partial release. The very vigour with which Pip dismisses these characters, moreover, leaves the reader in no doubt about how he is to interpret this world. Like Dullborough in *The Uncommercial Traveller*, this is a backward provincial society peopled by pompous bullies like Pumblechook and, worse, by those who respect Pumblechook and see in him a figure of local dignity and importance. As Pip grows older he becomes increasingly aware of what the narrative irony has implied from the outset: that life in this environment is coarse, violent, frustrating and humanly demeaning, and that it is profoundly inimical to the realisation of the potential within himself. Yet this recognition is itself a source of guilt and shame, because it involves admitting an inadequacy in the one character who had made his childhood tolerable. Joe Gargery may be said to represent the positive aspects of this otherwise limited world: he is simple and credulous and illiterate, but these limitations are in his case related to a corresponding strength. He is the possessor of a 'great nature' (ch. 57), and in a book where feelings take a violent and sometimes self-destructive form he shows Pip a constancy and generosity of affection, and an instinctive tenderness, which go a long way towards mitigating his wife's severity. He is also associated throughout with the fire and the forge (we meet him poking the fire and his first act is to rescue Pip from the wrath of Mrs Joe by shielding him in the chimney-corner), which in the novel's symbolism are the source of positive, life-giving energies, opposed to the 'extinguished fires' (ch. 8) of the defunct brewery in the sterile Satis House. Appropriately, it is Joe who marries Biddy at the end and becomes the father of a second Pip who will not suffer as his namesake has done.

Joe presents Pip with a continual problem throughout the novel. He grows in stature from Dickens's original conception of him as a 'good-natured foolish man', whom Pip looks upon as 'a larger species of child' (ch. 2), to the 'gentle Christian man' (ch. 57) he blesses in his illness, recognising in him a natural morality of the heart which his career of great expectations has, in a sense, betrayed. Yet it is in the nature of Pip's effort to cultivate himself that it should involve a betrayal of Joe, that the social pressures to which he is subject should ultimately be incommunicable to the human being he needs most. Although Joe can forgive Pip, he cannot redeem his guilty conscience because he cannot understand the complexity of motivation behind his behaviour.

This moral dilemma is illustrated at the outset of the novel. When Pip steals the food and file he does so under a compulsion which deprives him of moral choice: he is compelled by one authority-figure, Magwitch, to steal from another, Mrs Joe. Yet this of itself does not exonerate him from the guilt attached to his action, for although he only feels a fear of detection in relation to his sister, his theft from the forge is a violation of the intimacy he shares with Joe. Moreover, the deed has the effect of exposing a poignant inadequacy in that relationship, because Pip feels that Joe — by virtue of the very qualities which make him a sympathetic fellow-sufferer under Mrs Joe's regime — would be incapable of understanding the compulsion behind his action:

> It was much upon my mind (particularly when I first saw him looking about for his file) that I ought to tell Joe the whole truth. Yet I did not, and for the reason that I mistrusted that if I did, he would think me worse than I was. The fear of losing Joe's confidence, and of thenceforth sitting in the chimney-corner at night staring drearily at my for ever lost companion and friend, tied up my tongue. (ch. 6)

And Pip is right in his suspicion, for when he does attempt to explain a similar situation to Joe — his lies about Miss Havisham and Satis House — Joe is astounded, and can only respond with a conventional platitude: 'a sincere well-wisher would adwise, Pip, their being dropped into your meditations, when you go upstairs to bed' (ch. 9). Which, of course, only serves to compound Pip's already developed sense of guilt.

His first visit to Satis House and the subsequent interrogation he has to endure from Pumblechook and his sister is a turning-point in Pip's life. Like most of the other important events which happen to him, this encounter is thrust upon him by his elders, but the actual experience is a new and complicating one for him. It opens up a whole world to him, a world which simultaneously attracts and humiliates — attracts because it offers a glimpse of a hitherto undreamed-of elegance and refinement, and humiliates because, in the shape of Estella, this world impresses on him how profoundly unfit he is to occupy it. Yet there is even a certain attraction in Estella's contempt for his coarse hands and thick boots for, as Hillis Miller has observed, her reaction 'implies a very definite self which he fails to be, and which would transcend his state if he could reach it'.[31] Her class judgement, in other words, answers to and arouses Pip's own sense of thwarted potential. From this moment on, his justified discontents and unexpressed longings become confused with a class goal and a marital motive: to become a gentleman and to marry a lady.

When he is asked to explain his visit, Pip's natural resistance to the coercion of his elders is aggravated by an awareness that what has happened at Satis House is something unique and personal, something belonging to Pip *as Pip* and not as the mere representative of his inquisitive relatives. His response to their attempts to invade his privacy takes the characteristic form of a verbal defiance, the account he gives them being a sort of comic masque in which the truth is presented in extravagant symbolic terms:

'Now, boy! What was she a doing of, when you went in to-day?' asked Mr. Pumblechook.

'She was sitting,' I answered, 'in a black velvet coach.'

Mr. Pumblechook and Mrs. Joe stared at one another — as they well might — and both repeated, 'In a black velvet coach?'

'Yes,' said I. 'And Miss Estella — that's her niece, I think — handed her in cake and wine at the coach-window, on a gold plate. And we all had cake and wine on gold plates. And I got up behind the coach to eat mine, because she told me to.'

'Was anybody else there?' asked Mr. Pumblechook.

'Four dogs ... and they fought for veal-cutlets out of a silver basket.' (ch. 9)

This pantomime version embodies the contradictory elements in Pip's confused state of mind. The fantasy reconciles his initial response to the glamour and melancholy refinement ('black velvet coach') of Satis House with the abiding impression of social subservience he is made to feel there: 'I got up behind the coach to eat mine, because she told me to.' It is, as Joe says, a lie, since it is told to deceive, but also a lie in which a deeper truth is expressed in symbolic terms.

The effect of this wild imagining upon his audience is not, as Pip fully expects, to bring the wrath of Mrs Joe about his head, but in fact to expose the limits of their own knowledge of Miss Havisham's world. They are taken in by his story because they do not know any better. But when his sister then relates the story to Joe and Joe shows himself to be equally credulous, Pip is 'overtaken by penitence ... Towards Joe, and Joe only, I considered myself a young monster' (ch. 9). The realisation that Joe too can be taken in, that his horizon is as limited as that of Mrs Joe and

Pumblechook, appears a terrible betrayal of the one source of love and trust in Pip's life; and it has the effect of cutting him off from the simple morality of the forge and isolating him still further in his own consciousness. Joe's homely moralisings only make matters worse, for he fails to see that the subterfuges Pip is forced to practise are the natural reaction of a sensitive child to the behaviour of a strange and demanding adult world. And so just as his sister's upbringing has made him 'morally timid and very sensitive', Joe in his very different way causes Pip to feel a similar guilt and self-consciousness about his efforts to make sense of his experience.

VI

We are now in a position to define the central drama of *Great Expectations*: it is a fable of cultural emergence, of the development of sensibility and conscience in a child who grows up into a world incapable of understanding or sympathising with it. And here, too, we can begin to see the imaginative significance of the historical dimension in which Dickens has set his fable. Pip comes to awareness in what is still essentially an eighteenth-century environment, and it is a world observed with literal as well as moral and symbolic fidelity: the Hulks, the gibbet, the blacksmith's forge, the red-coated soldiers, the chaotic human misery of Newgate and the 'Bloody Code' — this is recognisably the 'radically untamed' society of Regency England, an age which is divided from the Victorian period by 'something that goes deeper than a change in shopping habits'.[32] Pip's situation in this world is analogous to that of the first-generation Romantic poets in the crude society of the late eighteenth century; like them he has a 'pitying young fancy' (ch. 5), an imaginative capacity for sympathetic penetration into the life around him which is altogether more complex and sensitive than the simple natural benevolence of Joe Gargery. His is a pioneering sensibility; he experiences what is, in effect, a new way of looking at the world. One might instance, as a parallel to Pip's obsession with crime and criminals, the rather earlier case of the *Lyrical Ballads* (1798) — Wordsworth's 'The Convict', for example, where the poet's sympathy for the imprisoned man passes beyond his appearance and 'the fetters that link him to death' to speculate on the moral effects of his imprisonment — 'Yet my fancy has pierced to his heart, and pourtrays/ More terrible images there'; or Coleridge's 'The Dungeon', with its insistent questioning of past brutality:

> And this place our forefathers made for man!
> This is the process of our love and wisdom,
> To each poor brother who offends against us.

The point to be stressed about this new spirit of social sympathy is its timing. In the early years of the nineteenth century, when Pip and his creator were children, there still persisted a barbarous criminal code which had changed little in centuries. When Dickens died in 1870, as Philip Collins has pointed out, 'the system for dealing with criminals was recognisably the one we have inherited; the system that obtained in his boyhood belongs to another world, at least as much akin to the sixteenth century as to the twentieth'.[33]

It is this sense of belonging to 'another world' that *Great Expectations* so powerfully conveys. Pip's consciousness is unique in the sense that the consciousness of his whole generation was unique. And Dickens, it need scarcely be said, belonged to this generation also; he too was born at the beginning of the nineteenth century, and his sensibility (as Gissing recognised) was deeply conditioned by the 'life of the young century — cruel, unlovely, but abounding in vital force'.[34] His lifespan corresponds to that of Dr Kitson Clark's hypothetical Victorian who, over 30 years of age in 1850, 'had lived in a world in which there were not only no railways, but also no police to speak of. When he was born, the old terrible criminal code would still be in force, the pillory still used and the cruel sports still legal.'[35] At this distance of time it is almost impossible to appreciate the contrast which this world presented to the mid-Victorian period. Walter Besant, writing in 1888 about the year of Queen Victoria's accession, spoke of 'a time so utterly passed away and vanished that a young man can hardly understand it'.[36] A modern scholar has seen in the coming of the railways a line of division in English life even more radical than that made by the First World War: 'The sense of division, of belonging to two ages... can never have been so strong as for those authors who grew up into the railway age.'[37]

There must have been many contemporary readers of *Great Expectations* for whom this sense of division was a felt reality, who shared the social and historical perspective which Dickens was exploiting. K. J. Fielding[38] has cited the case of Sir Henry Hawkins, Baron Brampton (1817–1907), the famous barrister whose most abiding childhood recollection was the sight of a 17-year-old youth, executed at Bedford Jail for rick-burning, being carried past his schoolroom window by the youth's parents. In his early years on the home circuit, Hawkins recalled in his *Reminiscences* (1904), 'they punished severely even trivial offences... while a sentence of seven years' transportation was almost as good as an acquittal'; that at every assize the law was 'like a tiger let loose upon the district' its victims being not so much the 'hardened ruffians' as 'ignorant rural labourers'. This was a time when the Old Bailey was 'the very cesspool for the offscourings of humanity', where even in 1852 Newgate had a room in which were stored the busts of hanged convicts, after the manner of Jaggers's office, with the indentation of the rope on the neck and 'the mark of the knot under the ear' — horrors which impressed Hawkins with 'a disgust of the brutal tendency of the age'.[39]

The experience of men like Hawkins helps us to see how much Pip's 'awakened conscience' (ch. 3), his extreme sensitivity to a pervasive 'taint of prison and crime' (ch. 32), is to be attributed to his historical situation. His tender conscience seems idiosyncratic to him precisely because it is a unique phenomenon, unsanctioned by the collective experience of his milieu. Pip is separated from the forge by all that is individual in his nature: his intelligence, curiosity, quick sympathy, 'pitying young fancy' — qualities which are frustrated not simply by the negative forces in his environment, as these reveal themselves in his sister and Pumblechook, but by what is best in it too, by Joe Gargery himself, whose simple code cannot accommodate these struggles within Pip's nature. His coming to self-awareness is at once an inevitable process (it has its origin, as we have seen, in his essentially defensive efforts to cope with the demands of the adult world) and a constant source of painful remorse, because it cuts him off from the security of Joe's love and from any recourse to the homely values which Joe represents. This moral deadlock issues in the tone of ironic resignation which is the controlling mood of the novel:

> How much of my ungracious condition of mind may have been my own fault, how much Miss Havisham's, how much my sister's, is now of no moment to me or to anyone. The change was made in me; the thing was done. Well or ill done, excusably or inexcusably, it was done. (ch. 14)

There is, then, a peculiarly intimate relationship between Pip's attempt to civilise himself and his pervading sense of guilt. He feels that the development of his sensibility has placed him outside the reach of received morality as he knows it, and since it was his initial act of sympathy for the convict that led to the breach in his intimacy with Joe, his 'pitying young fancy' and moral delicacy begin to appear to Pip as themselves unnatural. For although the convict represents everything from which Pip hopes to escape — brutal intimidation, moral coercion, coarse physical contact between individuals — at the same time he offers the only model available to Pip in his close-knit rural community for the loneliness and alienation which his career of self-improvement increasingly involves: that of the social outcast. As Q. D. Leavis has pointed out, the secret and barely acknowledged bond between them is signalled by Magwitch calling Pip 'my boy' and Pip always referring to Magwitch as 'my convict'.[40]

The historical setting of the novel provides the important clue to the nature of Pip's much-discussed guilt. His predicament is representative of a social class in the act of emergence; specifically, of the Victorian middle class in its emergence from primitive origins. He *needs* civilisation because he is so acutely aware (as the born gentleman Herbert cannot be) of its opposite, and consequently he overvalues it, purging his advance into gentility from all associations with the physical brutality which had formed his 'first most vivid and broad impression of the identity of things'. Satis House comes to symbolise 'everything that was picturesque' (ch. 15), and it captures Pip's imagination just because it seems to be the negation of all that he has known on the marshes. Estella is so utterly divorced in his mind from any association with criminality that (in one of the many brilliantly economical symbolic touches in which the novel abounds) he cannot bear Jaggers even to sit next her at the card-table, trumping 'the glory of our Kings and Queens...with mean little cards at the ends of hands' (ch. 29). While waiting for her at the coach-house near Newgate he feels contaminated by his recent visit to the jail with Wemmick:

> I thought of the beautiful young Estella, proud and refined, coming towards me, and I thought with absolute abhorrence of the contrast between the jail and her. I wished that Wemmick had not met me, or that I had not yielded to him and gone with him, so that, of all days in the year on this day, I might not have had Newgate in my breath and on my clothes. (ch. 32)

Yet the very intensity with which Pip repudiates this contrast betrays a nagging consciousness of interrelationship between the areas of his experience which he wants to keep apart. He is, one might say, the conscience of his environment, for he has to carry within himself a secret knowledge of the polarities which make up his world. The blacksmith's boy who aspires to being a gentleman can never know the certainty of status which Herbert inherits as a matter of course; at home in neither world, he experiences a continual remorse and a moral isolation which align him, paradoxically, with the criminal outcast who constitutes his most enduring image of all that the civilised life will free him from. Pip's sense of guilt, I would suggest, is the subconscious recognition of a truth which he deeply resents, in common with the Victorian middle-class culture of which he may be said to be a pioneer: that criminality and civilisation, violence and refinement, Magwitch and Estella, are not warring opposites but intimately and inextricably bound together.

The basic *donnée* of the book, the pivot on which Dickens's 'grotesque tragi-comic conception' turns, is the fact that Magwitch is Pip's benefactor and the father of Estella. But so firm is Dickens's control of his theme, so subtle his command of significant detail, that long before the convict's return he has been able to suggest this inherent contradiction in his hero's expectations. The narrative is indeed a fabric of wonderful richness and resonance. For example, when Pip visits Satis House for the second time the smoke from the dining-room fire reminds him of 'our own marsh mist' (ch. 11), just as the cobwebs on Miss Havisham's bridal cake recall the damp on the hedges, like 'a coarser sort of spiders' webs' (ch. 3), on the morning when he sneaks out of the forge to carry the food to Magwitch.

Such delicate tracery of interrrelationship serves to unify the atmosphere of the novel, undermining the opposition Pip is setting up between the savagery of the marshes and the refinement of Satis House, and thereby preparing the way for the revelations to come.

The separation of the two worlds is also undermined in the case of Bentley Drummle, Pip's rival for Estella, a minor character who foreshadows an important truth which is only fully manifest at the end of *Great Expectations*. As his name implies, with its suggestion of 'bend', 'drum', and 'pummel', Drummle is heavy, brutish, cruel and violent; he is an upper-class equivalent of the journeyman Orlick, with whom he is associated at the end of chapter 43. The function of this character in the scheme of the novel is to remind us that violence and brutality are not confined to life on the marshes, that they also exist in the supposedly refined society of London. And Estella's marriage to Drummle provides another dimension to our understanding of her character. This 'proud and refined' girl who is the very incarnation of the civilised life to which Pip aspires can prefer a coarse brute like Drummle because there exists, deep within her, a violent animal nature which Pip ignores. Dickens suggests this fact in chapter 11, where Pip fights and beats Herbert. Unknown to him, Estella has been watching the fight and when she comes down to let him out 'there was a bright flush upon her face, as though something had happened to delight her'. She offers to let Pip kiss her, and he does so, without realising the significance of her sudden response; he feels that 'the kiss was given to the coarse common boy as a piece of money might have been, and that it was worth nothing'. The brief scene enacts the supreme paradox of Pip's life: Estella can only respond to him when he exhibits those qualities of physical force and animal aggression which, in order to win her, he is at pains to civilise out of himself. It is her one spontaneous gesture to Pip and he misreads it, feeling only guilt and remorse at this exercise of his blacksmith's arm.

VII

Throughout this discussion I have stressed a quality of violence as the distinguishing feature of the imaginative world created in *Great Expectations*. We have seen that in this Dickens has been faithful to the period in which his novel is set, but also that through Pip's reaction he is dramatising an attitude which we can recognise as belonging to a later time, to the mid-Victorian era in which the book was written. It is Pip's self-conscious revulsion from the violence of life on the marshes which sets him apart from his home and decides him to become a gentleman, and it is this violence, in the shape of Magwitch, which provides the ultimate touchstone for the values and social position he has embraced. The most intimate meaning of

Dickens's fable of social evolution is finally revealed when the old convict returns, and brings with him not only the truth about the source of Pip's wealth, but also a fearful reassertion of the primitive forces from which he had thought to have escaped forever:

> The influences of his solitary hut-life were upon him besides, and gave him a savage air that no dress could tame; added to these were the influences of his subsequent branded life among men, and crowning all, his consciousness that he was dodging and hiding now. In all his ways of sitting and standing, and eating and drinking — of brooding about, in a high-shouldered reluctant style — of taking out his great horn-handled jack-knife and wiping it on his legs and cutting his food — of lifting light glasses and cups to his lips, as if they were clumsy pannikins — of chopping a wedge off his bread, and soaking up with it the last fragments of gravy round and round his plate, as if to make the most of an allowance, and then drying his fingers on it, and then swallowing it... there was Prisoner, Felon, Bondsman, plain as plain could be ...
>
> Words cannot tell what a sense I had, at the same time, of the dreadful mystery that he was to me. When he fell asleep of an evening, with his knotted hands clenching the sides of the easy-chair, and his bald head tattooed with deep wrinkles falling forward on his breast, I would sit and look at him, wondering what he had done, and loading him with all the crimes in the Calendar, until the impulse was powerful on me to start up and fly from him. (ch. 40)

Magwitch is the embodiment of everything Pip has tried to free himself from, even down to the 'heavy grubbing' which is only an exaggerated form of the clumsy table-manners Pip had acquired at the forge. He is also a violent criminal, and for all Pip knows a man with blood on his hands; he recalls with horror his childhood vision of the convict as a 'desperately violent man' whom he had seen 'down in the ditch, tearing and fighting like a wild beast' (ch. 39). Yet such is the symbolic suggestiveness of Dickens's conception, that this wild beast, a returned transport, is in his way a nightmare version of the Victorian self-made man. (Even here one can see something of Dickens's literal and imaginative fidelity to the period setting of his novel. It was a fact that in the early years of the colonisation of Australia many emancipated convicts did make huge fortunes. Giving evidence before the 1837 Select Committee on Transportation, John Lang, a Church of Scotland clergyman in New South Wales, cited the case of one convict who was reputed to have an annual income of £40,000, and agreed that there were many who had 'some thousands a year'. They made their fortunes 'generally very rapidly', Lang said, because they 'bent the whole energy of mind and body to money making'.[41]) Magwitch has pursued wealth with a single-mindedness which makes his career in Australia a bizarre parody of the classic economic success story: 'I lived rough', he tells Pip, echoing the paternal hopes of first-generation wealth, 'that you should live smooth; I worked hard that you should be above work' (ch. 39).

What is the significance of Magwitch in the novel? He is the father of Estella, the 'proud and refined' girl who is the very emblem and model of the civilised life to which Pip aspires; and theirs is a blood-relationship in a double sense, for we have already seen that Estella possesses an animal will and energy and passion, a deeply-seated physical nature which Pip ignores in his idealisation of her. The moral pattern of *Great Expectations* is only fulfilled when, in chapter 48, Jaggers hints that Bentley Drummle will beat Estella, and Pip, glancing at Molly's knitting fingers and flowing hair, realises that this woman is the mother of the girl he loves. The wheel has come full circle; the girl who had been the inspiration for his attempt to improve himself is found in the end to be the daughter of a transported convict and 'a wild beast tamed' (ch. 24), a woman so violent and powerful that she has been able to strangle another woman with her bare hands. And what in a lesser novelist would be a melodramatic linkage is here a symbolic structure of deep imaginative power and social implication. This triangular relationship of 'blood' ramifies throughout the novel, destroying the opposition Pip has set up between the worlds of the marshes, Satis House and London.

Magwitch is the ultimate source of all Pip's expectations. With his energy, his resourcefulness, his powerful will and rough sense of justice, his touching respect for the refinements of life expressed in admiration for his 'dear boy's' dubious accomplishments, he is a grotesque parody of the uncouth but successful self-made man, determined that his son shall be a gentleman. In recoiling from him, Pip, like the fastidious Victorian gentleman he has by that stage become, is understandably recoiling from contemplating the unpleasant social origins of the wealth that makes gentlemanliness possible — from facing the fact that the economic security which has enabled him to work out the beast was itself provided by bestial means. What Pip has to experience in the concluding third of the novel is the unweaving of the spell that has bound him hitherto; he has to learn that Magwitch is not an ogre but a human being, and a decent and generous one; that Estella, 'proud and refined', has the same blood flowing through her veins; and that the opposition he has set up between the two worlds is false. And in learning the truth about the ultimate interrelatedness of a society based upon class distinctions, he learns to overcome the division within himself, between the inhibited, guilt-ridden gentleman he has become and the blacksmith's boy he has locked away and failed to acknowledge in his pursuit of gentility.

The deepest irony of *Great Expectations* is Dickens's location of gentility in a context of violence — a violence that is defined in symbolic, almost Blake-like terms, as both creative and destructive, having its positive source in the life of instinct, energy, physical passion, as well as its negative manifestation in the barbarism of a brutal society. Pip wants to become a gentleman because he wants — rightly and, as I have argued, inevitably — to become a gentle man, to escape from the brutality and intimidation that characterise life on the marshes. But gentlemanliness in the nineteenth-century world involves exclusion and repression for someone like Pip, alienation from Joe and the warmth of instinctive life which the blazing forge symbolises. The novel is full of a wonderful unobtrusive poetry which suggests this beneath the level of narrative and character. In chapter 8, where Pip makes his first visit to Satis House, he stays with Pumblechook and notices the seeds tied up in little packets in the seedman's shop: 'I wondered ... whether the flower-seeds and bulbs ever wanted of a fine day to break out of those jails and bloom'; and the image anticipates and reinforces the sense of deadened life in that other jail, Satis House, where 'there were no pigeons in the dove-cot, no horses in the stable, no pigs in the sty, no malt in the store-house, no smells of grains and beer in the copper or the vat', and where he sees Estella 'pass among the extinguished fires' of the old brewery. Gentility is associated with the repression and defeat of instinct and vital energy. On his next visit to Satis House Pip fights and beats the 'pale young gentleman', Herbert, and when he meets him again in London Pip notices 'a certain conquered languor about him' (ch. 22); but Pip at this stage is neither pale nor a gentleman, and our sense of his instinctive vitality, and its associations with his blacksmith's arm, is underlined at the end of the chapter when we see the 'bright flush' on Estella's face and the light from Joe's furnace 'flinging a path of fire across the road' (ch. 11). One thinks of Blake and *The Marriage of Heaven and Hell*: 'The Giants who formed this world into its sensual existence, and now seem to live in it in chains, are in truth the causes of its life & the sources of all activity; but the chains are the cunning of weak and tame minds which have power to resist energy ...' Pip's instinctive life is put in chains by his pursuit of gentility, and these chains only start to loosen when he recognises and accepts Magwitch, and comes to work for his benefactor's escape. In the burst of activity which this involves, some of the buried energies within Pip are released and — significantly — the mists which have dominated the atmosphere of the novel start to clear:

Wednesday morning was dawning when I looked out of [the] window. The winking lights upon the bridges were already pale, the coming sun was like a marsh of fire on the horizon. The river, still dark and mysterious, was spanned by bridges that were turning coldly grey, with here and there at top a warm touch from the burning in the sky. As I looked along the clustered roofs, with church towers and spires shooting into the unusually clear air, the sun rose up, and a veil seemed to be drawn from the river, and millions of sparkles burst out upon its waters. From me too, a veil seemed to be drawn, and I felt strong and well. (ch. 53)

With the unveiling of illusion Pip overcomes his revulsion from Magwitch; the blacksmith's boy and the gentleman are integrated in the physical gesture of holding the old convict's hand in the boat and later, publicly, at his trial: 'For now, my repugnance to him had all melted away, and in the hunted wounded shackled creature who held my hand in his, I only saw a man who had meant to be my benefactor, and who had felt affectionately, gratefully, and generously, towards me with great constancy through a series of years. I only saw in him a much better man than I had been to Joe' (ch. 54). And it is appropriate that in the illness which follows Magwitch's death Pip should be nursed back to health by Joe in an episode which returns him, briefly and poignantly, to the old physical intimacy and dependence of childhood. Pip cannot be a child again, or preserve the old companionship once he has recovered; but Joe can heal him out of the 'wealth of his great nature' (ch. 57), his physical tenderness can penetrate the crust of genteel inhibition and release the flow of feeling which has for so long been trapped beneath. Again, this release and reintegration is signalled in the holding of hands:

At last, one day, I took courage, and said, '*Is* it Joe?'
And the dear old home-voice answered, 'Which it air, old chap.'
'O Joe, you break my heart! Look angry at me, Joe. Strike me, Joe. Tell me of my ingratitude. Don't be so good to me!'
For Joe had actually laid his head down on the pillow at my side, and put his arm round my neck, in his joy that I knew him.
'Which dear old Pip, old chap,' said Joe, 'you and me was ever friends. And when you're well enough to go out for a ride — what larks!'
After which, Joe withdrew to the window, and stood with his back towards me, wiping his eyes. And as my extreme weakness prevented me from getting up and going to him, I lay there, penitently whispering, 'O God bless him! O God bless this gentle Christian man!'
Joe's eyes were red when I next found him beside me; but I was holding his hand and we both felt happy. (ch. 57)

'O God bless this gentle Christian man!' Pip (and Dickens) separate the word 'gentleman' into its classless elements, the gentle man who, living by the Christian ideals of love and forgiveness, is the one type of gentlemanliness which the novel at the end unequivocally affirms.

In its historical depth, social range and psychological penetration, *Great Expectations* is the most complex and satisfying fictional examination of the idea of the gentleman in the Victorian period. The truth of a novel is of course something different from social and historical truth, but one cannot read Dickens's book sympathetically without feeling it taps a deep source of uneasiness in the Victorian cult of the gentleman. In the figure of Pip, this gentle man whose instinctive warmth and tenderness have been thwarted by his sterile passion for Estella and by the inhibitions involved in becoming Magwitch's 'brought-up London gentleman' (ch. 39), one senses a haunting knowledge of the social exclusions and psychological repressions that make gentility possible. This uneasiness can be felt elsewhere in the Victorian period; one comes across it, for example, in the recently published diaries of Arthur Munby (1828–1910), a minor poet, barrister, civil servant and man about town, who was fascinated by working women and married a servant, Hannah, after a long and secret engagement.

Munby was, by birth and education, a conventional gentleman who lived an eminently respectable professional life and had a wide circle of acquaintance among the well-to-do London upper-middle class and its artistic fringe. But he was also a man of great sensitivity, and as the friend and disciple of the Christian Socialist F. D. Maurice, of humanity and social conscience. His interest in working women had complex origins in his own character and psychology: it was compassionate, partly sexual, partly sociological and, as his relations with Hannah show, highly honourable. It gave him access to a world of which his own class was largely ignorant, and he was fascinated by the contrast. In an early diary entry he recounts an abusive and no doubt blasphemous shouting-match between a gang of dustwomen and two 'respectable workmen', and comments: 'Looking on at such scenes, one ought of course to feel properly shocked at the rudeness of the two workmen, and saddened at the coarseness & vulgarity of the dustwomen ... But what struck *me* most, was the piquancy of contrast between such manners and those of the civilised classes ...'[42] The diaries are full of this piquancy, and since Munby was chiefly interested in working women (dustwomen, servants, milkwenches, colliery girls), full too of an awareness of sexual contrast between these women and the drawing-room ladies he knew and for whom he was, as a gentleman, an eligible match:

Wednesday, 1 July (1863) ... Walked in the Green Park and Hyde Park from five to six p.m.; and eastward through May Fair. Near Grosvenor Gate, where carriages full of languid perfumed ladies were as usual flashing by, and other misses, less languid but not less sumptuous, sat or strolled elegantly in the quasi-private garden, I passed a milkwench, going home with her yoke and her emptied pails to the Grosvenor Dairy in Mount Street. A tall clumsy creature, with feet of inexpressible bigness. Looked at from behind as she moved heavily along, she seemed a brawny woman of middle age ...

But I passed, and saw her honest ruddy face; and she was a girl of twenty. The same age as those novelreading charmers & those reposing beauties in the barouches and on the garden chairs, between whom and herself so great a gulf is fixed.[43]

A year later he notes a similar contrast between the fashionables riding in Rotten Row and the dustwomen darting between their horses:

By way of absolute complete contrast to this (and it *is* the most striking contrast I know) the gangs of Paddington dustwomen were struggling through the equipages in the open near Apsley House. I stood by the rail awhile & watched this phenomenon. Close by, at Fools' Corner, a troop of exquisites sat motionless on their welltrained steeds: very elegant persons, in faultless gloves and sumptuous attire and aristocratic moustaches. Who shall describe their haughty idlesse, their refined & lofty ease, as they spoke & simpered languidly with the yet more languid belles who lay supine under a cloud of pink and white fluff in the barouches that waited near? And meanwhile among the wheels of those barouches & under the feet of those steeds the mob of coarse and ragged and ablebodied wenches were creeping and darting, anxious only to save their limbs and their loads of cinders. No one took heed of them.[44]

Like Pip, Munby had to conceal within himself his secret, intimate knowledge of the social polarities of the Victorian world ('the most striking contrast I know'). He never ceased to be the gentleman, nor indeed to value gentlemanliness; it is one of the most authenticating features of the diaries that he does not take a proto-modern glee in debunking the idea of the gentleman. Nor did Hannah who, knowing her man, refused to become a 'lady' and always called Munby 'Massah'. (Hands, incidentally, are a preoccupation of the diaries, as of *Great Expectations*: the contrast between Munby's clean gentlemanly hands and Hannah's rough servant ones, which he secretly delighted in though knowing them to be the clearest indication that she was not a 'lady'.) Yet what moves one most, perhaps, in his remarkable story is a sense of the strain which his secret imposed on Munby, leading to long periods of separation and even estrangement after the marriage in 1873, and preventing their living together as man and wife for more than a few days at a time. One is struck, too, by how reluctant or unable even his closest friends were to overcome the class barriers in their minds and welcome and accept Hannah, how rigid these barriers could be and how ruthlessly on occasion they might be asserted. There is, for example, an entry recording a conversation he had at the Eton and Harrow cricket match with one of his lady acquaintances, a Miss Williams, on the subject of *mésalliances*:

If she had known how nearly the question touched me, and how all I said had a secret reference to a certain maid of all work, I fear that the respect and preference with which she has lately honoured me would quickly disappear.

For she spoke with such bitterness and scorn of all servant maids and such-like, that I half fancied she had some private reason for doing so. She refused to believe that any such woman could by possibility be refined in nature, or be companionable for a man of education. She knew them by experience: their faces might be pretty and their manner modest, but within, they were full of baseness & vulgarity. And no man of refinement & gentlemanly feeling could *ever* degrade himself by such an union. *That* was absolute: there was *none* exception![45]

Had she perhaps guessed his secret? On this and many similar occasions in the diaries one is forcibly reminded of Pip, carrying into his new gentleman's world his secret, guilty knowledge of another seemingly antithetical world.

Munby's diaries touch on the same area of preoccupation, the same social ambivalence, as *Great Expectations*, and they illuminate the representativeness of the experience with which, as I have argued, Dickens's novel deals. Both Munby and Dickens were outsiders, and in their different ways they knew that the social contrasts which fascinated them had deep sexual and psychological as well as class origins. Throughout the diaries there runs an awareness, never explicitly formulated, that the life of gentility is enfeebled by the exclusions necessary to its existence, and that a society divided into 'languid perfumed ladies' in carriages and milkwenches with yokes means human impoverishment for both. This was not a division Munby could heal in the larger world, but he could heal it in himself, by marrying Hannah. A similar awareness lies at the heart of *Great Expectations*, a work in which Dickens's lifelong preoccupation with what it means to be a gentleman, and its relation to the contrasted worlds of Victorian England, is given definitive expression.

REFERENCES: CHAPTER 4

1 Quoted in G. H. Ford, *Dickens and His Readers*, 2nd edn (New York: Norton, 1965), p. 162.
2 G. K. Chesterton, *Criticisms and Appreciations of the Works of Charles Dickens* (London: Dent, 1911), p. 125.
3 P. A. W. Collins (ed.), *Dickens: The Critical Heritage* (London: Routledge and Kegan Paul, 1971), pp. 327–8.
4 G. Tillotson and D. Hawes (eds), *Thackeray: The Critical Heritage* (London: Routledge & Kegan Paul, 1968), p. 272.
5 J. Forster, *Life of Charles Dickens*, ed. J. W. T. Ley (London: Cecil Palmer, 1928), pp. 28–9.
6 Quoted in Collins, op. cit., p. 476.
7 E. Moers, *The Dandy: Brummell to Beerbohm* (London: Secker & Warburg, 1960), p. 215.

8. W. Dexter (ed.), *The Letters of Charles Dickens*, 3 vols (London: Nonesuch Press, 1938), Vol. III, p. 717.
9. Ford, loc. cit.
10. Forster, op. cit., p. 350.
11. K. J. Fielding (ed.), *The Speeches of Charles Dickens* (Oxford: Clarendon Press, 1960), p. 336.
12. H. E. Rollins (ed.), *The Letters of John Keats*, 2 vols (Cambridge, Mass.: Harvard University Press, 1958), Vol. II, p. 67.
13. Forster, op. cit., p. 641.
14. R. C. Lehmann (ed.), *Charles Dickens as Editor* (London: Smith, Elder, 1912), p. 158.
15. Forster, op. cit., p. 734.
16. J. Bayley, '*Oliver Twist*: "Things as they really are"', in *Dickens and the Twentieth Century*, ed. J. Gross and G. Pearson (London: Routledge & Kegan Paul, 1962), p. 53.
17. G. Gissing, *Charles Dickens: A Critical Study* (London: Blackie, 1898), p. 60.
18. G. B. Shaw, 'Charles Dickens and *Great Expectations*', in *Majority, 1931–52*, ed. H. Hamilton (London: Hamish Hamilton, 1952), p. 387.
19. G. R. Stange, 'Expectations well lost: Dickens' fable for his times', *College English*, vol. XVI (1954), p. 10.
20. L. Trilling, 'Manners, morals, and the novel', in *The Liberal Imagination* (London: Secker & Warburg, 1951), p. 211.
21. J. Moynahan, 'The hero's guilt: the case of *Great Expectations*', *Essays in Criticism*, vol X (1960), p. 60.
22. F. Harrison, 'A few words about the nineteenth century', *Fortnightly Review*, n.s., vol. XXX (1882), p. 12.
23. S. Smiles, *Self-Help* (London: John Murray, 1859), p. 262.
24. J. S. Mill, 'Civilization', *Westminster Review*, vol. XXV (1836), p. 12.
25. G. R. Porter, *The Progress of the Nation* (London: Charles Knight, 1851 edn), p. 681.
26. W. R. Greg, 'England as It Is', *Edinburgh Review*, vol. XCIII (1851), p. 330.
27. G. K. Clark, *The Making of Victorian England* (London: Methuen, 1962), p. 64.
28. M. Edminson, 'The date of the action of *Great Expectations*', *Nineteenth Century Fiction*, vol. XIII (1958), p. 31.
29. W. Cobbett, *Rural Rides*, ed. G. D. H. and M. Cole, 3 vols (London: Peter Davies, 1930), Vol. I, p. 215.
30. Edminson, op. cit., pp. 34–5.
31. J. H. Miller, *Charles Dickens: The World of His Novels* (Cambridge, Mass.: Harvard University Press, 1958), p. 267.
32. R. J. White, *Life in Regency England* (London: Batsford, 1963), pp. 4, 17.
33. P. A. W. Collins, *Dickens and Crime*, 2nd edn (London: Macmillan, 1964), p. 3.
34. Gissing, op. cit., p. 15.
35. Clark, op. cit., p. 60.
36. W. Besant, *Fifty Years Ago* (London: Chatto & Windus, 1888), p. 1.
37. K. Tillotson, *Novels of the Eighteen-Forties* (Oxford: Clarendon Press, 1954), pp. 106–7.
38. K. J. Fielding, 'The critical autonomy of *Great Expectations*', *A Review of English Literature*, vol. II (1961), pp. 75–88.
39. Sir H. Hawkins, *The Reminiscences of Sir Henry Hawkins*, ed. Richard Harris (London: Nelson, 1904), pp. 37, 87, 38, 121.
40. F. R. and Q. D. Leavis, *Dickens the Novelist* (London: Chatto & Windus, 1970), p. 294.

41 *Parliamentary Reports*, 1837, Vol. XIX, pp. 254–6.
42 D. Hudson, *Munby: Man of Two Worlds* (London: John Murray, 1972), pp. 50–1.
43 ibid., pp. 166–7.
44 ibid., p. 194.
45 ibid., p. 167.

CHAPTER 5

Trollope and the Squires

> The man was distasteful to him as being unlike his idea of an English gentleman, and as being without those far-reaching fibres and roots by which he thought that the solidity and stability of a human tree should be assured. But the world was changing around him every day.
> (A. Trollope, *The Prime Minister*, 1876)

I

To move from the radical analysis of *Great Expectations* to almost any Trollope novel is to become at once aware how much more at ease Trollope is with the idea of the gentleman than either Dickens or Thackeray. They are more deeply involved in the growing pains of their society, and gentlemanliness is problematic in their work for this reason; caught between the memory of aristocratic insolence and the promise of moralised gentility, neither can shake off the uneasy spectre of the dandy or quite forget that the gentleman's style, moralised or not, is made possible by money and by Ruskin's 'sacrifice of much contributed life'. Trollope did not on the whole share these tensions or the corresponding urge to redefine the idea of the gentleman. His notorious reluctance to say what he meant by a gentleman, which is sometimes taken as a sign of his confusion, implies just the reverse: he knew, or thought he knew, very well what a gentleman was, and his refusal to spell it out came partly from a feeling that gentlemen should not be too specific on such matters, and partly, I think, from a correct suspicion that many of his readers would be shocked to learn how very inegalitarian and unprogressive his conception was. Gentlemanliness is centrally important in his work, but it feeds the roots of his values and only rarely – as in *Doctor Thorne* or in the Lopez sections of *The Prime Minister* – emerges above the soil as a subject or problem in its own right. The reader, in his turn, must be prepared to dig a little below the surface to see what Trollope understood by a gentleman.

An important clue is to be found in his attitude to that most characteristic of Victorian enterprises, Civil Service reform. The replacement of patronage by open competitive examination was, as we saw in Chapter 3, a direct blow at aristocratic influence. Trollope hated examinations, and he hated even more the purpose they were designed to serve, the replacement of the old elite of 'gentlemen' by a new elite of professional bureaucrats. In a well-known passage in his *Autobiography* he argues that examinations only test the sort of knowledge which can be got up by cramming, whereas the system of patronage, evil though it may have been in many respects, did at least go some way to recognising that qualities of character were also important in judging an applicant's suitability for public employment:

> As what I now write will certainly never be read till I am dead, I may dare to say what no one now does dare to say in print, — though some of us whisper it occasionally into our friends' ears. There are places in life which can hardly be well filled except by 'Gentlemen'. The word is one the use of which almost subjects one to ignominy. If I say that a judge should be a gentleman, or a bishop, I am met with scornful allusion to 'Nature's Gentlemen'. Were I to make such an assertion with reference to the House of Commons, nothing that I ever said again would receive the slightest attention. A man in public life could not do himself a greater injury than by saying in public that commissions in the army or navy, or berths in the Civil Service, should be given exclusively to gentlemen. He would be defied to define the term, — and would fail should he attempt to do so. But he would know what he meant, and so very probably would they who defied him. It may be that the son of the butcher in the village shall become as well fitted for employments requiring gentle culture as the son of the parson. Such is often the case. When such is the case, no one has been more prone to give the butcher's son all the chances he has merited than I myself; but the chances are greatly in favour of the parson's son. The gates of the one class should be open to the other; but neither to one class or to the other can good be done by declaring that there are no gates, no barrier, no difference. The system of competitive examination is, I think, based on a supposition that there is no difference. (ch. 3)

There is a blend of honesty, realism, defensiveness and self-assurance here which goes a long way to explain why Trollope shrank from offering a definition of the gentleman in his novels. To have done so would have meant challenging the progressive attitudes of his day, something no popular writer could afford to do. This passage reveals how very conservative was Trollope's understanding of gentlemanliness, and how relatively unaffected by the modernising tendencies analysed in this study. In the confessional of a posthumously published autobiography he could make explicit attitudes that had to remain implicit in the novels. The fact that they were implicit, however, does not mean that they were confused, inconsistent, or stupid.

In the first place, then, gentlemanliness was a rank, and could not be prised away from rank without losing its meaning. This, and the corresponding disbelief in what he saw as the humbug of the notion of 'Nature's Gentlemen', has at least the merit of honesty; it is also realistic and modest. Realistic, because as he says those who challenged him to define the term knew perfectly well what was meant by it, even when they asserted its meaninglessness; and modest, because Trollope makes no extravagant claims for the rank. Attempts to moralise the gentleman tended, paradoxically, to inflate the concept out of all proportion, making it into a transcendent value. Trollope's certainty about rank saves him from these excesses; he nowhere states (though he may on occasion imply it) that the gentleman is superior to the good and honest man who is not a gentleman, only that he is different. Thus in *The Way We Live Now* (1875) Roger Carbury, the spokesman for Trollope's values, declares the grain dealer John Crumb to be the moral superior of his worthless cousin Sir Felix Carbury — 'I look on the one as a noble fellow, and regard the other as dust beneath my feet' (ch. 43) — but Trollope would have considered it humbug to have then called the 'noble fellow' a gentleman. Conversely, since a Church of England clergyman ought to be a gentleman, in Trollope's view, it matters for the successful discharge of his duties that the Rev. Samuel Prong in *Rachel Ray* (1863) is not one: 'I do not mean to say that he was a thief or a liar; nor do I mean hereby to complain that he picked his teeth with his fork and misplaced his "h's". I am by no means prepared to define what I do mean', Trollope goes on, characteristically, but he is clear 'that his efficiency for clerical purposes was marred altogether, among high and low, by his misfortune in this respect' (ch. 6). Perhaps these distinctions ought not to exist, Trollope often seems to be saying, but they do, and it is pointless to pretend otherwise. It is this honest realism, coupled with his lack of fuss about the gentleman, which makes Trollope seem a much less snobbish writer than Thackeray, although the latter's social analysis is a good deal more radical.

The realism and the lack of fuss are of course related in Trollope, and derive from the fact that, unlike Dickens and Thackeray, he had an intimate understanding of the landed order in Victorian society. The social priorities of landed society provide the conflicts and nourish the values of his fiction, and his attitudes to rank and gentility can be inferred from the affectionately mocking treatment he gives to those characters who combine kind hearts with unfashionable attachment to old ways, like the Thornes of Ullathorne in *Barchester Towers* (1857) or Miss Marrable in *The Vicar of Bullhampton* (1870). These figures provide the excess of Trollope's mean:

> Miss Marrable thought a good deal about blood. She was one of those ladies, — now few in number, — who within their heart of hearts conceive that money gives no title to social distinction, let the amount of money be ever so great, and its source ever so stainless. Rank to her was a thing quite assured and ascertained ... She had an idea that the son of a

gentleman, if he intended to maintain his rank as a gentleman, should earn his income as a clergyman, or as a barrister, or as a soldier, or as a sailor. Those were the professions intended for gentlemen. (ch. 9)

Miss Marrable's list of suitable occupations shows, like her preference of Fielding and Richardson to Dickens and Thackeray, that she is still living in the eighteenth century. She has doubts about the respectability of medicine, the Civil Service and civil engineering, 'but she had no doubt whatever that when a man touched trade or commerce in any way he was doing that which was not the work of a gentleman'. Trollope, a civil servant himself, means us to see her prejudices as out of date, but by no means absurd. She may be old-fashioned, but her sense of rank saves her from being mercenary:

> The strongest point in her character was her contempt of money. Not that she had any objection to it, or would at all have turned up her nose at another hundred a year had anybody left to her such an accession of income; but that in real truth she never measured herself by what she possessed, or others by what they possessed. (ch. 9)

For Trollope this is the heart of the matter. Whereas Dickens and Thackeray could not forget that the gentleman was made possible by money, Trollope saw the traditional system of rank as a defence against the encroachment of money-worship. This is especially important in his treatment of the squire, which I shall come to in a moment.

Like Miss Marrable, Trollope 'thought a good deal about blood', although the results of his thinking were inconclusive. She may have been quixotic to limit gentility to the old landed professions, and to believe that 'brewers, bankers, and merchants, were not gentlemen, and the world was going astray, because people were forgetting their landmarks' (ch. 9), but the landmarks existed for Trollope and it was important to remember them, even when one recognised that they were no longer quite meeting the case of modern society. The problem was to know what relative weight to give to birth, worth and breeding in deciding who could be called a gentleman or a lady. 'It was admitted on all sides that Ferdinand Lopez was a "gentleman"', Trollope observes at the start of *The Prime Minister*. 'Johnson says that any other derivation of this difficult word than that which causes it to signify "a man of ancestry" is whimsical. There are many, who in defining the term for their own use, still adhere to Johnson's dictum; — but they adhere to it with certain unexpressed allowances for possible exceptions. The chances are very much in favour of the well-born man, but exceptions may exist' (ch. 1). Lopez turns out not to be a gentleman, not because he is of low birth but because he conceals his origins, and to do that in Trollope's world is a sure sign of dishonesty. On the other hand 'blood' is no guarantee of principled conduct. Sir Harry

Hotspur of Humblethwaite, in the novel of that name, is described as deceiving himself with a 'muddled theory' on the subject of blood when he thinks that the Hotspur blood in his vicious cousin George may save him from the 'mud' into which he has sunk. Good blood 'will have its effect, — physical for the most part, — and will produce bottom, lasting courage, that capacity of carrying on through the mud to which Sir Harry was wont to allude; but good blood will bring no man back to honesty. The two things together, no doubt, assist in producing the highest order of self-denying man' (ch. 20).

Trollope's most thorough, though not perhaps most satisfactory treatment of the subject is in *Doctor Thorne* (1858). Mary Thorne, the illegitimate daughter of a Barchester working-class girl who had been seduced by Dr Thorne's brother, is adopted and brought up by her uncle. Dr Thorne is a gentleman, cousin to the Thornes of Ullathorne, and intensely but secretly proud of his family: 'He had a pride in being a poor man of a high family; he had a pride in repudiating the very family of which he was proud; and he had a special pride in keeping his pride silently to himself' (ch. 2). His inverted pride prevents his showing due deference to rank when it might suit his professional advancement, but it saves him from the snobbery of the Barchester doctors, who maintain a strict distinction between 'physicians' and 'apothecaries', for he mixes his own medicines and is not squeamish about asking for his fees. Mary inherits both his pride and his self-division. Partly a lady by birth, she is wholly a lady by breeding, having been educated at boarding school and spent much of her youth on intimate terms with the squire's children at Greshamsbury. Frank Gresham, heir to the encumbered estate, loves but cannot marry her because she is penniless and he must marry money.

The situation is familiar enough, reminiscent to some extent of *Mansfield Park* (Mary is a Victorian Fanny Price, the outsider brought up on the inside), and the denouement takes the conventional form of a legacy. The interest lies in the differing degrees of realism and sympathy Trollope brings to the question of 'blood'. There is little sympathy for Mary's 'low' uncle, Roger Scatcherd, the self-made man whose fortune enables her to marry Frank. He is the merest caricature, drunken, boorish and snobbishly determined that his son, Louis, shall be a gentleman. Louis is enfeebled, having 'been dismissed from his mother's breast in order that the mother's milk might nourish the young heir of Greshamsbury' (ch. 10), and drinks himself to death. In this way the fortune of the *nouveau riche*, like his mother's milk, goes to feed the Greshamsbury estate (the symbolism of this blood transfusion from trade to rank is not developed, in contrast to what Dickens was later to do with Magwitch in *Great Expectations*). On the other hand there is some telling satire at the expense of the De Courcys, the aristocratic Whig family into which Frank Gresham's father has married, ruining himself in the process by deserting the old Tory loyalties of his family. They are doubly hypocritical, as only

Whig aristocrats can be in Trollope, the daughters pursuing mercenary marriages themselves while at the same time looking down their noses at anyone else who deserts the rule of 'blood'. Amelia de Courcy advises her cousin Augusta Gresham, Frank's sister, against marrying the lawyer Mr Gazebee because he is 'after all, only an attorney; and, although you speak of his great-grandfather, he is a man of no blood whatsoever. You must acknowledge that such an admixture should be looked on by a De Courcy, or even by a Gresham, as a pollution' (ch. 38). Augusta allows herself to be persuaded, only to find that Amelia has taken up Gazebee and plans to marry him herself.

Between satire on the aristocracy and the conventional treatment of the self-made man, there is Trollope's sympathetic handling of Mary's predicament, as she ponders her fitness to marry Frank:

> She said to herself, proudly, that God's handiwork was the inner man, the inner woman, the naked creature animated by a living soul... Was it not within her capacity to do as nobly, to love as truly... as though blood had descended to her purely through scores of purely born progenitors? So to herself she spoke; and yet, as she said it, she knew that were she a man, such a man as the heir of Greshamsbury should be, nothing should tempt her to sully her children's blood by mating herself with any one that was base born. She felt that were she an Augusta Gresham, no Mr Moffat, let his wealth be what it might, should win her hand unless he too could talk of family honours and a line of ancestors.
>
> And so, with a mind at war with itself, she came forth armed to do battle against the world's prejudices, those prejudices she herself still loved so well. (ch. 8)

Mary's division of mind is her uncle's and, in a sense, Trollope's too. To insist exclusively on 'blood' leads to the injustice and hypocrisy of the De Courcys, but to abandon the criterion altogether would be to cut at the heart of the inheritance principle on which landed society was based. Trollope solves the problem much as Jane Austen does in *Mansfield Park*, by showing that Cinderella's foot fits the slipper of rank. Mary proves her fitness to marry the squire by the fineness of her capacity to doubt it, and Frank shows his good sense by recognising this fact. In their marriage the openness and adaptability of the gentry are affirmed against the challenge of new wealth and old snobbery, the parvenu and the aristocrat. By recognising Mary's worth, even though he will be a Tory squire, Frank becomes the kind of landed gentleman a middle-class reader could respect. It is hardly surprising that *Doctor Thorne* should have been Trollope's most popular novel with his contemporaries (according to the *Autobiography*), for many of them must have identified with Mary's predicament and been gratified by the way it was resolved.

Although gentlemanliness implies rank in Trollope, and although no one can be a gentleman without displaying the appropriate manners, one cannot be a true gentleman in his world without possessing what he calls in *The Prime Minister* 'the feelings of a gentleman'. He says of Lopez: 'In a sense he was what is called a gentleman. He knew how to speak, and how to look, how to use a knife and fork, how to dress himself, and how to walk. But he had not the faintest notion of the feelings of a gentleman' (ch. 58). These include the feelings we should expect, such as chivalry and unselfishness, and also 'manliness', which in Trollope means much what it means elsewhere in the Victorian novel, not hearty muscularity but a balance of masculinity, simplicity and directness of manners, and tenderness. 'Heart', as Frank O'Connor pointed out,[1] is also an important touchstone of worth in Trollope, and no man can be a true gentleman without it. Kindness, the capacity for warm sympathy, an instinctive rather than coldly moral or theoretical approach to life — these are involved in 'heart'. To possess it is not the same thing as being good-natured, indeed the easy-going and good-natured are sometimes those who have least heart, like the Stanhope family in *Barchester Towers*:

> The great family characteristic of the Stanhopes might probably be said to be heartlessness; but this want of feeling was, in most of them, accompanied by so great an amount of good nature as to make itself but little noticeable to the world. They were so prone to oblige their neighbours that their neighbours failed to perceive how indifferent to them was the happiness and well-being of those around them. The Stanhopes would visit you in your sickness (provided it were not contagious), would bring you oranges, French novels, and the latest new bit of scandal, and then hear of your death or your recovery with an equally indifferent composure. (ch. 9)

One cannot be a true gentleman without heart, although, curiously, it is possible to be a perfect lady. There is no doubt that Archdeacon Grantly's social-climbing daughter Griselda is perfectly bred and, as the world goes, a lady, 'but, as for heart, — what she had was, in such a matter, neither good nor bad. Her blood circulated with its ordinary precision, and, in that respect, no woman ever had a better heart' (*Can You Forgive Her?*, ch. 50). In contrast Clencora Palliser is impulsive and generous, drawing from Trollope the comical but revealing observation: 'I do not know that she was at all points a lady, but had Fate so willed it she would have been a thorough gentleman' (ibid., ch. 49).

It follows that the hottest room in Trollope's hell is reserved not for his rogues and cads (who tend to stimulate his remarkable powers of sympathetic imagination), but for the heartless, especially those technical gentlemen who combine heartlessness with lack of principle and selfishness.

Such a one is Captain Marrable, the old dandy and man about town in *The Vicar of Bullhampton*:

> He was good-tempered, well-mannered, sprightly in conversation, and had not a scruple in the world...To lie, to steal, — not out of tills or pockets, because he knew the danger; to cheat — not at the card-table, because he had never come in the way of learning the lesson; to indulge every passion, though the cost to others might be ruin for life; to know no gods but his own bodily senses...to eat all, and produce nothing; to love no one but himself; to have learned nothing but how to sit at table like a gentleman; to care not at all for his country, or even his profession; to have no creed, no party, no friend, no conscience, to be troubled with nothing that touched his heart; — such had been, was, and was to be the life of Colonel Marrable. (ch. 33)

The prose of moral description in Trollope is usually cautious and qualified, suggesting the difficulty of analysis and judgement; here the rhythm of rhetorical certainty indicates an uncharacteristic intensity of revulsion. Captain Marrable is the antithesis of almost everything Trollope believed a gentleman should be. He is heartless, selfish, dishonest, lacking in principle, incapable of loyalty or patriotism. But his worst fault, the fault which conditions all the others, is that he is incapable of thinking or feeling beyond the appetite of the moment. It is this that leads him to squander the legacy which should have gone to his son Walter, thereby blighting Walter's prospects in life. Now if there is one root-virtue in Trollope's true gentlemen it is their capacity to live beyond the needs of the moment, to look before and after, to transcend selfishness, to be disinterested. The characters most capable of this quality are those who have inherited it as a habit of mind and a way of life: his squires. It is significant that Captain Marrable can only live as he does because he lives in the town, where he can sponge off others. The squire has a wider responsibility, and it is in his interpretation of that responsibility that we can see the essential link between rank and morality in Trollope's conception of the gentleman.

In his squires the old idea of the gentleman as a man of ancestry is resurrected and reaffirmed. The landed gentleman inherits a name and an estate, and the spirit of inheritance means that he holds both not as a possessor, to squander at will, but as a steward, conscious of and sustained by what Burke called a 'partnership...between those who are living, those who are dead, and those who are to be born'.[2] This is not necessarily a Christian notion, although it can blend with Christianity. As Paul Elmer More said in his fine essay on Trollope, the idea goes back to the primitive cult of the dead, and 'the reverence for the home as something more than a mere place of shelter for those in possession', widening to a sense of the 'sacredness of the enclosed land about the house, originally revered as the underground abode of the buried which could not be alienated without interrupting the memorial rites of homage and so cutting off the communion of the living with the dead'.[3] But Christianised or not, this feeling for the name and the place could fulfil one of the functions of Christian morality, by providing a centre of authority outside the self powerful enough to restrain the self and hold it in the ways of righteousness. In fact several of Trollope's squires do look upon ancestral loyalty as a 'religion'. There are the Dales in *The Small House at Allington* (1864):

> It had been a religion among them; and seeing that the worship had been carried on without fail, that the vestal fire had never gone down upon the hearth, I should not have said that the Dales had walked their ways without high principle. To this religion they had all adhered, and the new heir had ever entered in upon his domain without other encumbrances than those with which he himself was already burdened. And yet there had been no entail. The idea of an entail was not in accordance with the peculiarities of the Dale mind. It was necessary to the Dale religion that each squire should have the power of wasting the acres of Allington, – and that he should refrain from wasting them. (ch. 1)

This passage makes explicit the link between rank and morality: the 'religion' is seen as fostering 'high principle'. Or there are Roger Carbury's words at the end of *The Way We Live Now*:

> The disposition of a family property, even though it be one so small as mine, is, to my thinking, a matter which a man should not make in accordance with his own caprices, – or even with his own affections. He owes a duty to those who live on his land, and he owes a duty to his country. And, though it may seem fantastic to say so, I think he owes a duty to those who have been before him, and who have manifestly wished that the property should be continued in the hands of their descendants. These things are to me very holy. (ch. 100)

Here Burke's 'partnership' has widened from the ancestral 'religion' to include duty to one's tenants and loyalty to one's country. Such are the roots of the patriotism which is declared to be the crowning quality of Trollope's ideal gentleman, Plantagenet Palliser.

Ancestral loyalty includes place as well as name. Trollope's descriptions of his squires' dwellings are nearly always subtle indicators of value in his work. Carbury Manor gets a chapter to itself in *The Way We Live Now*: 'The house itself had been built in the time of Charles II ... but had the reputation of being a Tudor building. The windows were long, and for the most part low, made with strong mullions, and still contained small, old-fashioned panes; for the squire had not as yet gone to the expense of plate glass' (ch. 14). The emphasis is on the modest, lived-in character of the house. 'The houses of the gentry around him were superior to his in material comfort and general accommodation, but to none of them belonged that thoroughly established look of old county position which belonged to Carbury' (ch. 14). Ullathorne Court in *Barchester Towers* is lovingly described; it too is Tudor in appearance, with mullioned windows and mellowed stone, 'of that delicious tawny hue which no stone can give, until it has on it the vegetable richness of centuries... No colourist that ever yet worked from a palette has been able to come up to this rich colouring of years crowding themselves on years' (ch. 22). The Saxon origins of the Thornes ('He counted back his own ancestors to some period long antecedent to the Conquest'), and the communal responsibility this implies, is indicated by the fact that Ullathorne Court has a large hall. 'Yes, kind sir; a noble hall, if you will but observe it; a fine old English hall of excellent dimensions for a country gentleman's family; but, if you please, no dining-parlour' (ch. 22). The squire's 'Great House' in *The Small House at Allington* is ironic, for it is nothing of the kind; again, it is built in the Tudor style with mullioned windows ('Of all windows ever invented by man it is the sweetest'), and stands near the village:

> And the house stood much too near the road for purposes of grandeur, had such purposes ever swelled the breast of any of the squires of Allington. But I fancy that our ideas of rural grandeur have altered since many of our older country seats were built. To be near the village, so as in some way to afford comfort, protection, and patronage, and perhaps also with some view to the pleasantness of neighbourhood for its own inmates, seemed to be the object of a gentleman when building his house in the old days. A solitude in the centre of a wide park is now the only site that can be recognized as eligible. (ch. 1)

Architecture and location proclaim the rootedness of the squire. Against this is set the isolated grandeur, the 'solitude in the centre of a wide park', of the Whig grandees and the *nouveaux riches*.

At one end of the landed spectrum in the Barsetshire novels is the 'Saxon' responsibility of the Thornes (the Ullathorne sports in *Barchester Towers*, often dismissed as padding by critics, help to establish this), at the other the 'Norman' insolence of the De Courcy family in their baronial keep. There is no hidden poetry in Trollope's description of Courcy Castle: it is a 'huge brick pile, built in the days of William III', with 'stumpy' towers and uninviting grounds, and the town of Courcy is similar, 'built of dingy-red brick... solid, dull-looking, ugly, and comfortable' (*Doctor Thorne*, ch. 15). No mullioned windows and mellow stone here, nor at Gatherum Castle, the 'immense pile' of white stone erected by the Duke of Omnium, with its Ionic portico and marble hall. 'But the Duke of Omnium could not live happily in his hall; and the fact was, that the architect, in contriving this magnificent entrance for his own honour and fame, had destroyed the duke's house as regards most of the ordinary purposes of residence' (ibid., ch. 19). The implications of the contrast between the hall at Gatherum and that at Ullathorne do not need to be spelt out.

None the less the Duke of Omnium and the appropriately named Gatherum are winning. At the heart of what I shall call Trollope's myth of the squire is his sense that the old-fashioned country gentleman faces an uphill struggle in the modern world. Many of his 'good' squires are childless: Wilfred Thorne, Christopher Dale, Roger Carbury are unmarried, Sir Harry Hotspur of Humblethwaite has lost his son and heir before the novel opens. Partly, of course, this shows the influence of literary stereotype, or archetype, going back to the last English gentleman himself, Sir Roger de Coverley. But Trollope breathes new life into the archetype through his understanding of the increasing social vulnerability of the small landed gentleman in the second half of the nineteenth century. His anti-Whig, Tory gentry bias in the Barsetshire novels is to some extent an inheritance from Jane Austen, but Trollope's gentry are under pressure in a way that hers are not, as R. H. Hutton pointed out in a brilliant essay. Writing in the *Spectator* shortly after Trollope's death in 1882, he compared Jane Austen's picture of rural society at the start of the century with Trollope's fifty years later:

> The former is, above all things, mild and unobtrusive, not reflecting the great world at all, and giving us the keenest sense of how easy it would be to drive oneself, even in a short drive, quite out of the reach of all the characters described in any one story; while the latter is, above all things, possessed with the sense of the aggressiveness of the outer world, of the hurry which threatens the tranquillity even of such still pools in the rapid currents of life as Hiram's Hospital at Barchester, of the rush of commercial activity, of the competitiveness of fashion, of the conflict for existence even in outlying farms and country parsonages...In a word, the society which in Miss Austen's tales seems to be wholly local, though it may have a few fine connections with the local capital, is in Mr. Trollope's a great web of which London is the centre, and some kind of London life for the most part the motive-power.[4]

As Hutton shrewdly realised, the rural gentry in Trollope's novels cannot escape the power of London, whether in the shape of public opinion, as in *The Warden* (1855), or the metropolitan types, the Slopes and the Crosbies, who come to challenge its pastoral values, or through the growth of the money markets, which in his later novels are seen to challenge the very economic basis of the squire's way of life. Although the only squire to go to the wall in the Barsetshire series is Nathaniel Sowerby in *Framley Parsonage* (1861), and that through his own fault, the truth of Hutton's insight into the 'conflict for existence' in Trollope's world is evident even here, for his country house, Chaldicotes, is only rescued from the rapacious Gatherum estate by the heiress Martha Dunstable. (Sowerby is yet another example of Trollope's 'religion' of landed inheritance. He is a rascal, but the most painful moment of his downfall, and characteristically the moment when Trollope evokes our greatest sympathy for him, is the remorse he shows at having to surrender his run-down estate: 'And then he would sit and think of his old family: how they had roamed there time out of mind in those Chaldicotes woods, father and son and grandson in regular succession, each giving them over, without blemish or decrease, to his successor. So he would sit; and so he did sit even now, and, thinking of these things, wished that he had never been born' [ch. 37].)

It would obviously be absurd to suggest that only a squire can be a gentleman in Trollope's fiction. But to counter the view that his notion of a gentleman was confused and inarticulate, or merely a vague sentiment, one would point to the precision of his social description and to the frequency with which, in successive novels, integrity is shown to have grown from ancestral loyalties. To be a gentleman in Trollope it is necessary to show 'manliness' and 'heart', but also to possess the 'hard' quality of principle which his squires have. This is perhaps best summed up, as Ruth apRoberts suggested,[5] by the Latin *honestum*, which Trollope in his *Life of Cicero* defines as a blend of 'honour' and 'honesty'.[6] Moreover, it is through the destiny of his landed gentlemen that Trollope's vision of society is presented. It is not a static vision. What changes, however, is not, as in Dickens and Thackeray, his concept of the gentleman, but his sense of the world in which the gentleman has to live.

II

Before considering this it is necessary to examine Trollope's myth of the squire in rather more detail. The purest expression of this myth, to my mind, is *Sir Harry Hotspur of Humblethwaite* (1870), one of Trollope's finest (and shortest) novels. Sir Harry is a commoner, but a very aristocratic commoner, with an income of twenty thousand a year from his huge estates in the North of England. The novel opens two years after the death of his only son: 'Sir Harry bore the blow bravely, though none who do not understand the system well can conceive how the natural grief of the father was increased by the disappointment which had fallen upon the head of the house.' The 'system' is primogeniture, and Sir Harry is a devout believer in the religion of inheritance:

But that an eldest son should have all the family land...and that that one should have it unencumbered, as he had it from his father, – this was to him the very law of his being. And he would have taught that son, had already begun to teach him when the great blow came, that all this was to be given to him, not that he might put it in his own belly...but that he might so live as to do his part in maintaining that order of gentlehood in England, by which England had become – so thought Sir Harry – the proudest and the greatest and the justest of nations. (ch. 1)

The qualifying parenthesis, 'so thought Sir Harry', hints at something quixotic, excessive in its zeal, but it is zeal for a principle capable of inspiring honourable and disinterested conduct, and so in Trollope's eyes worthy of respect. The description of Humblethwaite Hall, which Sadleir reckoned 'the longest and most arresting description of a big country house in the whole of Trollope's work',[7] contains all the features we have come to associate with squirearchical responsibility. It consists of 'various edifices added one to another at various periods' – a Caroline house on a Tudor original, made of brick, with a Queen Anne hall, modern drawing-rooms, and (inevitably) mullioned windows. The many different but harmonised styles of architecture testify to long and continued residence in the one spot.

Sir Harry has a daughter, Emily, who shares his pride and his looks, even to 'the same arch in her eyebrows, indicating an aptitude for authority' (ch. 2), and despite her parents' encouragement to look elsewhere, she falls in love with Sir Harry's cousin and heir, George Hotspur. George is 'a very black sheep indeed', an inveterate gambler, debt-ridden, dishonourable, yet just passing muster in certain sections of good society because 'he looked like a gentleman' (ch. 5). Indeed, he turns out to be worse than the usual run of Trollope's cads because, in addition to his mistress and his gambling, which are redeemable sins, he lies and cheats at cards, which are not. Emily, who does not know this, believes she can redeem him, and Trollope skilfully shows how the very virtues of heredity and breeding serve to confirm her in this illusion: her sheltered, lady-like upbringing, her endowment of the family pride and obstinacy, even the Christian training that leads her to think that she can wash this black sheep white. Sir Harry knows otherwise, but he is torn between his love for Emily and his love for the family name and estate, and at crucial points in the story he vacillates; first by allowing George to visit their London home, where he pays court to Emily, and later by admitting him to Humblethwaite, where he proposes and is accepted by her. As news comes in of the full extent of his cousin's 'blackness', Sir Harry reproaches himself bitterly: 'Could any duty which he owed to the world be so high or so holy as that which was due from him to his child? He almost hated his name and title and position as he thought of the evil that he had already done' (ch. 13). The catastrophe is inevitable. The day after George is reluctantly accepted at Humblethwaite as Emily's fiancé, a lawyer's letter arrives telling of his cheating at cards, and back in London he agrees never to see Emily again in exchange for payment of his debts and an annuity. The letter of renunciation drafted by his mistress is 'heartless', containing no word of love for her, and it breaks Emily's heart. He has proved himself 'a brute, unredeemed by any one manly gift; idle, self-indulgent, false, and without a principle' (ch. 22). Overcome by shame and loss, she dies in Italy, and her broken father wills the estate away to his wife's nephew, 'an Earl with an enormous rent-roll, something so large that Humblethwaite and Scarrowby to him would be little more than additional labour' (ch. 24).

As even this bald outline suggests, *Sir Harry Hotspur* is a little tragedy of a kind rare in Victorian fiction and unique in Trollope, for it springs from the conflict of two goods: a father's tender love for his daughter and his high conception of his duties as a landed proprietor. There is nothing mercenary or ambitious in his pride; he does not want a titled son-in-law: 'To have Humblethwaite and Scarrowby lost amid the vast appanages and domains of some titled family, whose gorgeous glories were new and paltry in comparison with the mellow honours of his own house, would to him have been a ruin to all his hopes' (ch. 4). The novel is a tragedy of the inflexibility that comes from an excess of nobility. When Sir Harry is trying unsuccessfully to convince Emily that her suitor is worthless, he looks into her face 'and saw there that mark about her eyes which he knew he so often showed himself; which he so well remembered with his father' (ch. 13). The little detail says it all: out of the treasured purity of birth and breeding has come the terrible constancy that will destroy them both. It is not cousin George who has brought about the downfall of the house of Humblethwaite, but stubbornness, a failure to adapt, an unworldliness, bred (literally) in the house itself.

'It is very nearly a new subject,' the *Spectator* reviewer said of *Sir Harry Hotspur*, 'for the ordinary novelists who have dealt with the pride of rank and wealth have either taken part against the worldly father who feels it, as if he were all but purely bad, or have made him the mere victim of some external necessity. Mr. Trollope does not make this mistake.'[8] What is new here is not so much the sympathetic portrayal of Sir Harry's downfall, with its echoes of Sir Roger de Coverley and the last English gentleman, as the way his downfall is traced to an innate vulnerability in his high-minded conception of his 'order'. The stark concentration of the novel lays bare the essential features of Trollope's squire myth: the landed gentleman, the cad and the noble girl who falls prey to the cad. The cad – the man who ought to be or pretends to be a gentleman, but is not one – is important in Trollope's fiction, taking the place occupied by the snob in Thackeray's; he is both a plot-spinner, since his entanglement with the English girl permits of almost endless variations, and, as the anti-type of the squire, a means by which gentlemanly conduct can be illustrated and the vulnerability of the squire explored. Although none of his other novels has quite the tragic force of *Sir Harry Hotspur*, the conflict of values between the landed gentleman and the cad is the subject of novels as different as *The Small House at Allington*, *Can You Forgive Her?*, *The Way We Live Now* and *The Prime Minister*, and can be seen to condition his treatment of landed society generally. The contour of Trollope's involvement with the idea of the gentleman is best traced, I would argue, through his changing vision of gentry society — as this is first defined in the early Barset novels, then challenged in *The Small House at Allington*, *The Last Chronicle of Barset* and *The Way We Live Now*, and finally reaffirmed in the character in whom the sins of aristocracy are redeemed, that perfect Victorian gentleman, Plantagenet Palliser.

III

'Whatever at different periods Trollope might think and call himself,' T. H. S. Escott wrote, 'his natural prejudices were always those of aristocratic and reactionary Toryism'.[9] The image of crimson-faced shires Toryism this summons up does less than justice to the thoughtfulness of Trollope's conservatism, as seen in his capacity to perceive what was vulnerable as well as valuable in his squires' way of life. But there is no doubt that the underlying ideology of the Barsetshire novels is that of country party conservatism. The whole series takes its character from the attack in *The Warden* on the moral imperialism of the reforming spirit, which is associated with metropolitan ignorance of rural ways (Tom Towers of *The Jupiter* never troubles to visit the scene of the abuses he denounces) and with what Trollope saw as the simplified sentimental radicalism of Carlyle and Dickens. Equally limited, he shows, is the dogmatic ecclesiastical conservatism of Archdeacon Grantly. Neither of the warring parties can understand the instinctive, untheoretical goodness of the Warden himself, Mr Harding. He is Trollope's natural gentleman, the embodiment of 'heart' and 'grace of character'; more than that, he is a good man, the one completely convincing good man in the series, and as such Trollope's touchstone of moral value. It is he, for example, who puts his finger on the uncharitable discourtesy which disqualifies Mr Slope from being a Christian gentleman: 'Believe me, my child, that Christian ministers are never called on by God's word to insult the convictions, or even the prejudices of their brethren; and that religion is at any rate not less susceptible of urbane and courteous conduct among men, than any other study which men may take up' (*Barchester Towers*, ch. 8). Although he is to some extent in the wings of the later Barset novels, the image of his goodness, and the example of 'urbane and courteous conduct' he sets, deeply influence the way we read them.

As the Barsetshire map grows, widening from Barchester Close and Plumstead Episcopi to take in Ullathorne, Greshamsbury (another 'Tudor' country house) and Framley, the conservatism of Trollope's social vision becomes more pronounced. *Doctor Thorne* opens with a salute to 'feudal England ... chivalrous England':

> England is not yet a commercial country in the sense in which that epithet is used for her; and let us still hope that she will not soon become so. She might surely as well be called feudal England, or chivalrous England. If in western civilized Europe there does exist a nation among whom there are high signors, and with whom the owners of the land are the true aristocracy ... that nation is the English. (ch. 1)

Such explicit statements are rare, and their ideological edge is blunted by two factors: the force of literary convention, which subsumes ideology in the Jane Austen novel-of-manners tradition and in the related tradition of pastoral, and Trollope's critical attitude to the nobility, expressed through the Saxon/Norman antithesis which is the Victorian novelists' version of the old 'Norman yoke' theory. This held that the original freedoms of Saxon England had been confiscated by the Norman invaders, and it was given new life in the nineteenth century by the popularity of Scott's *Ivanhoe*, which contrasted Norman chivalry and the 'manly' Saxons, with their 'plain, homely, blunt manners, and the free spirit infused by their ancient institutions and laws'.[10] The theory, or myth, inspired popular radicalism and provided a convenient metaphor for the middle-class assault on aristocratic dominance. It is in the latter sense that Trollope both mocks and validates the myth in his treatment of the Thornes of Ullathorne in *Barchester Towers*. Mr Thorne is so devoted to his Saxon ancestors that he cannot quite believe in even the oldest English nobility: 'He would gently sigh if you spoke of the blood of the Fitzgeralds and De Burghs; would hardly allow the claims of the Howards and Lowthers; and has before now alluded to the Talbots as a family who had hardly yet achieved the full honours of a pedigree' (ch. 22). And just as we are starting to think the Thornes absurd, their prejudices are borne out by the behaviour of Lady De Courcy – 'a vain proud countess with a frenchified name' (ch. 35) – who arrives three hours late for the Ullathorne sports and blames it on the Thornes' roads, and indeed by the sports themselves, which symbolise a generous concern for the rural community that the De Courcys altogether lack. 'Don't be too particular, Plomacy,' Miss Thorne tells her steward as the local people press in uninvited to the party, 'especially with the children. If they live anywhere near, let them in' (ch. 35).

Trollope's 'Saxon' bias meshes naturally with the pastoral values which, as James Kincaid[11] and others have pointed out, inform his presentation of Barsetshire. The conservative gentry values of the Cathedral Close and the 'small house' (as opposed to the Whig 'great house'), embodied at their finest in Mr Harding, are challenged equally by the baronial arrogance of the Whig aristocrats and by invasion from London: both are manifestations of what Hutton calls 'the aggressiveness of the outer world'. The outer world is cruel and competitive, the pastoral world sheltering, kind to the old and the unfashionable, living by 'heart' rather than calculation. And in the first four novels the challenge of the outer world is fought off successfully, victory bringing with it an enhanced sense of pastoral solidity and well-being. Mr Slope creates a temporary crisis in the Cathedral Close, but no one who matters has any difficulty in seeing that he is not a gentleman, and in the end he overreaches himself with Mrs Proudie and is expelled. Roger Scatcherd seems to challenge the rural order at Greshamsbury, but his challenge comes to nothing; he is rejected and his money is absorbed to re-establish the Gresham estate. In *Framley Parsonage* Mark Roberts gets into trouble at Gatherum Castle but the Lufton family bail him out, and although Mr Sowerby is ruined, Chaldicotes is saved by Martha Dunstable, whose fortune from the 'Ointment of Lebanon' goes, like Scatcherd's, to rescue gentry society; her marriage to Dr Thorne, in turn, is a victory for those sympathetic to pastoral values. Painful issues are raised in these novels, but everything is resolved happily and, in the case of *Doctor Thorne* and *Framley Parsonage* at least, almost too cosily.

All this changes with *The Small House at Allington* (1864). Here for the first time the pastoral world of the rural gentry is seriously wounded by the invader from London, and in the process its vulnerability to the modern world exposed. It is also, significantly, the first of the Barsetshire series in which the gentlemanliness of a principal character becomes problematic: no one takes Slope for a gentleman, almost everyone takes Crosbie for one. The Small House of the title is even more sheltered than small houses generally are in Trollope, for the Great House is only the squire's house (the real 'Great House' in the story is Courcy Castle, with its metropolitan orientation, while Squire Dale's nestles close to the village). 'The gardens of the Great House of Allington and those of the Small House open on to each other', Trollope tells us (ch. 2), and this detail is important, because it underlines the shared heredity of Lily Dale and her uncle, the squire — both are obstinate and true, and the squire anticipates Lily's fate in being 'unable to transfer his heart to another' (ch. 1) after having been rejected in love. The bridge separating the two properties is the setting for the love affair between Lily and Crosbie, where she offers herself to him passionately in the moonlight (ch. 9). The pastoralism is explicit: this is the paradise Crosbie loses when he betrays her, which is to haunt him in his loveless marriage to Alexandrina De Courcy; she is *Lily Dale*, a self-styled 'butterfly' (ch. 12), a 'wounded fawn' (ch. 31). Pastoralism is mocked by Courcy Castle in the worldly irony of Lady Rosina's letter to Crosbie, inviting him to stay:

We have heard of you from the Gazebees, who have come down to us, and who tell us that you are rusticating at a charming little village, in which, among other attractions, there are wood nymphs and water nymphs, to whom much of your time is devoted. As this is just the thing for your taste, I would not for worlds disturb you; but if you should ever tear yourself away from the groves and fountains of Allington, we shall be delighted to welcome you here, though you will find us very unromantic after your late Elysium. (ch. 12)

Crosbie's trouble is that he is susceptible to this irony, which hits just the spot where he has already doubted his future with Lily: 'He must give up his clubs, and his fashion, and all that he had hitherto gained, and be content to live a plain, humdrum, domestic life, with eight hundred a year, and a small house, full of babies. It was not the kind of Elysium for which he had tutored himself' (ch. 7). He is an alien in the rural world, unlike Lily's other suitor, Johnny Eames, and this is perhaps the clearest indication that he is not a gentleman. No doubt he got his post in the Civil Service by competitive examination.

The Small House at Allington is usually read as a love-story, but it is much more than that. The unhappy love-story mediates beautifully a change in the balance of forces in Trollope's world — 'small house' values are in retreat from modern society, the pastoral is blighted. It is true that Lily's sister marries Dr Crofts, but against this must be set a long list of the unmarried: Squire Dale is a bachelor, Mrs Dale a widow, Lord de Guest and his sister Julia are unmarried, Johnny Eames is rejected, Lily on the road to spinsterhood. She may be perverse and self-indulgent, but the perverseness is in the Dale blood and the self-indulgence in keeping with a gentry class now turning in on itself and away from the modern world. It is futile to say of her that if she were like Amelia Roper, the daughter of Johnny Eames's London landlady, she would have to snap out of her melancholy mood, as Amelia does over Johnny: 'I didn't think ever to have cared for a man as I have cared for you. It's all trash and nonsense and foolery; I know that. It's all very well for young ladies as can sit in drawing-rooms all their lives, but when a woman has her way to make in the world it's all foolery' (ch. 59). But Lily is not Amelia, and she does not live in London: that is just Trollope's point.

The Small House at Allington is an important transitional novel in his career. In its vision of small gentry society grown vulnerable to the outer world, he breaks decisively with the reassuring balance of the previous Barsetshire novels, and looks forward to later works like *Sir Harry Hotspur* and *The Way We Live Now*. Deciding the difference between a gentleman and a cad has become more difficult, not because the criteria have changed but because the social landmarks are shifting. At the same time Trollope has started to think through some of the simpler social oppositions on which the comic resolutions of the previous novels had depended. It is probably significant that the book introduces us to Plantagenet Palliser, in whose subsequent career Trollope will begin to examine his instinctive anti-Whiggery and take his examination of gentlemanliness into the great world which had hitherto been the antagonist of his squirearchical values. His next novel is *Can You Forgive Her?*, the first of the Palliser series. He had come, in effect, to the end of Barset, and when he returned to it three years later, it was from an altered perspective. In Crosbie he had examined the character of a man who looked like a gentleman but was not one; in the Rev. Josiah Crawley he examines the character of a society which honours the ideal of the Christian gentleman but fails, at crucial points, to live up to it.

The Last Chronicle of Barset (1867) asks some hard questions within the reassuring framework of a return to old friends and old places. Trollope had always been concerned with the small gentry, here he turns his attention to the poor gentry. Mr Crawley, perpetual curate of Hogglestock, is a gentleman by birth, by breeding and by profession; he is a devoted priest in a labouring parish and, besides, a better Hebrew scholar than the Dean of Barchester. But he is also wretchedly, undeservedly poor, and his poverty and sense of injured merit make him a difficult man at the best of times. When the worst comes, and he is suspected of stealing a cheque for twenty pounds, he becomes an impossible man – proud, brooding, obsessed, full of an understandable but corrosive self-pity and sense of degradation. 'He was a man who when seen could hardly be forgotten. The deep angry remonstrant eyes, the shaggy eyebrows, telling tales of frequent anger...the repressed indignation of the habitual frown, the long nose and large powerful mouth, the deep furrows on the cheek...No one ever on seeing Mr. Crawley took him to be a happy man, or a weak man, or an ignorant man, or a wise man' (ch. 18). He takes a perverse pride in refusing to conceal his humiliation, and as he walks through Barsetshire in his threadbare clothes and broken shoes he is a living reproach to the comfortable materialism of Barchester Close and Plumstead Episcopi.

Trollope, who had begun in *The Warden* by attacking importunate reformism, and had seemed to side with the fleshpots of Plumstead against the low church zeal of Mrs Proudie in *Barchester Towers*, now asks his readers to consider the injustice of the contrast between the pinched Crawleys and the 'comely roundness' (ch. 5) of the Archdeacon's prosperity. The Archdeacon delights in the system which creates such manifest injustices: 'The Church was beautiful to him because one man by interest might have a thousand a year, while another man equally good, but without interest, could only have a hundred. And he liked the man who had the interest a great deal better than the man who had it not' (ch. 83). These are no longer comfortably comic attitudes and Trollope does not spare the Archdeacon; his materialism is seen to contradict the spirit of Christianity and to consort oddly with the freemasonry implied in the code of the gentleman, for if Crawley really is a gentleman (and everyone in the novel agrees that he is), and his wife and daughter are ladies, then how can the church of the gentry tolerate the conditions in which they are forced to live? Matters are made worse by the fact that Crawley is the only clergyman in the series we see working hard, and working, moreover, among those the Christian is most enjoined to help, the very poor, in this case the un-pastoral poor of the Hogglestock brickworks. Through Crawley we make contact, for the first time, with the social outcasts of comfortable rural Barsetshire.

But although the poverty of the poor is terrible, Trollope says in a remarkable passage, 'none but they who have themselves been poor gentry, – gentry so poor as not to know how to raise a shilling, – can understand the peculiar bitterness of the trials which such poverty produces'. The 'normal poor' suffer more in absolute terms, since they may starve to death, but they do not know the bitter humiliations of lost caste:

> The angry eyes of unpaid tradesmen...the taunt of the poor servant who wants her wages; the gradual relinquishment of habits which the soft nurture of earlier, kinder years had made second nature; the wan cheeks of the wife whose malady demands wine; the rags of the husband whose outward occupations demand decency; the neglected children, who are learning not to be the children of gentlefolk; and, worse than all, the alms and doles of half-generous friends, the waning pride, the pride that will not wane...(ch. 9)

Trollope does not soften or sentimentalise this genteel poverty as another novelist might have done. There is no pretence that the man's essential nature is untouched by his sufferings. 'Nothing can degrade but guilt', Crawley's wife tells him as they go in to the magistrates' hearing; 'Yes', he replies, 'misfortune can degrade, and poverty' (ch. 8). This proud, humiliated man is a continual embarrassment to the proprieties of the genteel code, which requires such loss of face to be reticent and hide itself.

The characters are judged by the way they judge Crawley. The women (apart from Mrs Proudie), the poor, even the tradesmen at Silverbridge believe him to be innocent. 'But the gentlemen in Silverbridge were made of sterner stuff, and believed the man to be guilty, clergyman and gentleman though he was' (ch. 5). The Archdeacon, the church's most solid temporal pillar, comes out worst. When he learns that his son, Major Grantly, is planning to marry Crawley's daughter Grace, his 'thorough worldliness' (ch. 56) gets the better of him. He cares more for the shame this marriage will bring to his daughter Griselda, the heartless Lady Dumbello, than for the suffering of a fellow-clergyman or the happiness of the young couple. His is a failure of imagination and conscience rather than of heart, because when he meets Grace at Framley he perceives at once that she is both a lady — with the beauty 'which shows itself in fine lines and a noble spirit, — the beauty which comes from breeding' — and a 'dear, good girl' (ch. 57). When Crawley is acquitted the archdeacon shows himself magnanimous to father and daughter, although one cannot help feeling that magnanimity after the event comes a good deal easier than sympathy and charity before it would have done:

> Mr. Crawley, having been summoned by the archdeacon into the library for a little private conversation, found that he got on better with him. How the archdeacon conquered him may perhaps be best described by a further narration of what Mr. Crawley said to his wife. 'I told him that in regard to money matters, as he called them, I had nothing to say. I only trusted that his son was aware that my daughter had no money, and never would have any. "My dear Crawley," the archdeacon said... "my dear Crawley, I have enough for both." "I would we stood on more equal grounds," I said. Then as he answered me, he rose from his chair. "We stand," said he, "on the only perfect level on which such men can meet each other. We are both gentlemen."' (ch. 83)

This passage is often quoted to illustrate Trollope's concept of the gentleman, but read in context it surely raises more issues than it answers. Naturally Crawley is grateful for this acceptance and assertion of equality, and the Archdeacon's gesture removes the awkwardness from their situation. But is it any more than a gesture? And what has the gentlemanly solidarity meant when really put to the test? Handshakes and marriage at the end do not dispel the doubts raised in the body of the novel.

IV

In the last two Barsetshire novels, then, we can see Trollope beginning to test his idea of the gentleman by approaching it from different angles and exposing it to different contexts. *Can You Forgive Her?*, the first Palliser novel, partakes of the same spirit of questioning, although the real question here is not the coy one asked by the title but a transposed version of the problem tackled in the previous novel, *The Small House at Allington*. 'What is it about a modern gentleman like Crosbie that leads him to betray a perfect lady like Lily Dale?' leads on to another, 'What is it about the modern woman, Alice Vavasor, that she should find a perfect gentleman like John Grey so chilling?' Alice is independent and indecisive, and her predicament is explored in the contrast between her two suitors. Trollope uses the cad, her cousin George Vavasor, to sound out the limitations of the perfect gentleman. Crosbie had been a 'soft' cad, one of those men, as Lily says, 'who are so full of feeling, so soft-natured, so kind', but who in the end 'won't wash' (*Last Chronicle*, ch. 16). George is a 'hard' cad, dark-featured and violent, all whips, pistols and brandy. He is the reckless heir to an old Cumberland estate, but lacks the ancestral loyalty so important in Trollope's landed gentleman. 'What trash it is', he says of Vavasor Hall, 'hanging on to such a place as that without the means of living like a gentleman, simply because one's ancestors have done so' (ch. 38). His recklessness and masculinity intimate a sexuality lacking in Grey, and it is easy to see why Alice should be attracted to George. John Grey's fault is that he is too true to be good, his imperturbability maddening to her restless spirit; she rightly fears that his refusal to show himself troubled by her indecision, which he chooses to see as an 'illness', reveals a hidden urge to dominate. 'There was something in the imperturbed security of his manner which almost made her angry with him. It seemed as though he assumed so great a superiority that he felt himself able to treat any resolve of hers as the petulance of a child' (ch. 11). Trollope's psychological insights in this novel often seem at odds with his narrative attitudes, so that he can resolve Alice's dilemma only by blackening George, showing him going to the dogs, and not by dramatising any convincing change in her relationship with John Grey.

None the less, Grey is interesting for the light he sheds on Plantagenet Palliser in the parallel plot involving Glencora and Burgo Fitzgerald. Here too a spirited woman is caught between an attractive scoundrel and a sober, principled gentleman, although in this case the problem is more convincingly solved, not by the blackening of the scoundrel but by Glencora's discovery that her husband is a better, nobler man than Burgo, and that he does care for her even though he has difficulty in showing it. This may make it no easier for her to love him (although the birth of their child at the end brings them together), but it does suggest depths in his character that subsequent novels will develop. The Grey/Palliser parallel works in obvious ways to unify the novel by integrating the two plots: it is through his friendship with Palliser, for instance, that John Grey gets the seat in Parliament which reconciles Alice to her future life as a country gentleman's wife. But the more important point of the parallel is that it serves to reinforce the reader's developing awareness that Plantagenet Palliser, despite all the grandeur of the Omnium name, is at heart a Victorian gentleman and not a Whig grandee. His friendship and respect for this first-generation country gentleman, including his political sponsorship in helping him to election at Silverbridge, indicate that the future Duke of Omnium, unlike his uncle, is a Whig politician temperamentally and politically in sympathy with the responsible middle classes. This, I think, is the clue to what would otherwise seem a paradox: that Trollope, who in the Barsetshire series and elsewhere seems to locate his values in the gentry rather than the nobility, and the Tory gentry at that, should offer a Whig nobleman as his 'perfect gentleman' (*Autobiography*, ch. 20). Trollope may not have been interested in redefining the idea of the gentleman, but the Palliser novels are the most notable attempt in Victorian fiction to redefine the idea of a nobleman.

In the two Dukes of Omnium, in the decline of the old and the rise to power of the new, Trollope is portraying an evolution within the aristocracy which is the Victorian version of what Audrey Laski, who has written well on this aspect of the Palliser novels, calls the 'Myth of the Aristocrat'.[12] Initially, the contrast between uncle and nephew suggests that Trollope was influenced by Thackeray: the old Duke is the worldly nobleman of stereotype, from the stable of Lord Steyne, and Planty Pal a dull, conscientious, slightly priggish bluebook politician like the second Sir Pitt Crawley in *Vanity Fair*. The Duke has the seigneurial arrogance of a class that does not feel itself accountable to those beneath it, and from the gentry viewpoint of Barset he is grandly remote with the unconscious insolence of grandeur. It is the Duke's remoteness, coupled with his immense wealth, that is the secret of the 'almost reverential awe' in which he is held. 'I think the secret lay in the simple fact that the Duke of Omnium had not been common in the eyes of the people', Trollope comments in *Phineas Finn* (1869). 'He had contrived to envelope himself in something of the ancient mystery of wealth and rank' (ch. 48). But in *Phineas Finn* the spell of the ancient mystery is starting to dissolve. The Duke's pursuit of Madame Max Goesler brings him down to earth, no longer the sought but the suitor, a lonely old man hungry for the crumbs of love. In *Phineas Redux* (1874) he is dying, now (in Glencora's words) a 'poor old man', pathetically clinging to Madame Max's hand on his deathbed. The magic of the great nobleman has evaporated, and at his death we see him for what he is and has been: an idle and selfish old man.

The Duke of Omnium is Trollope's version of the unregenerate pre-Victorian nobleman, and he adds one touch to the picture familiar from Lord Steyne and Disraeli's Lord Monmouth: the Duke has been simply too selfish and lazy to trouble himself much with politics. His life has had no purpose beyond being a duke; he has put all his efforts into surrounding himself with 'the ancient mystery of rank and wealth'. But his nephew is not interested in being a duke as such, he only wants to serve his country. 'To him his uncle's death would be a great blow, as in his eyes to be Chancellor of the Exchequer was much more than to be Duke of Omnium' (*Phineas Redux*, ch. 25). The future Duke of Omnium is a new kind of nobleman, as the Victorian gentleman was a new kind of gentleman, in that he is an essentially disinterested public servant:

> Mr. Palliser was one of those politicians in possessing whom England has perhaps more reason to be proud than of any other of her resources, and who, as a body, give to her that exquisite combination of conservatism and progress which is her present strength and best security for the future. He could afford to learn to be a statesman, and had the industry wanted for such training. He was born in the purple,

noble himself, and heir to the highest rank as well as one of the greatest fortunes of the country, already very rich, surrounded by all the temptations of luxury and pleasure; and yet he devoted himself to work with the grinding energy of a young penniless barrister labouring for a penniless wife, and did so without any motive more selfish than that of being counted in the roll of the public servants of England. (*Can You Forgive Her?*, ch. 24)

The rather lofty opening of this passage may lead a reader of the Palliser series to expect more politically of Plantagenet Palliser than he will get. To jaundiced modern eyes, the remarkable feature of the man is the fact that he seems to lack the hunger for power which has come to seem the politician's basic attribute. He is much more important for what he is than for what he does, and in fact he does very little beyond working hard at the chores of office. He has no grand political visions like Disraeli's politicians, and when he becomes head of a coalition government in *The Prime Minister* he is at a loss to know what to do. His one cherished reform, to introduce decimal coinage, is portrayed as an endearing crotchet. For much of the time he seems not so much a statesman, more a kind of transcendental civil servant.

But he is a 'noble gentleman'. In the second Duke of Omnium the qualities of Trollope's landed gentlemen are raised into a higher sphere. Like the squire, he can be trusted because he has that 'rock-like solidity' which comes from the responsible stewardship of landed property:

It is the trust which such men inspire which makes them so serviceable; — trust not only in their labour, — for any man rising from the mass of the people may be equally laborious; nor yet simply in their honesty and patriotism. The confidence is given to their labour, honesty, and patriotism joined to such a personal stake in the country as gives them a weight and ballast which no politician in England can possess without it. (ibid., ch. 24)

Of course Trollope does not suggest that Plantagenet Palliser is the first politician to possess these qualities, only that he brings to the traditional serviceableness of the patriotic statesman a characteristically Victorian high-mindedness and devotion to principle. Out of the old Whig comes the new Liberal, a disinterested man who can turn his back in *The Prime Minister* on using the Palliser 'interest' in the Silverbridge election, and who is capable on occasion of talking with passion and articulacy about the principles underlying his political beliefs. But it is also a very unsectarian liberalism, and in the end it matters less in his characterisation than the integrity, unselfishness and old-world chivalry he shares with Trollope's other true gentlemen. Without being a Tory squire he is the kind of Whig nobleman that even a Tory squire could respect. The measure of his integrity, indeed, is that it works to his political disadvantage, as when he gives his first knighthood of the Garter to a deserving Tory peer, a social reformer, against the advice of his colleagues to use it as patronage to strengthen the coalition. The act leads directly to his political downfall.

When Plantagenet Palliser grows to his full stature as a gentleman and a politician in *The Prime Minister*, he does so against the background of Trollope's increasing pessimism about the decline of gentlemanly standards in his society voiced in the sombre satire of *The Way We Live Now*, published in the previous year, 1875. This novel, which Trollope described in his *Autobiography* as an attack on 'the commercial profligacy of the age' (ch. 20), reflects the misgivings he shared with the editor of *The Times*, John Delane, about the growth of stock jobbing in contemporary society. What troubled them both was the evidence from a number of recent scandals that the mania for share speculation had spread to the aristocracy and gentry, and was starting to undermine the standards on which landed society was based. Delane wrote in *The Times*'s first leader on 11 August 1875:

> It is a simple matter of fact that these last twelve months have been marked by a succession of disgraceful scandals...Gentlemen of family and station are competing for the honour of helping Canadian, American, French, and German adventurers to fleece English Society, and English Society has allowed its greediness for exorbitant gain to hurry it blindfold into the trap.

The Way We Live Now could be described as a novel about the treason of the gentlemen of England, and its controlling metaphor, or analogy, is that of gambling. Gambling is always a sign of incipient caddishness in Trollope, and to cheat at cards, as George Hotspur does, is the mark of the utter scoundrel. In this novel everyone is gambling, the young men in the Beargarden Club, their fathers in the Stock Exchange or on the boards of bubble companies, and the arch-gambler is the corrupt financier, Augustus Melmotte, a man who cannot be trusted, in Trollope's view, because no one knows where he comes from or what his antecedents were. And the English aristocracy, who of all groups in society should apply the criterion of ancestry, are falling over each other to cultivate Melmotte, to get on the boards of his companies and to marry their sons to his daughter.

The only man to stand out against the corruption of the day is, as we would expect, one of Trollope's bachelor squires, Roger Carbury, who speaks up for the gentlemanly standards that are being betrayed:

> Men say openly that he is an adventurer and a swindler. No one pretends to think that he is a gentleman. There is a consciousness among

all who speak of him that he amasses his money not by honest trade, but by unknown tricks, — as does a card-sharper. He is one whom we would not admit into our kitchens, much less to our tables, on the score of his own merits. But because he has learned the art of making money, we not only put up with him, but settle upon his carcase as so many birds of prey. (ch. 15)

The word 'gentleman' crops up again and again in the novel, but uncomfortably. Everyone knows that Melmotte is not a gentleman and that those who follow him are breaking the code, but only Roger says so and makes the uncomfortable (but to Trollope inevitable) link between gentlemanliness and honesty. In Roger we see all the old territorial decencies — the long-established estate, the squire's sense of responsibility to his tenants, the steadying conviction that 'he held the place in trust for the use of others' (ch. 15) — but we see them threatened by the very economic forces which are making Melmotte's operations possible. Trollope tends to portray his squires as vulnerable, as we have seen, but in *The Way We Live Now* he shows his awareness of the economic reality that in the long run (and of course after his own death) was to bring the reign of the squires to an end: land was ceasing to be a good commercial investment. In 1800 the Carbury property could maintain the house, but since then, even though rents have increased, 'the income is no longer comfortably adequate to the wants of an English gentleman's household. If a moderate estate in land be left to a man now, there arises the question whether he is not damaged unless an income also be left to him wherewith to keep up the estate. Land is a luxury, and of all luxuries is the most costly' (ch. 6). The Carburys have no other sources of income but land. 'There had been no ruin, — no misfortune. But in the days of which we write the Squire of Carbury Hall had become a poor man simply through the wealth of others' (ch. 6). The implications are plain and Trollope understood them very clearly: the institutions of landed society, especially the smaller gentry, could not long survive the decline of the income necessary to sustain them. Roger's is not only a lonely voice against the age, it is also an embattled voice (Carbury Manor is appropriately encircled by a moat) and, Trollope suggests, it may prove to be a doomed voice.

There are other signs in his fiction of the 1870s that he was aware of the democratic and plutocratic pressures threatening the reign of the Roger Carburys. The extension of the borough franchise to the counties, which was to enfranchise the farm labourer and so weaken the political power of the land-owning class, came in the 1884 Reform Act, but it is already on the political agenda for the Duke's coalition in *The Prime Minister*, much to the disgust of that old Whig and reluctant Liberal, the Duke of St Bungay. The new Duke realises that he cannot use the Omnium interest in Silverbridge elections as his uncle had done, or he himself in former days: 'It is not for me to return a member for Silverbridge...The influence which owners of property may have in boroughs is decreasing every day, and there arises the question whether a conscientious man will any longer use such influence' (ch. 21). This development will not much affect Matching, but it is part of a democratic wave that was to engulf the political influence of Carbury Hall. Trollope was aware of the many unsuccessful Bills to establish elected county authorities, and to take away the wide but unofficial powers of the old unpaid justices, who were usually squires; and his attitude was hostile, if we can judge from the caricature of Mr Cockey, the vulgar commercial traveller in *The Vicar of Bullhampton*, who challenges 'Squire' Gilmore to explain the 'use' of a country gentleman:

> 'Sometimes he's a magistrate.'
> 'Yes, justices' justice! we know all about that. Put an old man in prison for a week because he looks into his 'ay-field on a Sunday; or send a young one to the treadmill for two months because he knocks over a 'are! All them cases ought to be tried in the towns, and there should be beaks paid as there is in London. I don't see the good of a country gentleman. Buying and selling; — that's what the world has to go by.' (ch. 29)

And when Mr Gilmore offers the observation that they buy and sell land, Mr Cockey retorts that they know nothing about it: 'After all, they ain't getting above two-and-a-half per cent. for their money. We all know what that must come to' (ch. 29). What it came to, as Trollope knew, was the decline of land as a profitable investment and, as he could not know, the County Councils Act, 1888. This was the occasion of F. W. Maitland's great essay on the passing of the old form of local government by country gentlemen, 'The Shallows and Silences of real life'. Remembering the 'splendid past' of this institution, and pointing (prophetically) to the dangers of bureaucracy, Maitland wrote: 'As a governor he is doomed; but there has been no accusation. He is cheap, he is pure, he is capable, but he is doomed; he is to be sacrificed to a theory, on the altar of the spirit of the age'.[13]

Did Trollope see the squire himself as 'doomed'? Certainly he appreciated the underlying economic threat to the resident landed gentleman, as well as the overt democratic challenge. In the last analysis, though, his attitude to life was too positive and melioristic to let him surrender entirely to the elegiac enchantments of the last English gentleman myth. Even in *The Way We Live Now* Roger's pessimism is related to his unhappy love for Hetta Carbury and challenged by the Bishop of Ealing, whose conviction that the world is slowly improving (ch. 55) is similar to Trollope's own view as expressed in the chapter of his *Autobiography* in which he discusses the novel. 'That men have become less cruel, less violent, less selfish, less brutal, there can be no doubt; — but have they become less honest?' (ch. 20). It is his fear that 'a certain class of dishonesty, dishonesty magnificent in its proportions, and climbing into high places' (ch. 20), has started to loosen the traditional moral foundations of gentlemanliness, at a time when the social and economic foundations are being weakened, that lies behind his troubled preoccupation with true and false gentlemen in both *The Way We Live Now* and *The Prime Minister*.

The Prime Minister is a very interesting novel from our point of view: it shows Trollope's ideal gentleman at the peak of his career, and it contains an answer, in the Lopez plot, to those who were saying that the idea of the gentleman no longer mattered. As we have seen, Trollope held rather old-fashioned notions of what a gentleman was which he found difficulty in defining and justifying; and he realised that many in the modern world were impatient with these notions, without stopping to consider that they might have an existential justification, as it were, to make up for what looked like their theoretical absurdity. The novel has a twin purpose which is served by the interaction of its two plots: to show a perfect gentleman in action in the new Duke of Omnium, and to show a modern woman in Emily Wharton discovering the empirical truth of the gentlemanly code of conduct and judgement which she has come to regard as merely old-fashioned prejudice. Emily's father, Mr Wharton, appears to be, and is, a rather unattractively prejudiced old man, who bases his objection to Lopez as a suitor on the grounds that he is not an English gentleman and nobody knows who his father was, and moreover tells him so. Trollope shows that this is foolish, not because it is untrue but because it cannot be proved: everyone takes Lopez for a gentleman, and to assert otherwise is rude — 'Lopez is...a bad name to go to a Protestant church with, and I don't want my daughter to bear it' (ch. 3) — as well as bad tactics, for it cedes the moral advantage to Lopez and prevents Mr Wharton's asking the question which, as a lawyer, he ought to have known was the telling one: can you support my daughter? Lopez is a penniless adventurer but the father's quickness on the gentility trigger prevents this important fact from emerging in time.

Emily has to discover Lopez's mean, mercenary character the hard way, and in doing so she discovers the truth contained in the prejudices she has hitherto dismissed. Drawing a comparison between Lopez and her former lover, a gentleman, she is forced to concede that 'there was some peculiar gift, or grace, or acquirement belonging without dispute to the one, and which the other lacked'. She had in the past told herself 'that this gift of gentle blood and gentle nurture, of which her father thought so much...was after all but a weak, spiritless quality', and she had regarded the notion that it went with 'that love of honest, courageous truth which her father was wont to attribute to it' as simply part of the legend of chivalry. Her desired qualities in a husband had been intelligence, affection and ambition, and she 'knew no reason why such a hero as her fancy created should be born of lords and ladies rather than of working mechanics, should be English rather than Spanish or French'. Yet Lopez changes her view, against her will. 'But now, — ay, from the very hour of her marriage — she had commenced to learn what it was that her father had meant when he spoke of the pleasure of living with gentlemen' (ch. 31).

Emily Wharton's education at the hands of a non-gentleman demonstrates the continuing validity of gentlemanly standards, despite the fact that in her father these take the form of unthinking prejudice; and it points to the nobler, articulate gentlemanliness of the Duke of Omnium. It is, above all, honesty which marks the Duke's character, as the lack of it marks Lopez. The Duke of St Bungay tells Lady Glencora: 'This husband of yours is a very peculiar man...His honesty is not like the honesty of other men. It is more downright; — more absolutely honest; less capable of bearing even the shadow which the stain from another's dishonesty might throw upon it' (ch. 28). He is a living disproof of Lopez's cynical assumption that 'the most experienced of statesmen are talked out of their principles' (ch. 2). Such exigent honesty is a dubious political asset, as Glencora discovers over the Silverbridge election, and the Duke's colleagues when he makes what seems to them the quixotic decision to give the Garter to Lord Earlybird simply because the man has served his country well. It is continually stressed, too, that his conscientiousness makes him too thin-skinned for the dirty work of office, and that his remoteness and reserve prevent him from attracting the wide range of friends a coalition needs to survive. But to set against these political deficiencies, the Duke possesses a quality which in Trollope's view is much rarer than political skill, and which stems directly from the man's scrupulous honesty, and that is a kind of ultimate disinterestedness. This, the hallmark of the true gentleman, is the crowning nobility of his conservative-reforming Prime Minister.

Trollope was intrigued by the spectacle of great Whig noblemen actively involved in the championing of reforms which must, at some distant date, end in the reforming away of their own immense privileges. As Frank Tregear says in *The Duke's Children* (1880) to the Duke's son, Lord Silverbridge: 'A Liberal party, with plenipotentiary power, must go on right away to the logical conclusion of its arguments. It is only the conservative feeling of the country which saves such men as your father from being carried headlong to ruin by their own machinery' (ch. 55). The old Duke of St Bungay is endearingly aware of this irony in his own case, a bewildered Whig compelled to vote for measures he detests out of ancient loyalty to the party. 'There must surely have been a shade of melancholy on that old man's mind as, year after year, he assisted in pulling down institutions which he in truth regarded as the safeguards of the nation; — but which he knew that, as a Liberal, he was bound to assist in destroying!' (ch. 68). Plantagenet Palliser differs from both the old Duke of St Bungay, and the newer ideological Radicals like

Mr Turnbull, in his clear-eyed acceptance of the *moral* case against the privileges he enjoys, and his willingness to follow through the political consequences. The chapter of *The Prime Minister* from which the reflection on the old Duke just quoted comes is entitled 'The Prime Minister's Political Creed', and it contains the Duke of Omnium's impassioned outburst to Phineas Finn on the 'godlike' prospect of true equality:

> Equality would be a heaven, if we could attain it. How can we to whom so much has been given dare to think otherwise? How can you look at the bowed back and bent legs and abject face of that poor ploughman, who winter and summer has to drag his rheumatic limbs to his work, while you go a-hunting or sit in pride among the foremost few of your country, and say that it all is as it ought to be? (ch. 68)

In his uncharacteristic enthusiasm the Duke throws off his hat and looks up to heaven, his fist clenched. Then the excitement passes and he concludes soberly: 'Equality is a dream. But sometimes one likes to dream, — especially as there is no danger that Matching will fly from one in a dream' (ch. 68). Equality is as remote as heaven; Matching is not going to fly away, so perhaps the Duke can afford (as he realises) his democratic convictions. But then enough is shown of his true disinterestedness as a politician to suggest that when the time comes he could not, in honour, resist measures to close the gap between the ploughman and the duke. It is finally a matter of honour, of the true gentleman's last act of gracefulness, bowing out when his time is up. Nothing becomes the Duke's tenure of office like the leaving it, and the readiness to leave it. In this, perhaps, Trollope had a prophetic insight into the way the landed order was to meet its destiny, when the Matchings really did fly away. 'In the past the landed aristocracy has done great service as well as enjoyed great wealth', Professor F. M. L. Thompson concluded in *English Landed Society in the Nineteenth Century*, 'and the most important service has been the peaceful surrender of power'.[14] The Palliser novels show how much that peaceful surrender of power owed to the code of the gentleman.

V

With *The Duke's Children* (1880) Trollope's version of the myth of the aristocrat is completed. Here we see the Duke a widower, trying to understand the new generation to which his children belong. There are many signs of change: gambling has become an established habit among his son's friends (Lord Silverbridge loses £70,000 on the St Leger); American heiresses are starting to appear on the London social scene; relationships between parents and children are freer, and deference to rank and 'blood' is not quite so strong; the Duke's son has even gone over to the Conservatives. The drama of the novel turns upon the irony of the Duke's position: in principle a Liberal committed to narrowing the differences between a duke and a dustman, his personal sense of caste will not let him accept easily his daughter's proposed marriage to the penniless Frank Tregear or his son's to the American girl Isabel Boncassen. But his conflict with his children is happily resolved because the moral lines are clear, unlike the Wharton—Lopez plot in *The Prime Minister*. Tregear is a gentleman, and Isabel accepts the priorities of rank and is, besides, good and beautiful and rich. The twin stereotypes of the wicked nobleman and the bluebook prig with which Trollope began have grown and mellowed into our final picture of the Duke of Omnium as the Victorian family man, reconciled with his children and, through them, to the future.

It would be neat and convenient to leave this topic with the Duke of Omnium as we see him at the end of the Palliser series. But an account of Trollope's landed gentlemen would be incomplete without mentioning the curious twist given to his treatment of this subject in that remarkable late 'problem' novel, *Mr Scarborough's Family* (1883). This seems to contradict much of what has been said so far about the stewardship of property as a source of moral value in his work, as if Trollope had decided at the end of his life, like Mr Scarborough on his deathbed, to give his readers a shock (the novel was published posthumously). When the book opens Mr Scarborough is dying and in the process of enduring painful surgery. He has just announced that his eldest son and heir to his estate, Mountjoy, is illegitimate because he was not married to his wife at the time the son was born; his second son, Augustus, is legitimate and becomes the legal heir. Mountjoy is a reckless gambler who has raised money on post-obits that amount to the value of the property, but this new development enables Mr Scarborough to settle with the irate creditors and so save the estate. Just before he dies he then announces that he married his wife twice, before and after the birth of Mountjoy, and that the now unencumbered Mountjoy is the true heir after all. It is an ingenious plot by means of which a ruined estate is redeemed for a ruined man, but only at the cost of farther ruin — to his dead wife's reputation, to the prospects in life of his second son (whom he hates), and most of all, to the professional reputation of an honest, gentlemanly lawyer, Mr Grey, whose good name he shamelessly exploits.

Mr Scarborough's Family is a dark and puzzling book because in it Trollope's system of values seems, for the first time, to be split down the middle. It is hard to read it without being made to feel, as most of the characters do, that there is much that is humanly attractive in Mr Scarborough. He is brave, generous, a good landlord, capable of intense love (and hate), unselfish (as he frequently says, he schemes that good may come to others, not himself), audacious and ingenious. There is, as his medical attendant says after his death, something heroic in his struggle to outflank the law: 'One cannot make an apology for him without being ready to throw all truth and all morality to the dogs. But if you can imagine for yourself a state of things in which neither truth nor morality shall be thought essential, then old Mr Scarborough would be your hero' (ch. 58). But of course one cannot 'throw all truth and all morality to the dogs'. Nor can one accept easily the cynical flouting of the laws of Trollope's 'religion' of inheritance, even when the intention is to establish a rough natural justice. And in addition to the extensive harm for which Mr Scarborough is responsible, there is the simple fact that it is all pointless anyway, for Mountjoy will only gamble away his restored estate. What is most disturbing, however, is the almost violent separation in this novel between the Ciceronian *honestum* (honour plus honesty) and the passion for inheritance, which in previous novels had been a guarantee of honour.

Yet this is also, I think, the clue to the novel, and it all comes back again to Trollope's idea of the gentleman. There have been many interpretations of *Mr Scarborough's Family*, as a satire on the laws of inheritance, or as a study in obsession, or as a novel about the desperate shifts to which a good man is put in a corrupt world. But what seems to be most at issue is the notion of *honesty*. The most revealing passage, at least to anyone who has registered the importance of honesty and principle in Trollope's work, is the following account of Mr Scarborough's attitudes:

> He had a most thorough contempt for the character of an honest man. He did not believe in honesty, but only in mock honesty... The usual honesty of the world was with him all pretence, or, if not, assumed for the sake of the character it would achieve. Mr. Grey he knew to be honest; Mr. Grey's word he knew to be true; but he fancied that Mr. Grey had adopted this absurd mode of living with the view of cheating his neighbours by appearing to be better than others. All virtue and all vice were comprised by him in the words 'good-nature' and 'ill-nature'. (ch. 21)

The point can hardly be missed: whatever else Mr Scarborough may be, he is not a true gentleman, and Trollope nowhere says that he is. He is triply blind to the nature of honesty: in despising it, in failing to see that Mr Grey's honesty is the real thing and in believing that he is himself more 'absolutely honest' (ch. 21) than Grey — meaning by that his authenticity in living without illusions, rather than the principled conduct Grey holds to.

Mr Scarborough's Family is the novel of a man playing with the themes of a lifetime, but it does not follow that Trollope is playing with the morality of a lifetime. Mr Scarborough may be an attractive rogue, but he is devoid of honesty and without any remorse for what he has done, and he ends by ruining a good man. Trollope makes it clear that his 'death-bed triumphs' (ch. 55) have been won at the expense of Mr Grey's reputation, for it is only the lawyer's known character for scrupulous honesty that gets the initial act of disinheritance believed by the world and, more important, by the creditors who are to be bought off. When he re-inherits Mountjoy the lawyer realises he has been used and dishonoured: 'He has treated me as no one should have treated his enemy; let alone a faithful friend...He has utterly destroyed my character as a lawyer' (ch. 55). In Grey's defeat and retirement we can see that Trollope's essential morality has not changed, nor perhaps his pessimistic sense of the way the world now is for honest gentlemen. 'As things go now a man has to be accounted a fool if he attempts to run straight', he tells his daughter Dolly, explaining why he has decided to retire. 'Another system has grown up which does not suit me...It may be that I am a fool, and that my idea of honesty is a mistake' (ch. 62). To which might be added, as a final word, Dolly's reasons for not marrying her father's partner, that he is not a gentleman and lacks 'a sense of high honour': 'I should want my husband to be a gentleman. There are not a great many gentlemen about' (ch. 33).

REFERENCES: CHAPTER 5

1 F. O'Connor, *The Mirror in the Roadway* (London: Hamish Hamilton, 1957), pp. 165–83.
2 E. Burke, *Reflections on the Revolution in France*, ed. C. C. O'Brien (Harmondsworth: Penguin, 1968), pp. 194–5.
3 P. E. More, *The Demon of the Absolute* (Princeton, NJ: Princeton University Press, 1928), p. 122.
4 D. Smalley (ed.), *Trollope: The Critical Heritage* (London: Routledge & Kegan Paul, 1969), pp. 509–11.
5 R. apRoberts, *The Moral Trollope* (Athens, Ohio: Ohio University Press, 1971).
6 A. Trollope, *The Life of Cicero*, 2 vols (London: Chapman & Hall, 1880), Vol. II, p. 384.
7 M. Sadleir, *Trollope: A Commentary* (London: Constable, 1927), p. 184.
8 Smalley (ed.), op. cit., p. 342.
9 T. H. S. Escott, *Anthony Trollope: His Work, Associates, and Literary Originals* (London: Bodley Head, 1913), p. 166.
10 Sir W. Scott, *Ivanhoe*, The Edinburgh Waverley (Edinburgh: T. C. & E. C. Jack, 1901), Vol. 16, p. xvi.
11 J. Kincaid, *The Novels of Anthony Trollope* (Oxford: Clarendon Press, 1977).
12 A. L. Laski, 'Myths of character: an aspect of the novel', *Nineteenth Century Fiction*, vol. XIV (1960), pp. 333–43.
13 F. W. Maitland, 'The Shallows and Silences of real life', in *Collected Papers*, ed. H. A. L. Fisher, 3 vols (Cambridge: Cambridge University Press, 1911), Vol. 1, p. 472.
14 F. M. L. Thompson, *English Landed Society in the Nineteenth Century* (London: Routledge & Kegan Paul, 1963), p. 345.

Epilogue

> We have lost somewhat, afar and near,
>   Gentlemen,
> The thinning of our ranks each year
> Affords a hint we are nigh undone,
> That we shall not be ever again
> The marked of many, loved of one,
>   Gentlemen.
> (Thomas Hardy, 'An Ancient to Ancients', 1922)

Trollope ends the chapter of English literary and cultural history with which this book has been concerned. His later fiction holds in tension an intimate understanding of the old landed order of 'rank' and an awareness of the new, competitive, urbanised world of 'class', and it anticipates, without indulging, the note of elegy which is to sound for the English gentleman in the novels of Ford Madox Ford and Evelyn Waugh. The idea of the gentleman bulks larger in his vision than it does in that of a near contemporary like George Meredith, or a novelist of the next generation like Henry James, and yet this preoccupation does not strike us as a source of limitation in his work. To explore the relation between gentility and the moral life was still for Trollope, as it had been for the novelists before him, an enterprise compatible with major fiction offering a complex interpretation of contemporary life.

By the time of his death in 1882, however, the situation had changed. Gentlemanliness was ceasing to be the vexing question it had been twenty years earlier — at least for the middle classes. The greatly expanded public school system was then in full swing. A public school education is not a significant determinant of gentlemanliness in Trollope's fiction, but it came to be so for the later Victorians and Edwardians. The system solved the problem of defining gentility for the middle and upper classes, and helped to forge a new elite by exposing their children to a common, shaping ritual of education. It was both a triumphant example of the Victorian compromise and a development which was to lead inevitably to the dilution and urbanising of the idea of the gentleman. Five or ten years' schooling in a country house setting came to take the place of the old gentry's intimate knowledge of village life built up through long residence in the country and work on the Bench; indeed, the growth of the system may even have concealed the extent to which Trollope's squires were dying off, because the public schools encouraged identification with the style and habits of the country gentleman, including the traditional links with military service through the cadet force.

By the end of the nineteenth century the status of gentleman, as Tocqueville had predicted, was being claimed by those lower down the social scale. It is no accident, I think, that the really interesting literary development of the idea of the gentleman after Trollope occurs not in the novel-of-manners tradition of Meredith or James, but in works with a lower- or lower-middle-class protagonist such as George Gissing's *Born in Exile* (1892) and H. G. Wells's *Kipps* (1905) and *Tono-Bungay* (1909). These characters come from a 'respectable' class of clerks and small shopkeepers which stood in much the same uneasy relation to the established middle classes as, fifty years earlier, middle-class men like Thackeray and Dickens had done to the Victorian gentry and aristocracy. Nor is it an accident that Gissing and Wells were both admirers of Dickens, and that their treatment of the 'born in exile' theme was profoundly influenced by *Great Expectations*.

Apart from Gissing and Wells, however, who are hardly 'modern' in any case, it must be said that the modern writer has not been greatly interested in the idea of the gentleman. The idea undoubtedly lost some of its potency when it ceased to be problematic, and no longer had to carry the freight of the middle-class challenge to aristocracy. Then by the end of the century the 'woman question' had surfaced, and this meant, as Ellen Moers says, that 'the nature of the gentleman was a minor question. Wilde's era asked instead, and with a new urgency, what it meant merely to be a man.'[1] Related to that development, and to the dilution through democratisation of the gentleman as a cultural type, is the growing suspicion that he may be after all a rather conventional and colourless figure. 'There was something insipid and tasteless to her in the idea of a gentleman', Gudrun Brangwen reflects in chapter 29 of D. H. Lawrence's *Women in Love* (1921). The only considerable modern novelist to take the idea seriously is Evelyn Waugh in his *Sword of Honour* trilogy, and even here Guy Crouchback's moral development is signalled by an act of charity which goes against the whole tradition of ancestral honour, when he takes his ex-wife back and accepts her illegitimate child by another man as his heir. Like Newman, Waugh ends by saying that it is more important to do good than to be a gentleman.

Britain is a society of such strange survivals and continuities that it would be rash to conclude that the gentlemanly ideal itself is dead. The old world of 'rank' lives on in the armed services, and the modern professional man, when he honours the concept of disinterestedness, is in the direct line of descent from his gentlemanly Victorian great-grandfather, little as he may like to be reminded of the pedigree. Even the squire has survived, although his political power has waned. There is little doubt, however, that something essential has gone, that industrialisation and two world wars have put a great distance between us and the traditional image of the gentleman. And those recent writers who have taken up that image, like Evelyn Waugh, have done so in a spirit of conservative challenge, asserting the fact of the gentleman's decline and his inevitable alienation from the modern world. One thinks of Guy Crouchback's father in *Men at Arms* (1952), who 'had like many another been born in full sunlight and lived to see night fall' ('Prologue'), forced to give up the family home and live in the local hotel. Or of Simon Raven's composite, idealised figure, Colonel Sir Matthew Tench, who dies shortly after the Suez débâcle, seeing 'nothing but shame, crooked dealing and betrayal' around him'.[2] After two centuries of vigorous life, the last English gentleman seems finally to have run out of heirs.

In the end, I believe, the gentleman has faded from the literary landscape because he has been absorbed by democracy without being resurrected, as the aristocrat has been, into myth. This book has been to some extent a history of the family quarrel between the two types, and if the gentleman won the argument in the nineteenth century, then it looks as if the aristocrat has had the last word in the twentieth. Like Simon Raven, I am on the gentleman's side in this debate, and agree with him when he writes that the tendency of members of the upper class 'is to rely on externals, such as prestige, power, rank, money, or privilege, whereas the gentleman, whether or not he also belongs to the upper class, has always been more concerned with justice, obligation and duty'.[3] But 'justice, obligation and duty' are unspectacular, even 'bourgeois' virtues, and they have not fed the modern imagination, hungry for myths of apocalypse. The figure of the aristocrat has. Supposedly doomed, he has been in touch with the springs of passion and power in a way that the gentleman has not, and Yeats's 'dream of the noble and the beggar-man' has been a potent one for the modern writer in recoil from middle-class civilisation. The gentleman has had nothing so glamorous to offer the imagination. But the last word here, at least, should not be of his limitations or harmful legacy, but of his positive contribution: that at a crucial period of history the idea of the gentleman provided a home for the spirit of disinterestedness. We have yet to do justice to that fact.

REFERENCES: EPILOGUE

1 E. Moers, *The Dandy: Brummell to Beerbohm* (London: Secker & Warburg, 1960), p. 308.
2 S. Raven, *The English Gentleman* (London: Blond, 1961), p. 90.
3 ibid., pp. 15–16.

Additional Bibliography

The following works, not mentioned in the text, are also relevant to this topic, and have been consulted:

Briggs, A., 'The language of class in early nineteenth-century England', in *Essays in Labour History*, ed. A. Briggs and J. Saville (London: Macmillan, 1960).
Faber, G., *Proper Stations: Class in Victorian Fiction* (London: Faber, 1971).
Green, M., *Children of the Sun* (London: Constable, 1977).
Houghton, W. E., *The Victorian Frame of Mind* (New Haven, Conn., and London: Yale University Press, 1957).
Mason, J. E., *Gentlefolk in the Making: Studies in the History of English Courtesy Literature, 1531–1774* (Philadelphia, Pa: University of Pennsylvania Press, 1935).
Perkin, H., *The Origins of Modern English Society, 1780–1880* (Routledge & Kegan Paul, 1969).
Rosa, M. W., *The Silver-Fork School: Novels of Fashion Preceding 'Vanity Fair'* (New York: Columbia University Press, 1936).
Smythe-Palmer, A., *The Ideal of a Gentleman* (George Routledge, 1908).

Index

Addison, Joseph 10, 11, 12, 13, 22–30 *passim*, 33–4, 39, 86, 91
Albert, Prince Consort 2, 29
Allen, Walter 13
apRoberts, Ruth 160
aristocracy, and idea of gentleman 5–6, 184; and middle-class reform 92–4; in Trollope 170–2
Arnold, Matthew 58, 92, 98
Arnold, Dr Thomas 2, 58, 88, 92, 109; reforms at Rugby 93–6; *see also* Stanley, A. P., *Life of*
Auden, W. H. 70, 82
Austen, Jane 11, 19–20, 85; and Richardson 31–2; and Trollope 13, 153–4, 159, 164; *Emma* 19–20, 31; *Mansfield Park* 20, 32, 153–4; *Pride and Prejudice* 6, 32

Bagehot, Walter 4, 8, 39, 95
Bayley, John 116
Besant, Walter 136
Blake, William 141–2
Blessington, Marguerite, Countess of 57
Bonaparte, Napoleon 50, 59; and Brummell 52, 55–6; and *Vanity Fair* 61, 63–4
Briggs, Asa 2, 102
Brontë, Charlotte: *Shirley* 98
Brummell, George ('Beau') 44, 50–4, 55–6, 59, 62, 72; Thackeray and 57–8
Buckle, H. T. 123
Bulwer, Edward (1st Baron Lytton) 48, 53, 108, 113; *Pelham* 48–51, 53–5, 106
Burke, Edmund 1, 90, 156, 157
Burney, Fanny 31; *Cecilia* 62
Byron, George Gordon, Lord 50, 52, 53, 55, 61–2, 64

Carey, John 38, 80
Carlyle, Thomas 11, 18, 74, 102, 119, 163; *Sartor Resartus* 50, 66
Cervantes, Miguel de: *Don Quixote* 34, 76, 79, 81
Chaucer, Geoffrey 4, 17

Chesterfield, Philip Dormer Stanhope, 4th Earl of 4, 13, 22, 31, 32, 55, 100, 122; *Letters discussed* 16–21; and Dickens 20–1, 122; and Newman 91; and *Pelham* 54
Chesterton, G. K. 37–8, 105, 107
Christian gentleman, ideal of 88–92
Cicero 160, 180
Civil Service, reform of and gentlemanly ideal 93–4; Northcote-Trevelyan report on 93; Trollope and 93, 149–50
Clarendon Commission 96, 97
Clark, G. Kitson 125, 136; quoted 99
class *see* rank and class
Clough, A. H.: *Amours de Voyage* 92
Cobbett, William 127–8
Cobden, Richard 29
Colburn, Henry 51
Coleridge, S. T. 135
Collier, Jeremy 26
Collins, John Churton 16, 18, 20
Collins, Philip 136
Collins, Wilkie 110
Congreve, William 26, 30
Conrad, Joseph 14, 75
Coverley, Sir Roger de *see Spectator*
Craik, George Lillie 120
Craik, Mrs G. L.: *John Halifax, Gentleman* 85, 101–2, 108, 120, 125
Crewe, John, 1st Baron 106
Culler, A. Dwight 91

Daiches, David 9
Dallas, E. S. 60
dandyism 11; Dickens and 108; *Fraser's* attack on 48–50; and novel of fashion 53–8; and Regency 50–3; and Restoration 50–1; Thackeray and 57–8, 65–6, 70–3
Davidson, John Thain 102
Defoe, Daniel 23, 25, 31
Dekker, Thomas 49, 88
Delane, John 173
Devonshire Commission 96–7
Dickens, Charles 2, 7, 11–12, 13, 18, 20–1, 32, 33, 40, 41, 74, 82, 89, 93, 103, 105–46, 149, 151, 152, 160, 163, 183

Barnaby Rudge 17, 20–1
Bleak House 34, 75, 108, 125
David Copperfield 74, 87, 106, 107, 112–13, 114–18, 129, 131
Dombey and Son 85, 108
Great Expectations 12, 74, 84–5, 87–8, 101, 103, 105–46 *passim*, 153, 183
Hard Times 21
Little Dorrit 93, 125
Nicholas Nickleby 85, 108, 112
Oliver Twist 108, 112, 113–15, 130
Our Mutual Friend 74, 75, 89, 108, 125, 130
A Tale of Two Cities 108
The Uncommercial Traveller 110–12, 132
Digby, Kenelm 88
disinterestedness, and gentlemanly ideal 97–8, 184
Disraeli, Benjamin, Lord Beaconsfield 51, 54, 60, 62, 71, 171, 172; *Coningsby* 55, 67–8, 61
D'Orsay, Count Alfred 53, 71
duelling 27–30; Thackeray and 40–1

Edminson, Mary 126–7, 129
Elgar, Sir Edward 14
Eliot, George 32, 126; *Felix Holt the Radical* 101
Empson, William 33
Escott, T. H. S. 163
Etherege, Sir George: *The Man of Mode* 24, 25, 48
Evelyn, John 51

Fagin, Bob 116
Faraday, Michael 120
Fielding, Henry 25, 32–3, 44, 67, 79, 152; *Tom Jones* 9, 33, 74, 76–7
Fleishman, Avrom 59
Ford, Ford Madox 13, 34–5, 182
Forrester, James: *The Polite Philosopher* 91
Forster, John 74, 105, 110
Fraser's Magazine 11, 43; and *Pelham* 48–51
Friswell, James Hain: *The Gentle Life* 84, 86; quoted 21

Gad's Hill Place 110–11
Gaskell, Mrs Elizabeth: *North and South* 85, 86; *Wives and Daughters* 6
'genteel' 85

gentleman, definitions of a, 3–9, 84–92; by Dekker 49; Etherege 48; Friswell 86; Harrison 6–7; Newman 88–92; Ruskin 4, 86–7; Sewell 89; Smiles 99–100; Steele 10; Thackeray 42, 69–70; Trollope 12–13
gentry, and idea of gentleman 5–7; and Richardson 10; and Trollope 151–81 *passim*
George III, King 127
George IV, King 50, 51, 53, 55, 56
Gibbon, Edward 90
Gissing, George 14, 117, 136; *Born in Exile* 183
Gladstone, W. E. 93
Gleig, G. R. 59
Gore, Mrs C. 51, 53; *Cecil* 55–6, 62; *Cecil, a Peer* 56
Green, J. R., quoted 22–3
Greg, W. R. 124–5
Gregory, Dr John 18

Hannay, James 37, 40, 62
Hardy, Thomas 182; *Jude the Obscure* 101; *Mayor of Casterbridge* 101
Harrison, Frederic 119–20, 125
Harrison, William 6–7
Hawkins, Sir Henry, Baron Brampton 136–7
Hayward, Abraham 41
Henley, W. E. 38
Hertford, Francis Seymour Conway, 3rd Marquis of 63, 57; and Lord Steyne 60
Hobhouse, John Cam 52, 61
Honey, J. R. de S. 96
Hook, Theodore 53; *Fathers and Sons* 56–7
Hopkins, Gerard Manley 1, 2, 4
Hudson, George 45, 46
Hughes, Thomas 94, 96; *The Manliness of Christ* 85–6; *Tom Brown's Schooldays* 95
Hutton, R. H. 159–60, 165

James, C. L. R. 96
James, Henry 14, 182, 183; *The Ambassadors* 98; *The Wings of the Dove* 37
James, H. A. 96
James I, King of Great Britain and Ireland 3
Johnson, Charles: *Caelia* 26

Index

Johnson, Dr Samuel 17, 22, 46, 61, 152
Johnston, William 124

Keats, John 17, 109
Kincaid, James 164

Lang, Rev. John 140–1
Laski, Audrey 171
Laski, Harold 1
Lawrence, D. H.: *Women in Love* 183
Leavis, Q. D. 119, 137
Lever, Charles 65
Lewis, C. S. 22, 25, 33
liberal education, and gentlemanly ideal 89, 97–9
Loftis, John 25, 26
Lubbock, Percy 48
Lytton, Bulwer *see* Bulwer, Edward

Macaulay, Thomas Babington 22, 23, 32, 35, 39; *Report on Indian Civil Service* 93
Maginn, William 48–50
Maitland, F. W. 175
'manliness' 17–18, 85–6, 109, 155
Martineau, Harriet 60
Masson, David 39–40
Marx, Karl 8
Maurice, F. D. 144
Melbourne, William Lamb, 2nd Viscount 50
Meredith, George 14, 182, 183; *Evan Harrington* 85
Mill, John Stuart 123
Miller, J. Hillis 134
Mingay, G. E., quoted 5
Modern English Usage (Fowler) 1
Moers, Ellen 12, 51–2, 107–8, 120, 183
More, Hannah 88
More, Paul Elmer 156–7
Moynahan, Julian 119
Munby, Arthur 144–6
Munby, Hannah 145–6

Newcomen, Thomas 120
Newman, John Henry 2, 12, 183; *The Idea of a University* 88–92
novels of fashion 48–51, 53–6; Thackeray and 55–8, 61–2, 73–5

O'Connor, Frank 155
Oliphant, Mrs M 106

Peel, Sir Robert 126
Pepys, Samuel 51
Porter, G. R. 123–4
Prince Regent, the *see* George IV
public schools 8; classical bias of 96–7; reform of, and Thomas Arnold 93–6; solved gentility problem 182
Punch 45, 49, 119

rank and class 8, 182
Raven, Simon 184
Ray, Gordon N. 38–9, 41, 70
Reader, W. J. 93
Richardson, Samuel 9–10, 35, 152; *Clarissa* 10, 26–7, 32; *Sir Charles Grandison* 9, 11, 12, 28–9, 30–2, 34, 76, 101
Roberts, William 88
Roscoe, W. C. 106
Rothblatt, Sheldon 19
Rower, Nicholas: *The Fair Penitent* 26
Rugby School 94–6
Ruskin, John 2, 4, 7, 12, 119, 149; *Modern Painters* 86–7; *Sesame and Lilies* 102–3
Russell, Bertrand 5

Sadleir, Michael 161
Saintsbury, George 38, 82
Scott, Sir Walter 29, 32, 50; *Ivanhoe* 164
self-help 99–103; Dickens and 108–9, 120–3; *see also* Smiles, Samuel
Sewell, William 88–9
Shaftesbury, Anthony Ashley Cooper, 3rd Earl of 90, 91
Shakespeare, William 109
Shaw, George Bernard 118
'silver-fork' novels *see* novels of fashion
Smiles, Samuel 2, 7, 99–102, 109; *Self-Help* 99–101, 120, 122–3, 125
Smith, Phyllis Patricia 31
Smythe, Hon. George 58
Sophocles: *Oedipus Rex* 118
Spectator 10–11, 13, 22–35 *passim*, 48, 76; Coverley papers 13, 24, 25, 33–5, 78, 81, 159, 162
Spenser, Edmund 9
Stanley, A. P.: *Life of Dr Arnold* 58, 88
Steele, Sir Richard, 10, 11, 22–30 *passim*, 33–4, 48–9, 86; *The Christian Hero* 28, 30; *The Conscious Lovers* 25–6, 28
Stephen, Sir James Fitzjames 4–5

Stephenson, George 101
Stevens, Joan 59
Stevenson, Robert Louis 81
Sudrann, Jean 47
Sutherland, John 74, 80

Taine, H. 98
Tatler 22
Temple, Frederick 97
Tennyson, Alfred 2, 16, 27, 32
Ternan, Ellen 110
Thackeray, William Makepeace 2, 7, 11–12, 13, 14, 16, 32–3, 35, 37–82, 93, 105–7, 109, 126, 149, 151, 152, 160, 162, 183
   Barry Lyndon 43–5, 48, 81
   The Book of Snobs 37, 42, 45–8, 50, 76, 77, 84, 119
   Catherine 42–3, 48, 49
   'The Diary of Jeames' 45
   'De Juventute' 12, 71
   The English Humourists of the Eighteenth Century 26, 33, 34, 86
   The Four Georges 42, 84
   The History of Henry Esmond 11, 29–30, 44, 59, 76, 81
   The Newcomes 13, 32, 34, 37, 41, 76–82, 84, 86, 89
   Pendennis 40, 53, 56, 71–6, 77, 81, 92
   Philip 38, 81
   'Punch's Prize Novelists' 49, 55, 65
   The Second Funeral of Napoleon 42
   A Shabby Genteel Story 42–3
   Vanity Fair 38, 39, 40, 41, 42, 48, 50, 53, 55–71, 76, 77, 82, 87–8, 92, 171
   The Virginians 38, 81
   The Yellowplush Papers 42
Thompson, F. M. L. 178
Tillotson, Geoffrey 59
Tillotson, Kathleen 59, quoted 136
The Times 173
Tocqueville, Alexis de 3, 4, 6, 14, 183
Trilling, Lionel 118, 119

Trollope, Anthony 2, 12–14, 37, 41, 149–83
   An Autobiography 12–13, 81, 150, 170, 175–6
   Barchester Towers 12, 32, 151, 155, 158, 163–5, 167
   Can You Forgive Her? 155, 163, 167, 169–70, 171–2
   Doctor Thorne 6, 85, 149, 153–4, 158–9, 164, 165
   The Duke's Children 13–14, 177, 178–9
   Framley Parsonage 160, 165
   The Last Chronicle of Barset 163, 167–9
   The Life of Cicero 160
   Mr Scarborough's Family 179–81
   Phineas Finn 29, 171
   Phineas Redux 171
   The Prime Minister 149, 152, 155, 163, 172–3, 174–8, 179
   Rachel Ray 151
   Sir Harry Hotspur of Humblethwaite 153, 160–3, 166
   The Small House at Allington 157, 158, 163, 165–7, 169
   The Vicar of Bullhampton 151–2, 156, 175
   The Warden 159, 163, 167
   The Way We Live Now 34, 151, 157–8, 163, 166, 173–4, 175–6
Twain, Mark 19

Victoria, Queen 127

Waugh, Evelyn 13, 35, 182; *Sword of Honour* 183–4
Wellington, Arthur Wellesley, 1st Duke of 29, 50, 52, 53, 55, 59, 72, 74
Wells, H. G.: *Kipps* 183; *Tono-Bungay* 183
Wordsworth, William 111, 135
Wyatt, Matthew 59

Yeats, W. B. 184
York, Frederick, Duke of 72
Young, G. M. 97–8